RAVENWING

Men and cannon were engulfed by a hail of bolts, ripping through padded jackets and metal, filling the gun pit with blood and splinters. Annael fired another burst to be certain, brick dust from the embrasure and fragments of torn cloth and shattered bone spraying across the snaking power cables of the multi-laser.

'The enemy are abandoning the citadel.' Grand Master Sammael's report was softly spoken, yet clearly heard over the din of war. 'First wave to encircle and contain. Second and third waves to follow across the bridge. Resistance faltering.'

Annael's squadron were part of the first wave, and it was their duty to cut off further escape across the bridge, while those that had already fled would be herded towards the second compound, providing pause for the gunners within and cover for the following Dark Angels.

'Be vigilant,' warned Sergeant Cassiel. 'The cornered animal fights without fear. This battle is not yet won.'

By the same author

• THE LEGACY OF CALIBAN •

Book 1: RAVENWING
Book 2: MASTER OF SANCTITY
(Coming 2013)

• THE ELDAR PATH •

Book 1: PATH OF THE WARRIOR
Book 2: PATH OF THE SEER
Book 3: PATH OF THE OUTCAST

ANGELS OF DARKNESS
A Dark Angels novel

THE PURGING OF KADILLUS
A Space Marine Battles novel

DELIVERANCE LOST
A Horus Heresy novel

RAVEN'S FLIGHT
A Horus Heresy audio drama

THE SUNDERING

(Contains the novels *Malekith, Shadow King* and *Caledor*,
and the novella *The Bloody-Handed*)

A Time of Legends omnibus

A WARHAMMER 40,000 NOVEL

RAVENWING

THE LEGACY OF CALIBAN BOOK ONE

GAV THORPE

BLACK LIBRARY

Dedicated to Mike, because he happens to be sitting next to me.

A Black Library Publication

First published in Great Britain in 2012 by
Black Library,
Games Workshop Ltd.,
Willow Road,
Nottingham,
NG7 2WS, UK.

10 9 8 7 6 5 4 3 2 1

Cover illustration by Fares Maese.

A CIP record for this book is available from the British Library.

UK ISBN 13: 978 1 84970 330 7
US ISBN 13: 978 1 84970 331 4

See Black Library on the internet at

www.blacklibrary.com

Find out more about Games Workshopand the world of Warhammer 40,000 at

www.games-workshop.com

Printed and bound by CPI Group (UK) Ltd, Croydon, CR0 4YY

It is the 41st millennium. For more than a hundred centuries the Emperor has sat immobile on the Golden Throne of Earth. He is the master of mankind by the will of the gods, and master of a million worlds by the might of his inexhaustible armies. He is a rotting carcass writhing invisibly with power from the Dark Age of Technology. He is the Carrion Lord of the Imperium for whom a thousand souls are sacrificed every day, so that he may never truly die.

Yet even in his deathless state, the Emperor continues his eternal vigilance. Mighty battlefleets cross the daemon-infested miasma of the warp, the only route between distant stars, their way lit by the Astronomican, the psychic manifestation of the Emperor's will. Vast armies give battle in His name on uncounted worlds. Greatest amongst his soldiers are the Adeptus Astartes, the Space Marines, bio-engineered super-warriors. Their comrades in arms are legion: the Imperial Guard and countless planetary defence forces, the ever-vigilant Inquisition and the tech-priests of the Adeptus Mechanicus to name only a few. But for all their multitudes, they are barely enough to hold off the ever-present threat from aliens, heretics, mutants - and worse.

To be a man in such times is to be one amongst untold billions. It is to live in the cruellest and most bloody regime imaginable. These are the tales of those times. Forget the power of technology and science, for so much has been forgotten, never to be re-learned. Forget the promise of progress and understanding, for in the grim dark future there is only war. There is no peace amongst the stars, only an eternity of carnage and slaughter, and the laughter of thirsting gods.

ONE

HADRIA PRAETORIS

VETERAN REBORN

How did the Lion die?

It was a simple question, innocently asked, and Brother Annael had wondered why, in over four hundred years of service to the Dark Angels Chapter, it had not occurred to him before. It was the question that had propelled him from an assault squad in the Fifth Company to the ranks of the Second Company, the lauded Ravenwing, and that was when he had found out the truth.

Horus, arch-traitor, thrice-cursed, had murdered the primarch of the Dark Angels.

So he had been told by Brother Malcifer, Chaplain of the Ravenwing, when Annael had been inducted into the lore of the Second Company. Annael had understood immediately why such knowledge was so closely guarded; that the Dark Angels had been brought to the brink of destruction by other Space Marines had been a testing revelation.

He had known that there were always the weak-willed, even amongst the Adeptus Astartes, who put themselves and their ambition above the call of duty and their oaths of dedication to the Emperor. He had fought against such heretics on eight different occasions, bringing the justice of death to them with chainsword and bolt pistol, but had never suspected the full horror of the temptations that draw good warriors away from the service of the Emperor.

Weeping, Annael had listened as Malcifer had related the tale of the Horus Heresy, a cataclysmic civil war that had threatened to destroy the Imperium at its birth. The Dark Angels, the First Legion, greatest of the Emperor's warriors, had fought against the evil of Horus and those primarchs who had been corrupted by his silken-tongued promises, and they had triumphed. The victory had been won at great cost, and Lion El'Jonson, the primarch of the Dark Angels had given his life to defeat the enemy.

Now that he was a member of the Ravenwing, it was Annael's duty to hold to that knowledge and keep it as a sacred fire in his heart to lend strength to his sword arm and to fuel his courage in battle. Armed with such understanding, it was the Ravenwing that sought out those traitors who had turned on the Emperor, so that they might be brought to account for their sins. As a Space Marine of the Dark Angels, Annael had never lacked conviction, honour or valour, but as a chosen warrior of the Ravenwing he now understood the importance of discretion and brotherhood even more sharply.

As the attack sirens sounded again across the strike cruiser *Implacable Justice*, Annael considered the sacrifice of the Lion and knew that he was willing to make the same sacrifice to protect the Chapter and the Emperor's dominion. His existence was not for a normal life, but to be an instrument of the Dark Angels' vengeance against those who had so wronged them.

While he pondered his change of perspective, Annael continued with his pre-battle preparations. He had already donned his armour, allowing the adepts of the Techmarines to perform their consecrations to the Machine-God before attending to his mount.

That machine, called *Black Shadow*, was as much a symbol of his position in the Ravenwing as the emblem on his knee and the markings on his shoulder pad. In the Scout Company he had been taught to honour his weapons and his armour, and they had served him well for four centuries of battle. Now that same honour extended to his steed, and Annael was attentive in his application of the unguents to the engine and suspension, and conscientious as he spoke the dedications to the spirit of the motorbike.

It was a fine mount, and it had a history no less acclaimed than his own. In the yellow light of the boarding bay's lamps the black enamelled fairing gleamed with polish that he had applied himself only an hour before. A serf of the armoury was checking the belt feeds of the twin bolters housed in the front cowling above the handlebars, muttering invocations that would ward away jams and misfires.

'Are you excited, brother?' Still with a hint of his Lauderian accent, Zarall's deep voice was unmistakable. Annael looked around and saw his squadron-brother standing at the back of *Black Shadow*, his helm in one hand so that his features could be seen. Zarall had a broad chin and rounded cheeks, a flat nose and bright, blue eyes, and his head was topped with white hair cropped almost to the scalp. His black armour was festooned with purity and devotional seals – strips of parchment on which were written the sacred oaths and texts of the Chapter, fastened with red wax. There were twenty-eight in all, each awarded by the Grand Master of Chaplains, Sapphon, for heroic deeds and clarity of faith; Annael had six and was one hundred and fifty years Zarall's senior.

'I am always excited by the prospect of purposeful endeavour,' replied Annael, standing up. Zarall raised his eyebrows doubtfully and Annael relented in his attempt at nonchalance. 'All right, I feel as I did the first time I dropped as a full battle-brother. It is as if the last four hundred years had never happened.'

'You have a fine steed and attend well to its requirements, there is no need for apprehension,' said Zarall.

'I did not say that I was apprehensive,' replied Annael. He patted the saddle of *Black Shadow*. 'I said I was excited. I am accustomed to the drills and procedures of the squadron. I have no doubt that I will acquit myself with honour and courage.'

'Yes, but you are to be blessed on your first drop with us,' said Zarall. 'Grand Master Sammael himself will lead the attack. Be sure that his eye will fall upon the deeds of his newest recruit.'

'And his eye will see only that which pleases him,' Annael assured the other Space Marine. 'Did Sergeant Cassiel ask you to ensure I was aware of the importance of my inaugural performance?'

'Not at all, brother,' said Zarall. The Space Marine smiled, realising that his questions were intrusive. 'I meant no disrespect. I wished to pay my regards and tell you that I am pleased to have you serve as my squadron-brother. The Emperor is equally pleased to count you amongst the First.'

Annael grasped the hand that Zarall offered, acknowledging the apology and the praise. It was unbecoming of a Dark Angel to feel prideful, but Annael gained some satisfaction from his battle-brother's confidence.

'We shall bring honour to the squadron and the

company, together,' Annael said. Another armoured figure appeared behind Zarall. 'Brother Araton, have you word yet of when we embark?'

'Sergeant Cassiel is still in briefing with the Grand Master,' said Araton. Stepping past Zarall, Araton looked over Annael's bike, his experienced eye taking in every detail at a glance. He was more slender of features than Zarall, his hair shoulder-length, nose regal and eyes deep blue. 'You have yet to calibrate your sighting arrays, brother.'

'I was about to attend to that,' said Annael, opting to take Araton's comment as observation rather than criticism.

He swung a leg over the saddle of *Black Shadow* and powered up the control panel set underneath the twin bolters. The screen flickered into life with a green light, showing a selection of scanning options. With a sub-vocal command Annael brought up the sighting display inside the lens of his right eye and activated the link between his armour and the machine. After a brief burst of static, the data from the bike's array transferred into his autosenses, half of Annael's view becoming a schematic of the mustering bay, the other members of the squad and their bikes highlighted by glowing red runes.

Annael deactivated the link and stepped off the bike, returning his attention to his companions. Brother Sabrael had joined the group, the white of a freshly painted chevron bright on his right greave amongst several other battle honours. Annael had heard at length from Sabrael how the honour had been earned against the orks of Pahysis; several times, in fact.

'Be sure to keep up when we attack, brother,' said Sabrael, the hint of a laugh in his voice. His aristocratic tone had become familiar to Annael during his induction into the company, a remnant of the Dark Angel's upbringing in the privileged classes of Aginor Sigma.

How the son of a coddled elite had managed to pass the harsh initiation tests of the Chapter was a mystery to Annael, but Sabrael had proven himself a capable, if impetuous, warrior over decades of battle, his name frequently appearing in the *Honoris Registarum*. 'And try not to fall off that fine machine.'

'I will take especial care,' replied Annael, wondering when the novelty of his induction would cease to provide amusement for his squadron-brethren. 'When you dash into more trouble than you can handle, be sure that I will not be far behind to drag you out.'

Sabrael laughed and walked away to his own machine, his armour managing to replicate the slight swagger in his step.

'Forgive Sabrael's exuberance,' said Zarall. 'He is a good warrior, despite the constant vexation he causes the Chaplains.'

'Do not be too swift to follow his example,' said Araton. 'We fight as a squadron. The line between enthusiasm and foolhardiness can be crossed all too easily.'

'I can hear you over the vox-net, brothers,' Sabrael's response came to Annael's ear via his helmet communicator. 'I know well the time for action and the time for contemplation, in right proportion.'

Annael was about to reply when Sergeant Cassiel's voice broke over the comm.

'Embarkation in ten minutes, stand by your mounts. Final briefing in five minutes. Be glad, for Grand Master Sammael has found us a worthy target of attention. There will be honour aplenty to spare for all of us.'

Zarall and Araton departed to their machines, leaving Annael to complete his pre-battle checks. Mounting *Black Shadow* he ran a series of diagnostic tests on the bike's systems and all seemed to be functioning within tolerable parameters. He made a vocal note in his battle log to commend the Techmarines of the armoury on their diligence in preparing the machine for its new rider.

When he was ready, Annael thumbed the ignition rune and the engine of his mount growled into life. *Black Shadow* came alive beneath him, trembling with suppressed power. Gunning the engine, he monitored the performance display in front of him and was satisfied that all was in working order. In time, he had been told by Cassiel, he would know by sound and feel whether all was well with his steed, but for the moment he relied upon the internal systems to warn him of any cause for concern.

Engaging the gearbox, Annael allowed *Black Shadow* to roll forward a short distance, thick tyres gripping the meshwork of the deck, blue-grey smoke chugging from the exhausts. He wheeled the bike around and saw that the other squadron members were lining up by the gateway to the docking hangar.

The attack siren sounded three times: five minutes until the drop would begin. Easing into his place at the back of the squadron, Annael felt his excitement rising again. Inside his helm, he grinned, amused at himself for feeling like a neophyte at his first battle.

MUSTER

Accompanied by the calm voice of Grand Master Sammael instructing his warriors, the rising and falling attack siren filled the decks of the Dark Angels' strike cruiser *Implacable Justice*. All across the two and a half kilometres-long ship motors were growling into life and anti-grav engines whined. Hydraulics wheezed so that immense pistons moved Dark Talon and Nephilim fighters from their transport berths into the launch hangars that took up the majority of the ship's bulk. The clank of chains and thump of pneumatics moved cascades of specially-constructed drop pods into position above yawning bay doors.

Exhaust smoke billowed along wide corridors and across the metal aprons of the mustering halls; the clouds sucked away through atmosphere processors that would reclaim trace elements of minerals before the raw gases were shunted back into the air refinery plant and moisture extracted to keep alive those aboard the space-ship. Built to patrol for decades at a time, the *Implacable Justice* wasted nothing.

The growl of engines became deafening as ten bike squadrons assembled, their high-density tyres leaving marks on the ferrocrete-lined passageways. Black as night were these machines, and black as night were the warriors that rode them, clad in armour of thick, rounded plates. Such was the nature of the Space Marines' power armour that they seemed as much machine as the heavy motorbikes on which they rode; half-mechanical, half-living avatars of the Emperor's vengeance.

Each rider bore the markings of his Chapter: a white-winged sword upon his left shoulder guard, squadron markings and rank identifiers on the right. Each machine was marked with the symbol of the company upon its armoured flanks and wheel guards. Some bikes bore devotional scripts painted by the riders. Others were decorated with intricately painted wings and feathers in white. Each bike bore a name, an honorific given to the machine by the armourium when it was built. The riders knew the names and deeds of their mounts as well as they knew their brothers, though the secret of the name was shared only by the rider and the Master of the Forge.

In the launch bays, Land Speeders glided into position to be locked into their drop-shields, the crews and machines encased in slabs of reinforced ceramite and plasteel. Warning lights flashed red as the drop-bay doors opened, the air within the launch chambers expanding into the vacuum as pale gusts of vapour and glittering ice.

Every warrior was filled with purpose and the comm-net was quiet of chatter as Sammael steered his mount into the fuselage of a waiting Thunderhawk gunship. A relic of the ancient past, *Corvex* was a larger, more heavily armed and armoured cousin to the bikes ridden by the rest of the company, suspended a few feet from the ground by powerful anti-grav engines, the workings of which had defied replication by the Chapter's Tech-marines. Upon the front fairing, above the polished white rendering of a great eagle with wings unfurled, was bound the *Liber Corvus*, the pages of which were inked the names of all the Ravenwing who had died on the hunt. *Corvex*'s power plant growled quietly as the jetbike slipped forward, energy pulsing through armoured cabling to the plasma cannon and storm bolters mounted under the cowling.

Unlike the other machines of the Ravenwing, *Corvex*'s name was well-known to all, its history entwined with the myths of the many Masters of the Ravenwing that had come before. It was this lineage, this legend, that Sammael now continued.

Sammael was garbed in the black armour of his company, adorned with personal heraldry in red and white, inscribed with litanies of remembrance and devotion. Over this he wore the white robes of a veteran of the Deathwing, for no Dark Angel could become a company Grand Master without first passing through the ranks of the First Company. Gilded skulls and scrolled honours upon his ebon plate stood testament to centuries of battle and victories. From his backpack flowed his adamantine mantle, the white cloak woven with fibres taken from the cloak of the Lion himself.

Within the transport compartment of the drop-ship his command officers waited for him on their bikes: the company Chaplain, Brother Malcifer; Brother Gideon the Apothecary; the honour guards Athelman and Daedis; and with them in the blue armour of the Librarium sat Epistolary Harahel. The command squad raised fists to welcome their leader. The ramp closed behind him, sealing them into the ruddily-lit belly of the Thunderhawk.

Acknowledging their salutes of fealty, Sammael killed the engine of the *Corvex* so that the machine drifted gently down to the deck. Locking bolts rose up in response to its weight on the floor, fastening the jetbike with padded grips, embracing it as tightly as a lover. Dismounting, Sammael activated his vox-caster and switched to fleet address so that his words would be heard by all aboard the *Implacable Justice* and the companion strike cruiser *Penitent Warrior*.

'Warriors of the Ravenwing, honoured brethren of the Fifth Company, we stand upon the brink of battle. All here have proven their worth to the Emperor time and time again, and it falls to us to honour oaths once more. On the world below us, vile rebellion has slithered like a serpent into the hearts of men who once dedicated their lives to the Emperor. This snake has bitten hard and its venom flows deep, so that only the most bloody excision of the wound will rid the populace of its fatal taint.

'We each know our measure and we acknowledge the duty expected of us. We are the Dark Angels, the First, who carry the pride of the Emperor upon our shoulders. In wars uncountable we have prevailed against the heretic, the alien and the mutant, and today shall be no different. Justice demands that we seek reparation for the wrongs done to the servants of the Emperor on this world. Let us be about our purpose with bold hearts and faith in our brothers. Look to your armour to protect you, your steeds to carry you and your weapons to honour you. Turn thoughts to those oppressed and fragile men we will rid from the tyranny of heresy, and be righteous in the knowledge that we do the Emperor's bidding. Only in death does duty end. Only in death can justice be earned.'

Sammael paused, waiting for the chronometer displayed above the assault ramp of the gunship to reach the appointed hour. As the red numerals ticked over and turned green, he laid a hand upon the aquila symbol embossed upon the gorget of his armour.

'Warriors of the Dark Angels, attack!'

THUNDERHAWK INSERTION

Sitting on the inner bench of the Thunderhawk's transport chamber, his armour joints locked into position, Brother Telemenus barely felt the swaying and buffeting of the drop-ship as it crashed down through the planet's atmosphere. Beyond the armoured window opposite he saw the sky on fire, a sheet of orange and yellow carpeting the heavens as the *Penitent Warrior* powered out of the upper atmosphere on plumes of plasma.

As the dark of near-space resolved into the cyan hue of thicker gases, Telemenus caught glimpses of drop pods, hurtling past as dark blurs, and the shape of other Thunderhawks plunging towards planetfall. Dragging his eyes from the stirring view, Telemenus attended to the bolter held across his lap. Around him the other members of the three squads embarked upon the gunship made their final checks too. Though he had thrice run through the rituals before boarding the Thunderhawk, Telemenus once more cleared the magazine and inspected the breach for obstructions. He disengaged the locking pins and used the magnification of his autosenses to look for small pieces of dirt that may have been picked up from the exhaust smoke of the Ravenwing's vehicles. Satisfied that his weapon was clean, he locked the magazine back into place.

'Let us hope that the Ravenwing leave some foes for us,' he said, turning his head to the right to look at Sergeant Amanael.

'The Second Company are not famed for their generosity,' replied Amanael. 'We can but wish that the enemy see sense and flee from their attack into our deadly welcome.'

'I am convinced that it shall be as you hope,' said Brother Cadael, sitting on Telemenus's left. 'These rebels are cowards at heart. They will attempt to fall back at the first sign of retribution. Such faithless men lack true conviction of purpose.'

'And we shall not be swayed from ours,' said Telemenus. 'I am but seventeen kills from achieving the honour of First Marksman. I would see that accomplished before the mission is complete.'

'An honour that would bring credit to the whole squad,' said Amanael. There was good humour in his voice. 'Yet do not think that we will leave our targets to your attention to see it bestowed.'

'I shall endeavour to leave some foes for you to practise your art upon whilst completing my tally, do not fear,' Telemenus replied with a laugh. 'My glory will be tempered by the knowledge that if I miss my mark you have opportunity to improve lacking aim and might one day equal my standard.'

'Take not credit for yourself that belongs to the artifice of your helm,' argued Brother Daellon, who had long contested that Telemenus' remarkable accuracy was the result of superior optics in his battlegear rather than the result of long hours' dedication to firing drill coupled with a calm head.

'And do not be so eager for painted honours that you are sparing in your attention to wider battle,' said Amanael, his voice carrying soft warning.

'Put aside such fears, brother-sergeant,' said Telemenus. He raised his right arm, showing on the vambraces a winged sword picked out in silver, a red star upon the blade. 'I would not add laurel to this at expense of duty. Nor would I see such honour engraved upon my tomb slab in place of decoration for my armour.'

A data-screen flickered into life at the head of the compartment, silencing the talk. The display resolved into a schematic of Hadria Praetoris, the rebel-held city that would be the target of the Dark Angels' attack. The view zoomed in and panned across to the eastern flank of the city, where the insurrectionists had made their stand in a series of fortified villas on the city outskirts. In the absence of the company commander, Grand Master Zadakiel, mission leadership of the Fifth Company had been conferred to Sergeant Seraphiel, the most senior warrior present. It was his voice that sounded over the comm-net, repeating the briefing given aboard the *Penitent Warrior*.

The battle plan was simple but had proven effective in countless joint-company actions in the Chapter's past. The Dark Angels of the Fifth Company were being deployed under cover of darkness, in a line to the north and west of the target buildings, where they would create prepared positions. The Ravenwing would assemble to the south and east and attack in a dawn spearhead, driving the enemy towards Telemenus and his fellow Space Marines. The shock and speed of the Ravenwing assault would swiftly break the enemy's fighting spirit and the resultant rout would take any survivors directly into the guns of the waiting Dark Angels. If the Ravenwing were to meet stubborn resistance and their attack stalled – an unlikely circumstance in Telemenus's experience – the Fifth Company warriors would push in from their positions and catch the enemy between the two forces.

As each sergeant sounded off the deployment schedules and dispositions of their individual squads, runes denoting each group of warriors flashed into existence on the schematic. Telemenus noted that he and the rest of Third Squad would be at the western end of the line, flanked only by Sergeant Athrael's devastators. Theirs was a lynchpin position securing the flank of the force, and it was proof of Sergeant Seraphiel's estimation of their resolve that they were assigned such an honourable duty, but Telemenus considered his chances of achieving his First Marksman's honour diminished; the fiercest fighting would be at the centre.

Outside, the sky darkened again as the Thunderhawk formation passed across the terminator into night. An alert in Telemenus's helm display warned him that they were fifteen minutes from planetfall. All intelligence had suggested that the rebels lacked long-range monitoring equipment and the passage of the gunships would go undetected, but there was always the risk that some observant lookout might see the streak of engines in the upper air and not mistake them for shooting stars. The dropsite would be considered hostile until secured, and the strike force would be on constant alert from the moment they touched down, anticipating enemy attack.

'Let the Ravenwing race and roar about as is their wont,' concluded Seraphiel. 'We gladly bestow to them the mantle of hammer to our anvil, for the hammer is worthless without a foundation against which it will strike. Stay true to your oaths and to your brothers and we will return to Grand Master Zadakiel with a new honour to place upon the battle standard of the Fifth.'

'Praise the Lion!' Telemenus added his voice to the time-honoured chorus that concluded the briefing. 'For the Emperor!'

FIRST DROP

Situated atop three hills, the compounds of the rebels were grey, walled forts ringed with towers connected by covered trenchworks. Gun emplacements broke the line of the walls and armoured gatehouses barred the road bridges between them.

As the first glow of dawn touched upon the walls of the easternmost fort, the fury of the Dark Angels fell upon the keeps of Hadria Praetoris like a storm of vengeance. In the skies above the compounds, attack craft plunged down, appearing as a storm of shadowy blades against the gold-tinged clouds. Black-hulled Thunderhawks swooped after the fighters, plasma jets bright in the dawn. Around them plummeted drop pods and entry-shielded Land Speeders.

As the arrestor thrusters of the drop-craft fired, dark blurs streaked past them, slamming into the curtain walls of the compounds: high-velocity munitions from the strike cruisers' bombardment cannons. The impact of the shells hurled rock and ferrocrete into the air and sent a cloud of pulverised masonry blooming over the citadels.

The blast wave from the bombardment uprooted trees lining the roads that wound up the hills and slashed through gun pits and bunker slits, shredding those inside with shrapnel and debris. Those who survived suffered blasted ear drums and internal compression, doomed to a slow death of internal bleeding and organ failure.

Grit and boulders fell like rain across the hillsides and the thunderous detonation rolled across Hadria Praetoris setting flocks of birds to flight above the city.

Missile and battle cannon fire raked the entrenchments as the aircraft of the Ravenwing strafed through the boiling cloud engulfing the compounds. Shells and las-fire flickered into the heart of the nearest fort as gunners picked out their targets on thermal scanners and high-acuity sensor arrays.

In the skies above the devastation, the remains of ablative drop-shields peeled away from plunging Land Speeders. Descending on their anti-grav engines, the anti-grav craft spiralled around the diving Thunderhawks, spewing fire from assault cannons and heavy bolters. Vengeance-class speeders spewed a torrent of plasma fire at the smoke-shrouded walls while rockets slammed into the ferrocrete barrier from the Tornadoes.

As the Land Speeders circled the compound, Darkshrouds followed the descent. Modified from the standard Land Speeder chassis, each anti-grav vehicle carried a pitted, ancient statue from the Chapter's fortress-monastery. The solemn hooded figures glowed with power, coils of cable sending nascent warp energy through arcane generators that threw out an all-concealing blanket of darkness. As they joined the attack, the shadow of the Darkshrouds enveloped the dropsite, obscuring the Thunderhawks as they touched down on plumes of plasma.

Protected from attack by the fire of their brethren and the screen of the dark-generating Land Speeders, the bike squads of the Second Company disembarked, racing from their gunships. Joining the squadrons were two-man attack bikes, their heavy weapons directed at the rebel fortress. Above them a flight of three Dark Talons took up station, pouring a torrent of fire from their hurricane bolters into the rebels trying to muster on the broken ramparts of the wall. A flight of Nephilim fighters swept over the compound, their Avenger weapons systems raking the open space between the wall and inner citadel with explosive bolts while Blacksword missiles streamed from their wings, turning the courtyard into a killing ground.

The assault ramp of the Thunderhawk carrying Annael's squad slammed down even while the gunship was still shuddering from landing. He saw a pink and scarlet sky silhouetting the hills, across which billowed a swathe of smoke that was swiftly blotting out the dawn light. The nearest citadel was two hundred metres away, a massive breach in its curtain wall like a broken-toothed smile.

'Full speed,' ordered Cassiel.

Within seconds they had plunged down the ramp. The sergeant was the first to disembark, the smoke of his exhausts filling the gunship as Annael and Zarall followed, Sabrael and Araton taking up the rear. Reaching the ground, the squadron spread into a V-formation to avoid the dirt and rocks thrown up in the wake of the others' bikes, engines roaring as they charged towards the opening made by the bombardment. Moments after they had left, the Thunderhawk's engines fired again, lifting it skywards on columns of flame, its weapons ready to provide supporting fire.

As he charged up the slope of the hill with the others, Annael's vision was filled with a superimposed view of the landscape ahead. The dust and smoke obscured normal sight, as did the cloaking field of the Darkshrouds, but those were no barrier to the surveyor array built into *Black Shadow*. With soft movements he guided the bike around jutting boulders and piles of shattered ferrocrete, seeking the telltale blur of red and orange that signified a heat source. He saw the smudge of colour amongst the ruin of the breach, but nothing that moved; the warmth leaking from the bodies of the dead quickly turned from yellow to orange.

His armour easily compensating for the jolt of his bike as it crashed over fallen slabs and blocks, Annael looked left and right, searching along the top of the remaining wall for threats. A squadron of Land Speeders curved around ahead of him, lifting up to the height of the rampart, their weapons unleashing a blaze of fire at unseen foes.

'Lance.'

The command from Cassiel was calmly spoken as the closest shadow-wreathed Speeder pulled back to cover the second wave of the attack. Annael slid into place behind Zarall as the squadron narrowed its formation to take the breach. He glanced back to see a squadron of Black Knights following fifty metres behind. The elite of the company, Sammael's chosen warriors, carried hammers with beaked heads and the gleam from the muzzles of their bikes' plasma weapons shone from beneath black cowlings. He glimpsed their Huntmaster raising his corvus hammer to point to the left, the squadron curving away as they were swallowed by the black cloud of the Darkshroud.

Just twenty metres ahead, the bikes of Sergeant Hephrael's squadron raced across the tumbled masonry, disappearing into the smoke and fire. Muzzle flashes flared in the gloom and Annael heard the echo of the squadrons' bolters ringing back from the broken wall.

In front, Cassiel and then Zarall dropped from view. A second later Annael hit the rim of a crater and for a moment he felt weightless as *Black Shadow* became airborne, plunging down into the smoking dip. With an impact that tested the reinforced suspension of his steed, Annael hit the sloping side of the crater, the tyres skidding him sideways for an instant as they regained traction. Hauling hard on the handlebars he righted his course, just three metres behind Zarall.

The explosion had torn a hole almost two hundred metres wide, most of that inside the compound. As soon as the squadron were through the breach they were greeted by a storm of flickering projectiles from within the central fortification. Few of the poorly-aimed volleys hit, but now and then something pinged from Annael's armour or the slanted fairing of *Black Shadow*. Something heavier – autocannon shells probably – threw up clods of earth just ahead of the onrushing squadron.

A brighter flash of red pulsed from a firing point on the citadel's roof and seared into Hephrael's squadron. From its elevated position, the lascannon shot punched through the leg of one of the riders and exploded into the engine of his mount. Fuel ignited, sending the unfortunate Space Marine spinning through the air as his bike's engine blew up.

Retribution for the loss was near-instantaneous. A ripple of missiles from a Land Speeder converged on the firing port from which the lascannon bolt had come, turning the embrasure into rubble and smoke. Heavy bolter rounds from another skimmer sparked amongst the debris, turning shattered ferrocrete into lethal shrapnel.

'Hard right.'

Leaning his weight over, Annael followed Cassiel and Zarall as they steered down a ramp into the trenchworks. The sergeant's bolters flared along the curving path, cutting down men hunkered against the wall ahead. Easing his bike towards the right-hand wall of the trench, Annael staggered their formation, allowing him to see past Cassiel. He saw a rebel in grey and green fatigues running for the cover of a shell slit. Pressing the trigger pad on the grip of the handlebars Annael opened fire, unleashing a short salvo of six bolts. The sparks of their propellant charge shrieked along the trench, ripping holes into the wood-reinforced wall and tearing three fist-sized chunks from the man's back.

In a moment Annael had raced past, but he knew that the shots had been fatal – no normal man would survive such injuries. The bike controls juddered in his grasp as he rode over the uneven footing planks and bumped over the bodies of those slain by Cassiel.

Another squadron of Land Speeders zoomed overhead, weapons spewing death, the wash of their jets momentarily flaring across Black Shadow's sensors. They recovered in time to show a blur of orange fifty metres ahead; a rebel soldier pulling up some kind of heavy weapon. The man fired as Annael activated the bolters, the missile from his launcher screaming down the trench towards the squadron even as Annael's fusillade turned him into scattered body parts.

The missile passed between Zarall and Annael, exploding on the wall to the Dark Angels' left. The blast showered Annael with dirt while pieces of shrapnel clanged from his backpack and left shoulder guard.

'You'll be spending some time repainting that,' came Sabrael's voice from behind. 'Consider it your first honour scar.'

'Back up top,' ordered Cassiel before Annael could throw back a reply.

The squadron turned up a ramp used for bringing supplies down into the trenches, racing past the burning corpses of half a dozen rebels caught by a heavy flamer. Just a little further up the trenchworks a blossom of flames rose into the air as an ammunition depot detonated; secondary explosions continued to bark and snap as Cassiel led the squadron around the smouldering wreck of an armoured ground car pulverised by a Blacksword missile, curving back towards the main building.

Hitting open ground, Annael could see the battle in its full fury. The compound, stretching three hundred metres from wall to wall, was carpeted in drifting smoke and ash. Whirling contrails cut through the gloom as bikes and Land Speeders converged on the central citadel. From above, gunships and strike craft continued to rain down fire, pinning the rebels inside the shell-pocked building while the rest of the company advanced.

'Battle speed,' commanded Cassiel, slowing at the head of the squadron. Annael eased down on the throttle and glanced at the surveyor sweep on the display. There was a mass of enemy contact returns several hundred metres ahead, flooding towards the bridge leading to the next compound; left intact to allow such a retreat.

Cruising through the smog and fire, Annael was alert, blood pumping hard through his body. In four centuries of battle he had raced into the fight shooting from the hatch of a Rhino transport, and he had performed jump pack drops from a hovering Thunderhawk, but nothing matched the exhilaration of the mounted charge. The machine beneath him was an extension of his armour, responding to the slightest nudge and touch, bumping over the uneven ground and curving easily past shell craters and the tangled ruins of gun batteries.

'With the Emperor as my witness, this is the way to fight!' he told the others.

'Our newblood has found his calling at last,' replied Sabrael. 'Who would have thought that such youthful joy lingered within such old bones?'

'A fine calling it is, to bring swift death to the Emperor's forsaken,' said Zarall. 'Many are the blessings we must give thanks for.'

'Enemy, third sector, two hundred metres,' said Araton. The position indicated was almost at a right angle to their line of attack, behind the lead elements of the force.

'Put tongues to rest and weapons to purpose,' chided Cassiel as he steered the squadron to the right.

Annael could see nothing, on display or in his helm view, but the sergeant trusted the report of his brother without question. Several seconds later Annael caught a glimpse of a multi-barrelled weapon beneath a camouflaged canopy, turning towards the lead squadrons. Annael admired the courage of the gunners, to remain hidden while the ferocity of the Dark Angels passed them by, though he cursed them for the cause they had chosen.

'The net must be woven of some kind of scrambling material,' he said, still not seeing any reading on the bike scanner. 'How did you see it, brother?'

'By putting mind to task and not to chatter,' replied Araton.

The timely chastisement focused Annael's thoughts, putting him in mind of the instructions he had received in the Scout Company.

'Apologies, brothers, if novelty of experience softened my discipline,' he said, accelerating to come alongside Zarall.

The cannon opened fire before the squadrons' weapons

could be brought to bear, unleashing a stream of las-fire at one of the Land Speeder squadrons swooping around the right side of the citadel. Smoke billowed from one of the craft and it veered wildly to the right, dipping towards the ground. Annael glimpsed the two crew leaping from the dropping machine moments from its impact, hitting the ground hard as the Land Speeder exploded against the inside of the wall.

'Avenge the spirit of our fallen steed,' snapped Zarall. A flurry of bolts screeched from his bike's weapons, slamming into the embrasure of the gun pit concealing the weapon. Annael looked directly at one of the gunners, his left thumb pressing a targeting rune. The guns on his bike elevated and swivelled to follow his gaze. A red lock-on gleamed in his view and a chime sounded in his ears. Muzzle flash lit up the front of his bike as he opened fire, the machine-spirit of *Black Shadow* keeping the bolters on their target even as the motorbike bounced across the ground and Annael strafed left and right.

Men and cannon were engulfed by a hail of bolts, ripping through padded jackets and metal, filling the gun pit with blood and splinters. Annael fired another burst to be certain, brick dust from the embrasure and fragments of torn cloth and shattered bone spraying across the snaking power cables of the multi-laser.

'The enemy are abandoning the citadel.' Grand Master Sammael's report was softly spoken, yet clearly heard over the din of war. 'First wave to encircle and contain. Second and third waves to follow across the bridge. Resistance faltering.'

Annael's squadron were part of the first wave, and it was their duty to cut off further escape across the bridge, while those that had already fled would be herded towards the second compound, providing pause for the gunners within and cover for the following Dark Angels.

'Be vigilant,' warned Sergeant Cassiel. 'The cornered animal fights without fear. This battle is not yet won.'

RETRIBUTION

The bridge was wide enough for three dozen men to walk abreast, yet it was still a killing ground. Many of the rebels that had fled at the very start of the attack had reached false sanctuary at the far end, and those wise enough to commandeer half-tracks and ground cars were racing across the half-kilometre span. There were scores still on foot, ill fate, or perhaps misguided bravery, keeping them in their positions for minutes longer than their wiser or more cowardly companions.

The barrel of the storm bolter mounted on Sammael's steed was glowing hot from firing and he ceased the fusillade unleashed into the mass of humanity pouring onto the bridge. Some rebels, desperate men who at the last chose to spit back at their attackers, turned to fire their weapons at the oncoming Ravenwing. Gunfire flashed past Sammael as he angled *Corvex* between the towers that guarded entry to the bridge. Smoke poured from the summits of these thirty-metre high bastions, and their upper storeys were cracked and pitted from battle cannon and missile hits. Most importantly, their gun batteries were silent, as were those at the far end.

Sammael's command squad fanned out to either side of him, guns roaring. The men ahead were cut down in twos and threes, legs ripped from beneath them, bodies shredded by explosive bolts. Drawing his power sword, the Grand Master of the Ravenwing fell upon the rear-most stragglers. His blade cut the head from the first, who had not the time to turn to see his death approaching. The next, a brief moment later, was sent tumbling to the ferrocrete with spine severed and arm spinning through the air.

On Sammael's left, Epistolary Harahel held a gleaming force axe, psychic fire licking along its edges. He swung the blade between the shoulders of a fleeing rebel and wrenched the axe free in a mist of steaming blood. Chainswords snarling, Brothers Daedis and Athelman slashed and hacked as the squadron caught up with a group of fleeing rebels. The aquila-headed crozius arcanum of Chaplain Malcifer shimmered with a powerfield as it smashed in the skull of another running trooper.

Alerted by a warning signal in his ear, Sammael swerved *Corvex* to the right, moments before a rocket sent up a shower of ferrocrete shards from the road ahead. It had come from a small half-tracked wagon halfway along the bridge; a litter of broken track links from a weapon hit testified to the reason for its immobility.

More rockets screamed from the launcher atop its rear compartment, many of them passing overhead to explode between the towers behind Sammael. One rocket impacted on the high guard wall to the left, showering Daedis with blocks of jagged ferrocrete. Fighting to control his bike, the Dark Angel veered into a clutch of bodies piled on the roadway. Bone splintered and flesh spattered across the ferrocrete as the heavy bike ploughed through the human debris. Smoke dribbled from damage to the bike's engine.

'Lion curse it,' snarled Daedis as his mount slowed to a halt and the command squadron swept on.

Sighting on the half-track as two crewmen appeared on its roof, hurriedly trying to reload the rocket launcher, Sammael powered up his steed's plasma cannon. He felt the shudder of the energy coils peaking through the constant throb of *Corvex*'s anti-grav engines and pushed the firing rune. The plasma cannon spat a ball of azure-and-white lightning that slammed into the side of the half-track a few moments later, rocking the vehicle and hurling the half-disintegrated remains of the crewmen from the top. Another second passed before a lascannon beam from a circling Thunderhawk punched through the armoured compartment.

Pulling back on the controls, Sammael soared over the flaming ruin of the half-track and plunged down on the other side; straight into a knot of men who had been heading for cover behind the vehicle. One was flung aside, body smashed by the prow of the *Corvex*. Acting without thought, Sammael lashed out with his sword, slicing through the chest of two more.

Arrestor vanes flared as he hauled his mount sideways and braked, spinning to confront the three survivors, the storm bolter stitching a line of small explosions across the side of the half-track before the cannonade cut down the men. Maintaining the momentum of the turn, Sammael wrenched *Corvex* full circle before firing the thrusters.

Within seconds he had caught up with the rest of his squadron.

Ahead, the second citadel loomed large, its light grey walls lit by the rising sun. Sammael activated the command link to Sergeant Seraphiel.

'Closing on second objective, commander,' he said. 'What is your status?'

'The rebels started fleeing the third objective right after the bombardment, Grand Master Sammael,' Seraphiel reported. 'They are heading straight for us.'

'Good. Let your guns give them the greeting they deserve.'

ESCAPE THWARTED

To the north of the fortresses the hills banked up into wooded mountains with snow-capped peaks. It was from hidden caves and secluded valleys that the rebels had first attacked, and they would return to these lairs if given the chance. To prevent escape, the squads of the Fifth Company had landed alongside the road that looped around the outskirts of Hadria Praetoris, and stretched twenty warriors on patrol across the heathland directly north of the compounds.

Squad Amanael had been assigned to the road, and were deployed alongside the Devastators of Sergeant Athrael. The heavy weapon-armed Space Marines were split either side of the road, sited with a view down a straight stretch coming down the hill from the forts. Telemenus and the others were sweeping the woods to the south, right of Athrael's position, to intercept any rebels trying to escape cross-country. Sergeant Amanael had split his squad into two combat teams, each five-strong, to cover more ground, with Telemenus in the sergeant's section along with Menthius, Daellon and Apollon.

Century-old pines speared into the sky across the hillside, but there was little undergrowth beneath to block visibility. The crisp chill of autumn created vapour from the heat exchanges in the Space Marines' backpacks as they advanced across a carpet of brown pine needles. Apollon held the auspex, gently swinging the scanning device left and right seeking a return. The distant boom of cannons had put all of the birds in the vicinity to flight, so the woods were tranquil as the combat squad advanced.

'Let us hope that the rebels seek cover beneath the canopy,' said Daellon. 'If they are foolish enough to use the road Athrael's squad will score a great tally.'

'Concerned for my honour badge, brother?' asked Telemenus. 'Your support will be remembered in my litany of acceptance.'

'Apologies sergeant, for swelling his damned head further, but it was not my intent,' said Daellon.

'I shall inform the armoury that Telemenus's helm will need replacing on our return,' replied Amanael. 'He can pick it up when he has made suitable recompense to the Chaplains for his prideful words.'

'It is not pride to take pleasure in the slaying of many foes,' argued Telemenus. 'My accomplishments increase the honour of the Chapter, not diminish it.'

'Contact, four hundred and fifty metres.' Apollon's warning silenced the Dark Angels, who waited for further information. It was forthcoming a few seconds later. 'Definitely enemy, moving at an angle to our advance. Large mass, I would say twenty or more. On foot.'

Amanael held a hand up for the squad to stop and joined Apollon to read the display for himself. The sergeant looked around and pointed to a rise in the ground off to the squad's right.

'They will have to cross that ridge. We shall wait for them at the top.'

Now with a focused purpose, the Dark Angels lengthened their strides and moved swiftly up the slope, their dark green armour blending naturally with the gloom beneath the canopy. Ten metres ahead of Telemenus, Apollon came to a sudden stop.

'Something else in the woods ahead, below the lip of a cliff. Getting high metallic readings.'

The sergeant ordered them into a run to investigate, leading the squad along the ridge line as it rose up from the forest floor, with the ground on their right dropping away steeply until it became a near-vertical gorge. Keeping watch along the line of the enemy advance, Telemenus saw nothing of the rebels, though a check with Apollon confirmed that they had not deviated from their route.

'I see nothing,' said Telemenus. He intensified the magnification of his autosenses and scanned between the trunks of the trees, but the slope of the ground worked against him and he could see no more than two hundred metres.

'I have found their destination,' declared Menthius, who had moved ahead several dozen metres. 'A small facility, built into the face of the cliff. Some kind of bunker, I think. No weapons systems visible.'

They caught up with Menthius, who stood at the edge of the precipice looking down. Joining him, Telemenus saw a ramshackle collection of outbuildings with sheet metal roofs surrounding a ferrocrete emplacement that looked as though it had been extruded from the rock of the cliff. Just beyond the shacks was a circular expanse of black plascrete, the trees cleared for it. A two-rotored gyrocopter sitting on the landing apron made its purpose obvious.

'Tunnels,' said Apollon, attracting the looks of the other squad members. 'The readings are indistinct because the enemy are approaching via tunnel. They seek to slip away without attention.'

'Perhaps the tunnels stretch all of the way back to the fortresses,' said Telemenus. 'An escape route long-planned.'

'And likely known only to the upper hierarchy,' concluded Amanael. He strode to the lip of the ridge and examined the drop. 'Too deep to jump. Too far to go back down and come around below. We must trust to our aim from here. Achamenon, new orders. Converge on our position with all haste. Keep to the low ground.'

An affirmative returned over the vox from the leader of the other combat squad.

'They are almost here,' said Apollon. He hooked the auspex to his belt and gripped his bolter in both hands. 'One hundred metres behind us, seventy metres below.'

Telemenus lowered to one knee at the very edge of the cliff and brought up his bolter to the firing position. In his right eye the aiming reticule of his targeter sprang into life as his finger settled on the trigger. The angle made it hard to see the opening of the tunnel, but the atmospheric craft was in plain sight.

'Hold fury until my word,' said Amanael. 'We must wait until they are too far to retreat back to their hiding place, in case there are other exits to which they will head. I have no desire for a sewer hunt.'

Taking his sergeant's words to heart, Telemenus lowered his weapon a fraction, lest the instinct to fire betrayed him. He watched as two men clad in camouflaged fatigues walked from the fortified tunnel entrance. They carried lasguns at the ready but were poor lookouts, their gazes turned to the forest floor around them rather than the clifftop above. One of them turned and waved and a few seconds later three more men emerged, to move out through the outhouses into the woods to either flank in an amateurish attempt at creating a perimeter.

Another half-dozen rebels followed, running across the apron to the low, broad form of the gyrocopter.

'We risk discovery,' said Menthius. 'If they reach their transport we have no weapon to bring them down.'

'Hold fire,' replied Amanael, speaking calmly. 'Wait for my command.'

Three of the rebels clambered into the cockpit of the aircraft and soon the whine of its engines drifted up to the Space Marines, accompanied by the acrid smell of poorly refined fuel. Thick smoke chugged from the exhausts as the twin rotors began to turn, gathering speed as the pitch of the engine increased.

'Sergeant?' said Telemenus, lifting his weapon once more. He moved his aim until the visor reticule settled on one of the rotor hubs. A good hit would be enough to ground the craft. 'An immobile target is much easier to hit.'

'I thought your aim better than that,' said Amanael.

'The rebel leader may already be aboard,' said Telemenus. 'We should attack now.'

'Not so,' said Apollon. 'The verminous traitor makes his appearance.'

Looking below, Telemenus saw a huddle of men dashing from the tunnel entrance. Most were garbed in the military gear of the others, but two wore black robes threaded with gold and silver. They certainly had the look of demagogues as they hurried towards their aircraft.

'Open fire.'

The words from Amanael came as a relief to Telemenus. He softly squeezed the trigger, sending a single bolt flaring down the cliff side. The round hit one of the minders in the shoulder, its detonation blowing off his arm. Even before the rebels had reacted, Telemenus's next shot took another bodyguard in the back, ripping out flesh and organs just above his hip.

Panic gripped the gaggle of rebels, but the guards stayed true to their purpose and closed around the two robed men as they broke into a run for the landing apron. Bolts from the other Space Marines cut through the air, striking down the men sent out on sentry as they turned their lasguns up to the clifftop. The bark of the squad's bolters echoed down the gorge and from the trees around them while bolt propellant cut criss-crosses of fire in the air around the tunnel entrance.

Telemenus ignored everything else as he focused on the patches of gold amongst the reds and browns of the camouflaged bodyguards. He fired another single round, aimed at the bald head of one of the leaders. Even as the bolt sped from his gun a minder stepped unknowingly into its path. A second later the rebel's skull exploded, spattering the demagogue with blood and brains.

'Caliban's fate,' Telemenus cursed as he took aim again. 'Luck guards these men better than any armour.'

There were exchanges between the other Dark Angels as they fired, passing information on the positions of their targets and voicing alerts to return fire. Telemenus absorbed the talk without consciously hearing the words, his focus on the group heading for the gyrocopter. The party had made it to the apron and was splitting apart as bodyguards fell to fire or turned to bring their weapons to bear on their attackers. Las-bolts spat up to the clifftop but they were of no concern to Telemenus.

'Speed death to the unworthy,' he whispered to his bolter, settling the sighting reticule once more on a black-robed figure.

This time there was no intervention to prevent the bolt striking the bald-headed man in the back of his neck. The demagogue's head flopped to one side, spine shattered, as his body crumpled to the plascrete.

'All fire on the craft,' declared Amanael. Shifting his view, Telemenus saw the blur of black robes disappearing into an open hatchway just behind the cockpit. He silently cursed that he had missed his second mark.

The scream of the engines increased even further as the gyrocopter lifted off, the downdraught of its rotors sending the men remaining on the apron tumbling to the ground. With a flick of his thumb, Telemenus switched his bolter to burst fire and unleashed a salvo of three rounds into its hull, slivers of metal and paint spraying around the door where the leader had climbed aboard. He stood up as the aircraft rose straight up from the apron. It was slowly turning towards the Space Marines and Telemenus took aim at the canopy. Bolter fire from the others sparked from the rotors and fuselage, to little effect against the armoured plate.

Slowly the cockpit was swinging into view as the gyrocopter lifted higher and higher, bringing the pilot towards Telemenus. It would be almost level with the clifftop before Telemenus could see inside. He waited, the reticule dancing a little as the ground shook from the thumping of the rotors.

Two more seconds would bring the pilots into view. Telemenus's finger was tightening on the trigger in expectation.

'Assault cannon!'

Menthius's shouted warning came a moment too late. Angled as far as its mount allowed, the multi-barrelled gun slung beneath the gyrocopter's nose came to bear before Telemenus's target came into view. A storm of shells scythed along the clifftop and engulfed him, slamming into his armour. The outer layer of his suit shattered, sending shards of ceramite spinning in all directions. The impact of the heavy shells on his left side turned him slightly as he fired, sending his salvo of bolts flaring past the canopy without effect. His autosenses picked up the rip of the cannon's fire a split-second later.

Pain flared through his left arm. He ignored it as he sighted again, but the distraction had cost him his shot. The gyrocopter soared up over the trees, its nose dipping as it accelerated towards the north.

'Brother, are you wounded?' said Menthius, glancing back at Telemenus. He looked down at his left arm. His shoulder guard was nothing more than a few scraps of ceramite attached to the actuators. Blood poured from the cracks in the armour around his upper arm. He became aware of four neat holes punched into the left side of his breastplate, the shells from the assault cannon buried within, deep, but not enough to penetrate to flesh.

'It is usually better to fire first, you damned idiot,' said Daellon.

'Noted, brother,' Telemenus replied sourly, turning his attention back to the soldiers still firing from below as Amanael broadcast on the company-wide channel.

'All command, we have priority target escaping in airborne transport. Last heading approximately twenty by fifteen.'

'Already aware, sergeant,' came Seraphiel's reply. '*Paladin Four* tasked for intercept.'

Telemenus glimpsed the head of a rebel glancing around the corner of a shack below and fired his bolter one-handed. The rounds tore through the flimsy walls and two men in fatigues staggered away, one holding the stump of his right wrist, the other with a hand clamped to a wound gushing blood from his thigh. Telemenus emptied his magazine with two more bursts, cutting down the injured men.

He looked up as he heard the scream of plasma jets above. His hands moved on instinct, ejecting the spent magazine and inserting another as he followed the dark blur of a fighter soaring overhead, the dull ache in his arm ignored. With a flare of light, the aircraft fired a missile, which left a curving trail of vapour as its internal cogitator steered it after the departing gyrocraft. A few seconds later a distant but distinct crack was picked up by Telemenus's autosenses.

'Target has ditched in the foothills,' announced the pilot of *Paladin Four*. 'Crash-landed. Survivors probable. Grid epsilon-four-eighty.'

'Get ready to move to the crash site,' announced Sergeant Amanael. 'Sergeant Seraphiel, Squad Amanael preparing to investigate crash. Brother Achamenon and the others can finish off the stragglers here.'

'Negative, brother-sergeant,' Seraphiel replied quickly. 'I have received orders from Grand Master Sammael. All Fifth Company squads attend to your orders. Hold the line against rebel evacuation. Do not approach the crash site. Ravenwing forces despatched to investigate survival of the priority target and will advise if assistance is needed.'

Amanael looked at Telemenus and then the others before replying.

'Please confirm, brother-sergeant. Squad Amanael is less than five kilometres from the crash site.'

'Orders are confirmed, brother. Acknowledge.'

'Acknowledged, brother,' said Amanael. His next words came from the external speaker of his helm. 'Looks like the glory hounds of the Ravenwing want to have a hunt.'

THE HUNT

As the squads of the Fifth Company swept through the woods towards the final citadel, Squadron Cassiel received orders to make all speed to rendezvous with Grand Master Sammael on the road leading north. There was little resistance at the first objective and they were able to withdraw from the fortification without incident before speeding down to the main highway that ran between the citadels and Hadria Praetoris. On the open road they opened up their engines, the wooded embankments lining the road speeding past in a blur, the growl of engines loud in Annael's ear.

'This is the truth of the Ravenwing,' said Sabrael. 'A foe to hunt, a fine steed and an open road.'

Annael admitted to himself that the sensation was uplifting, almost as pleasurable as the heat of battle. Despite the light spirits of the squadron they remained alert for possible ambush and rebels fleeing the fighting. Occasional flutters of scanner returns flared in Annael's display, but they were not conclusive enough to warrant investigation. Their orders had been specific: make all speed to rendezvous with their commander en route to the priority target's crash site.

Three kilometres north of the final citadel, the highway was joined by a smaller road winding down from the heights. Just as the squadron reached the junction, Grand Master Sammael and his command squad powered into view. Cassiel slowed the squadron a little, allowing the Grand Master and his attendants to come alongside.

'Well met, brothers,' said Sammael, glancing across towards Cassiel and his warriors. 'Let us run down this traitorous dog and his henchmen. We shall discover the truth behind this unseemly insurrection.'

'As you command, Grand Master,' replied Cassiel.

'I see that you have fine company, Brother Annael,' remarked Chaplain Malcifer, steering his bike to ride beside the Ravenwing's newest recruit.

'I am honoured,' replied Annael, keeping his answer short so that he could concentrate on controlling his mount; the experience of the others allowed them to steer their bikes guided by instinct alone. Short answers also gave the Chaplain less opportunity to find fault.

The highway started to curve westwards, away from their objective, and the two squadrons moved off the road, racing up the embankment before plunging into the shadows of the forest. The squadrons split further to negotiate the rough terrain. Annael kept his gaze fixed on the scanner return, using its artificial eyes to guide his bike between trees, avoiding ruts and boulders that were too large to traverse.

'Do you think we should slow down for our new brother?' said Sabrael. 'I would not see a good machine ended on a tree.'

'Would that you should suffer such a fate to spare us

your prattling, brother,' said Malcifer. 'If you could control your tongue as skilfully as you master your steed we would be blessed by your silence.'

'I must reveal that the secret of my skill is to let both mount and tongue free to follow their own spirit,' said Sabrael. 'I simply let them take me where they wish to go.'

'Is he always this boastful?' Annael asked, his bike dipping down a shallow incline, dead leaves and mulch spraying in its wake. He glanced across to Malcifer. 'Have not the penitent cells taught him good manners by now?'

'Sabrael is the bane of the Chaplaincy, it is certain, but enthusiasm is not a crime,' said the Chaplain. 'It is the nature of the Ravenwing that it provides home to those of restless or wayward spirit.'

'Is that what I am now?' asked Annael. He leant to his right and guided his bike past a moss-covered fallen tree. 'A wayward spirit?'

'You take reproach where none is intended. Your inquiries revealed a questing mind seeking answers best provided by service in the Ravenwing. As now we hunt a physical foe, so we also run the truth to ground.'

'Then I shall be content that I have found my place.'

'You are welcome amongst us, brother,' added Sammael. 'It was not chance that I picked your squadron, Annael. I would have you experience the deepest nature of the Ravenwing and set before you the reward of service in the Second Company.'

'I am doubly honoured, Grand Master, to be in your consideration,' replied Annael, humbled by the attention of his superior.

'Good, for the matter will swift come to resolution,' said the Grand Master.

A warning chime attracted Annael's attention to his

scanner. They were within two kilometres of the crash site, which showed up on the display as a reading of dense artificial materials and heat; the burning wreck of the traitor leader's aircraft. Glancing up, the Dark Angel could see smoke drifting across the cloudless sky through gaps in the forest canopy. Even though he had looked away for only a moment, when he returned his gaze ahead he was forced to duck down to his handlebars to avoid a low-hanging tree limb. Smaller branches snapped around him, raking across his backpack as he powered through the thick foliage.

'Rightly it is that the Chaplains warn of eternal vigilance,' said Malcifer, who had seen Annael's close call. 'Let us put distraction aside and focus on the hunt.'

They soon came across a scatter of broken branches and pieces of snapped rotor blades, and a short distance away Sammael signalled as a crackle of flames and a cloud of smoke drifted through the trees. A check of *Black Shadow*'s scanner showed no sizeable life forms nearby, only the heat from the fires.

The two squadrons slowed as they reached the downed gyrocopter, its mangled wreckage propped against a thick trunk, debris scattered all around. Fire had licked up from its engine, scorching the tree trunk and setting fire to the leaves of the tree. A corpse dangled halfway out of the shattered cockpit, skull smashed.

Cassiel ordered his squadron to form a perimeter around the wreck while Sammael and his squadron circled the site, checking for survivors. None were evident within the crashed gyro, and the Grand Master confirmed as such.

'Three more bodies inside,' said Sammael, bringing his jetbike to a halt not far from the wreckage. 'Focused heat scan shows a residual trail leading west. Someone escaped the crash. One, possibly two targets. Spread out, echelon primus.'

The riders fanned out into their search formation, twenty metres between each Dark Angel. Annael narrowed his scanner array to detect the slightest variation from the ambient temperature and his vision lit up with signals of birds and small mammals fleeing from the oncoming bikes, and a ghostly trail that meandered between the trees ahead.

A Space Marine on nearly a tonne of motorbike was not built for a stealthy approach and the woods trembled with the noise of engines as the Ravenwing advanced, scattering birds from the trees. The heat trail grew more definite as they advanced, and it was Araton who made the first sighting.

'Heat mass, quadrant four, two hundred and fifty metres.'

'Cassiel, Zarall, Sabrael, circle around. All others, close on signal,' ordered Sammael. Annael picked up speed as the three nominated riders peeled away to the left to cut off escape – not that escape was likely with the warriors of the Ravenwing bearing down on their prey.

Annael could see the telltale glimmer of heat from behind a tree not far ahead and switched from thermal view to catch a glimpse of gold catching a shaft of sunlight. The rebel made one last attempt for freedom, bolting from the cover of the tree, cutting to the right. His bald scalp glistened with sweat, his heavy black robes impeding him as they caught on the thorns of a low bush, pulling him to a halt.

Sweeping around from the right, Sammael reached the rebel first, an outstretched hand grabbing hold of the fugitive's robe as he ripped himself free from the tangling embrace of the bush, lifting him from his feet as easily as a normal man picks up a child. The Grand Master of the Ravenwing turned towards the others and brought his jetbike to a halt, flinging the man to the ground where he tumbled through fallen leaves and dirt and lay unmoving.

'Priority target detained,' announced Sammael. 'We have their leader, but there are more rebel scum to be brought to justice. Rendezvous with the Fifth Company squads and scour the hills of the filth. This one I leave to your attentions, Brother Malcifer.'

Annael wondered why a Chaplain would be interested in a rebel commander, but had no time to consider the answers; Sergeant Cassiel was already ordering the squadron to form up on his position to return to the battle.

DISAPPOINTMENT

Two mind-scrubbed servitors were lifting the body of the captured rebel leader, the corpse wrapped in a bloodstained white shroud, as Sammael entered the chamber. Malcifer had conducted the interrogation of the prisoner, Ansat Neur Hakol, in a sub-basement of one of the captured citadels, and was wiping blood from his gauntlets with a rag. Epistolary Harahel stood to one side, in the shadows cast by the flickering light globe hanging from the ceiling, his hands clasped to his chest in contemplation. Aside from the small metal chair that Hakol had occupied, the only furniture in the room was a table on which Malcifer's crimson-flecked interrogation implements glinted.

'No taint,' said Malcifer. The Chaplain tossed the bloodied rag onto the shrouded corpse as the servitors clanked past on bionic legs. He looked at Harahel to continue.

'Just a man with misplaced ideals,' said the Librarian. 'Not a hint of possession or corruption.'

'The other commander, the one that died in the crash, was the instigator,' said Malcifer with a slight shake of his head. Sammael knew that it was not a gesture of sorrow, but maybe one of disappointment. 'This one's confession gives no cause to suspect that the Ruinous Powers are at work in the system. There has been no contact with external influence, and nothing to suggest this is part of any grander scheme.'

Sammael was not sure whether to be pleased or not by this news. On the surface, the fact that the local rebellion was a straightforward anti-Imperial insurrection and nothing more sinister meant that there was no further threat to nearby star systems in contact with the world. Weighed against that was the distraction it had been for the Ravenwing, who had other rumours to investigate, other calls for aid to address. On balance, Sammael was frustrated by the mundane nature of the enemy. He had arrived hoping to encounter one of the true targets of the Ravenwing, foes the specialist company had been created to hunt, or at the least the mark of such an insidious enemy at work. Instead he had simply killed disillusioned labourers led astray by ambitious demagogues.

'Very well,' said the Grand Master. 'There are pockets of resistance remaining, but nothing of significance that would require us to tarry here. I shall inform the Imperial Command that our mission has been concluded.'

'Where does the hunt take us next?' asked Harahel.

'I am inclined to respond to news of attack in the Raedal system,' replied Sammael. 'The astropathic messages are not definitive, but hint at possible incursion by followers of the Ruinous Powers. The speed with which orbital protection was breached hints at prior knowledge of the defences. It is not conclusive, and I will weigh alternative suggestion.'

'Raedal is only three hundred light years away,' said Malcifer. 'It warrants scrutiny.'

'I have no counsel to offer that would sway decision,' Harahel said as Sammael moved his gaze to the Epistolary.

'Raedal it shall be,' concluded the Grand Master.

'And what shall we do with the rebel's remains?' asked Malcifer.

'Have it presented to the Imperial Commander,' replied Sammael. 'A gift from the Dark Angels and a message for others to heed.'

OMENS FROM AFAR

The door to Harahel's cell opened to admit two robed figures with sunken faces and blank eyes. The Librarian turned, his plain wooden stool creaking under his weight, and beckoned for the astropaths to enter. He stood up from his desk, where he had been penning a report on the knowledge gleaned from his foray into the mind of the rebel commander.

'You received a vision?' he asked.

'One of terrible import,' replied Bayoth, the eldest of the two. The astropath looked at Harahel with pale eyes, seeing him with a sense other than normal vision. 'We seek your guidance in its interpretation before we speak with Grand Master Sammael.'

'We are but five hours from translation to the warp,' said the Librarian. 'A timely omen.'

The astropaths nodded inside their hoods but said nothing.

'Very well, we shall commune,' said the Librarian. He rolled up the sleeves of his blue robe, revealing arms covered with the scars of old burns, the legacy of a plasma gun malfunction when he had been but a novitiate in the Scout Company. Lacking later adaptations that would have healed the wounds with barely any trace, Harahel had borne the scars without thought ever since.

He held out his hands, palms up. Bayoth laid his fingers upon the Epistolary's right hand and the other astropath, Neim, did the same of the left. The Librarian closed his eyes. It was not necessary for the projection of his psychic potential, but he disliked staring into the blind orbs of the astropaths when they entered their trance-like transmission state.

The astropaths murmured a mantra to dislocate their conscious state, moving their minds from the bonds of corporeal form. Harahel needed no such ritual, but simply freed his thoughts from the tether of his synapses, his soul enmeshing with the spirits of the two astropaths.

'Show me,' he whispered.

The first sensation was of scorching heat; the residue of the soul-binding the astropaths had undergone. The fire of the Emperor's soul burned within them, a fiery shield against possession. Harahel let the burning subside before pushing on, feeling connection with the astropaths as they opened up their minds to his inquiry.

He felt a gulf opening beneath him as he was drawn into the warp-memories of the psykers. All three became floating motes on the immaterial seas, rising and falling on the insubstantial waves of energy. The background noise of the universe hummed in the Librarian's ears while echoes from past, present and future flitted around him just out of reach.

The sound of a sword unsheathing. A black blade glinted with inner light. The key-symbol of the Dark Angels.

A fortress dark against a setting sun. The Tower of Angels, fortress-monastery of the Chapter, known also as the Rock.

An angel's wings spread from a blade that hovers above the battlements of the castle. The sigil of Supreme Grand Master Azrael, Chapter Grand Master.

Harahel drew in a deep breath, knowing why the astropaths had come to him. A signal with the seal of the Supreme Grand Master was rare. The vision unfolded, sent across the void of the warp by the psykers of the Rock, carried by a flock of fluttering ravens. The message was for Sammael, for the Ravenwing. Steel claws and beaks glinted in the black mass: a summons to battle.

A starship circled a world. Its name floated through Harahel's thoughts. Blade of Caliban. *He knew the ship, and from where it had come. Piscina, a recruiting system of the Dark Angels. Not so long ago the warriors of the Chapter had fought a war against an ork invasion of the world. Harahel sought confirmation that the ork threat had returned, but it was not a green-skinned beast that was carried upon the ship.*

Instead there appeared a Space Marine, clad in black armour, a skull-face helm concealing his face beneath the cowl of a white robe. A Chaplain. The robes caught fire, the armour of the figure becoming black flames that consumed the white of the Deathwing. The meaning was unclear until the Chaplain was reduced to ashes, and from the embers rose another figure. A hooded warrior, angel wings splayed from his back, a sword inverted in his hands.

Harahel broke the communion, pulling back sharply. The urgency of his retreat brought gasps from the astropaths and Harahel was forced to take another deep breath to steady himself. He opened his eyes and saw questioning looks on the faces of the two men in front of him.

'We saw but a fraction of the vision,' said Neim, wiping sweat from his face with the cuff of his robe. 'Can you interpret its meaning?'

'Scour these memories, and speak not of them to

another soul,' said the Librarian. 'I comprehend its meaning and will bear this news to the Grand Master. Return to your posts and be ready to transmit a reply to the Tower of Angels.'

'As you command,' the two astropaths chorused, bowing their heads once more.

They turned and left. Harahel sat down with a grimace once they were gone and allowed himself a groan as the images from the Supreme Grand Master pulsed through his thoughts. To one who knew the secret signs of the Chapter, there was no confusion. The Epistolary took a moment to collect his thoughts, hands trembling as he rested them on his knees.

The reception of the message had been timely indeed. They would need to lay in a new course.

THE HUNT BEGINS

Malcifer arrived in Sammael's quarters just a few minutes after Harahel had entered. The Chaplain was dressed in the vestments of the sacristy, a cloak of black over his white robes. Sammael sat at the head of the oval table while Harahel paced back and forth beside the Grand Master, hands clasped together behind his back.

'Sit,' said Sammael, waving the Chaplain to the chair on his right.

'I detect disquiet,' said Malcifer as he seated himself, sweeping his cloak over the ornately carved back of the chair. Wood creaked under his weight. 'And urgency. You said that we have received a message from Azrael, brother?'

Sammael looked to Harahel to reply. The Librarian's communication that convened the council had been brief and Sammael had waited for Malcifer to arrive so that there was no need for repetition. The Librarian ceased his pacing and sat down opposite Malcifer. With sparing words, Harahel described the images from the message, clarifying the source and sender.

'There is trouble at Piscina,' said Sammael. 'The inverted blade signals treachery, but I do not know what to make of this dark Chaplain.'

'We cannot know for sure,' said Malcifer. 'There was a small squad left to oversee the protection of the Chapter Keep and the initial training of the recruits, led by Brother Boreas. The message must relate to him, but I find it hard to accept that he has turned against us. Boreas is one of the most stalwart upholders of the Chapter's honour, a hero of the Piscina campaign and many others.'

'We cannot ignore the image,' said Harahel. 'It has been several years since the Tower of Angels last had contact from Piscina, and much can happen in that time.'

'Not to the loyalty of a Brother-Chaplain,' Malcifer argued vehemently. 'Perhaps we read the signs wrong. The Chaplain has been consumed by dark flames of treachery, but that can mean victim, not perpetrator.'

'Questions that can be answered when we arrive,' said Sammael. 'The intent of the Supreme Grand Master is clear. Something sinister has happened at Piscina and the Ravenwing must investigate.'

'We must consider that this message was meant for you alone, brother,' said Harahel. 'It is for the Ravenwing. There must be other forces open to despatch to Piscina, and therefore the choice of the Supreme Grand Master to call to us leaves only one conclusion – that the Ravenwing alone is suited to solve the mystery of Piscina. That in turn leads me to believe that Azrael suspects the involvement of our particular foe.'

'The Fallen.' Sammael whispered the word with a grimace.

'Indeed,' said Malcifer. 'It is not coincidence that one of our home worlds is threatened, I fear.'

'It also leaves us with a more pressing issue,' said Harahel. 'Do we take the warriors of the Fifth with us? They may be exposed to truths that are beyond their calling.'

'A risk we must take,' said Sammael, reaching a decision instantly. 'To send them back to the Rock without explanation would only invite curiosity. The Ravenwing will be the vanguard, and we shall shield our brothers from uncomfortable fact if necessary. This is not the first occasion we have encountered such issues and it shall not be the last.'

'As you command, Grand Master,' said Malcifer. 'I sense that we cannot expect further support from the Chapter for the foreseeable future.'

'I think not,' said Harahel. 'The Tower of Angels will certainly make for Piscina as swiftly as is possible, I am sure, but as ever we shall be the first light to penetrate the shadow.'

'Let us be thankful then that we are not embroiled in further complications.' Sammael leaned back. 'Why so glum, my brothers?'

'The taint of the Fallen is always cause for regret,' said Harahel. 'To think that they cast a shadow upon one of our worlds again heralds concern.'

'Not at all,' replied Sammael. He smiled. 'When one of the Fallen casts ripples for us to see, it is a blessing, not a curse. One more name to be struck from the ledger of shame. This is our purpose. This is why we hunt!'

TWO

PISCINA IV

A WORLD OF ANARCHY

'Something is certainly amiss, Grand Master,' reported Judoc Pichon, bridge officer of the *Implacable Justice*. A rangy man, Pichon was almost as tall as Sammael, whom he addressed in the middle of the strike cruiser's bridge. An unaugmented human in his middle ages, the bridge officer bore the sigil of the Chapter as a red tattoo on his left cheek; a symbol of one who had been accepted as an aspirant but ultimately failed the subsequent testing by the Librarians and Chaplains. Unsuitable to undergo the transformation into a super-human warrior, Pichon instead served as the ranking non-Space Marine officer of the bridge crew.

'Hails to the Chapter Keep receive no response,' he explained, passing a sheaf of transparent reports to the Grand Master of the Ravenwing. 'We have detected no intercepting craft from the system defence fleet, nor have we received any hail from orbital defence.'

'A matter of concern,' agreed Sammael. He flipped through the scanner readouts, processing the information at a glance. 'Scattered communications traffic describes considerable turmoil on the surface.'

'Yes, Grand Master Sammael, it would appear so. With your permission, I will begin an all-frequency hail. There are certainly active defence forces. Somebody will be paying attention.'

'Very good, Pichon. Move us into low orbit and conduct a full sweep scan. I want a clearer picture of what is happening below.'

The officer lifted his hands to his chest and bowed before turning away to issue the orders. Sammael pondered the meaning of the reports and concluded that the lack of attention paid by the defence forces had to indicate a pressing threat on the surface. He recalled the data entries he had read on Piscina IV, and much mention was made of the residual ork presence left in the wake of the invasion. Despite all efforts, the aliens continued to be a threat and this seemed the likely source of the turmoil.

Though this explanation offered a likely reason, Sammael could not dismiss the possibility that something deeper and more sinister was wrong at Piscina. The nature of the message from the Rock lent credence to the Grand Master's suspicion that treachery was a contributing factor.

'Signal alert to full combat readiness, Pichon,' he said. 'I want to be ready to intervene or react should events require it. Relay orders to the *Penitent Warrior*.'

'As you command, Grand Master,' replied the officer. He made his way to the communications console and moments later his voice echoed from the address system, announcing the call to combat status. Pichon turned to step away when one of the Chapter serfs manning the comms monitoring station called him back. There was a brief exchange and then Pichon hurried over to Sammael.

'Contact made, Grand Master,' said the officer. 'We are receiving transmission from the command staff of a Colonel Brade.'

'Commander-in-chief of the Free Militia defence force,' said Sammael, remembering the name from his studies. 'Send summons to Brothers Harahel and Malcifer to meet me in my command chamber, and ask the colonel to be ready to make a full report. Transfer reception to my secure channel.'

'As you command, Grand Master.' Pichon bowed again and attended to his orders as Sammael crossed to the door leading to his chamber adjoining the bridge. As the double doors swung open on hydraulic hinges, the Grand Master turned back to issue one last command. 'Signal Sergeant Seraphiel of the Fifth Company to stand ready to receive drop orders.'

Sammael stepped through the doors without waiting for the officer's acknowledgement, walking into a sparsely furnished chamber dominated by a hololithic projector and a bank of communications equipment. He activated the display and accessed the strike cruiser's data store to bring up an image of Piscina IV. His fingers moving quickly over the controls, the Grand Master zoomed in on the principal island, Kadillus, and the planet's capital, Kadillus Harbour. A blinking icon not far inside the city marked the position of the Chapter Keep where recruits from the feral tribes of Piscina V underwent initial recruitment testing and training.

Overlaying the data stream from the current sensor sweep, Sammael noticed an automated transmission sourced from the Chapter Keep. He recognised it immediately as a standard beacon signal, activated as a warning that the keep was under threat.

The doors wheezed open behind him and he turned to see Harahel and Malcifer enter. The two of them wore their armour, as did Sammael; standard doctrine when approaching a potentially compromised star system. They carried their helmets in their hands, the faces of both showing concern.

'We receive word from the planet,' Sammael informed them, moving to the communications array. He spoke briefly with one of the attendants and a few seconds later a garbled signal screeched from the speakers. Sammael keyed in his personal code to decrypt the channel.

'You are addressing Grand Master Sammael of the Adeptus Astartes. Confirm identification. Issuing decryption signal now.'

It took a moment for the link to be established, a grey screen at the centre of the panel flickering into static and then resolving into the monotone image of a broad-faced, aging man wearing a peaked cap decorated with the Imperial aquila. Sammael transferred the link to the hololith and turned back to the centre of the room as the man's face appeared, floating above the schematic of Kadillus.

'Colonel Brade, Commander of the Piscinan Free Militia. Thank the Emperor you have arrived! It is anarchy down here.'

Sammael glanced at his companions before replying.

'Be specific, colonel. What is the nature of the threat?'

'Where do I start? We have widespread civil unrest in the capital, a burgeoning famine, resurgent ork attacks and a divided planetary command.'

'What is the status of our Chapter Keep?' asked Malcifer. 'Where is the Dark Angels garrison squad?'

'We have had no word from the keep for months.' Brade shook his head despondently. 'We tried to enter, but it is sealed and we thought it better not to attempt a breach of a Dark Angels facility.'

'A wise choice. What is your current military status,

colonel?' asked Sammael. 'Why have you not restored order?'

'I have tried, by the Emperor, believe me I have tried.' Brade's face was haggard, eyes dark-rimmed even in the poor resolution of the display. 'A mob broke into the palaces of Imperial Commander Sousan, aided by some of my own men. She was tried for treason against her own people and executed before I could intervene. Her cousin has taken on the role of Imperial Commander under my supervision, but the people are refusing to accept her command. Between the uprising and the orks, we do not have enough forces. The mega-trawlers are refusing to dock at the harbour and people are starving. Part of the city is infested with greenskins but I cannot clear them out whilst protecting what little food stores remain.'

'When the Tower of Angels last departed Piscina, we left behind an ordered, stable world. How is it that such a parlous state has so rapidly come about, colonel?' said Malcifer.

'Not to cast blame, but your warriors have not helped the situation. Lord Boreas and the others deserted the keep before the trouble began, and another force from the Chapter arrived in their place. They started a massacre, gunning down civilians and Free Militia. The people were terrified, thinking that the Emperor had turned against them. It was as if His divine judgement was being meted out upon the city. Hundreds were slain.'

'By Dark Angels?' Sammael demanded, sickened by the thought. He heard a snarl from Malcifer and a glance showed the Chaplain clenching his fists with anguish. Harahel met Sammael's gaze with a meaningful look. Sammael calmed himself and turned back to the hololith. 'You are certain, colonel?'

'That is what it seemed at the time, though when Lord

Boreas returned he gave the impression that these Space Marines were not acting under orders. But we haven't seen nor had word from the original garrison since they entered the keep. The people feel abandoned and with the orks on the verge of overrunning the city everything has descended into madness. Half my men have deserted or joined the uprising.'

Brade turned away and Sammael heard voices in the background, too quiet to be heard over the link. The colonel nodded a few times but his face was grim when he turned back.

'I have to go. The orks have broken through again and are advancing on Northport. The shuttle terminal is our only supply route, we cannot let it fall. Your assistance would be an Emperor-sent blessing, Lord Sammael.'

'I will contact you again shortly, colonel,' replied Sammael. He cut the link before Brade could make any further requests. The Grand Master turned his attention to his companions. 'Black flames of treachery indeed.'

'There can be no other reason,' said Malcifer. 'The Fallen have instigated this conflict. It is a malicious attack against the Chapter, one we cannot ignore.'

'I have no intention of ignoring it, brother, but it is not clear which course it is best to proceed upon. I would welcome your counsel.'

'Though the colonel did not state as such, it appears that the Fallen are no longer on Piscina,' said Harahel. The Librarian laid his helmet on the surface of the hololith, blanking out half the display. He looked thoughtful, fingers raised to his chin, palms pressed together. 'If we become embroiled in this conflict it will take considerable time to resolve. Judging by the reaction of the populace to the Fallen's slayings we cannot expect widespread cooperation.'

'I am of the same mind, brother,' replied Sammael.

'Even with our brethren from the Fifth Company, the Ravenwing is not ideally suited to this battle.'

'Regardless, we will only find the answers we seek on the surface,' said Malcifer. 'We must gain access to the Chapter Keep. It is possible that Boreas and the others, beset by an angry populace, have decided that isolation is the best course of action. To turn their weapons on the rebels might be seen as further betrayal by the Chapter and fuel the rebellion rather than quell it.'

'Why no answer to our communications?' asked Sammael.

'Their array may have been damaged in fighting, or perhaps disabled by the Fallen whilst the garrison was absent,' suggested Harahel.

'There are too many questions to which we have no answers, brother,' said Malcifer. 'You are correct, we must avoid the entanglements of this insurrection, but we cannot avoid making a planetfall. I suggest we devise a strategy to segregate the Chapter Keep from threat and then proceed to see what we can discover.'

'I concur,' said Harahel. 'The Tower of Angels is in transit to Piscina. If there is no resolution to the conflict by the time of their arrival, the intervention of the rest of the Chapter will settle matters. To that end, we must send warning of what they can expect to encounter.'

Sammael turned away from the pair and considered his options. He had been chosen as Grand Master of the Ravenwing for his initiative, and his position always entailed balancing the needs of the hunt with the duty the Chapter owed to the Imperium. He did not have to think long before he turned back to Malcifer and Harahel.

'The Fallen have already inflicted grievous injury on Piscina,' he told them. 'Our purpose must be to apprehend them before they can cause such harm again. At the moment there is no trail for us to follow, so we must secure the Chapter Keep and whatever intelligence it contains. We will launch overflights of the keep and have a perimeter secured by the rest of the company, while the Fifth Company creates a cordon between the orks attacking the city.'

'And Colonel Brade? He will make further requests for aid.' Harahel's expression betrayed inner conflict at the decision, something Sammael could understand but not share.

'We will give assurances that the Dark Angels will set to right the wrongs done to his people, and that is all. Brother-Chaplain, prepare the company for battle. We drop in three hours.'

STRATEGIC PRECAUTIONS

Pounding down the ramp of the Thunderhawk, Telemenus and the other members of Squad Amanael fanned out quickly, joining the other squads securing the landing site. The gunships had placed the Dark Angels amidst the ruins of abandoned entrenchments and bunkers; fortifications of cracked ferrocrete overgrown with vegetation. A stubby tree was growing up through the flak boards of a gun pit to Telemenus's right, crawling plants spilled from the firing slits of a bunker directly ahead.

Dust billowed as the gunships lifted off, the downdraught from their engines flattening wild grass and kicking up dead leaves that had gathered in the lee of the defensive wall. Through this litter the squad advanced, weapons at the ready though no enemy were expected. The constant ticking of negative returns from Apollon's auspex sounded in Telemenus's ear.

'As expected, long abandoned,' said Sergeant Amanael.

Sergeant Seraphiel's instructions split the force,

despatching Squad Amanael to secure the south-western end of the defensive line with Squad Atleus. The twenty Dark Angels forged along the hill, their shadows long in front of them as a new day dawned over the isle of Kadillus. The morning light shone bright from the distant curtain wall of Kadillus Harbour to the west, but the sky above the city was dark with smoke. The Free Militia were defending the starport on the other side of Kadillus Harbour. The Space Marines heard the constant crack of artillery in the distance and a perpetual chatter of gunfire. The muted growl of tank engines resounded across the city and Telemenus thought of the battle raging only a few kilometres away; stark contrast to the peaceful surrounds that greeted the arriving Dark Angels.

There was no threat here, and there were no signs of any impeding ork attack. As far as Telemenus could tell, the Fifth Company were nowhere near the fighting, for reasons he could not fathom. He wondered – hoped – that they were not simply being kept out of the way of their brethren in the Ravenwing, but he had suspicions. Yet if that was Sammael's aim, it would have proven simpler to keep the Fifth Company in orbit.

'Be aware of unexploded munitions and orkish traps,' warned Seraphiel, breaking Telemenus's train of thought. 'We know these bunkers were occupied by the orks less than twenty days ago.'

Following Amanael's lead, Telemenus dropped over the lip of the trench, crunching onto fractured plascrete two metres down. There were holes in the wall where roots and plant tendrils had broken through, the years since the construction of the fortifications enough for the wilderness to begin healing the scar made upon it.

The bleak landscape, endless kilometres of grassland and scrub leading up to the more verdant slopes at the island's volcanic heart, reminded Telemenus a little of the barren plains of Bartia where he had been raised.

It was warmer here, the wind not as icy; the sky darker from a more distant star.

His memories of Bartia were little more than fragments. He could not picture his parents' faces, nor the other children of the large family with whom he had shared a yurt for twelve years before the Dark Angels had returned to the midsummer hunt. Even his testing was a blur, of running and blood, and ultimately victory. None had run swifter nor slain more beasts than Telemenus that day; the youth he had been was more proficient with the short bow of his people than many four and five years his senior.

He stopped as Amanael turned to check a bunker leading off from the trench line, his bolter covering the lip of the line ahead. It was instinct to do so, requiring little thought, especially with no expectation of enemy.

One memory in particular did stand out though, a moment towards the end of the midsummer hunt when the gunships of the Dark Angels had descended like chariots on pillars of fire. The elders had crowed glories to the Emperor that the Dark Angels had returned and the competitors in the hunt, those with less than ten winters behind them, had been gathered for the inspection.

Telemenus – he had not been named as such back then – had been slightly shorter than the other youths, and to him the giants that had marched down the assault ramps had been walking gods. He remembered the glint of the setting sun on dark green armour and bolters, and the image of the winged sword in red upon the white of a flag snapping from the banner pole of the captain leading the recruiting squad.

Some of the boys had made fearful remarks when the Chaplain appeared, a skull-faced shadow that matched the ancient paintings of the Long Death that could be seen on the cliffs at Casoron Ford. Telemenus had not been afraid as he watched the deathly warrior approach; he had thought of a great-uncle – a name now forgotten with his own – who had been taken by the Dark Angels. It was a source of much pride and influence for the family to have such an ancestor.

When the other boys had stepped back from the advance of the armoured giants, Telemenus had kept his ground. The Chaplain had loomed over him, seeming larger than the aridovores that roamed the taiga in thousand-strong herds. With the confidence and impudence that only a youth could possess, young Telemenus had looked up into that skull face and asked, 'Are you my uncle?'

Such was the way of the Chapter initiation – love of home and kin replaced with love of the Emperor and the Dark Angels – Telemenus had never found out if his great-uncle had survived the trials and been accepted into the Chapter. There were certainly other Dark Angels who hailed from Bartia, Sergeant Seraphiel being one of them, but there was no way to know who they were before they had become Space Marines; they could not remember and the Chapter records did not contain such details. If his uncle was indeed still amongst the ranks of the Chapter, he was a brother to Telemenus now, a brother of battle.

Listening to the growl of the gunships prowling overhead and the sussurant whisper of the wind in the grass put Telemenus in mind of that day many decades ago, but it was a memory he recalled with intellectual detachment; something that seemed to have happened to another person, which he had later been told about. He no longer felt or thought the way that enquiring youth had felt and thought, his younger self as alien to him as any other human.

'Sweep clear,' announced Amanael as they came to a revetment at the end of the trench line, the glimmer of the sea visible many kilometres further down the sloping shore of the island.

There were other reports and acknowledgements from the other squads, confirming that the maze of trenches and fortifications was deserted. Amanael and his squad were ordered to hold ground, while patrols were sent out to secure the land to the north.

Watching thirty of his battle-brothers striding across the grasslands, the smoke and flame of the battle for Northport staining the air in front of them, Telemenus realised that something was not as he expected.

'Sergeant, our patrols are heading the wrong way,' he said. 'They are advancing towards Kadillus Harbour.'

'Your eyes are as sharp as ever, brother,' replied Amanael. He pointed to the north-west, where the stone of the Dark Angels' garrison citadel could be seen rising over the wall of the city, not far from where Kadillus dropped steeply down towards the port. 'We are not here to guard the city, we are to ensure that the ork attack does not move from Northport around the city towards the Chapter Keep. Imperial Guard and planetary forces are already holding the city. Those are our orders from Grand Master Sammael.'

'Curious,' said Cadael. 'I would have thought the Ravenwing better suited to patrol the open ground while we secure the citadel. Land Speeders and bikes are not ideal for urban conflict.'

'I am sure Grand Master Sammael has good reason to position our force as he has,' said Achamenon. 'One does not rise to the position of Company Grand Master by making fundamental mistakes.'

'I have the feeling we are somewhat redundant in the Grand Master's thoughts,' said Cadael. 'I look forward to the day that I learn the intricacies of strategy so that I may understand what plan requires sixty Space Marines to guard an empty patch of wilderness.'

'Watch your words, brother,' said Amanael. 'It is not our place to second-guess our orders, nor to doubt the decisions of superiors. Be assured that Grand Master Sammael set us here for a purpose.'

'The Ravenwing do things their own way,' said Telemenus. 'Sometimes they act more like White Scars or Space Wolves than Dark Angels.'

'And our current duty will be fulfilled with the dedication and decorum for which we are known,' said Amanael. 'Attend to your sectors and, while we have peace, reflect upon what we have witnessed today. It is evident that the Imperial Commander and her forces were lax in their scourging of the orks following the departure of the Chapter. That they have been able to multiply again, to grow to become a force that threatens the city once more, is a damning testimony to the peril of complacency. Be vigilant, as the Emperor stands vigil over us.'

Knowing that his sergeant's words forestalled any further debate, Telemenus nodded acquiescence and raised his bolter, his view telescoping through its targeter to magnify a stand of stunted trees half a kilometre away. He scanned left and right and saw only his battle-brothers continuing their patrol. Despite the battle raging for Northport only kilometres away, there were no enemies here and he would remain eleven kills short of his laurels for the time being.

ARRIVAL IN KADILLUS

The streets of the city were eerily empty as the lead squadrons of the Ravenwing entered by the south gate, opened to them by Brade's soldiers in the Free Militia. The returns from *Black Shadow*'s scanner showed that there were plenty of people around – several thousand in the immediate vicinity – but none showed themselves. Whether it was the ork warriors still prowling in other parts of the city or the presence of the Dark Angels that made the inhabitants hide, Annael did not know. The faces he glimpsed in windows were pale, expressions shell-shocked from a long, harrowing ordeal.

Against a backdrop of cannons and mortars, tanks and smalls arms fire from the north of the city, the growl of bike motors and whine of anti-grav engines echoed back from the low buildings. Glass was scattered across the roads, little danger to the reinforced tyres of the Ravenwing's machines, and in places narrower side streets and alleys between the grey tenements were blocked by improved barricades made of piled furniture, tyres, ferro-crete slabs and overturned vehicles.

There were bodies amongst the debris and draped over the obstacles. Vermin, furred and feathered, fought with each other over the spoils, though Annael noticed that the defenders of Kadillus had been wise enough to remove any orkish dead though they had not been able to do the same for their own kin. The bodies were almost picked clean, the fighting that caused them having passed to another part of the city some time ago; weeks more likely than days. From what the Dark Angels had gleaned from the planetary defence force commander, the city had been under incessant attack for some time, as the orks emerged in waves from their lairs in the wilderness, sometimes hundreds of them, occasionally a thousand or more.

It seemed impossible to believe that this had once been a recruiting world for the Chapter. Ever since Ghazghkull the Beast had brought the green horde here, Piscina had never quite known peace. The Dark Angels had done all they could, hunting down the aliens on the flanks of the volcanic island, purging their hidden camps. Other concerns had taken them away; campaigns that required their strength far more than Piscina, leaving the planet's defence in the hands of the local militia. Apparently they had not been as diligent as the Supreme Grand Master had expected. Annael was not surprised. The Piscinan soldiers were, after all, only human.

Reaching a large intersection with the rest of his squadron, Annael came across the burnt out wrecks of two Chimera troop transports. The vehicles had been stripped of weapons, track links, running gear, hatches and even some armour panels. Across the junction, about half a kilometre away in the direction the wrecked transports were facing, a line of chassis of destroyed ground cars choked the road, evidently targeted trying to approach the position of the Chimeras.

A bike squadron and two Land Speeder Typhoons peeled away to secure the far side of the intersection as the Ravenwing column turned left towards the Chapter Keep. More squadrons were despatched to secure the area around the citadel and Sergeant Cassiel passed on the order for Annael and the others to follow him into a wooded parkland.

The trees were losing their blossom, scattering pink and white petals in the wind as the black-armoured bikers guided their mounts along a winding road that cut through the park. The grass was heavily trampled and Annael saw scorch marks on a rise to his left in a pattern he recognised.

'Thunderhawk landing,' said Araton before Annael could make the same observation. 'Opposed, it seems.'

Annael was not sure what these last words meant until he was almost level with the black marks on the flattened turf. There were charred bones in the grass, tatters of clothing still clinging to them. Magnifying his autosenses, Annael saw that they were definitely humans not orks, and the clothes were of different colours and fabrics; civilians not soldiers.

'A gunship landed on them?' Zarall's voice was a whisper. 'There must have been good cause for such an act.'

'Let us concentrate on determining the present threat,' said Cassiel.

Annael tore his eyes away from the grisly tableau atop the hill. He had seen many corpses, human and alien, but there was something disturbing about the bodies scattered on the rise in the middle of the landscaped parklands. He could see no obvious damage to the surrounding buildings to indicate a battle had been fought here, though at the far side of the park he did see another destroyed Chimera at one of the gates in the wall surrounding the public gardens.

'Nobody is coming out,' said Sabrael. 'I have a mass of signals but they are all inside the buildings. I was worried we would be swamped by citizens celebrating our coming.'

'Perhaps they know better than to leave the safety of their homes during battle,' suggested Annael. 'The people of Kadillus Harbour know war very well.'

'That must be it,' said Sabrael. 'I would not like to contemplate any other reason why the Dark Angels would be shunned by loyal Imperial citizens.'

Annael knew that Sabrael made oblique reference to the bodies on the hill, and what they might signify, but like his battle-brother he did not voice any suspicion openly. Ever since he had been informed that they were securing the city around the Chapter Keep, Annael had wondered at the nature of the mission. It was clear that there was heavy fighting around the space port – the boom of shells and crackle of gunfire on the edge of his augmented hearing testified to the continuing conflict – but Grand Master Sammael had made a priority of the Chapter's citadel. Coupled with the deployment of the Fifth Company outside the city wall, it was a confusing situation.

It was not in Annael's nature to doubt the competence of his superiors, and he certainly trusted Grand Master Sammael's judgement in all strategic matters, but he wished that the upper echelons of the company had better communicated the mission objectives. Context was an important part of any tactical understanding and Annael felt that he and his brothers in the squadron were under-prepared to make correct decisions if the current situation changed. There seemed to be an overdependence on Grand Master Sammael to take personal command in all events.

It was not a great concern, and Annael knew well enough he had a lot to learn about the Ravenwing despite his induction into some of the company doctrine. After Chaplain Malcifer's remark, as good-natured as it had been intended, Annael was not going to get himself a reputation as a wayward spirit by voicing such opinion openly. It was the weakness in himself that gave rise to doubts, not some shortfall in the conduct of those around him; such was the teaching of the Chaplaincy.

When the park had been swept and declared secure, Grand Master Sammael's Thunderhawk blazed overhead, landing in the park not far from the corpse-littered hill. The Grand Master of the Ravenwing and his squadron sped from the gunship's belly, cutting directly across the park towards the citadel. The bikes disappeared along the street, no word received from Sammael as to the next phase of the mission.

'We wait for orders,' confirmed Cassiel, motioning the squadron to form a mobile patrol around the perimeter of the parkland. 'If we are needed, Grand Master Sammael will send word.'

GRIM DISCOVERIES

Under Sammael's guidance *Corvex* slid to a halt at the end of the street. Ahead, the Chapter Keep rose up at the centre of five hundred metres of bare rockcrete, its shadow stretching far across the grey slabs. Once this had been an industrial complex, flattened by the Dark Angels to create a kill zone around their citadel. The keep itself was not a grandiose building, simply a five storey slab-sided tower surrounded by a ten metre high curtain wall. Two squat bastions flanked the armoured gate, red sensor globe lenses staring impassively from within chamfered niches. There were ramparts on the keep roof and a gun tower at each corner.

It was the gun towers that were the focus of Sammael's attention.

As the rest of his command squad halted around him, Sammael checked the scan readings from his machine.

'No active sensors detected,' he announced. 'Gun towers inactive.'

He tried one more time to contact anyone inside

the keep, sending his personal identifier across several secure channels. There was no reply except for the insistent tone of the warning beacon.

'No sign of damage,' said Athelman. 'I cannot see any cause for the attack beacon to have been activated.'

'A subtle danger is the most perilous,' warned Malcifer, edging his bike forward to come alongside Sammael. He spoke to the company Grand Master over the command channel, heard only by Sammael and Harahel. 'If what we suspect is true, the attack was not external.'

'Daedis, Athelman, perimeter sweep,' announced Sammael, motioning for the squadron to move on. As the two battle-brothers accelerated off to the right, the Grand Master led Harahel and Malcifer directly towards the keep. Seeing multiple signal returns on his scanner in the buildings ringing the kill zone he looked around. Scared men and women, young and old, peered at the Dark Angels from the narrow windows of the housing blocks.

'I sense their fear,' said Harahel.

'Given the circumstance, not unexpected,' replied Malcifer.

'No, it is not just a general dread of the orks or the battle,' replied the Librarian. 'They are terrified of *us*. Colonel Brade and his men are in a minority if they are pleased to see us return.'

'Further reason to keep our presence here brief,' said Sammael.

They approached the gate of the curtain wall and still there was no sign of activity from the keep. Daedis and Athelman had disappeared from view, the return of their ident-markers on the scan display showing their progress around the far side of the citadel.

'You have the lock codes, brother?' Sammael looked at Malcifer as he asked the question.

'My override codes will gain us entry,' the Chaplain replied. Sammael's comm picked up the telltale buzz of a tight-channel transmission and a second later motors inside the wall snarled into action, the gate sliding to one side to reveal the courtyard within.

Sammael slowly moved into the compound and curved left towards a ramp that led down to the broad gate of the keep's underground garage. Behind him the outer gate rumbled back into place. Another transmission from Malcifer caused the reinforced steel slabs of the garage doors to retract. Sammael descended the ramp as lights flickered into life.

'Power generation still functioning,' the Grand Master remarked as *Corvex* slid through the gateway.

Two Rhino armoured carriers sat side-by-side, with three bikes lined up in maintenance cages along the left-hand wall. All seemed to be in order, the machines showing no signs of battle damage. The armoury garage stretched out as far as the foundations of the curtain wall, with plenty of room for the three Dark Angels to park their machines. Dismounting, Sammael ordered Malcifer to close the gates and made his way across the plascrete floor to a data terminal. He entered his ident-code and accessed the armoury logs while his companions performed a quick search of the garage.

'Nothing untoward,' reported Harahel.

'Nor here,' said Sammael. 'More than fifty days since the armoury was last accessed. Last entry is an ammunition and weapons withdrawal. To be expected if the orks presented a threat again.'

'Why are the Rhinos still here?' asked the Librarian. 'Surely they would not have departed on foot.'

'The Thunderhawk is missing,' said Malcifer. 'If they abandoned the keep for some reason, they flew out of here.'

'After setting the warning beacon. Also their ship, the *Blade of Caliban*, is not in the system,' added Sammael. 'I assume that the strike cruiser returned to the Rock with some news of what happened here, prompting the message we received. If the keep was not under direct assault, why was it evacuated?'

The other two Dark Angels had no answer to this question and remained silent.

The tread of their booted feet was loud as they strode to the doorway leading to the main body of the keep. Sammael drew his blade, the Raven Sword forged from a piece of meteorite inlaid with a crystal matrix powerfield. A blue aura flickered along the edges of the blade as Sammael activated the field generator with a touch of his thumb. Behind him Malcifer readied his bolt pistol and crozius and Harahel's force axe gleamed with psychic power.

Sammael keyed in an override access code and the locks of the door hissed open. It swung open easily at his touch, revealing a winding stairwell leading up into the first storey of the keep. With Malcifer beside him, Harahel a few steps behind, the Grand Master of the Ravenwing advanced quickly up the steps.

They came to an archway at the top that opened out into the entrance hall behind the citadel gate. Sammael was keenly aware that his autosenses detected nothing that suggested the keep was occupied; only the thrum of the building's power grid. Stepping into the hallway his eye was drawn to red stains on the bare rockcrete floor, and spots of crimson on the brushed metal cabinet of the gate access terminal.

'Blood,' he said heavily. 'Old.'

'No bodies,' added Harahel. 'I sense no life in this place. Not even vermin or insects.'

Sammael accepted this statement without comment,

turning to his left and heading beneath another archway into the chamber beyond. It was only a few metres square, the floor and ceiling bare ferrocrete. Red-cushioned benches made of dark timber lined the chamber to each side, beneath wooden carvings hung on whitewashed walls; a gilded Imperial aquila on the left, the winged sword of the Dark Angels on the right in enamelled black. There was material spattered on the walls and floor, amongst more bloodstains; small droplets of something grey. Sammael prodded one of the tear-shaped droplets and it came free, falling to the floor.

'Molten ceramite,' he told the others. 'Judging by the amount, it was a considerable blast. Plasma probably.'

'Other pieces of debris here,' said Malcifer, crouching to point at a scatter of metal splinters and plasteel filaments caught in the fabric of the bench cushions.

They moved through the remaining chambers of the lower floor – storerooms, the communications centre and a well-furnished holding area for visitors – and found nothing to further explain the absence of the garrison except for more bloodstains. They found a gleaming metal staircase at the heart of the keep and continued to the second storey. Here they found the dorters of the Space Marines and the keep's serfs, beds arranged along the walls, all neat and in order. The armour stands of the Dark Angels were empty, the weapon brackets above their cots also vacant.

'They left armed and armoured,' said Malcifer, walking between the massive bunks used by the Space Marines of the garrison. 'The evacuation was not hasty. Or at least, not under direct duress.'

'There are still belongings here,' called Harahel from the serfs' chamber across the hallway. 'Personal effects, clothes.'

'Which tells us nothing more about what happened,'

said Sammael. A feeling of unease was steadily grow-ing in his gut. He could not stop the image described to him by Harahel surfacing in his thoughts: a Chaplain consumed by treachery. He pushed aside his misgivings, focusing on the investigation. He was the Grand Master of the Ravenwing, the eyes of the Chapter, and he could not afford to miss any clue. 'Continue upwards.'

The bloodstains on stairs and floors diminished as they ascended to the third floor. Here were more dort-ers and a range of cells, for the initiates that had been accepted into the Chapter. Like the dormitories below, the rooms were clean and tidy, though Sammael imme-diately noticed something was missing.

'There are no bedclothes on the cots,' he mentioned to the other two Dark Angels, pointing at the bunks. 'Stripped.'

'Blood has seeped into the mattresses of several,' said Malcifer, examining the beds more closely. He stood up and there was a hush to his voice that betrayed an unset-tled mind. 'The initiates were attacked in their sleep.'

'Here, a mark.' Harahel drew their attention to a hole in the wall, the size of a Space Marine's fist. Magnifying his autosenses, Sammael could see pieces of shrapnel embedded in the plaster within the gash.

'Bolt detonation,' he said grimly. 'It seems that it was one of our own that perpetrated the killings.'

'Or one of their weapons was taken,' Malcifer answered quickly. 'A single bolter round is not conclusive, brother.'

'You may be right, but I sense that something terrible has happened here,' replied the Grand Master. 'Harahel, can you glean nothing with your powers?'

'All is dead here, brother,' replied the Epistolary. 'I was taught to delve into the minds of living men, the walls here do not remember.'

'You sense nothing?' Sammael could not believe that

there was no psychic trace of the massacre that seemed to have been carried out. 'Nothing at all?'

'Nothing more than your instincts are telling you, brother. A darkness has claimed this place.'

Sammael grunted and shook his head. Librarians could be superstitious at times. On the next landing there were more signs of fighting, bolter impacts and bullet holes stitched across the walls. Most of the floor was taken up with the access chambers and ammunition stores for the roof turrets. There was nothing to be found there and they swiftly continued to the top of the keep.

A RIDDLE OF CORPSES

The uppermost storey was split between three rooms; two small cells for the personal use of the garrison commanders and the keep's chapel. It was the last that Sammael entered first and what he found inside stopped him in his tracks.

'Brothers...' The sight that confronted him was beyond reckoning and he heard pained gasps from his companions as they entered the chapel behind him.

In front of a marble symbol of the Chapter was a low altar set with a few relics, amongst them the crozius arcanum and rosarius of a Chaplain. It was dark, the candles in the sconces and on stands around the hall melted to stubs. In the gloom there were shapes on the floor, their outlines visible in the light from the hallway.

Along one wall were laid more than twenty bodies, covered in bloodstained shrouds stitched with the icon of the Dark Angels. At the end of the line, closest to the door, a much larger figure lay covered, the shroud turned about so that the symbol lay inverted. Sammael did not need to pull aside the covering to know that a Space Marine lay beneath; the bulk of the body made that clear.

Yet more astounding were the five armoured figures sprawled before the altar.

The middle corpse was clad in midnight black, his helm skull-faced: a Chaplain. To each side lay a Dark Angel in the livery of a Techmarine, and three others whose dark green armour was marked by the symbols of the Third Company. Each Space Marine had a ragged hole through his body, armour melted, innards charred.

'That is the heraldry of Boreas,' said Malcifer, pointing at the corpse of the Chaplain, disbelief in his voice. 'How could he be dead? What foe could best five of the Adeptus Astartes and cause such wounds?'.

'No foe, save perhaps doubt,' said Sammael, crouching by the body of the Techmarine. The fingertips of the dead Space Marine's gauntlets were missing, each sliced cleanly through and cauterised. Turning over the Techmarine's hand he saw molten swirls on the palm. The Grand Master looked at the other corpses and found the same injuries. There were tiny globules of molten metal and ceramite coating the insides of the wounds in their chests. The conclusion he reached was incredible and he chose not to voice it, seeking another explanation.

While Sammael pondered the meaning of what they had found, Harahel investigated the other bodies, pulling back the shrouds to reveal the faces of the dead. There was no sign of decay, skin and flesh untouched as if the keep was sterile.

'The initiates and serfs,' announced the Librarian as he continued along the line. 'Knife wounds, bolt detonations. Oh...'. Harahel shook his head and looked at Sammael. The Grand Master could see nothing of his companion's face but his posture spoke of great distress.

To see such a thing from a veteran of Harahel's standing gnawed at Sammael's own resolve. 'The necks of the young ones have been snapped.'

'They took their own lives,' Sammael announced, standing up. The revelation was just as disturbing, but at least it distracted the other two from the dead novitiates. 'Melta bomb held against the breastplate.'

'Why?' Malcifer voiced the question that had been nagging Sammael since he had first entered the chapel, somewhat pointlessly.

'Am I to conjure answers from dead flesh and broken armour?' snapped Sammael, his anxiety forcing out the words. He immediately regretted them, wishing to show no sign of weakness in front of his companions. 'Apologies, brother, I have nothing to tell you that you do not know.'

'My apologies also,' replied Malcifer. 'What we have found defies rational explanation.'

'And the situation grows more curious,' said Harahel, pulling back the shroud of the Space Marine body to reveal the white armour of an Apothecary. There was no head on the body, only the blackened stump of a neck.

'Brother Nestor,' said Sammael, recalling the name with a little effort. 'He was Apothecary to the garrison, integral to the recruitment.'

'And more,' Malcifer said quietly. 'Piscina was chosen as one of the secret repositoria for the Chapter's gene-seed.'

'Nestor was a gene-guardian?' Sammael knew of the gene-seed caches located on some of the Dark Angels' recruiting worlds, held away from the Tower of Angels to ensure future generations could be created if something disastrous happened to the fortress-monastery. However, only a few of the Inner Circle knew the locations and the names of the gene-guardians from the apothecarion who watched over them. 'There was nothing in the report.'

'There would not be any,' said Malcifer with a hint of apology. 'It is a secret closely guarded, even within command-level documents.'

Accepting this without comment, Sammael examined Nestor's remains. Aside from the absence of the Apothecary's head there were no other visible injuries. There was significant charring of the armour around the cauterised wound, the paint obliterated and the ceramite melted down through several layers.

'Though I do not comprehend the significance, I would say that we have found the victim of the blast by the gate hall. A single plasma shot to the head.'

'The Techmarine has a plasma pistol,' announced Malcifer, stooping to pull the weapon from a holster on the dead Dark Angel's belt. The Chaplain inspected it for a moment, an orange icon springing into life with the whine of power cells charging. 'The only shot fired, it would seem. Stacked cells contain ninety per cent reserve.'

'No need to give voice to the obvious question,' said Sammael, before someone asked why a Dark Angels Techmarine would shoot a Brother-Apothecary. 'We have but one hope left to explain the mystery. We must open the vaults and see what we can find within the action reports and logs. I do not hold out much hope for enlightenment.'

BROTHER BOREAS SPEAKS

The vocal log entry started playing as soon as Malcifer accessed the Chapter Keep records. Sammael was surprised, and glad that he had not entrusted the investigation of the keep to any warrior not of the Inner Circle. There were bound to be revelations not suitable to the ears of the lesser ranks.

The voice of Chaplain Boreas was calm and thoughtful, issuing after death from the grille of the vault's main data terminal.

'This is Interrogator-Chaplain Boreas of the Emperor's Dark Angels Chapter,' he began. 'This is my final communication from Piscina, as commander of the Dark Angels in the system. Our ancient foes have struck a blow against our Chapter. The reviled enemy has wounded us severely. We are entangled in a plot that goes beyond our comprehension. The events I relate stretch beyond this world, beyond the furthest reaches of this star system. Great and dark powers are at work, I see their hand manipulating us, bending us to their twisted goals.'

There was a pause in the voice and Malcifer stopped the recording, turning to Sammael.

'Is this a confession?' the Chaplain asked, incredulous.

'We shall see,' replied Sammael. He gestured for Malcifer to continue the log playback.

'For ten thousand years we have sought redemption.' There was more life to Boreas's voice now, an animation fuelling words that cut to the core of Sammael as he listened. *'We have pursued that which shamed our brethren when our time of triumph was at hand. It was a grave, unforgivable sin, which must be atoned for. That is beyond doubt. But these last days, an even greater sin has come to light. It is the sin of ignorance. It is the sin of past errors repeated.'*

Sammael gestured for Malcifer to interrupt the log, disturbed by the dead Chaplain's message. For many decades he had hunted the Fallen, following every clue and trail that might lead him and the Chapter to the capture of one of the Dark Angels that had turned on their primarch ten thousand years before. It was a heinous burden, to know of the Chapter's shame and the true reasons for it, but all of those granted access to those secrets were chosen for their strength of will and dedication to the Dark Angels. The Interrogator-Chaplains were integral to the hunt and the strongest-willed of the Chapter, save perhaps for the Supreme Grand Master himself. To hear Boreas speak from beyond the grave, to listen to a testimony that threatened to cast doubt on the teachings of the Chapter shook Sammael in a way that no physical foe could.

'I do not think this is the time or the place,' he said. 'If what we hear is true, we must wait for the rest of the Chapter before continuing. What we have heard hints at a heresy deeper than anything we have witnessed before.'

'You think that Brother Boreas has turned against us?' Malcifer shook his head. 'Then you hear different words to I, brother. This is not a confession, it is a warning. If we are to know what has destroyed our brothers we must listen to the rest of the testimony.'

Deep inside, Sammael knew that he did not want to hear anything further. Talk of errors repeated set in motion a chain of thoughts that led to a devastating conclusion. Had Boreas discovered something within the Dark Angels that meant another schism would divide them? When even a Chaplain's integrity was in doubt, was it wise for his words to be heard by Malcifer and Harahel? Sammael wondered even if it was wise for him to hear them. Words carried ideas, and ideas could sow doubt; doubt that had evidently caused the garrison of Piscina to turn upon each other.

Unseen by the other two, he closed his eyes, trying to accept what Malcifer had said. Reluctantly, he motioned for Malcifer to continue the playback.

'I ask myself what it means to be one of the Dark Angels. Is it to hunt the Fallen, chasing shadows through the dark places of the galaxy? Is it to pursue our quest at any expense, forgoing all other oaths and duties? Is it to lie, to hide and to plot so that others will never know of our shame? Is it to keep our own brethren unacquainted with the truth of our past, the legacy we all share in? Or is it to be a Space Marine? Is it to follow the path laid down by the Emperor and Lion El'Jonson at the founding of this great Imperium of man? To protect mankind, to purge the alien, cleanse the unclean?'

Sammael's misgivings gave way to a simmering resentment, to hear his calling disparaged by one who had been a brother. That Boreas had not considered the Fallen a blight upon the galaxy was fast becoming clear. Somehow their corruption had passed to the Chaplain, twisting his view of the Dark Angels. To throw back solemnly held oaths spoke of a mind wandering in dark places.

The forlorn sight of the dead Space Marines upstairs had stirred sorrow, but listening to Boreas's testimony turned that to anger; anger that the Chaplain had failed those who had looked to him for leadership; failed them to the extent that his lies had led them to kill themselves. The log continued, but Sammael barely registered the words, his attention caught by the intensity of the dead Chaplains voice, bordering on manic. The clash between Boreas's words and the crimes he had perpetrated against his brothers told a tale of deep hypocrisy.

'We must act as a shining brand in the night, to lead the way for others to follow. We are the warriors of the Emperor, guardians of mankind. Roboute Guilliman called us bright stars in the firmament of battle, untouched by self-aggrandisement. Yet we, the Dark Angels, commit the supreme sin. We put ourselves before our duty. We have buried our traditions, masked our real history in legend and mysticism to confound others. We are not bright stars, we are an empty blackness, a passing shadow that serves nothing but its own purpose.'

When the recording continued, Sammael detected weariness. The words came slowly again, softly spoken. The tone was one of utter resignation, evidence that Boreas had strayed from the path of a Dark Angel. No true warrior who knew of the sacrifice of the Lion would weary of the task of hunting down those who had betrayed the primarch. Of the many sins it seemed the Chaplain had committed it was this lack of fortitude that condemned him the most in Sammael's eyes. A Space Marine of more fortitude would have overcome moments of doubt and remained strong to the beliefs of the Chapter.

'Included in this log is a complete account of the disaster that has befallen Piscina and us.' The three Dark Angels exchanged glances and Malcifer bent to the runepad, tapping the keys swiftly as he searched for the report. *'For this I take sole responsibility. Our enemies know us too*

well. We have become anathema to ourselves, as this plot of the Fallen demonstrates. Everything that has transpired has led us to this place and time, and there is nothing left to do what we must. Ten thousand years ago our soul was split. We tell ourselves that the two halves of us are the light and dark. I have learnt a bitter lesson, that it is not true. It is a comforting lie, which keeps us safe from doubt, so that we do not ask questions whose answers we fear. There is no light and dark, only the shades of twilight in between.'

Sammael had heard enough and was eager to find out what the accompanying log entry contained, but Boreas's message continued.

'If once there was a chance to redeem ourselves, it passed away ten thousand years ago. For a hundred centuries it has driven us, and consumed us at the same time. Not while one Fallen stays alive can we know peace within ourselves.'

The words sounded all too familiar, the reasons that drove him and brought him purpose as Grand Master of the Ravenwing, but to hear them spoken by Boreas they sounded like a curse. The Chaplain's tone grew stronger again, more fervent, almost desperate if such a thing was possible for a Dark Angel.

'But what then? If not, there will never be salvation, and all that we aspire to will come to nothing, all that we have achieved will be in vain. I beseech you not to allow this to happen. We are to make the ultimate sacrifice for the people of Piscina, and to safeguard our future. Do not make the deaths of my Brethren be for nothing.'

The log hissed and then the chamber fell into silence. Sammael flexed his fingers in agitation, but Boreas was not done. The recording started again, the Chaplain's voice not much louder than a whisper, the last words sounding as if spoken through gritted teeth.

'I have one more message to deliver. Walk that dark road through the rooms of the interrogators, past the catacombs

into the deepest chambers. Go to that solitary cell at the heart of the Rock and tell him this: you were not wrong.'

The log finally finished with a short high-pitched tone. Sammael exhaled sharply, having not realised he had been holding his breath, the tension in him building towards the Chaplain's final words. He looked at Harahel and saw the Librarian's gaze was on the floor, hands clasped at his waist as he contemplated the contents of Boreas's speech.

'Do not spend too long pondering the words of a heretic,' warned Sammael. 'It is folly to welcome their lies into your thoughts.'

'Yet that is what the Interrogator-Chaplains must do,' Malcifer said quietly, 'each and every time they bring one of the Fallen to repentance. It seems to me that Boreas was wounded in soul long before coming to Piscina.'

'What did he mean? About a solitary cell?' asked Harahel. 'Who was not wrong?'

Sammael looked at Malcifer, who had straightened at the question. The Chaplain glanced at the Grand Master, shook his head slightly and returned to his work at the terminal, leaving Sammael to deal with the question. It was not for the Grand Master of the Ravenwing to divulge the greatest secrets of the Dark Angels to an Epistolary – such matters could only be dealt with by one, the Supreme Grand Master or the Master of Sanctity. If there was one piece of knowledge that could destroy all faith in the Chapter it was this and he could not even bring himself to think of it.

'One of the Fallen Boreas interrogated, most likely,' Sammael lied, trying to sound nonchalant. 'I doubt it is of significance.'

Fortunately Harahel's next question was cut off by an urgent communication across the company channel.

'This is Sergeant Cassiel. We have a potential threat developing.'

HERESY BEGETS RETRIBUTION

For several minutes, the scanner readings had been changing. The mass of life signals within the buildings surrounding the park was dispersing. Annael could see the citizens of Kadillus hurrying out onto the roads, moving further into the city, some of them leading and carrying children, others with armfuls of clothes and other belongings.

'What is the significance of this?' asked Araton. 'What has put them to flight?'

Though the exodus had cleared out many of the augur returns, there were still several dozen heat signals registering in the tenements overlooking the squadron's position. It was a situation Annael had not encountered before and it made him uneasy as he looked at the buildings with magnified autosenses. There were people at the windows, far fewer than before, moving from floor to floor and room to room. On the roofs of several of the buildings he saw the glint of the sun on lenses.

'We're under magnocular observation, sergeant,' he

said quietly, running through another targeter calibration on his guns.

'Confirmed, brothers,' said Araton. 'Four separate observers. Civilian clothing.'

'What are they watching for?' asked Sabrael.

'Report.' Sammael's command cut through the squadron's observations. Cassiel relayed a brief description of what was occurring but offered no conclusion.

'Stay alert,' the Grand Master instructed them. 'Thunderhawk overflight incoming to appraise the situation.'

'I think I see a heavy weapon,' said Zarall. 'Sector two, third storey, left corner window.'

Annael saw movement to the north, where Zarall indicated. He edged his bike forward, turning the bolters towards the possible threat. There were two men at the window, holding something bulky between them.

'Missile launcher!' snapped Cassiel. 'Evasive action!'

Engines screamed as the squadron burst forwards. A projectile blurred from the window leaving a faint trail of vapour, the missile arcing down towards the position the Dark Angels had occupied a moment before. The explosion sent a shower of dirt high into the air, the noise of the detonation drowned out by the bark of bolters as the squadron returned fire. The ferrocrete wall around the window exploded into fragments and dust and Annael saw the two men cut to pieces by bolt impacts, tumbling out of view.

Accelerating to full combat speed, the squadron changed course, following Cassiel as he swerved left. The red beam of a lascannon seared overhead, missing by several metres. Annael's autosenses picked up the zip and crack of smaller las-weapons as more fire erupted from the tenements. The distinctive whine of falling mortar shells caused the squadron to turn again, zigzagging towards the scorched, body-littered hill at the centre of the park. Three bombs landed a dozen metres behind the swiftly-moving bikes.

'Under sporadic fire from armed civilians,' Cassiel barked over the vox. 'Fifty-plus targets surrounding us in dominant position. Returning fire.'

There was little the bikers could do as the insurgents popped out of hiding, loosed off a few wild shots and then disappeared into cover once more. The tenement walls absorbed the fire of the bolters, and the enemy were scattered across several buildings, giving no single target onto which the squadron could concentrate their fire. Along with the others, Annael fired off short bursts where his thermal imaging indicated attackers moving towards the windows, able to cut down three of them as they came into view.

'Why are they shooting at us?' demanded Sabrael. 'What is happening here?'

A las-bolt struck the cowling on the front of Zarall's bike, sending up a puff of paint and ceramite dust. The rattle of autogun fire heralded a hail from a second-storey balcony to the squadron's left. This was not the sort of battle the bikes of the Ravenwing were prepared for. The open space of the park gave them plenty of room to manoeuvre and the enemy fire was inaccurate, but the Dark Angels could not afford to linger in one place to unleash a full fusillade at their foes.

'The canker of heresy sets grip on Piscina,' said Zarall. His bike's gun unleashed a blast into the lower floor of one of the buildings, the thumb-sized bolts leaving brief streaks of yellow in Annael's thermal display, punching a hole through the ferrocrete to tear into a knot of attackers hiding within. 'Fortunate it is that we are here to purge the taint from a world we thought loyal to the Chapter.'

'As you say, brother,' replied Sabrael. 'Such ingratitude seeks a reckoning.'

'Keep moving,' said Cassiel as more mortar bombs detonated several metres to the right of the squadron. 'Fire at any presented targets.'

An explosion tore through the upper floor of a tenement directly ahead of Annael as he swerved his bike to the left, away from the mortar impacts. The roar of plasma jets accompanied the Thunderhawk as it launched another salvo of missiles from its stubby wings, obliterating the entire top storey of the building. Chunks of ferrocrete, glass and mangled bodies spilled down onto the street bordering the park to the east. Several fires started, smoke and dust billowing up on the thermals to join the cloud that already swathed much of Kadillus.

'They are withdrawing,' announced Araton. Annael glanced at his sensor display and saw that the registers were moving away. Looking up he could see nothing on the streets though.

'Where have they gone?' Annael said, turning his bike about so he could check the buildings to the west. The roads were likewise empty in that direction too.

'Sub-levels, basements, sewers perhaps,' said Cassiel. 'West. Rendezvous with the rest of the company. We cannot do anything meaningful here.'

The Thunderhawk's battle cannon sent shells into the buildings to the north as it came to a hover over the park. The downwash of its jets caused temperature warning symbols to blink into life across Annael's display as the squadron raced beneath the gunship, a pall of dirt and dust kicked up from bikes and the Thunderhawk.

'Request orders,' barked Cassiel as the Dark Angels raced onto a winding track between rows of blossoming trees. Scatters of white and pink filled the air as they roared west across the park.

'Establish safe cordon to the south gate,' came

Sammael's reply a few seconds later. 'Prepare to extract from the city.'

'Are we leaving already?' said Sabrael, obviously disappointed. 'We just withdraw?'

'We have our orders, brother,' replied Cassiel.

Zarall was in the lead now. He slowed as they reached the boundary fence, crashing his bike through a wide gate leading to the main road. Land Speeders whirred overhead, towards the attack, their assault cannons, missile pods and heavy bolters sending a storm of fire into the tenement buildings, though there were few targets left inside them.

Hitting the ferrocrete of the road, the squadron turned south, towards the Chapter Keep. Annael glanced back across the park, his senses alight with adrenaline. One of the tenements was slowly collapsing under the bombardment of the Thunderhawk, the others were half-ruined, their facades shredded by fire from the converging Land Speeders.

Slowing his bike as Cassiel brought the squadron to a halt, Annael checked his armour and bike for damage. There were some superficial marks and scattered cracks in the fairing of *Black Shadow* but all of his mount's systems were working well. His armour was equally intact and he took a deep breath, shaking his head, still confused as to why the people of Piscina had turned on the Dark Angels.

THE TRAIL OF THE FALLEN

In the bowels of the Chapter Keep the only evidence of the conflagration of fury unleashed by the Dark Angels less than a kilometre away was an occasional tremor and the reports of the company across the comm-net. While Sammael attended to the tactical needs of his warriors, Malcifer had been kept busy at the data terminal, accessing the records of Chaplain Boreas.

'We have another sensor build-up to the east, around the transit station. Large number of civilians on foot. Some sidearms and improvised weapons. Threat currently minimal. How should we proceed, Grand Master?' Sergeant Orphaeus's report was just the latest to suggest that there was a much wider anti-Imperial sentiment on Kadillus. The attack on Squadron Cassiel had been a spark, falling upon the tinder of resentment that had been kindled by the attack of the Fallen.

Sammael wrestled with the thought of opening fire on what, to the heavily armoured Space Marines, amounted to unarmed citizens. To strike against insurgents who had opened fire on the Dark Angels with heavy weaponry was one matter; to gun down disaffected, desperate civilians was of another order of magnitude entirely.

The damage to the reputation of the Chapter had already been inflicted but there was no point in adding fuel to the fire of rebellion. If the Ravenwing responded in force there would be a bloodbath, solidifying opposition against the Dark Angels. As the situation stood, there was a chance that a peaceful settlement could be reached when the Tower of Angels arrived. That would become impossible if the true Dark Angels slaughtered those they had been sworn to protect. Such aggression would likely turn even Colonel Brade and others trying to restore order against the Chapter, at a time when their efforts had to be focused on the resurgent ork attacks.

'Do not engage civilians unless threat increases,' he announced over the command channel. 'Withdraw perimeter by five hundred metres. We will be ready to extract shortly.'

As affirmatives chorused over the comm-net, Sammael switched his attention to Malcifer.

'We will be ready to extract shortly, I hope,' he said to the Chaplain. 'What have you learnt?'

'I have decrypted Boreas's account of the actions he took prior to the intervention of the Fallen,' said Malcifer, still looking at the flow of script moving across the screen in front of him. 'It will take some time to evaluate its significance.'

'Anything contained in the report that suggests our next step?' asked Harahel. 'The longer we remain here, the greater the feeling of injustice and resentment I am sensing. If we stay here much longer, we will be facing thousands, not hundreds.'

'Noted, brother,' said Malcifer. 'In summary, Boreas learned of a transport ship known to be in use by the

Fallen and led the garrison away from Piscina to seize the vessel. It seems that this was just a ruse, calculated to draw the garrison out of position. The Chapter Keep was compromised while they were absent and the Fallen... Oh Emperor, the Fallen broke into the storage vault and retrieved the gene-seed within.'

'They took the gene-seed cache?' Harahel was horrified by the thought. 'To what purpose would the Fallen turn such a thing?'

'We can think about that at a time more convenient,' Sammael said, cutting off Malcifer before he could offer opinion on the matter. 'What does it say about the Fallen after they took the gene-seed? Does Boreas know where they went?'

'No, there is no further record,' said Malcifer. 'However, there is a cross-reference to one of the other logs. It is from Boreas's personal records, an account of one of his interrogations of a Fallen named Astelan.'

'Reference to any matter of importance?' Sammael listened as a fresh wave of reports announced that the initial insurgents had resurfaced further to the east and were targeting the Ravenwing with more heavy weapons and mortar fire. His desire to be away from Kadillus was growing swiftly and his impatience made his tone curt. 'What does this have to do with Piscina?'

'Nothing, brother, that I can see,' confessed Malcifer, stepping away from the terminal with a shake of his head. 'It will take some time to analyse the testimony of Astelan to see what Boreas was trying to highlight.'

'We have a city on the verge of outright attack; we do not have the luxury of time. Make a copy and erase all data files.'

'This is too sensitive to transmit over any channel, no matter the level of encryption,' said Malcifer. He went to one of the shelves lining the terminal chamber and looked through the metal containers stored there. Locating what he looked for, the Chaplain opened a slender box stencilled with the symbol of the Chapter on its lid. From within he produced a cube of emerald green. 'I shall transfer all logs and accounts to data crystal.'

'All warriors, this is Grand Master Sammael. I want a five hundred metre cordon between the Chapter Keep and the south gate. Athelman, Daedis, meet us at the keep gate. On my word, perimeter collapse and withdrawal to position of the Fifth Company. All aerial assets to prepare for extraction.'

'Assist Malcifer with the cleansing of the datacore,' he added, looking at Harahel. 'Let us not tarry here a moment longer than necessary.'

THE SEED OF DOUBT

Watching a third Thunderhawk strafing across Kadillus, its heavy bolters firing at the rooftops of a processing plant, Telemenus had to wonder what the Ravenwing had encountered inside the city. Certainly the whole southern district of Kadillus had come under intense fire. He could see columns of smoke from several burning buildings and the thunder of battle cannons rolled across the plains as the gunships continued their bombardment. There had been next to no information on the Fifth Company's comm-net and Sergeant Seraphiel had refused all inquiries as to what was happening inside the city.

'It must be the orks,' said the Dark Angel, gaze fixed on the ongoing attack. 'We should be moving to support our brothers.'

'We remain here,' Sergeant Amanael said curtly. 'Wait. Receiving new orders.'

'It seems our brothers might need some assistance, after all,' said Cadael.

'And there may yet be opportunity for the kill tally to rise on our account,' added Telemenus. 'It is self-ish of our brothers to deny us equal opportunity for valour.'

'If we had gone into Kadillus first, I doubt there would have been need to see such fury unleashed,' said Daellon. 'It will take many years to rebuild that district.'

'I am not surprised,' Telemenus replied. 'The Raven-wing excel at encountering trouble where others would walk more softly. I suppose we will be clearing cellars and hallways for the next few days, clearing up the orks they cannot reach.'

'A stairwell is no obstacle to the warriors of the Fifth Company,' said Cadael. 'The Ravenwing must submit to that eternal truth.'

'We are not going into the city,' announced Amanael. 'We are to defend an extraction zone, four hundred metres from the southern gate. Gunships are already en route to pick up our brothers.'

'Let us be sure that they receive a warm welcome,' said Telemenus. He slapped a hand against the side of his bolter. 'When the Ravenwing have been removed from our path, we will show these orks the ferocity of the Dark Angels in proper fashion.'

'Negative,' said the sergeant. 'Our orders are to wait for second wave extraction.'

Amanael's announcement was met by silence; proof that it was unexpected and highly controversial. Tele-menus knew better than to make further remark as the sergeant signalled for the squad to begin the march north. Whatever trouble in which the Ravenwing had found themselves embroiled, it was enough to trigger the withdrawal of the whole force. For the Dark Angels, any retreat was remarkable. To do so when there were

clearly still enemies to fight was unheard of by Telemenus and his flippant mood was quickly replaced by
concern for his brothers in the Ravenwing.

REARMING

The clatter of machinery and autoloaders rang around the muster hall. Servitors, legs reinforced with heavy gauge callipers, arms replaced with hoists and crane arms, lifted the bikes of Squadron Cassiel onto the service ramps. Unaugmented serfs in the livery of the armourium swarmed over the machines with ratchets, bolt drivers, parts and replacement armoured plates, while others connected up diagnostic terminals and recharger cables. This activity was overseen by two Techmarines, their armour black like the rest of the Ravenwing except for their dark red shoulder pads.

The Space Marines were also surrounded by menials, offering protein-replenishing synth-loaves and ewers of thick, nutrient-enriched fluid. Hanging his helmet on his belt, Annael took the proffered drink and downed the contents of a jug in four long gulps, the sweetness of the liquid a salve to the acrid taste that always built up in his mouth during combat; a side effect of the Betcher's gland that modified his saliva, he had once been told by an Apothecary.

He waved away the armourium attendants, who descended on Zarall instead, fussing over the cracks in his shoulder plates from several autogun hits. Zarall stood impassively munching on a synth-slab while they removed the shoulder guards from his armour and replacements were fixed in their place.

Pushing through the throng, Annael watched the serfs taking apart the fairing of *Black Shadow*, amazed at the number of las-marks and bullet holes. In the heat of the battle he had not realised how much enemy fire had found its mark.

'You were lucky, brother.' This came from Techmarine Naethel, who was on the opposite side of the service ramp, inspecting the innards of the bike.

Annael clambered over the ramp to join the Techmarine, who crouched down and pointed to a blackened chip in the casing of the bike's secondary fuel tank.

'Another two centimetres further forward and a fuel line would have been caught,' explained Naethel. 'Lucky indeed.'

'It was bad luck to be hit in the first place,' replied Annael. 'Their marksmanship was woeful. I would have expected better of men trained in a planetary defence force.'

'That is why we trust to speed as well as armour, brother.' Annael stood up and looked over *Black Shadow* to see Sabrael approaching, a jug in each hand. 'I told you that you ride too slowly.'

'I am in no mood for your jests, brother,' Annael replied. 'You should attend to your own steed.'

'What for?' Sabrael shrugged and took a mouthful of drink. 'There is not a dent upon it.'

Annael turned to Naethel to disprove the boast but the Techmarine shook his head.

'Our brother speaks truly, the worst his mount suffered is some scratched paintwork,' said Naethel. 'Would that you were all so blessed with such fortune, the armourium would be a quieter place.'

'Do not confuse me for a braggart, Brother Annael,' said Sabrael, his expression grim. 'You will learn to be as one with your mount, so that it moves without your conscious thought. Then you too will be able to ride through the fury of the storm without concern.'

There was nothing to say to that, and Annael let Sabrael depart without retort. He lowered himself down to the deck, murmuring thanks to the spirit of *Black Shadow*, and voicing more loudly his appreciation of Naethel's work.

'Your steed will be ready for you soon enough, brother,' the Techmarine informed Annael when he asked how long the repairs would take. 'When the order comes for the next drop, you will be reunited with your faithful mount.'

'May it come swiftly,' said Annael, feeling dishonoured by Sabrael's words. 'I would stand to rectify my account with the rebels below.'

'Do not wish such a thing too swiftly,' cautioned Araton. The other squadron member had been silently attending to his machine, and rose up from behind it, leaning forward to rest on the saddle. 'Not to second-guess Grand Master Sammael's intent, but I do not think we should be returning to Kadillus soon.'

'How so? The city was in uproar when we left, between insurgents and the orks. We have fought only a brief skirmish, the real battle remains to be won.'

'And had Sammael the desire to prosecute that battle he would have done so while he still had the company on the ground,' replied Araton. 'To pull back from battle engaged is no easy decision, but it is one he has already made.'

'What of our losses? Will they not be avenged?'

'Five there are, never to ride with us again, but their deaths will not find greater meaning in the blood of innocents.'

'Innocents?' Annael could not believe Araton's argument. 'It was they that opened fire upon us. We did not bring this war to Piscina.'

'Yet it is Piscina that will suffer if we continue to wage it,' Araton said evenly, stroking a gauntleted hand along the handlebars of his bike. 'If we are to unleash the full weight of our fury, will you be able to set apart the guilty from the bystander? If the Ravenwing falls upon Kadillus, it will be to destroy the city, not to save it. City-fighting is no arena for the Ravenwing.'

'So we must leave it to the Fifth Company squads to restore our honour?' Annael surprised himself with the vehemence of his words. It was not long since he had been a member of another company, but already he felt the acute sense of duty and honour that was the preserve of the Ravenwing to uphold. 'It is the blood of the Ravenwing that stains Kadillus, and it is the Ravenwing that should balance the scales.'

'Justice, brother?' Annael stiffened as he recognised the voice of Sergeant Cassiel behind him. 'Or revenge?'

'Insurrection against the Emperor cannot go unpunished,' Annael said as he turned, believing in his heart that it was not revenge he sought. 'If the Dark Angels do not respond, it will be a sign of weakness, and that I cannot abide.'

'It is not for you to decide, brother,' Cassiel continued, his words softly spoken. 'If it is the choice of Grand Master Sammael that this matter is left to the Piscina Free Militia to resolve, that will be the end of it.'

'Of course, brother-sergeant,' Annael replied quickly, realising his words had bordered on insubordination. 'No dissent was intended.'

'Either way, we have not yet received orders to stand down,' Cassiel said. 'Repair and rearm. I suggest that when the present mobilisation is concluded, you should seek out Brother Malcifer if you continue to have questions regarding our duty here.'

Annael realised the words were sincerely meant, advice rather than chastisement. He considered the sergeant's words as Cassiel walked away, and tried to come to terms with what had happened in Kadillus. Combat was second-nature to him, and in the heat of battle he had not given a moment's thought to the nature of his enemies. Looking at the dents and scratches on *Black Shadow*, thinking of how a lascannon blast or missile might have struck him down as it had five other members of the company, he realised that he would have died without knowing why.

It was his purpose to fight for the Emperor and Annael knew that he was fated to fall in battle one day. Even the greatest Supreme Grand Masters of the Dark Angels eventually succumbed to a lifetime of war, one way or another. Yet he had been taught also that his death was to have purpose, and if rebels were allowed to rise up without reply – to attack the Adeptus Astartes, the Emperor's Angels of Death no less – then he was not quite sure what purpose he was now serving.

The contrast between Hadria Praetoris and Kadillus could not be starker and Annael was left to wonder what divide there was between the foes he had encountered. His first two engagements with the Ravenwing were causing him more doubts and raising more questions than he had experienced in the previous four hundred years. Heeding the advice of Cassiel, he resolved that a conversation with the Chaplain might well be what he needed to reinforce his conviction.

A CURSED NAME

The name spoken by Malcifer hung in the air of the command chamber, reverberating through Sammael's thoughts like the tolling of a great bell. It was a name that had haunted the Dark Angels for ten thousand years, and plagued Sammael ever since he had first heard it from the lips of Grand Master Gideon two centuries before. That had been at Kaphon, when Sammael had still been a sergeant in the Ravenwing. Now that he thought about the situation on Piscina, Sammael was surprised he had not recognised the similarities with the uprising on Kaphon Betis; a world under threat from alien attack driven into anarchy by the acts of a handful of Fallen. Kaphon Betis had been repeatedly assaulted by eldar pirates who had provided cover for the diabolic Fallen and his band to destabilise the rule of the Imperial Commander. Now the traitors had used the ork resurgence to repeat the misdeed on Piscina.

It had been a regret of Grand Master Gideon that they had been so close to catching the Dark Angels' greatest threat at Kaphon. The Fallen had still been in-system when the Ravenwing had arrived, supported by warriors from the Third Company and the Deathwing, though the Dark Angels had not known at the time that their elusive quarry were still nearby. By the time the Dark Angels had driven off the eldar attacks, the Fallen had slipped away once more. Sammael had taken several dissident prisoners and overheard their discussions of 'Lord Cypher', intimating that this mysterious individual had been the architect behind the overthrow of the Imperial Commander. Faced with Sammael's questions, Gideon had chosen to take Sammael into his confidence, inducting him unofficially into the Inner Circle; an induction that was formally ratified when they had returned to the Chapter.

Though he recalled Kaphon Betis with anguish and chastised himself for not seeing similar manipulation on Piscina, Sammael took heart from the fact that he had once more crossed trails with the greatest enemy of the Dark Angels. Such opportunities were rare, and if there was any hope of catching the worst of the Fallen, it had been rekindled in the Grand Master. Piscina had been laid low by the Fallen, but the Ravenwing were on hand, ready to hunt down the fiend once more. With dedication, initiative and perseverance, Sammael could be the one to succeed where so many previous Masters had failed before.

Malcifer said nothing more, allowing the import of his announcement to sink in. There was a growl of distaste from Harahel and the Librarian leaned forwards, head bowed, fists resting on the dormant display console.

'You are certain?' Sammael asked when he had collected his thoughts, seeking more than just similarity to the events at Kaphon before getting ahead of himself. 'He was at Piscina?'

'As certain as one could ever be when considering the actions of such a deviant,' the Chaplain replied. 'Descriptions of the Fallen gathered by Boreas strongly indicate that their leader bore wargear identical to that witnessed in previous encounters.'

'That he was here is informative, but it does not give us further intelligence regarding where he is now,' said Harahel, straightening. He folded his arms and shrugged. 'It has been many days since the Fallen quit Piscina, who can say where they have gone?'

'Boreas, for all that he strayed from the righteous path, did not abdicate his duties fully,' replied Malcifer. 'I have read through the sections of his interrogation of Astelan that Boreas referenced. It deals with Astelan's actions at an independent star fort named Port Imperial. A den of pirates and outcasts, Astelan and two other Fallen frequented Port Imperial for several years. Though I cannot confirm that the one we seek is connected to Port Imperial, we have the testimony of Astelan that it was certainly used by the Fallen.'

'I remember the name,' said Sammael, dredging up decades-old memories. 'Boreas passed me this information not long after I became Grand Master. The trail was a dead end from the outset, with no clue from Astelan's account regarding where we might find this Port Imperial. And, by that same account, Astelan claimed that he and his fellow Fallen destroyed the star fort when they decided to part company with the pirates.'

'A claim that we can now test,' said Malcifer. 'Annotated on the transcript of the interrogation are navigational details that I believe will lead us to Port Imperial. I would say that, like so much of his testimony, Astelan delivered up falsehoods to justify his actions and protect the other Fallen.'

'You thought to save this information until now?'

Sammael was taken aback by the news, having forced himself to be pessimistic regarding the Ravenwing's chances of finding a worthy lead to follow.

'Apologies, brother, but I thought that context would be important,' said Malcifer. 'The time stamp of the Port Imperial coordinates places the addition at the same time the Chapter Keep vault was accessed during Boreas's absence.'

'How can that be?' said Harahel. 'If Boreas did not make the entry, who would?'

'One of the keep serfs, most likely,' said Malcifer.

'Or one of the Fallen,' the Grand Master said after a moment's thought.

'A false lead to cover their trail,' suggested Harahel. He gestured towards Malcifer. 'Brother, activate the display and let us see where we would be heading.'

The Chaplain busied himself with the console while Sammael considered the implications of what Malcifer had discovered. He was faced with two unlikely possibilities, for it would be against all protocol and doctrine for Boreas to entrust the keycodes of the vault to a menial. Weighed against that was the incredible notion that one of the Fallen had deliberately left the information. On balance, it seemed to Sammael that the former was the more probable, considering Boreas's other breaks from Chapter tradition.

The hololith gleamed into life, displaying a network of Imperial star systems ranging out a thousand light years from Piscina. A red dot appeared in wilderness space roughly halfway between the Adeptus Mechanicus forge world at Casiorix, and the sparsely populated Orlean system, almost nine hundred light years from the Ravenwing's current position.

'It could be a trap,' said Sammael, returning to the idea that the Fallen had tampered with the records. Malcifer moved aside as the Grand Master stepped up to the runepad and keyed in a series of instructions. In the hololith display a swathe of systems started to blink with green icons, almost surrounding the location highlighted by the Chaplain. 'These are ork-held worlds, catalogued by Imperial Navy patrols a little more than thirty years ago. It is possible that the xenos have encroached further or were not detected by the Navy. The Fallen may be trying to lead us into an ork-infested system.'

'That is not reason enough to pass up this opportunity,' said Malcifer.

'I did not say that we would not go,' Sammael replied sharply, displeased by the Chaplain's tone. 'We must be prepared, that is all, brother.'

'And what of our brothers in the Fifth Company?' asked Harahel. 'If Port Imperial is truly a haven for the Fallen, perhaps several of them, there is a significant risk that our brethren will be exposed to knowledge that is too dangerous to share.'

'It would seem prudent to leave them to assist in the fighting here,' said Sammael. 'Both to mend the damage done by the Fallen and to shield them from uncomfortable truth.'

'I think that would be unwise,' said Malcifer. He shut down the hololith display and turned, leaning back against the console edge. 'If we take the Fifth Company with us we can continue to observe and control their interaction with the Fallen. Left on Piscina, we cannot determine what they will learn, whether truth or rumour. By Boreas's account Colonel Brade certainly knew of the Fallen's arrival, and the hostility of the populace will lead our brethren to question the foundation of such anger towards the Chapter. They are without their company Grand Master or Chaplain to forestall or divert such questions, and dangerous knowledge would easily come to the ears of our brothers if they remain behind.'

'Your appraisal has merit, brother,' said Sammael. 'I sense that there is some resentment from Sergeant Seraphiel, and for the Ravenwing to seemingly abandon their brothers at the outset of a difficult campaign would cause grievous injury to our reputation.'

'Brothers, do not cast the warriors of the Fifth Company as a hindrance to our cause,' Harahel said with some annoyance. 'They are Dark Angels still, and their presence would be a boon to any endeavour, whether we find Port Imperial or not.'

Sammael bowed his head, shamed by the Librarian's admonishment. Such was the nature of the hunt and the risk posed by knowledge of the Fallen, that those of the Inner Circle stood apart from the bulk of the Chapter, forced to endure the secrets of the past and the lies to protect them.

'Let us not countenance further division,' said Malcifer. 'The Fifth Company shall be with us, Dark Angels together.'

Sammael nodded his agreement, though he knew that as was so often the case when the Ravenwing fought alongside any but the Deathwing, brotherly union would have to take second place to secrecy. If necessary, the Fifth Company could be despatched elsewhere to keep them from learning anything of harm, even if that entailed longer-term consequences.

'Commune with the astropaths, brother,' he instructed Harahel. 'Send a message to the Tower of Angels that they must come to Piscina as soon as they are able.'

'And of our mission, what do I say?' asked the Librarian.

'Simply that the hunt continues.'

SOLACE AND PUNISHMENT

The crack of the bolt-round rang dully from the metal bulkheads of the range. Telemenus watched the flickering trail of its propellant for seventy metres until the round struck the target, dead centre. The ferro-resinous alloy of the target sphere shattered as the bolt detonated, spraying silvery-red shards to the floor. In his mind's eye, Telemenus saw an ork's head ripped apart.

Though the firing range was large enough for twenty Space Marines to hone their marksmanship, Telemenus was alone. There was purity in this place, where he could concentrate solely on the mechanics of his craft without distraction or external consideration. There was just him, his bolter and thirty targets; free from the commands of his superiors, the din of battle and the threat of enemy attack.

He closed his eyes for the next shot, using his boosted musculomemetic sense and armour systems to target the next globe on the rack. His shot was rewarded by the telltale smash of a direct hit. Without opening his eyes, he moved his aim, adjusting to the target three along to the left. Another round, another clean hit.

The door pistons hissed as he opened his eyes and took a one-handed grip. Turning his head, he saw Sergeant Seraphiel enter. The provost-commander of the Fifth was dressed in his dark green surplice, cowl pulled back, eyes shadowed in the low lighting of the firing range. Telemenus fired without looking, a frown creasing his brow as the heard a screech of his shot ricocheting off the dense target ball; a hit but not a clean kill.

'The Chaplaincy tells us that it is a sin to be wasteful of the Emperor's resources,' said Seraphiel as Telemenus returned his attention down range, taking up his weapon in both hands again.

'Not a single shot misses its mark,' replied Telemenus. He switched the bolter to burst fire and his aim to an elongated oval at the one hundred metre mark, past the remnants of the globes. A three-shot salvo smashed into the target, evenly spaced between top and bottom, turning it to a cloud of fragments and glittering dust. 'Where is the waste?'

'To expend ammunition and targets in an attempt to improve already flawless marksmanship, perhaps,' said Seraphiel, standing to Telemenus's right.

'It is not my aim I seek to improve, brother-sergeant, but my spirit.'

Another three-round volley and another shattered target.

'So it is that you remove yourself from evening contemplation to come here, away from brothers who might provide solace?'

'My brothers do not need to hear complaint from me,' said Telemenus. He fired again, the last three shots in the magazine, a trio of closely-spaced targets disintegrating from the impacts. 'I find this exercise to be most enlightening.'

He ejected the magazine but Seraphiel placed a hand on his arm as he took another from his belt to reload. Turning to the sergeant, Telemenus lowered his bolter, the next magazine still in hand.

'I know that which gives you cause for complaint, brother,' said the sergeant. 'The withdrawal from Kadillus was untimely. It is rare for us to deploy and yet not see conclusion to battle.'

'There were many foes on Piscina, yet we head out-system on the whim of Grand Master Sammael with those foes unrepentant.'

'And laurels for the honour of First Marksman still unearned?'

'I do not place my own glory above that of my duty,' snapped Telemenus, pulling his arm away. 'My honours are a testament to my dedication to our cause, not to my ego, brother-sergeant. If laurels go unearned it is because traitors and xenos filth go unpunished!'

'And you would place yourself in judgement of Grand Master Sammael for his decision?'

The words were softly spoken but Telemenus detected their disapproval with ease. He had known Seraphiel for many decades and reasoned that he could speak freely, as warrior to warrior.

'Does it not give you concern, brother? First Hadria Praetoris and now Kadillus. Two cities where forces move against the rule of the Emperor, abandoned to the uncertain attention of others when the Dark Angels were present to sway the balance. Is this our duty, brother?'

'Grand Master Sammael must attend to a higher duty,' Seraphiel said, his expression stern. 'He would weigh decisions on a scale that we cannot see. It is in his judgement that the Supreme Grand Master places trust, and detached from the command of Grand Master Zadakiel we are subject to that authority.'

'We leave Piscina, a world that lies under the aegis of the Chapter, to fight pirates?' Telemenus did not hold back his scorn, feeling that it would be a greater dishonour to dissemble rather than voice his disapproval of a Grand Master's decisions. 'Towards what great goal does that strive?'

'We may be detached from company command but you will show due respect!' bellowed Seraphiel, and Telemenus knew he had gone too far, but was unrepentant.

'Servants of the Emperor are dying on Piscina while we chase star pirates, brother-sergeant. How can your honour bear such a thing?'

'My honour is my concern, brother,' growled Seraphiel. 'And if you choose to place yours above the honour of the Chapter, you are at fault, not Grand Master Sammael. You will pass ten days in the penitentium to transcribe the *Angelis Hierarchia*. Heed well its doctrine and contemplate your insubordinate behaviour as you do so.'

'Yes, brother-sergeant,' said Telemenus, briefly bowing his head in acceptance of Seraphiel's punishment. He turned towards the door, hiding a frustrated glower.

'Your weapon, brother,' said the sergeant, holding out a hand for Telemenus's bolter. The command bit deep into Telemenus's heart. 'You will regain it when you have served your penitence.'

Telemenus hesitated. To be relieved of his bolter was a greater punishment than the seclusion. As he made his way to the penitentium the other Dark Angels would see that he was without a weapon and would know his shame. Reluctantly he handed his bolter to Seraphiel, his antagonism replaced with vexation.

'I shall repent of my deviant thoughts, brother-sergeant,' he said apologetically, head hanging.

'Pass your armour to the Techmarines for maintenance, so that it can be cleansed as you cleanse your soul.'

'Yes, brother-sergeant.' Telemenus spoke softly, humbled by the realisation that perhaps his distress was caused by arrogance rather than sincere concern. 'I offer apology and entreat forgiveness for my rash words.'

'Ten days contemplation, brother, and you shall be forgiven.'

THE PREY REVEALED

Attending to the summons of Brother Malcifer, Annael entered the ship's Reclusiam with seven other brothers of the Ravenwing. He knew them all and immediately realised they each shared something in common: they were the latest recruits to the company.

The Reclusiam was dark, lit only by three large candles behind an altar made of titanium, the flames reflecting from the black marble sigil of the Dark Angels worked into its surface. Censers hung from the ceiling, a trio of them above the altar, spilling the scent of musky incense through the chamber. The haze of it diffused the candle-light, casting the chamber in an otherworldly air.

Dressed in their black robes, the eight Space Marines filed down the centre of the Reclusiam – large enough for a hundred Space Marines to attend to the sermons of the company Chaplain – and knelt in a line facing the altar.

Silver plaques on the walls were etched with the names of the one hundred and seventy-two Grand Masters who had led the Ravenwing in battle. It was a high number, much higher than those who had been Grand Masters of the other companies, standing testament to the daring and dedication expected of Sammael and those that had come before. Annael had known before he had joined the Ravenwing that attrition was high in comparison to the rest of the Chapter, and that his remaining term of service before he died was now most likely numbered in decades not centuries. It was the price to pay for being the first in the attack. The bravery of all Dark Angels was beyond question, but amongst their brethren the Ravenwing were given regard for being the quickest to place themselves in danger.

Before he had been inducted into the mysteries of the company, Annael had thought, with due respect, that such an attitude had perhaps been pride or foolhardiness. Certainly warriors such as Sabrael did nothing to dismiss the myth that the Ravenwing were arrogant in their courage and suffered high casualties as a consequence. Yet now that he had ridden alongside them, even if only twice, Annael understood better the dangers they had to face to perform their duty. It was their secret lot to uphold the honour of the Chapter, to delve into peril on the hunt so that the shame of the past could be laid to rest. To know what the Ravenwing knew and to hold back from the fight was impossible; honour demanded action.

It was with this thought in mind that Annael watched Brother Malcifer enter from a side chamber. The Chaplain wore a robe also, the white of the Deathwing. His bare arms were covered in a tracery of tattoos that depicted links of mail, each inked ring lettered with words of devotion; a representation of the armour of faith that protected the Chaplain's soul. More black and grey could be seen on his chest, the two heads of an aquila whose wings were hidden by the robe. Malcifer was not bare-headed like the rest. His face was covered with a skull mask, identical to the fashioning of his battle helm, and his eyes were hidden in shadow.

The assembled Space Marines bowed their heads in acknowledgement of the Chaplain, their hands on their knees. Annael straightened along with the others, all eyes set to Malcifer as he stood behind the altar and laid his palms upon its dark surface.

'You are the Ravenwing's freshest blood,' he said, voice solemn and quiet. 'But this you already know, because you are Ravenwing and you are observant. You have been taught much about your duty since you came to the company, and have all undergone the First Rite of the Raven. Now, as we stand upon the brink of a new battle, you are to be elevated in knowledge and esteem, to be welcomed into the body of the company by the Second Rite of the Raven.'

Annael wondered at this. It was the first he had heard of such rites, by that title at least. He knew that even as he had learnt of the Horus Heresy and the betrayal of the Dark Angels by their brethren there were further mysteries not yet explained. He trembled at the thought of what new secret might be revealed by this second rite and he could feel the anxiety and anticipation of the others in the reclusiam.

'When I inducted you into the company, I spoke to each of you, passing on the secret of the past. The history of our Chapter is a troubled one, and it takes courage greater than that required to face an enemy to accept it. You have all demonstrated that courage and today you will be rewarded for your service.'

Malcifer bowed his head, silhouetted against the light of the candles, a shadow that loomed over the kneeling Space Marines. The skull mask seemed to float in the air and the incense was strong in Annael's nostrils, sweet yet acrid. Malcifer stayed silent for some time, and when he next spoke his words seemed to drift on the haze of the censers, softly spoken but carrying to Annael's ears with ease, pushing aside other thought so that the words alone filled his mind.

'In our next battle it is likely that we will face one of the renegades that turned on the Dark Angels and the Lion.' There was a collective intake of breath and the incense fog stirred into whirls and coiling wisps. 'Yes, my brothers, the hunt of which I have spoken before now takes centre place in our duties. This renegade was once a Space Marine, but you cannot think of him as such. Should you set eyes upon him, do not be deceived by his appearance. In body he may be alike to you and I, of great build and giant stature, but remember that inside he is as small as an insect. He is a traitor to everything that we hold to our honour, and it is a privilege for us to bring him to justice.

'He is corrupt, as others you have seen before are corrupt, in soul even if there is no sign of it upon his body. Do not be mistaken if he feigns ignorance of his treachery, for he is a liar and a thief. He spoke an oath to the Emperor and turned away from the words. He took the gifts of the Emperor – a body built for war and a purpose purer than any other to destroy the Emperor's foes – and he turned those gifts against those that had called him brother.'

Blood. Annael smelt blood.

He could not hear the words of Malcifer as he continued, not as something separate from himself. He was in accord with the teaching, becoming one with the lesson handed forth by the Chaplain. It was the blood of Dark Angels on the hands of the traitors that Annael could smell. He heard growls and snarls from his brethren and realised that he too had given voice to the anger that had been brought forth by the thought. The incense was like fire, the smoke of the ruin brought to beautiful Caliban by the treachery of the renegades.

Images formed in his head, of towers toppled and forests razed, and innocents put to slaughter by gun and blade wielded by a monster. Annael's hands formed fists and his body quaked as Malcifer painted the picture of calamity and shame, of the sky torn asunder by a storm of energy and the traitors plucked from the jaws of justice by the infernal powers to which they had enslaved themselves.

The renegade was a pitiful, mewling thing, concealed within the body of a magnificent warrior in shining armour. He was deceit incarnate, his serpent's tongue spilling forth lie upon lie, claiming innocence and fraternity with those that would see him slain.

Such crimes deserved retribution. It would come, but not swiftly. The cowardly, feeble thing that had taken hold of one of the Emperor's finest would be driven out, brought forth from the darkness by the attentions of the Interrogator-Chaplains so that the soldier of the Emperor who had been brought low could redeem himself in the eyes of his Chapter. Only repentance would bring justice. The renegade was to be captured, not slain.

Again and again Annael felt these commands pulsing through his thoughts. His hearts were racing as if in full battle, muscles corded with tension, his breath coming in long, deep draughts that brought in the taste of blood and incense. His throat burned with the taste, like ashes in his mouth, and his lungs were filled with the bitterness of shame. Only the capture of the renegade would bring release, his repentance a gale of fresh air that would cleanse the foulness of treachery that was tainting Annael's body. To cleanse himself Annael had to cleanse the soul of his quarry. Only then would he know peace.

Slowly, as if surfacing from a long dream, Annael became aware of his surroundings again. Overhead a filtration unit buzzed into action, drawing away the fume of the incense. Malcifer paced around the Reclusiam, lighting more candles with a spark-rod, bringing a warm glow to push back the darkness that had enveloped Annael. The Space Marines looked at each other and there was a fierce light in the eyes of Annael's brethren, matching the heat of resolve that lingered still, burning inside like an ember set into his heart.

Malcifer completed his circuit of the chamber and came back to the altar. Tattooed mail rippled as he brought his palms together, his hands at his chest. Annael copied his pose, feeling a state of calm pushing aside the anguish he had felt as his hands came together. Once more the Chaplain bowed his head, his words strong but not forced.

'Give praise to the Emperor for the life that flows within us,' he intoned.

'We are his weapons,' replied the kneeling warriors, lowering their gazes.

'Give praise to the Lion for the purpose that drives us.'

'We are his loyal servants.'

'Give praise to the Chapter for nurturing the wrath within us.'

'We are the Dark Angels.'

THE BLACK KNIGHTS

When his first assembly had departed, Malcifer pulled off his skull mask, a puff of vapour escaping from its rebreather unit. He had a few moments before attending to his second congregation and took the opportunity to compose his thoughts with some silent contemplation. He walked around the altar and knelt down, reaching up with one hand to touch the sigil upon its surface. Feeling the cold stone beneath his fingers Malcifer closed his eyes and turned his thoughts to what it meant to bear the symbol of the Dark Angels.

For him, and the others of the Chaplaincy, to be a Dark Angel was to walk along a precipice between light and dark. It was his duty to ensure the shame of the Chapter remained a secret, even from those he led into battle, but it was also his task to oversee the wellbeing of the company's warriors. He was the bastion against doubt that would hold against the questions his charges would ask, always ready to provide explanation to the worthy and to offer assurance to those not yet ready for the truth.

As Sammael prepared the battle plan that would see the Ravenwing and warriors of the Fifth Company victorious, Malcifer faced a labour no less daunting: to ensure the faith and resolve of the warriors was fortified, the mysteries of the Chapter upheld.

He had accepted that fate, and took honour from the fact that he had been chosen for the Chaplaincy, for there were few with the strength of mind to utter the half-truths necessitated by his calling. Even Sammael, lauded Grand Master, did not know everything that Malcifer knew. There were layers of truth even within the Inner Circle, and Malcifer was keenly aware that everything he thought was true might one day be revealed to be not quite as he believed. Revelation and acceptance were the burden of the Chaplain, and to keep apart the disparate levels of truth was a stretch on his willpower.

Boreas had been left alone for too long. The weight of the truth had broken his spirit, with no guiding hand from the Inner Circle to show him the path of righteousness. The dead Chaplain's warning was timely, but it was not the content of Boreas's message that held a deep truth, but the manner of its delivery. Malcifer knew there would be an inquest when he returned to the Tower of Angels and he would give voice to the opinion that members of the Inner Circle and Chaplaincy should not be allowed to remain away from their brethren for so long. The sturdiest faith could be shaken by abandonment, each passing day becoming a torture on the spirit. Boreas had been one of the most devout members of the Chapter and yet even he had been broken by solitude and the machinations of the Fallen.

That it was sometimes necessary to lie to those that trusted him was another duty of the Chaplaincy that Malcifer was willing to bear. The Space Marines who had just departed had been manipulated to believe what the

Chapter required them to believe. Most of them would die, later rather than sooner he hoped, not knowing fully the treachery that had brought the Dark Angels to the brink of destruction. It was a blessing for them to be ignorant, and a mercy for their souls that Malcifer did not encumber them with the unabashed truth. Even within, if the knowledge that the Dark Angels had turned upon themselves was widely known the Chapter would be destroyed.

This way was better, he reminded himself.

He stood up as the reclusiam doors hissed open, admitting the next congregation. There were fifteen of them, the Black Knights, their ebon robes stitched with a red Chapter symbol on the right breast. Hardened warriors all, their clean-shaven faces and close-cropped hair showed the scars of battle on cheeks and scalps. Some had silver and gold service studs in their brows, marking half-centuries and centuries of war.

The small procession was led by the two Huntmasters, Tybalain and Charael. The left breast of their robes was embroidered with a silver hammer shaped like the head of a raven, duplicating the weapons the Black Knights wielded from their bikes. Tybalain had a scar on his right cheek, a slash of white from nose to ear, pierced with tiny dagger-shaped pins. Malcifer remembered the day an eldar power blade had cut through the Black Knight's helm, moments before the alien had its head crushed by Tybalain's hammer. That night, following the battle, Tybalain had replaced slain Gethion as Huntmaster. Charael was more orthodox in appearance, free of brand, scar or tattoo, though his right eye had been replaced by a plasteel and adamantium augmetic, the red lens glinting in the candlelight that bathed the reclusiam.

The two were fearsome warriors and after this campaign

Malcifer expected one or both of them to be elevated to the ranks of the Deathwing. They had certainly earned the honour of such promotion and their service to the Chapter deserved reward. The Black Knights were Sammael's elite; amongst the highly specialised Ravenwing that was a profound honour. The Huntmasters had to exemplify the tenets of the Company, both military and spiritual, and as the warriors knelt in front of the altar, Malcifer wondered which of the others would be suitable replacements for Tybalain and Charael should they be elevated.

Such concerns were for later thought and consultation with the Grand Master, for there were much more pressing matters to address. Malcifer sat between the Black Knights and the altar, facing them, the gathering more informal than the previous service. These warriors were as much Malcifer's progeny as Sammael's, inculcated in all seven Rites of the Raven, possessors of knowledge above their brethren; though not yet made aware of the Fourth Level of Initiation. Such truths were only passed on to the Deathwing, but the Black Knights knew enough for Malcifer to be candid about the foe they hoped to face.

'We embark on a battle to claim one of the Fallen.' The Black Knights exchanged pleased nods and grim smiles. This was their true purpose brought to the fore. 'We suspect that they have made lair on an ancient star fort, dubbed Port Imperial by the renegades. You will learn the battle plan from Grand Master Sammael, but it is my duty to make you aware of the possible consequences. In the close confines and hectic fighting of a boarding action you must stand ready to respond immediately if there is a possibility that one of your brethren from the Fifth Company will come into contact with the Fallen. You must ensure that all protocols and cordons are maintained, and by preference ensure that one of you or the Grand Master conducts the apprehension of the renegade.'

'What tapestry is to be woven for the other warriors of the force?' asked Charael.

'Our brothers in the company are aware that we may face a traitor Space Marine at Port Imperial. I have agreed with Sergeant Seraphiel that those in the Fifth will be told that the enemy are led by an Imperial officer turned renegade. His capture is necessary to locate other forces that broke from Imperial governance with him. Standard communications protocols will apply. The target is marked as Diabolus and will be referred to as such in all broadcasts.'

'And if there is a Fallen on this station, what of other witnesses?' asked Tybalain.

'Knowledge of the Fallen must be contained. All archives will be searched for data. This is a renegade base – there are no innocents,' Malcifer replied, looking at each of the Black Knights in turn. 'No one is to be spared.'

THREE
PORT IMPERIAL

OPENING SALVO

It was with relief that Sammael heard from Judoc Pichon of the arrival of the second strike cruiser. The *Implacable Justice* had been waiting on the edge of the system for the other ship for six days, the vessels having been separated by the tides of the warp during transit to the Polgoth system. For those six days, passive sensor readings had detected the mass of Port Imperial and three small vessels. Fortunately none of the rebels had attempted to leave the system, which would have forced Sammael into action before the arrival of the Fifth Company. Now that the *Penitent Warrior* had arrived, the Dark Angels could move on their target. Fortunately the two strike cruisers had translated in close proximity to each other and the star fort was only four days away at cruising speed.

Lacking any powerful scanning equipment or psykers to detect the arrival of the Dark Angels' ships, the pirates were wholly unaware of the two strike cruisers that prowled in-system. They made swift progress, the outer reaches of Polgoth relatively free of asteroids and other stellar phenomena that would slow their progress. Forty-two standard hours after the *Penitent Warrior* had arrived both ships were in position to scan for the enemy.

On the command bridge of the *Implacable Justice*, fully clad in his armour and his warriors at their battle stations, Sammael monitored the situation with Harahel by his side. The two of them stood on the gallery overlooking the main floor of the bridge, their voices soft so that the non-augmented serfs below could not hear their conversation. On the main screen, magnification at maximum, Port Imperial was a small blur of grey and silver against the stars. Not wishing to risk discovery with aggressive scanning, the Dark Angels had not yet determined the exact nature of the base and its capabilities were as yet unknown.

This gap in his knowledge was of minor concern to Sammael, trumped as it was by the sense of satisfaction he felt at finding the star fort where he had hoped, intact and operational. To have arrived at Polgoth to find an empty system after much anticipation would have been a serious setback. Sammael felt justified in leaving battle-ridden Piscina, though he tried hard not to let optimism run wild.

'Astelan lied in his testimony,' said the Librarian. 'Port Imperial was not destroyed.'

'As we suspected,' replied Sammael. 'No void shields detected, which is good news. I do not think our foes have the means to maintain their base to any competent standard. Certainly they lack the means to move from the system. They are deficient of tech-adepts. One of the many disadvantages of being renegade. I am surprised they can even find this place after their raids, lacking navigators.'

'There is a warp-beacon within the lair,' said Harahel. 'I

could feel its signal before we translated. The navigators reported detecting several more surrounding the system out to fifty light years. The pirates' hunting ground is small.'

'Yet those same beacons are the bait that draws in the unwary. A lone ship, perhaps needing to re-establish its bearings, would make transition at one of the beacon sites, only to be ambushed by these pillagers.'

'I scoured the datalogs but there is no mention of how the fort comes to be here. Do you think the Fallen were the founders or did they simply discover the turncoats' nest?'

'Malcifer tells me that there are no clues to the origin of this place in the transcript of Astelan's confession, and he has read the log many times since we left Piscina. This system is almost cut off by ork encroachment that has been expanding for several hundred years. I would not be surprised to learn that the garrison turned renegade after being forgotten. These pirates are probably descendants of the crew.'

'Or were seduced from service to the Emperor by the Fallen,' suggested Harahel. 'A secure base such as this would be valuable to them.'

'Three ships poses a dilemma,' said Sammael, deciding not to speculate further. 'Any one of them may be carrying our quarry and if they split from each other, we can only chase two.'

'What sort of vessels are they?' asked the Librarian.

'Two smaller ships, equivalent to a destroyer or rapid strike vessel in size, and what appears to be a rebel Imperial Navy frigate.'

'Our prey will be on the largest ship,' said Harahel. 'The Fallen are driven by selfish needs, and to command a smaller vessel than another would be a thorn to their pride. Target the frigate first if you fear they will escape.'

'Good advice,' said Sammael, nodding in appreciation. He raised his voice. 'Assign primary target to enemy frigate. Designation Mongrel. Report range, repeat on standard intervals.'

'Four hours until optimum range, Grand Master,' Pichon replied. 'No enemy sensor sweeps detected.'

'Very good, Pichon. Designate smaller vessels as Rat One and Rat Two.'

'Designations assigned, Grand Master.'

Sammael waited, the distance-to-target reports slowly creeping down. The watch below changed over the intervening hours, though Pichon did not relinquish his command position. Just after the two hour mark. a serf appeared with a tray of food and drink for the Grand Master and his companion. The two of them withdrew to Sammael's command chamber confident that Pichon would notify them of any urgent news.

'First a trio of citadels and then a city, and now a star fort,' muttered Sammael as he broke off a chunk of heavy, blackened soyslab. 'This latest patrol has not been kind to the Ravenwing in the battlegrounds it has offered.'

'We fight where we must, brother,' replied Harahel.

'True enough.' Sammael chewed mechanically, the dark loaf of synthetic food almost tasteless. 'At least we know that if there are the Fallen aboard Port Imperial they cannot escape.'

'It is your hope that we follow the trail of our hated foe, brother,' said Harahel. 'Do you really think we may have cornered him at last?'

'No,' said Sammael. He wolfed down the last of his meal and pushed the silvered platter across the dull slate of the hololith projector. 'The security here has lapsed so badly I am under no illusion that the arch-quarry will be found at Port Imperial. He is far too cunning to be so easily trapped.'

'But one of his companions, perhaps?'

'The coordinates appended to Boreas's log have proven correct and Astelan admitted the Fallen frequented this place, even if he tried to mislead us about its destruction. I am confident.'

Sammael looked at Harahel, who returned his gaze with an intent stare.

'This is what we do, brother, the long hunt,' said Harahel. 'I share your confidence. The Fallen have been here and we take another step closer to redemption.'

'A road the Chapter will continue to tread long after you and I have departed this mortal plane,' said Sammael.

'Yet along the road we still move, as inexorable as the turning of the stars. Have faith, brother. From the fruit of our labours shall be sown the seeds of the new Dark Angels. One day the Lion shall know peace and one day our Chapter can forget the legacy of Caliban lost.'

'No, we shall not. We must never forget, lest we are doomed to repeat the mistakes of the past.' Sammael smiled. 'You are fortunate that Brother Malcifer is not present to hear such words from your lips. Your ears would ring with his chastisement for some time.'

'Each of us knows his own righteousness,' laughed Harahel. 'Malcifer simply knows it a little more than the rest of us.'

With still an hour left until the attack began, Sammael and Harahel returned to the bridge and took up station at the centre of the command deck, surrounded by the bustling of the serfs and technicians. Servitors wired into the scanner arrays and communications consoles whispered and croaked a constant chatter of information, monitored by the attending crew. Dataslabs were exchanged and reports made, everything of routine importance passed to Pichon so that Sammael was able to concentrate on the wider situation.

'Send word to Sergeant Seraphiel,' the Grand Master announced, seeing that one of the ships docked at Port Imperial was showing a spike in its energy signature. 'Have the *Penitent Warrior* increase separation. I want to be sure that we catch these scum between us.'

Pichon signalled an affirmative and passed on the order, before returning to his customary position a few metres from the Grand Master. They continued to wait, alert for any sign that the enemy knew their doom approached.

'Have all torpedoes readied, full spread,' Sammael commanded. 'Increase thrust to full battle speed. Signal the alert.'

Moments later the warning klaxon sounded across the bridge. The volume of communication increased rapidly as reports were relayed from station to station, while the buzz and grind of metriculators and babble of servitors intensified as scanner readings were correlated and firing solutions calculated.

Amongst the hum of voices a low tone sounded from the sensor array terminals. Sammael knew its meaning immediately, but waited for Pichon to receive confirmation and pass on the report.

'Active scan detected from the enemy base, Grand Master,' said the deck officer. 'Also picking up magnified energy output from Mongrel and Rat One. No sign yet of Rat Two responding.'

'They see us,' replied Sammael. 'The scum are preparing to bolt. Launch torpedoes, four salvos, arc four-sixteen, declination thirty. If they try to power directly out-system they will run into the torpedo spread.'

'As you command, Grand Master,' said Pichon, bowing before repeating Sammael's instructions to the torpedo officers.

'Are you still confident that our prey will use the frigate, brother?' Sammael asked Harahel. The Librarian nodded. 'Good, then we can afford to destroy the smaller vessels and concentrate on crippling Mongrel.'

'It is with hope rather than expectation that we should proceed, brother,' said the Epistolary. 'It is rumour alone that we chase.'

'Rumour and shadow have ever been the spoor we follow.' Sammael paused as the weapons technicians announced the launch of the first salvo. On the main screen, four immense torpedoes powered away from the prow of the *Implacable Justice*, the blaze of their engines swiftly dimming to pinpricks of light against the backdrop of stars. 'The next few hours will shed light on the matter.'

What would happen next depended upon the actions of the pirate ships. The Dark Angels strike cruisers could easily outpace the smaller vessels in a straight pursuit, given that the enemy would take some time for their plasma reactors to come to full power while the Space Marine ships were already at combat velocity. Sammael had aimed successive torpedo spreads not at the enemy star fort, but on a trajectory that cut off an avenue of escape for the docked ships. They would have to dare the torpedoes to take the most direct route away from their berths, and more likely would come about, heading to port across the bows of the approaching attackers.

Sammael hoped that the renegades would be foolish enough to remain for battle, and was confident that the two strike cruisers had sufficient strength to quickly best their opponents. More likely the pirates would attempt to break away, heading for the outer reaches of the system so that they could escape into the warp.

Lacking torpedoes, the *Penitent Warrior* was on a curving course ahead and to port of the *Implacable Justice*. Sergeant Seraphiel and his bridge officers were under orders to contain any escaping ship, acting as an outrider to force the enemy back into the path of the Ravenwing strike cruiser. Caught between the two Space Marine vessels, the pirate ships would be crippled and rendered irrelevant, to be boarded and cleared once the raid on the star fort had been complete.

Throughout, Sammael had emphasised the need for swift and decisive action. Their main purpose in coming to the system was to sweep for evidence of the Fallen, and to capture any that were present, rather than engage in a lengthy battle with their foes. Three phases of battle would see the deed done. The opening phase had started and once the threat of the starships had been neutralised the second phase – the attack on Port Imperial itself – could begin. The third and possibly most dangerous phase was the extraction of the Dark Angels from the space station.

Sammael was full of energy, but resisted the urge to pace the bridge. He had to remain calm and capable of reasoned thought, weighing his decisions carefully rather than acting on instinct alone. A space battle was not the sudden cut and thrust of a Ravenwing assault, but a more measured, almost balletic process. The distances were vast and the time required to correct a mistake could well leave a gap for his enemies to escape their punishment. It would be at least another hour until the *Implacable Justice* was in effective range with its gun batteries, but that hour would require all of his poise and attention.

NO ESCAPE

The vessel designated Rat Two had not properly loosed its berthing locks as it tried to pull away from the Port Imperial docks. Gantries tore apart, leaving twisted metal scrap and hunks of broken plascrete in the wake of the ship. Several bodies were hurled from the star fort's quay by decompression, the spinning corpses rapidly freezing in the void amidst a plume of ejecting gases. The ship commander was too hasty to escape from his moorings to adhere to safety protocols and as Rat Two's plasma engine fired up white heat bathed the superstructure of the harbour wharf jutting from the station, melting a welt along the side of the docking spar.

Rat Two slowly gathered speed, but was already far behind Mongrel and Rat One. There being little honour amongst pirates, the dawdling vessel had been abandoned as the frigate and its destroyer-sized escort made a bid to escape. Rather than attempt to catch up with its departing companions, Rat Two powered ahead, veering to starboard to avoid the onrushing wave of torpedoes launched by the *Implacable Justice*.

Concerned that the opposing flotilla was splitting, Sammael held a brief discussion with Sergeant Seraphiel and the two of them agreed to divide their attack. While the *Penitent Warrior* continued on its intercept course towards Mongrel and Rat One, the *Implacable Justice* altered its heading to pursue Rat Two. Without knowing whether one of the Fallen was aboard one of the ships, it was imperative that none were allowed to escape and the ship carrying the Fifth Company would have to contend with the frigate and destroyer alone; a match in which it would not be outclassed.

Sammael briefly considered another torpedo salvo, but decided against such a course of action. Rat Two was only a few hundred metres long, less than a quarter of the size of the *Implacable Justice*. Each torpedo from the strike cruiser contained several dozen warheads of which only three or four would need to hit to utterly obliterate the fleeing pirate craft. It was Sammael's task to capture the Fallen so that they could be taken for interrogation and the chance of repentance; the risk of a torpedo strike killing the Grand Master's prey was too great.

Instead, the Ravenwing vessel would have to close the range and cripple Rat Two with its guns. This would be a more time-consuming course of action, giving those left aboard the station more time to prepare their defence, but it could not be avoided. Under Sammael's command the *Implacable Justice* moved to full-speed, describing a long arc until it was directly behind Rat Two.

Having moved into the stern chase, it was only a matter of time until the strike cruiser overhauled the enemy ship and brought it into range.

The gap between the *Implacable Justice* and the *Penitent Warrior* was widening every minute, and they were now separated by a large swath of space. Sergeant Seraphiel and his ship could not expect any assistance from their fellow Dark Angels and would take on Mongrel and Rat One by themselves.

To the good fortune of the Fifth Company's interim commander the renegades decided that they were better placed to remain close to each other rather than breaking away and heading in different directions. Watching the scanner blips of the two ships on the main display of the bridge, Sammael remarked on this to Harahel.

'Surely they cannot be contemplating an attack?' said the Grand Master.

'If one of those we hunt is aboard Mongrel, perhaps overconfidence might be expected,' replied Harahel. 'More likely, neither wishes to be the one to draw the strike of the *Penitent Warrior*, for surely if they divide their course one of them will be overwhelmed while the other escapes. They are too afraid to part ways lest they are the one that becomes the subject of pursuit.'

'A fair assessment brother,' said Sammael. 'I see that each ship has made bearing alterations and the other has swiftly followed to keep station. Their selfishness dooms them both.'

'It is the old story of the two squires and the varglion,' said Harahel. 'One does not need to outrun the varglion, only the other squire.'

Sammael laughed. It was a story he had not heard since leaving the Scout Company, and to be reminded of it after so long lightened his mood.

'I always thought it would be better for the two squires to face the varglion together,' said the Grand Master.

'I believe that the moral of the tale is that it is better to sacrifice one's self to allow a brother to live,' said Harahel. He nodded towards the huge display screen. 'I also believe that *Penitent Warrior* is about to demonstrate why your course of action would be brave but pointless.'

Sammael checked the chronometer and range readings. Rat Two was still accelerating hard and *Implacable Justice* would not be within weapons range for fifteen minutes.

'Main display, *Penitent Warrior*, maximum magnification.' The Grand Master folded his arms and watched as the image moved away from the glow of Rat Two's plasma wash and centred on the Dark Angels strike cruiser. Superimposed over the star-filled screen were three glowing reticules, one in red highlighting the position of the *Penitent Warrior* and a pair of white circles around the pirates. Sammael glanced at Harahel as he watched their intersecting courses. 'Let us hope that Sergeant Seraphiel understands the importance of taking the ships intact.'

'He understands well his role, brother,' said Harahel. 'He will temper fury with finesse.'

For the next few minutes the two ships ahead of the *Penitent Warrior* engaged in several drastic changes of heading, perhaps fearing another torpedo attack. They cut to starboard and inclined sharply down through the system plane, and then broke to port and rose up in the hopes of making their course too unpredictable. As the *Penitent Warrior* possessed no torpedo tubes, the only result of this manoeuvring was to allow the strike cruiser to gain even more quickly on the evading ships.

'Though clumsily executed, their attempts at evasion are not without some strategy,' said Harahel. 'I think that our pirates have had experience against the Imperial Navy. It may indicate the presence of a superior military mind...'

'No, I disagree, brother,' replied Sammael. 'If their commander had received training in fleet tactics they would not waste time with their torturous convolutions, but instead make all power perpendicular to the *Penitent Warrior*'s angle of attack. And if they had experience of the Imperial Navy, they have never encountered anything larger than a Sword-class frigate.'

'Why do you assume that, brother?'

'They are turning to fight,' said Sammael, pointing at the screen. The white circles were slowly coming about, turning to a heading directly towards the oncoming strike cruiser. 'If they had fought a light cruiser before, they would know that they are outgunned and certainly in a position of weakness to attempt a head-on attack.'

Sammael saw desperation, even panic, in the tactics of the foe. Having twisted and turned every way they could the commanders now threw caution to the wind and confronted their attacker directly. Mongrel and Rat One were keeping close together, arrowing directly for the *Penitent Warrior*. Sammael did not know what weapon systems the pirates possessed, but if they hoped to overload the void shields and penetrate the metres-thick hull of a strike cruiser the captains were about to be sorely disappointed.

A range scale counted down between the reticules on the screen and then flashed red to confirm the enemy had come into firing range of the Dark Angels ship. From a dorsal turret atop the spine of Mongrel a lance battery opened fire, sending the beam of a laser towards the *Penitent Warrior*. The blue streak slashed across the heavens for several seconds, missing the strike cruiser by a wide margin. Its capacitors drained, the lance beam disappeared. The *Penitent Warrior* was not yet in range with its weapons and was forced to endure another lance beam before it could bring its guns to bear. This time the pirates' fire was more accurate, the beam of high energy causing the strike cruiser's void shields to activate. Warp energy flared in a purple and green corona around the

Penitent Warrior as the enemy's lance ran from the starboard bow to the port stern. As the searing energy of the beam dissipated, the strike cruiser was left undamaged, the energy of the attack absorbed by the void shield.

Thirty seconds later, the Dark Angels were in range to respond.

Tracking Mongrel as the strike cruiser closed on the pirates, the turret housing *Penitent Warrior*'s bombardment cannon turned, sophisticated sensor arrays locking on to the frigate's position and course while inorganic cogitators calculated the firing trajectory required. The bombardment cannon was mostly used in orbital support – bringing devastation from afar as they had at Hadria Praetoris – but it was no less effective against enemy ships. Additional stabiliser engines flared into life to keep the strike cruiser on course as the bombardment cannon opened fire, a plume of igniting gas ejecting from the barrel of the immense gun. For several minutes the cannon unleashed shells the size of gunships, filling the vacuum around Mongrel with hurtling ordnance.

Three of the shots struck the incoming frigate, two amidships and one to the stern. The void shield generators flared into life for the first, shunting the energy of the shell's impact into the warp, but the second and third hits scored directly against the ship's hull. Velocity alone was enough for the shells to punch through metres-thick armour, and time-delayed fuses ignited inside the frigate, activating the plasma cores of the bombardment shells to rip out building-sized chunks of superstructure. Hundreds of crew were incinerated in a moment; dozens more pulped by the blast wave and shredded by explosive decompression. Plasma and debris blossomed from the wounds, heeling the ship over to port, the expulsion of energy forcing Mongrel from its original heading.

The lance turret on the frigate responded, but its beam weaved harmlessly back and forth above the strike cruiser, its targeting sent awry by the bombardment cannon hits. Rat One and Mongrel parted slightly as the frigate headed to starboard of the *Penitent Warrior* and the destroyer was on course to pass down the port side. Armoured shields slid back from the gun decks of the Dark Angels vessel, revealing battery after battery of missile launchers, plasma drivers and macro-cannons.

Rat One's own meagre batteries started firing early, sending a barrage of laser and shell fire towards the strike cruiser. Most of the storm missed, but as the *Penitent Warrior*'s broadside came to bear the strike cruiser's void shields lit up once more, saturated with the welter of fire erupting from the small enemy vessel.

Fire and laser beams erupted along the hull of the *Penitent Warrior*, moving from bow to stern on both the port and starboard sides as the strike cruiser passed between the two approaching ships. For several minutes the weight of fire fell upon the Dark Angels' foes, by which time the strike cruiser was already turning sharply to starboard to come around behind Mongrel.

The missiles and shells hit the two vessels with dozens of direct impacts. Rat One's dorsal buttresses disintegrated under the weight of fire, the spine of the ship breaking so that a fifty-metre-long portion of decks tore away from the hull. Mongrel, already breached by the bombardment cannon, was wracked by internal explosions as the storm of fire breached weapons batteries and magazines. Fortified gun turrets turned to dust and debris as they were blown apart from within and crew dorms were swept through with white-hot shrapnel and plasma.

Both ships were badly damaged, trailing wreckage in their wake. The engines of Rat One were faltering, the plasma flare growing dim due to severed energy lines. Mongrel powered on as best as the crew could manage, turning away from Rat One, leaving their fellow renegades to their fate.

With the frigate still mobile, the *Penitent Warrior* swung around, bringing the starboard broadside against Mongrel's engines. The gunnery crews were ordered to fire as they each came to bear, a half-volley of laser and plasma that slammed into the unshielded engines of the frigate. Armour and fuel couplings were breached with secondary plasma detonations, and finally the huge exhaust nozzles of the ship grew dark and the frigate was left drifting without power.

While the *Penitent Warrior* had been occupied with its foes, the *Implacable Justice* was overhauling Rat Two. The strike cruiser's bombardment cannon fired several ranging shots at the aft sections of the destroyer, the shells screaming past the fleeing ship. The gunners adjusted their targeting matrices and through Pichon informed Sammael that they were locked on and ready to fire when the strike cruiser came into optimum range.

With the fight between the *Penitent Warrior* and the pirates all but finished, Sammael ordered the main display to focus on Rat Two. The ship looked to be some kind of heavily modified short-range cargo hauler. She was wide in the beam, at least four hundred metres from port to starboard, and perhaps only two hundred metres high. Three-quarters of a kilometre long, most of the ship was taken up with cargo holds and engines, with just a small crew space and bridge along the dorsal decks. Two freight bays had been converted into gun mountings, an array of asymmetric laser batteries and energy relays clumsily protruding from poorly armoured turrets and gantries.

Three engine nozzles obscured most of the ship, and

Sammael frowned as the plasma discharge intensified, turning from a deep orange to yellow edged with blue and white. He looked over at the navigational team as they turned and made a report to Pichon.

'Rat Two accelerating,' the officer of the deck told Sammael. 'Velocity increasing by five per cent.'

'They are overcharging their reactors,' the Grand Master said, the words directed to Harahel. 'It will not be enough.'

'Acceleration reaching ten per cent additional,' reported one of the navigation serfs. 'Velocity still increasing.'

On the main screen, Rat Two was pulling away, adding to the separation between pursued and pursuer every second.

'Report our reactor status,' snapped Sammael. In half a minute the target ship would be beyond effective range again.

'Optimal and eighty-five per cent, Grand Master,' Pichon replied immediately, not even having to check with the engineering attendants.

'Increase to one hundred per cent, all speed ahead,' said Sammael. 'We shall...'

His words petered out as he saw what was happening on the screen. Rat Two's plasma trail was almost solidly white, leaving a shimmer of energy in the ship's wake. Steam was bursting from overheating valves, the hot gases vented from the reactor meeting with the icy coldness of space to creating swirling clouds of crystal and congealing vapour. The ship's systems could not cope with the increased heat output from the overcharging engines and Sammael saw exhaust ports rupturing into fountains of molten metal.

Something inside the pirate vessel was going catastrophically wrong as a jet of plasma punched out from the engine blocks, sending armoured plates and twisted lengths of immense piping spinning into the void.

'Belay last order,' Sammael said quietly as the chain reaction engulfed Rat Two. The last third of the ship disappeared into a ball of expanding white light, a miniature star that swiftly engulfed the rest of the ship, vaporising it. 'Full power to navigational and void shields. Brace for debris. Engines full back, new heading one-zero-nine.'

Despite breaking thrusters and a sharp turn to port, the momentum of the *Implacable Justice* took the strike cruiser into the expanding cloud of gas and debris. Navigational hazard warnings flashed and sirens wailed as the ship ploughed into the superheated fog. There were shrieks and whines from the servitors of the sensor banks, the half-human half-machine interfaces crying out in pain as the scanner arrays were overloaded with data. The comms network screeched for several seconds until one of the serfs shut down the open channels, plunging the bridge into silence, cutting off the reports that had started to come through from engineering and the gun decks.

Sammael could feel the ship shuddering as it continued to turn through the dense zone of collapsing plasma, the low-frequency navigational fields pushing aside what remained of Rat Two while the void shields absorbed the energy of the artificial star.

A circuit exploded across a cogitator to Sammael's left, blasting sparks into the face of a serf. The young man cried out, falling back from his station as suppressant gas bloomed from a nozzle above the flickering fire creeping across the console.

'They did more damage destroying themselves than their guns would have caused,' snarled Sammael. He called for Pichon, who was supervising a medicae team coming forward from the shadow beneath the bridge gallery. The wounded attendant cried out and flailed in his blindness but Sammael ignored the distraction. 'Full damage report. Set course for Port Imperial. All flight crews to stand by and all torpedo tubes readied.'

'As you command, Grand Master.' Pichon darted a look at the fallen serf to assure himself that all was being done that could, and then started to snap off orders. Only phase one of the battle had been finished. A lot more fighting remained between the Dark Angels and their objective.

PRIMARY INSERTION

With one ship destroyed and the other two unable to manoeuvre, the Dark Angels were able to press towards their primary target quickly, leaving the crippled vessels to be dealt with once the station was secured. Converging on Port Imperial at ninety degrees to one another – the *Penitent Warrior* approaching from above the star fort with the *Implacable Justice* below – the two strike cruisers made ready for the attack.

Port Imperial looked like a city floating in the void. From a square foundation of plasteel-reinforced ferrocrete and tapering spires nearly ten kilometres across, four docking arms jutted out a kilometre from each corner of the station. Atmosphere still billowed from the spar damaged when Rat Two had broken its moorings, creating a cloud of gas and ice around the mess of twisted gantries and broken buttresses. Hab-towers banked up steeply, growing taller towards the centre of the station, but the majority were dark, only the central spire and the towers clustered directly about it shining light from scores of windows.

In armoured bastions built around the docking spars where they met the main hub, missile batteries and macro-las cannons turned towards the approaching ships. Gigantic archways opened, spilling the gleam of launch bay lamps into the darkness beneath the station, illuminating communications dishes, sensor arrays and maintenance gantries.

From a safe distance, outside the range of any of the fort's batteries, *Implacable Justice* launched another salvo of torpedoes, targeting the closest defence turrets. In the wake of the torpedoes the Ravenwing cruiser spilled forth a cloud of fighters and gunships; another wave of Thunderhawks sped from the flight deck of the *Penitent Warrior*.

Long-range laser fire sprayed from the station, cutting the void with intermittent beams of red and blue. The torpedoes and attack craft were too small to be targeted by these main weapon systems, which instead were focused on the incoming strike cruisers. Laser energy met void shields in multicoloured blasts but the Dark Angels continued on, engines at full power to bring their weapons into range.

The fighters in the vanguard of the attack wave split, half of them staying on course with the Ravenwing gunships and the other half cutting across the vacuum to take up position with the Thunderhawks of the Fifth Company. A cloud of dark shapes spewed from Port Imperial's bays as the pirates launched their own fighters to intercept the incoming attack.

In one of the lead Thunderhawks, Brother Telemenus ran through his final pre-battle rituals, checking his wargear while Daellon inspected Telemenus's armour seals and ensured there were no obstructions in his battle-brothers' backpack vents. With a final full-spectrum diagnostic of his autosenses, whispering benedictions to the spirit of his armour, Telemenus completed his preparations and turned his attention to Daellon to make a return investigation of the other Dark Angel's armour. All was in order and he slapped his companion on the shoulder.

'We are ready, brother,' said Telemenus.

'Let us trust to the skill of the pilots and the ineptitude of our foes,' replied Daellon.

Telemenus nodded but said nothing. Since returning to the squad following his punishment, the Dark Angel had endeavoured to remain focused on the mission at hand. Now that they were in flight, their fate prey to forces he could not control for the moment, Telemenus found his doubts had evaporated. With missiles and las-blasts filling the void, the wider cause for battle mattered little. He had been presented with an enemy and it was his duty to slay them. Ten days in solitary reclusion had not tempered his misgivings wholly, but he had come to realise that dissenting action would not be the solution. Whatever the cause for Sammael to abandon Piscina and come to this Emperor-forsaken place, Telemenus was honour-bound to see the mission completed. The sooner these renegades were destroyed, the sooner the Dark Angels could move on to more important enemies.

'You are quiet, brother,' remarked Sergeant Amanael. 'I would think that your First Marksman laurels are ensured this day. A boarding action against a trapped enemy will see you surpass the needed tally by dozens.'

'As you say, brother-sergeant,' replied Telemenus. 'The awarding of the laurel will be pleasing, but its attainment against such enemies lessens the honour.'

'There are merchant crews and Imperial Navy captains who would argue that point, brother,' said Achamenon. 'This nest of serpents has required cleansing for decades, it would seem. Remember that they are traitors to a man, preying upon the loyal servants of the Emperor.'

'Do not mistake my sentiment, brothers, I am glad to destroy this scum and see their perfidy ended. Yet it is an engagement not worthy of remark, merely a footnote in the Chapter annals. I would see my laurels awarded in a glorious battle that would echo down the generations to come.'

'Brother Telemenus.' He looked to the right and regretted his words as Sergeant Seraphiel approached from the bow of the gunship. The commander's approach was punctuated by the thump and whine of the mag-locks in his boots connecting with the metal decking. 'Have you forgotten so soon the content of my briefing?'

'No, honoured brother, I have not,' Telemenus replied. 'I remember well that our foes may well be commanded by a renegade of the Adeptus Astartes. If I cut down this traitor whilst achieving my laurels I shall consider it a great honour.'

'Yet you also recall that this traitor is to be apprehended not executed, if possible,' said Seraphiel, stopping in front of Telemenus. 'Those are your orders.'

'And I shall obey them, brother-sergeant,' said Telemenus, looking up at his commander. 'I do not think there will be opportunity to do otherwise, considering our role is simply to secure the landing zones and allow the Ravenwing to make ingress.'

'We are about to board a space station, brother,' said Seraphiel. 'Our brethren on their bikes and Land Speeders will be limited in their manoeuvring. I suspect that the warriors of the Fifth Company shall prove the more successful hunters today.'

'I will give thanks to the Emperor if that proves to be so, brother. If we are the ones to deliver this miscreant to justice, it will be to the honour of the company, even if no others shall be allowed to know of it.'

'Just so. The Supreme Grand Master will hear all accounts, and our actions shall be recognised by him if no other.'

'Praise the primarch, in whose shadow we all follow,' Telemenus said softly, bowing his head.

Seraphiel nodded and turned away.

'If Sammael has his way, I will be left guarding the ramp of a Thunderhawk,' muttered Telemenus.

'Cease your grumbling or I will make it so,' Sergeant Amanael said sharply, stilling further protest.

Several minutes passed during which Telemenus listened to the general comms reports. The *Implacable Justice* was moving within firing range of Port Imperial, its weapon batteries ready to pour fire into the station to cover the approach of the attack craft. The screen of Ravenwing fighters powered ahead of the gunship wave to engage the enemy interceptors. A warning chime sounded, alerting the force to incoming attackers and the subdued conversation aboard the Thunderhawk fell silent as the Dark Angels followed the progress of the pilots.

The pirate craft were a mix of single and two-man fighters, armed for the most part with missiles and autocannons. While the strike cruisers and star base duelled over thousands of kilometres, between these behemoths the small craft of both sides engaged over hundreds of metres.

The swarm of foes appeared as a glittering spray of plasma jets against the dark bulk of the space station, spreading out as the Ravenwing craft powered onwards, their sleek black hulls disappearing into the void.

Stabs of blue light spat out from the four lascannon-armed Nephilim forming the tip of the Dark Angels attack, causing the motes of plasma trails to scatter.

Flurries of Blacksword missiles followed swiftly after, swerving and jinking as their artificial brains guided them towards the energy signatures of the enemy craft. The pirate craft were built only for void battle, stubby boxes of bare metal illuminated by the glare of attitude jets and main thrusters, whirling away from the Raven-wing onslaught with plumes of red and orange. Rockets rippled from side-mounted pods, spraying out towards the Ravenwing, filling the vacuum with trails of fire.

As the spearpoint thrust through the dispersing cloud of enemy fighters the second wave of Nephilim, six craft, opened fire with their megabolters. Flashes of propellant flickered between the converging squadrons, filling the firmament with a storm of tiny explosions. One craft turned into a ball of plasma as it crossed the path of hundreds of rounds, its engines punctured by the fusillade. Behind it another fighter split apart, shredded from cockpit to thrusters by a lascannon beam.

All semblance of order disintegrated as the two forces passed each other. In a haze of manoeuvre jets the Nephilim rolled and stooped, while pirate fighters span wildly, unleashing streams of shells at their foes. Bright plasma trails criss-crossed with tracer shells and hurricane bolter salvoes as the Dark Talons came into range. Engines flared to spin the craft, ships exchanging flurries of fire as they parted and turned, hulls gleaming as another fighter was engulfed by its detonating engines. Shell fire from the heavier renegade craft littered the battlespace with explosions, hurling shrapnel into the gunship formation.

Telemenus felt the Thunderhawk tremble as its battle cannon opened fire. The large-calibre ordnance was more suited to blowing apart ground targets, but the fusillade of shells erupting from the onrushing gunships parted the enemy fighters, punching a path through their midst. Heavy bolters chattered from the Thunderhawks' wings as they sped on, trusting to the fighters to protect them against attack from behind.

The Nephilim and Dark Talons formed up into hunting pairs, chasing the enemy as they tried to slip past the screen to bring fire upon the gunships. Occasionally Telemenus heard the rattle of weapons fire or the clang of debris against the hull, but nothing heavy enough to breach the armoured transport compartment. The vox-net was alive with the chatter of the pilots, snapping out target designations and grid coordinates, exchanging attack vector information and warnings.

There was nothing that Telemenus could do, and he waited patiently and in silence as they sped towards their objective. Another announcement over the comm warned that the attack fleet was coming within range of the star base's defence grid. Much of the close-range weapons systems had been targeted by the strike cruisers, but as the gunships passed enemy range mark, ripples of cannon fire and rockets hurtled from the station's remaining defence turrets.

Lacking the more sophisticated targeting matrices of the Ravenwing craft, the pirate fighters and the base gunners opted for weight of fire over accuracy. Their spewing salvoes created a blanket of missiles and shells through which the gunships were forced to pass. The impacts against the hull grew in intensity and frequency and every few seconds the Thunderhawk would rattle from a close detonation. The pilots rolled and banked their craft through the storm; the support of their harnesses rendering the Space Marines oblivious to the evasive manoeuvres being performed. To Telemenus they might well have been cruising gently through the void, as straight as a bolt shot.

Red lights flashed and a warning klaxon filled the compartment. Moments later, a second warning lit up in Telemenus's helm display, indicating a rapid loss of atmospheric pressure. Sealed inside their suits the Space Marines were protected against decompression; the parchment tabs of their purity seals fluttered wildly as the pressurised air evacuated through a hole somewhere towards the rear of the gunship. Everything else had been locked down as a precaution, preventing stray magazines and other items becoming dangerous debris.

The breach was not significant, judging by the time it took for the interior atmosphere to utterly deplete. By the time Telemenus's autosenses detected zero pressure they had passed the five thousand metres mark.

He performed one last check on his bolter and the spare magazines clamped to his cuisses and greaves. Sergeant Seraphiel appeared again, standing by the ramp at the nose of the gunship. The lighting dimmed, Telemenus's autosenses compensating for the gloom, and the ramp whined down into the assault position.

Through the open maw of the Thunderhawk, Telemenus could see the ceramite slabs of the space station's ablative plates, many of them cracked or shattered, a haze of debris coalescing against the superstructure, drawn in by the artificial grav-field. Plasma fires raged in several of the outer towers and as Telemenus watched another streaking fusillade from one of the strike cruisers slammed into Port Imperial. Ferrocrete and metal was ripped apart by the impacts, spraying jagged metres-thick chunks into the void.

The Thunderhawk dipped and Telemenus's view changed. A slit of light appeared as the vista passed underneath a docking spar and a red sigil appeared in Telemenus's view, the range to target counting down beside it: one hundred kilometres.

Arrestor jets fired hard, killing the speed of gunship as it banked towards the opening of the fighter bay. Black blades against the grey of the port, Dark Talons swept past, opening fire with their rift-cannons. Warp generators unleashed coruscating beams that rippled with power from the immaterium, tearing through the fabric of reality. The streaming warp particles struck the plating and buttresses surrounding the fighter bay entrance, creating ravening warp holes that collapsed the armoured bulkheads in upon themselves. Iridescent implosions blossomed across the docking bastion, ripping struts and casements apart, leaving the bay entrance a ragged mess.

The lascannon of the Thunderhawk opened fire, blowing apart the larger pieces of debris in its flight path, turning plascrete to cinder and metal to clouds of molten droplets. The fighters made one final pass, sweeping across the jagged bay entrance with missiles and heavy-gauge bolt cannons. Into this maelstrom of fire plunged the Thunderhawk, the restraining harnesses holding the Space Marines in place snapping up with hydraulic hisses.

Telemenus took his place as the squads thudded towards the ramp, the dark of the looming fighter bay broken by the flare of the gunship's bolters and arcs of electricity forking from ruptured power lines.

'For the Emperor!' roared Seraphiel, wing-hilted power sword held aloft as he led the charge down the ramp even as the Thunderhawk slammed into the pock-marked ferrocrete of the landing apron. His autosenses adjusting to the flickering light, Telemenus was greeted with a scene of utter ruin.

The bulkheads to the right had collapsed entirely, filling half of the docking area with a tangled mass of plasteel struts and fractured ferrocrete. Power cables spitting sparks draped over the rubble, while split gas lines and fuel feeds spewed gouts of green and blue flames. The charred wrecks of several large fighter craft had been buried by the avalanche, glinting shards from their crystalflex canopies scattered across the dull grey of the ferrocrete deck.

A quick sweep from right to left showed no living thing except for Telemenus and his fellow Dark Angels. Broken limbs protruded at odd angles from the slag heap that had been a control bastion and dozens more bodies were littered across the apron, dangling from broken gantries and mangled amongst fallen masonry.

The screech of landing pads scraping across the ferrocrete announced the arrival of a second Thunderhawk while the thirty Space Marines from the first gunship swiftly advanced through the piles of rubble. Amanael's squad were despatched to the right by a terse command from Seraphiel. Telemenus followed on the shoulder of his sergeant, bolter at the ready. His steps felt light as he took a stride over a crumbled pillar, seeming to float for a split second.

'Artificial gravity is compromised,' he remarked.

'Running at approximately ninety per cent,' replied Cadael. The ignition flame of his weapon burned into life as the star fort's atmosphere swept back into the bay, the breeze kicking up dust and fluttering clothing on the bodies protruding from the rubble. The otherworldly scene was bathed in blue for a moment as another arc of electricity surged across a mound of rubble ahead.

The chamber, nearly three hundred metres long and almost as broad, reverberated to the roar of gunship thrusters as more Thunderhawks touched down, bringing the rest of the company onto the space station. Telemenus glanced back for a moment, watching thirty more green-armoured warriors pounding across the landing apron, heading towards a half-ruined archway in the left bulkheads.

'Back!' snapped Sergeant Amanael, waving for the squad to retreat. The sergeant was looking up and Telemenus followed his gaze. A girder warped by a rift-cannon hit snapped the last threads connecting it to the wall. The heavy strut smashed into the ground a few metres ahead of Telemenus, sending shards of metal pinging against his armour.

Switching on their suit lamps, the squad advanced more cautiously, Cadael moving a little ahead of the others, checking the footing as they clambered atop a mound of debris. Reaching the summit, they could see into the corridors and chambers above where the floor had fallen in. Telemenus saw a blur of movement at the edge of the breach and opened fire, the flare of the bolt-round highlighting the shocked expression on a thin face a split second before the man's head was blown apart.

'Enemy above,' Telemenus warned, transmitting over the company channel, though he saw no further move-ment for the moment. Amanael covered the opposite side of the hole as the squad passed beneath, and once they were clear and heading down the other slope of rubble Telemenus backed away and joined them. Ama-nael followed two seconds later, his pistol still trained on the floor above.

'Opening, grid-east, twenty metres,' announced Apol-lon, studying the screen of his auspex. 'Inoperative pressure door, I think.'

The squad turned their lamps on the opening, reveal-ing a wide portal; a massive armoured shutter lodged halfway down, stopped by a crumbled pile of masonry. Dust trickled across the rubble and a motor whined within the structure of the bulkhead as the emergency door continued to push down on the obstruction.

'Control panel,' said Telemenus and pointed to a runepad glowing dimly to the right of the door. A red light blinked incessantly on the display.

Amanael, Apollon, Cadael and Achamenon secured the entrance, bolters trained into the darkness beyond, while Telemenus took his bolter in one hand and approached the keypad, the rest of the squad spreading out to watch their backs. The interface was immediately familiar to Telemenus; he had seen hundreds like it aboard Imperial ships and in buildings all across the galaxy. He prodded a finger into the override key and the whining motor stopped. With a screech of metal gears grinding against each other, the blast door slowly withdrew back up into the bulkhead, revealing the corridor beyond.

Cadael opened up with his flamer, the wash of yellow fire illuminating several ragged-looking pirates who were crawling through a tangle of collapsing ceiling tiles and broken support beams. The three men were dressed in dark-red pressure suits, helmetless; no defence against the ignited promethium streaming from Cadael's flamer. The renegades' agonised shrieks lasted a few seconds only as they flailed around the flames and then collapsed, their bodies smoking, the fabric of their suits melting into charred flesh.

'Clear on this grid,' Amanael reported, adding his voice to those of other sergeants announcing that their sectors were clear. Now and then bolter fire rang out, isolated shots and short flurries that spoke of minimal resistance.

'Primary insertion complete and on time,' Seraphiel announced. 'All positions secured. Awaiting confirmation of secondary insertion success. Prepare to advance.'

CONFUSION AND FEAR

'In the darkness, we shall be the light.'

Chaplain Malcifer's words over the comm-net were comforting to Annael as he waited in the dark, crouched over *Black Shadow*, mount and armour locked into position.

'In the light, we shall see true.'

Annael focused on the litany, driving other thoughts from his mind; thoughts such as the fact that he and the rest of the squadron were in a boarding torpedo hurtling towards the armoured skin of Port Imperial at several thousand miles per hour.

'In the truth, we shall see victory.'

Victory. The word resonated through Annael. Victory was all that mattered. His honour depended upon it, and his honour was stronger than weak desire for safety. Courage was truth. Fear was false. One such false fear briefly fluttered on the edge of Annael's comprehension as something rattled against the outer casing of the boarding torpedoes. Shrapnel most likely. No threat.

'In the victory, we shall be honoured.'

It was no better or worse than a drop pod, Annael

told himself. Whether speeding across the void in an armoured missile or falling through the sky towards an uncaring planet's surface, his fate was beyond his control. Better to relax, to breathe deep and enjoy the sensation of life. These might be his final moments, his life ended in one of many horrendous ways: the torpedo's plasma propellant could misfire and incinerate them all; a shot from Port Imperial's defence batteries could turn their carriage into slag in an instant; the retro-thrusters could malfunction and slam them sideways into their target to crush them instantly; the melta-jets could fail to penetrate the metres-thick hide of the space station so that they crashed against the surface rather than punched through.

'In the honour, we praise the Emperor.'

The Emperor probably never did this, a rebellious part of Annael thought. Even when he had walked amongst his followers it was doubtful that the Master of Mankind had ever hurled himself at an enemy fortress in what was little more than a guided rocket, astride the large fuel tank of a motorcycle. That privilege the Emperor had saved for his loyal Adeptus Astartes.

'In the Emperor, we find our protector.'

Annael smiled, fighting back a childish laugh at the thought of the golden form of the Emperor falling upon the armies of Horus riding bareback on a torpedo. Ever since he had learned of Horus from Malcifer, Annael had wondered how the Emperor had slain the Warmaster. If Horus had been powerful enough to destroy the Lion, he had been powerful indeed. Though this thought process took his mind from possible causes of his imminent demise, the route it took led to greater uncertainties than those posed by questions regarding his near-future.

'In our protector, we claim faith.'

Faith could be in short supply sometimes, Annael

figured. When the people of Kadillus had opened fire on the Ravenwing, Annael had felt his faith sorely tested. He had been led to believe the Piscinans were loyal, not only to the Master of Mankind but through oaths of brotherhood with the Dark Angels. What could vex a populace so badly that they would turn on their benefactors and protectors? What force could break the faith of millions so that they would turn their weapons on the Emperor's Angels of Death? If not respect and honour, fear alone should have stayed the hands of the Piscinan rebels, but something more powerful than fear of the Dark Angels had led them to desperate acts. Had it been the same force that had turned Horus's hand against the Emperor and the Lion? Had it been desperation and fear that had brought the Warmaster to blows with the primarch of the Dark Angels?

'In our faith, we are invulnerable.'

When Annael had heard this litany before, it had filled him with zeal, firing his blood for the battles to come. It stirred him still, to think of the Emperor and all that he sacrificed for mankind. Faced with that, Annael could do nothing less than offer his life and death for the protection of the Imperium the Emperor had built, and the countless trillions of humans who came under that auspice. Yet for all that he desired to serve, to bring honour to himself, his squadron, his company and his Chapter, Annael heard something cold and hard about Malcifer's words. In the darkness, contemplating his death, the Dark Angel felt that his life was incomplete. No more was he satisfied by the notion of a life of battle in the Emperor's name. He had been ready to die content, but ever since Malcifer had spoken of the Horus Heresy Annael had more questions than answers. It irritated him that he might die before he knew those unfound truths.

'Brace for impact!' Sammael's words cut sharply through Annael's mind, sweeping away all other musings. The warning sent floods of adrenaline washing through the Space Marine and he forced himself to keep calm.

'Like a sword into their gut!' Sabrael said with a laugh, his words edged with battle-mania.

'Impact in five... four...' Sergeant's Cassiel's countdown was delivered in a measured monotone.

'For the Emperor!' Zarall's bellow drowned out the last of Cassiel's count.

'For the Emperor!' Annael echoed with gritted teeth.

Retro-thrusters still burning, the boarding torpedo sped into the hull of Port Imperial. Seconds before impact fusion-flares ignited, turning the nose cone of the manned missile into a white-hot spearhead. Proximity-triggered melta-charges detonated milliseconds before impact, vaporising the first two metres of armour-plate. The fusion flares and diamond-tipped drill-shards churned through the remaining two metres while shockplates splinted and crumbled, disintegrating to dust as they absorbed the energy of impact. The metre-thick outer casing of the torpedo crumpled like foil and slewed away, secondary boosters thrusting the inner missile through the molten ruin of the star fort's outer skin.

Annael's eyes and ears were filled with a barrage of pressure and impetus warnings from his autosenses, a blaze of flashing icons and blaring chimes. Sitting nose to tail, the warriors of the squadron slid forwards a dozen metres, their steeds clamped onto shock-absorbent rails that glowed red-hot as ablative ceramite padding shattered and the inner braking pads gripped titanium.

Reaching the extent of their run, the bikes came to a

shuddering stop and then recoiled a few metres, sliding to a halt as the torpedo settled into its self-made breach. Assault launchers mounted in the prow of the missile detonated, scattering shrapnel and white-hot filaments into the star fort's interior, moments before the nose cone exploded outwards, showering even more shards of metal and ceramite.

Activated by the torpedo's systems, Annael's armour was flooded with energy once more, the joint lockdown breaking as soon as he moved to sit upright. Explosive bolts holding *Black Shadow* to the braking carriage beneath detonated as he revved the engine and engaged first gear. Ahead of him, Cassiel launched from the remnants of his carriage, his bike wheeling up momentarily as he roared out into the breach. Zarall was next, a second later, and then Annael gunned the engine and released the clutch to hurtle after his squadron-brothers.

The telemetric display on *Black Shadow* confirmed that they had breached exactly as planned, the boarding torpedo depositing them midway along a broad connecting corridor between one of the harbour spars and the central spires. The boarding torpedo had struck as a group of turncoats had been heading out from the hub, littering the immediate area around the impact with melta-blasted and shrapnel-ridden corpses. Ash and cooling droplets of metal were sprayed across the deck for nearly twenty metres, and beyond that a scene of carnage; dismembered bodies and severed limbs leaving the transitway awash with blood.

Along the far side of the access tunnel ran a narrow gauge track, bordered by metre-high ferrocrete walls. Bodies were draped over the barricade and scattered across the rails. They were dressed in a mishmash of clothes – some with plated ceramite armour, others with bulky environment suits, most in leggings, shirts and jackets. As his gaze passed over the corpses in a moment, Annael took in details: a broken autogun in the hand of one pirate, pistols stuffed into belts or held in holsters, spare magazines and energy packs carried in bandoliers and spilling from shoulder bags. The enemy were no better armed than the dissidents on Piscina.

Leaving swathes of dark rubber on the metal deck, Cassiel, Araton and Annael slewed hard to the left, heading in-station towards the inner towers. Sabrael and Zarall skidded their bikes to the right and opened fire on a group of survivors fleeing towards the sanctuary of the harbour gate. Red dots of life signals faded on the sensor screen of *Black Shadow* as the roar of bolters filled the tunnel.

'Rear clear of enemy,' announced Zarall, 'rejoining main advance.'

The exhaust smoke of their steeds was drawn up into overhead extractors as the squadron raced hubwards, the thunder of engines reverberating from bare metal walls. Four hundred metres ahead was a blast door through which they had to pass to gain the inner towers, and a cluster of signal returns indicated that there were enemies at the portal. If they were allowed to bring down the emergency shutter, the attack would stall before it started.

Unleashing a hail of bolts from their steeds, the squadron sped towards the opening, the weight of fire intended to suppress any foe trying to reach the portal controls. Annael fired short bursts every couple of seconds, *Black Shadow*'s bolters tracking left and right as he passed his gaze from one side of the open blast door to the other, lighting up the darkness beyond with flickering trails and small explosions.

Ahead, Cassiel drew a chainsword, the growl of its whirring teeth lost in the noise of the bikes. The sergeant braked heavily and bounced over the lip of the entrance, hauling his bike to the right as he did so. Annael split to the left, his mount snarling as he leaned over hard, Space Marine and machine crashing sideways through the portal, bolters firing again. Caught in the blaze of fire, three pirates were torn apart where they had been crouching just ahead of Annael. Braking hard, he brought *Black Shadow* to a standstill, guns pointed past the dead foes down a corridor several metres wide. Behind him, the rest of the squadron came to a halt, awaiting orders from Cassiel.

'Which way?' asked Araton.

'Does it matter?' asked Sabrael. 'Either direction will take us hubwards. Our orders are to rove at will, are they not?'

'True,' replied the sergeant. 'We are to sow confusion and fear, keeping the enemy off-balance while the Grand Master and Fifth Company establish a foothold and push on in numbers. Follow me and engage at will.'

Turning his bike about, Annael joined the rear of the squadron as they moved off after Cassiel, passing into an archway-lined corridor that ran for about a hundred metres. They travelled at cruising speed, ready to respond to attack though the scanners showed no enemy readings in the vicinity. Looking left and right through the arches as he passed, Annael saw empty chambers – most likely once used for storage and ship supplies. With time now to consider his surroundings, he noticed that the station was in serious disrepair. Maintenance hatch panels had been pulled off the walls and there was a filth of oil dripping from pipes that ran along the junction of wall and ceiling to his right.

Here and there he passed anti-Imperial slogans daubed on the walls in black and red paint, interspersed with more mundane graffiti boasting personal prowess and sexual conquests. There was rust around rivets and bolt heads, and dark-blue lichen was growing out of one of the storage bays. Through the olfactory filter of his helm, Annael could smell rotting vegetable matter nearby.

'They live like animals,' muttered Zarall. 'It is a wonder that they have managed to keep the station running at all.'

'Ill-discipline shows in many ways,' replied Cassiel. 'It is the mind of the traitor to seek selfish ends, forgoing all other considerations. Their weakness of will makes them poor warriors.'

'I see more than selfish sentiment in some of these slogans,' remarked Annael. 'There is hatred here, and though loathing of the Emperor is misguided it can bring forth stubbornness.'

'Yet it is ultimately a hollow hatred, born out of insecurity and doubt,' said Zarall. They came to a halt at the end of the corridor, further progress barred by a metal door. 'Do not confuse righteous hatred with the nihilism of our foes. We hate out of love for the Emperor. They hate for nothing save hate itself.'

'Annael, see to the door controls,' said Cassiel.

Dismounting, Annael strode the last few metres to the portal and inspected the panel beside the door. There was a simple runepad with four buttons, two of them more marked than the others.

'It is an elevator, probably for transport of supplies,' he told the others, pushing the call button. Chains clanked above him as the carriage motors groaned into life. 'Do we ascend or descend?'

'Contact! Signals incoming.' Sabrael's warning sent Annael hurrying back to *Black Shadow*. He looked at the sensor display as he swung a leg over his steed and saw several dozen signals converging, directly above the squadron.

With a hiss of pneumatics the elevator door opened, revealing an empty car a few metres wide and ten metres long. A flickering yellow strip did little to light the grimy interior. There was another piston-driven door at the far end. The cluster of life signals was gathering around the shaft on the levels above.

'They are lying in wait for us,' said Araton.

'Let us not disappoint,' said Sabrael, gunning his bike onto the elevator without waiting for word from Cassiel.

Annael looked at his sergeant, who was studying the bike's telemetry display carefully.

'The next three levels are too dense to operate effectively,' said Cassiel, moving into the elevator after Sabrael. The rest of the squadron edged their bikes into the remaining space, Araton and Zarall turning their bikes around and backing in to cover the direction from which they were entering. 'Punch the control for four levels up.'

Annael was closest to the keypad, and he noted that the elevator served twelve floors, three below and eight above their current position. Jabbing a finger into the button for the eighth floor, he returned his attention to the scanner. There were several dozen signals, at least forty or fifty enemies waiting on the levels above.

With a clang the elevator door shut and a screech of gears accompanied the clank of chains as the conveyor started to rise. The main car was little more than a mesh cage with a solid floor, and looking up Annael could see red lights marking the floors above. He saw light spilling through a crack above and drew his pistol.

'Enemy forcing the doors, two levels up, forward,' he warned the others, sighting on the widening splash of light.

The elevator rose painfully slowly, creaking loudly as

it passed one floor and then the next. Annael saw two figures silhouetted against the light above and opened fire, the spark of his bolts disappearing into the yellow glare. A pained shout echoed down the shaft and a pirate plummeted from the opening, slamming into the top of the cage, her right arm missing below the elbow. Blood poured down onto Sabrael, splashing across his black armour. The woman wore black coveralls tucked into heavy boots, a tattered white shirt beneath the straps.

She stared down with horror at the Space Marines, still alive. Annael's next bolt ripped apart her chest, spraying blood and bone down into the carriage.

'The corpse is blocking my view,' snarled Annael, leaning over as far as he could but not able to see the open door past the mangled remains of the woman.

Enemy fire whined down the shaft, pinging and clattering from the cage and surrounding walls. A round scraped down Annael's left arm, leaving a livid scratch through the paint on his armour. The others had drawn their pistols and those that could see – Araton and Cassiel – fired back, the bark of bolt-rounds ringing loud in the confined space. Exhaust smoke from the chugging engines of the bikes drifted up the shaft and Annael heard coughs and chokes from the pirates as they leaned out to fire down at the rising Space Marines.

Another flurry of las-beams cut through the haze, several shots hitting Araton, puffs of ceramite and paint blossoming across his armour. He coolly returned fire with his pistol, the headless body of a renegade falling onto the cage roof a moment later. Blood dripped down, joined by more sprays of crimson as autogun rounds from above hit the corpse, the impacts making the body jerk as if still alive.

When the elevator reached the floor beneath the pirates, it shuddered to a stop. There were signals in front, behind, above and below the squadron and Annael holstered his pistol, focusing on the opening door ahead. Bullets flashed into the elevator as the portal slowly cranked open.

When there was just enough room, Sabrael hit the throttle and surged out of the carriage, his bolters blazing into the enemy waiting in the chamber outside, bike slamming through their falling bodies. With just enough room to pass Cassiel and hit the gap, Annael accelerated, exiting the car a second before the sergeant could follow.

The handlebars jerked in Annael's hands as he rode over a pile of bodies, cries of pain cut short indicating that at least two had still been alive. Wheels throwing up a spume of body parts and crimson, *Black Shadow* hurtled into the mass of enemies while Annael kept the trigger rune pressed, unleashing a constant hail of bolts into the broad space where the foe had lain in ambush.

Remarkably, a man beside the elevator door had been missed by both Sabrael and Annael and he hurled himself at them with a chainsword, the teeth of the weapon sparking across Annael's backpack. Annael braked and hauled the bike sideways, using it as a weapon, the pirate disappearing beneath the rear wheel, the Dark Angel's mount juddering as it pulped the man's remains into the decking.

Fire from Zarall and Araton announced the opening of the other elevator door but Annael could spare no attention for his brothers. The elevator had deposited them in a warehouse-like chamber, several hundred metres square, and from gantries above and behind enemy fire descended like a storm. Cassiel whirled his bike around, the bolters at maximum elevation as he cleared a gantry above the elevator door, while Sabrael was racing to the far end of the chamber, his weapons gunning down several foes who were making a break for a stairwell up to a mezzanine floor.

Below the walkways more pirates used bulky cargo-lifters and metal-cased extractor vents as cover, poking out to snap off shots that were wide of their targets more often than they hit. Annael slewed his machine around and fired at a handful of foes skulking in the shadow of a bulk-hauler, the flash of bolts sparking from the upraised lifting blades on the front of the vehicle. Las-fire snapped back as he cruised across the warehouse, still firing, the fusillade puncturing balloon tyres and severing hydraulic hoses. Noticing a pool of fluid spreading out from beneath the engine, he directed his next salvo towards the floor, the explosive bolts igniting the leaking fuel.

A blue fireball engulfed the bulk-hauler and several pirates, who staggered from their hiding places with clothes and hair aflame. Annael ignored them, aiming his next burst of fire at the uninjured enemies scurrying for cover behind a row of cylindrical canisters; four of them were cut down before they reached safety. The surviving pair continued to run as Annael continued to sweep his fire to the left, the tyres of *Black Shadow* screeching as they gripped across the blood- and oil-slicked deck.

'Maintenance access, quadrant four, high,' he told the others, spying more enemies issuing from a metre-high crawlspace. One of them was dragging a heavy stubber into view as a companion set up a tripod for the machine-gun. Sabrael cut back along the storage hold, bolt pistol in hand, and fired up through the mesh of the walkway. His volley tore the legs from the renegade with the stubber and sent another pitching back into the bulkhead minus his left arm.

Trusting that the threat would be dealt with, Annael continued his circuit, picking up speed as he curved across the open space in the centre of the warehouse, searching the piles of crates and stacks of barrels for targets. He opened fire in brief bursts at any signature on his thermal scan, driving the pirates further back into the darkness behind the stores.

Switching his fire to full automatic, his brought his bike to a stop facing a pallet laden with metal drums. Splinters filled the air as the bolts punched through the containers, splashing blood against the wall as the rounds found their mark inside the bodies of the men behind. A man crawled into view, his face a bloody mess from a jagged sliver of steel jutting from his cheek, his right leg trailing uselessly behind him.

Opening up the throttle of *Black Shadow* Annael roared past, lifting his foot to connect with the wounded pirate's head. Spine snapped, the man was flung like a rag doll across the floor.

There were only a handful of enemies left, but one of them had a final surprise for the Dark Angels. A blue plasma bolt shrieked down from overhead, smashing into the rear of Sergeant Cassiel's steed. Molten metal, ceramite and hardened rubber sprayed into the air and the sergeant was flung from his mount as it careened past Annael, trailing sparks across the floor.

As he turned his bike to face the threat, Annael saw that Cassiel's right leg was missing below the knee. Undeterred, the sergeant pushed himself up, drew his pistol and fired at the plasma gunner. A round hit the combustion chamber of the weapon and it detonated, enveloping the pirate in superheated gas. Skin blistering, flesh slewing away from the bone, the man toppled over the walkway rail and span crazily to the floor, his impact punctuated by another small plasma detonation.

'Brother-sergeant?' Zarall drew his bike to a stop beside Cassiel, shielding the sergeant from the fire of the few remaining enemies.

'I will signal command with my position. My steed is no more, anyway. Araton, you have the lead.' The sergeant looked down at the remnants of his leg, his augmented blood clotting the injury, the spurts of dark red slowing to a trickle. 'It looks like I will be not riding with you for some time. Not until we return to the Rock and I can have a bionic fitted.'

'Nonsense,' said Sabrael as he and Annael turned their bikes' bolters on the remaining enemy. 'You can still ride gunner in an attack bike. I will drive for you.'

'I am obliged for the offer, brother, but if I am to be at the mercy of another's riding, I will choose Zarall or Araton. You are too fast for my liking!' There was a hint of a laugh in Cassiel's voice, which was remarkable considering his condition.

The last of the opposition died when a volley from Sabrael cut him in half across the chest. The warehouse suddenly fell quiet save for the throb of idling engines, the ping of cooling metal and the clink of settling shell cases. Annael scanned around once, both with his own eyes and the sensors of his mount, but nothing save for the Dark Angels was left alive in the chamber.

'Area clear,' he announced. He joined the others as they gathered around Cassiel. Zarall dismounted and helped the sergeant across to the gantry stair where he was able to sit down, the metal steps sagging slightly under the Space Marine's weight.

'Keep pushing hubwards and then come around to sector four to meet up with the Grand Master's advance,' Cassiel told them. The ruined stub of his leg was now a black and brown mottled mass of coagulant and Larraman cells, the scab thick and leathery. Reloading his pistol, the sergeant gestured towards the wide warehouse doors. 'No delays. Get moving.'

'We will return for you, brother,' said Sabrael, slapping a fist to the aquila on his chest as he turned his bike away. 'Unless the Apothecaries reach you first.'

'Concentrate on the mission, brothers. I am not the first casualty we have ever suffered.'

'Vengeance shall be ours,' said Zarall. 'Every drop of blood shed by our own will be atoned for by a river from our foes.'

Annael said nothing, though he bowed his head in respect to the sergeant as he rode past, receiving a raised hand in thanks.

'You are doing well, Annael,' Cassiel said as Annael turned away and gunned his steed after the others. 'A true brother of the Ravenwing.'

Annael smiled at the praise but did not reply. Ahead, Sabrael had pulled up alongside the door controls. The shutters creaked open on runners, flooding the warehouse with white light. Checking the status display of *Black Shadow* Annael saw that he had already used up more than forty per cent of the bike's ammunition.

'We will be using fists and pistols before we are done,' he said as the squadron rolled out through the opening doors.

'We shall smite the enemy, brother,' replied Zarall. 'Any way that we can.'

The last thing Annael heard before exiting the chamber was Cassiel signalling the Grand Master, reporting the squadron's ongoing commitment to the completion of the mission.

THE UNWORTHY

'Understood, brother. Remain in position. There is a squadron within two kilometres of your location, await their arrival.' Sammael cut the link with Sergeant Cassiel and turned to Brother Gideon, the Apothecary. 'Join with Sergeant Charael and his Black Knights. They will perform escort for you. Of the casualties, which is your priority?'

'Brother Gabrael needs my attention swiftly,' replied the Apothecary. 'The others are stable as far as I can judge by the reports.'

'Very well.' Sammael brought up a schematic created from the close-range scans of the strike cruiser as the Dark Angels had launched their attack. It showed the broad layout of Port Imperial, though much of the display was filled with static where the sensors had been blocked by the density of the station's structure. Telemetric feedback from the advanced squadrons was being transmitted to the *Implacable Justice* and the digital chart was being regularly updated. 'Tell Charael you can cut through a maintenance hangar grid-north-west of here. That should take you to Gabrael and his squadron with least delay.'

'As you command, Grand Master,' said Gideon. The Apothecary turned his bike around and headed back towards the docking spar where the majority of the Ravenwing had inserted aboard their gunships.

As soon as Gideon was gone, Sammael turned his attention to Malcifer. The two of them sat astride their mounts, the remainder of the command squad around them. At the far end of the passageway bolter fire resounded from plastered walls as squads from the Fifth Company extended their perimeter. Sammael motioned for the squadron to move, accelerating softly towards the open blast doors leading to the closest of the hub towers. 'Three brothers' dead, another five incapacitated. However, the breaches have been made and the landing secured.'

'You mean to press on immediately?' the Chaplain asked.

'Not too swiftly, we must maintain contact with the Fifth Company,' replied the Grand Master. 'I have four bike squadrons on roving patrols along the transitways circling the hub spire, and Land Speeders moving in from grid-north to cut off any counter-attack on the main breach. Latest report from Pichon indicates the pirates are split into three groups, with the majority in the central spire. We will eliminate the outlying pockets of resistance first.'

'We have attained our position through speed and precision, brother, are you sure you wish to risk the attack losing impetus? If the enemy are given time to secure their positions, the fight will be all the more difficult.'

'Unless their leader is foolishly arrogant, provision will have been made to defend the station against attack.

Scanner reports on the enemy movements convince me that they are falling back to prepared positions. The two outlying groups have had their line of retreat severed but they must be dealt with if we are to secure our flanks for the thrust to the inner spire. We need the Fifth Company to provide that security.'

'Very well, brother. I do not seek to dissent from your plan, but it is imperative that we secure the enemy commanders as soon as we are able. Every minute risks them escaping the station.'

'Have no fear on that account.' The squadron slowed to negotiate the opening at the end of the passage, passing two abreast onto a skybridge that arched across the base towards the upper levels of one of the hub spires. 'Defensive batteries have been silenced and both strike cruisers are moving into range for close sensor sweeps. I have fighters on standby to intercept any craft that attempt to leave Port Imperial.'

'Then we have nothing to fear,' said Malcifer as the group accelerated once more, passing underneath a thick armourglass canopy held up with plasteel arches. Through the transparent panes Sammael glimpsed flares of blue as a pair of fighters swept overhead. The squadron reached the crest of the bridge and began their descent, the arching tunnel reverberating with the noise of their steeds' engines. 'Our prey will be trapped.'

'If they are here...'

Sammael's confidence that the Fallen were aboard Port Imperial was waning fast. Regardless of their loyalties, the Fallen were Space Marines and the poor discipline and shocking lack of maintenance evidenced by the renegades made the Grand Master doubt that their leaders were at all competent. It had been a slim chance, he recognised, but the likelihood was that the Fallen had long quit Port Imperial and left their followers to fend for themselves. It was not in Sammael's mind to give voice to this pessimism, if only so that he could maintain a small nugget of hope himself. If he spoke his doubts they would be confirmed in his mind, and he did not desire to give up the hunt just yet.

'We need to secure prisoners,' Harahel announced. 'If we can take some of the enemy alive we may learn more concerning their leaders.'

'A sensible plan,' said Malcifer, 'though I would not burden our brothers with the task when we are suitably placed to perform it ourselves.'

'So be it,' said Sammael. Knowing that Athelman and Daedis could hear everything that passed between the Grand Master and Chaplain, he addressed the two Black Knights following a short distance behind their superiors. 'Take no risks, but if we can take some of the enemy alive for interrogation, it will be for the better.'

'As you command,' the honour guards replied in unison.

'It may not be simple,' said Daedis, a hint of humour in his voice. 'These pirates die very easily. Bolters and bikes are not the ideal weapons for taking prisoners.'

'Do what you can,' said Sammael. 'I am sure you can improvise a solution.'

The squadron fell silent as they reached the far end of the bridgeway. Sammael slowed *Corvex*, suspicious that the emergency doors had not been sealed. He had been expecting to use the plasma cannon on his jetbike to blast through, but the doorway stood open like a dark cavern beyond the lights of the bridge. Looking at his bike's scanner, the Grand Master saw a mass of returns, but nothing conclusive; the signal was blurred by converging power conduits. Switching to thermal scan did little to clarify the image and his armour's autosenses did not detect anything waiting in the darkness.

'Prepare yourselves for close assault,' he told the others, drawing his power sword. Malcifer held up his crozius and Harahel his force axe, while Athelman and Daedis signalled their readiness with their corvus hammers. 'Combat speed!'

The squadron accelerated along the last hundred metres of bridge, the lights of their bikes glaring bright into the opening ahead. As the beams glinted upon metal, Sammael heaved his bike to the right out of instinct, a moment before a pulse of plasma spat from the opening. The flash of las-fire erupted along the bridge as the enemy launched their ambush, catching Malcifer in a storm of energy blasts. The Chaplain's rosarius blazed into life, enveloping Malcifer in a shining aura of red as the field within the ancient device converted the incoming fire into light. Arcane technology also protected Sammael from the worst of the volley; the night halo fixed upon the gorget of his armour encasing rider and machine in a forcefield that glimmered with small forks of black lightning where the las-bolts struck. Those blasts not deflected by the night halo scored marks across the Grand Master's armour but lacked strength to melt or crack the plates of ceramite that protected him and *Corvex*.

In the gleam of the bike's lamps, Sammael saw the walls of the chamber ahead lined with enemy, skulking behind buttresses and pillars. The room seemed to be some kind of junction chamber, spreading out from the bridge to join with rampways, stairwells and conveyors to the left and right.

'Douse lamps!' he commanded, realising that the squadron were making themselves easy targets as they plunged into the lightless hall. His autosenses compensating as the lights on *Corvex* faded, Sammael slid his mount to the right, swinging his sword low to cut through the arms and stomach of the nearest enemy. Around him the other riders obeyed his command instantly, shrouding the squadron in shadow.

The black-clad Ravenwing were not entirely invisible, their polished armour gleaming in the light of criss-crossing las-beams and plasma stars, their weapons giving off the glow of power fields in the blackness. Steering close to the right-hand wall, Sammael plunged his blade into the chest of a woman armed with a chainsword and pistol, her face a screaming mask for a moment in the haze of the sword. She disappeared as Sammael swept on, ripping the sword free to slash the leg from a man who had turned to run, cleaving his thigh with one blow.

The crack of discharging energy punctuated the blows of the corvus hammers wielded by Athelman and Daedis, breaking the darkness with flashes of white, their victims falling to the floor with arcs of the same energy coruscating across their bodies. Harahel's force axe left a glittering trail of psychic sparks as he swept in wide arcs, severing limbs and heads to his left and right.

Another plasma shot screamed into Malcifer but his conversion field took the brunt of the blast, the Chaplain momentarily disappearing in the heart of a nova of white light. Scattered autogun rounds snapped and rasped around Sammael as the pirates tried to track his arcing progress across the hall, the bullets whining wide of their mark, defeated by the speed of the Grand Master's attack. The storm bolters of *Corvex* snarled into life at his touch, sending a hail of fire cutting through a group of foes clustered behind an archway leading off from the foyer on the right. Killing his speed and turning sharply to the left, Sammael spun his steed to face a stairwell opposite the bridge entrance, from which a fierce fusillade was emerging.

With a slow whine, the magnetic accelerators of *Corvex*'s plasma cannon charged, funnelling energy from the machine's miniature reactor. With a high-pitched shriek and a crack of super-expanding air the plasma bolt sped from the ejector muzzle beneath the front fairing, filling the chamber with flickering blue and purple light for a moment. Hitting the stairwell, its containment field disintegrating, the plasma charge exploded, engulfing everybody on the first flight of steps in a ravening corona of heat and electrical discharge. Those whose bodies were not vaporised immediately fell screaming down the steps, flesh burned to the bone, nerves and blood vessels shredded by the energy unleashed.

One of the enemy fighters came to the conclusion that the dark served the Space Marines better than the ambushers and a switch was thrown. Lumen strips hanging from the ceiling crackled into life, bathing the chamber in a yellow glare. In a moment Sammael's autosenses had adjusted, dimming the view so that the Grand Master was not blinded.

Able to better see their enemies, the pirates let forth another hail of firepower, the weight of the attack falling upon Malcifer as his bike's bolters roared forth a volley into a group of foes sheltering behind a rusted vat. Adelman fired his bike's mounted grenade launchers, the frag devices sending shrapnel scything along a walkway to the left. Harahel's axe spat lightning as he swept it towards the pirates, forks of psychic energy arcing across the warehouse to earth through the bodies of half a dozen foes. There were at least two dozen dead and the same again still fighting. Despite the pandemonium of combat, Sammael remembered his instruction from a few moments earlier.

'Prisoners if you can,' he reminded the others, cutting

off the plasma cannon recharge and powering down his bike's storm bolter ammunition feed. He sheathed the Raven Sword and sped forwards, heading directly into a stream of las-fire coming from three men sheltering behind an overturned metal cabinet. Las-bolts flared from the night halo field around him and skimmed across his armour, but he did not waver from his course. The toppled furniture was less than a metre high, easily cleared by *Corvex* as the Grand Master ploughed directly into the enemy using the sloped prow of the jetbike as a ram.

The trio of pirates were thrown to the ground by the impact, rolling over and over until they came to a stop lying awkwardly. From the way he lay at an unnatural angle, one of the men had his back broken, but the other two were still alive, though they could barely move. Bringing *Corvex* low, Sammael leaned over and grabbed one of the men by the throat, squeezing just hard and long enough to render the man unconscious. He let the pirate flop back to the floor. The other was trying to crawl away, fractured arm cradled underneath him. A boot to the back of his head served the same purpose as the choke hold.

Hearing the whine of a power cell behind him, Sammael turned in the saddle in time to see a young pirate, no more than fifteen or sixteen Terran years old, crouched behind a pile of rotting pallets. He held a laspistol in trembling hands, eyes wide with fear, face soaked with sweat that darkened the white bandana tied across his head.

'Murderer!' snarled the youth, opening fire as Sammael pulled free his bolt pistol.

The las-shot crackled harmlessly from the Grand Master's protective field. Sammael fired a single bolt in return, cracking open the youth's head from within. He watched without feeling as the headless body toppled against the pallets, blood seeping into the wood.

The junction chamber had fallen quiet save for the moans of the renegades incapacitated by the Dark Angels. A quick visual sweep confirmed to Sammael that the rest of the enemy were dead, though the scanner showed more foes massing a few hundred metres beyond the hall's main doors.

'Athelman, Daedis – overwatch.' The two Black Knights moved to cover the closed doors while Sammael, Malcifer and Harahel gathered together the prisoners; six remained alive although three were unconscious. The others struggled feebly as they were dragged to the centre of the chamber and deposited roughly on the metal deck. Ringed by the trio of Space Marines on their steeds, the captives were defiant, glaring sullenly at their captors.

'We require information,' Sammael told them as he dismounted, leaving *Corvex* hovering just above the floor. Malcifer and Harahel followed, looming over the pirates with weapons bared.

'We'll tell you nothing, Imperial scum!' snarled the oldest of the group, grey in his shaggy black beard and hair. He wore baggy worker's trousers and a padded tunic, nursing his left wrist, which was clearly broken. 'We are ready to die for the Divine.'

'Your deaths are not in dispute,' said Malcifer, grabbing the man's injured hand and twisting, eliciting a yelp of pain. 'Your lives were forfeit the moment you took arms against the servants of the Emperor. Only the manner of your demise remains to be determined.'

'Torture?' This came from one of the others, his face bloodied from a cut above his eye, swelling with bruising where he had been punched by one of the Dark

Angels. 'How like the attack dogs of the Emperor to be so cowardly.'

Malcifer released his grip and crouched in front of the pirate that had spoken. The man's face reflected in the glassy lenses of the Chaplain's skull helm, sneering through his fear.

'I can coax a confession from Space Marines.' Malcifer's voice, edged with the metallic tone of his external augmitters, was a barely-heard whisper full of menace. 'Warriors that can survive injuries and withstand pain that would kill a man such as yourself. Harbour no illusion that you will remain silent against my attentions.'

The man swallowed hard, his sneer replaced by a nervous glance towards the other two. He clamped his mouth shut and narrowed his eyes, refusing to say anything further. Malcifer nodded in acknowledgement of the man's defiance and turned his stare upon the third conscious prisoner. He was the youngest, face marked with the boils and spots of adolescence, his red hair long and lank across his face.

'And what of you?' asked the Chaplain, deactivating his crozius and hanging it on his belt. 'Do you choose excruciation over swift mercy?'

The youth spat at Malcifer, the gobbet of saliva landing on the brow of the Chaplain's helm. Malcifer did not react immediately, but stood up and turned to Harahel. When he spoke, it was in conversational tone.

'The old one is weakest, he will not last long. When the others see what is in store for them, they will see the error of their decision.'

Harahel nodded and grabbed the oldest pirate by his jerkin, pulling him to his feet with one arm. The gleam of the psyker's force axe shone blue on the man's pale skin as Harahel held its blade close to his throat, the brightness forcing the man to blink rapidly.

'Watch,' Malcifer told the other two as Harahel laid his hand on the scalp of the pirate. Dark sparks glittered along the cabling of the psychic hood surrounding the Epistolary's helm and the renegade jerked, baring his teeth in pain, growling profanities through gritted teeth. The Librarian's eye lenses grew bright, lit from behind by small stars of red that fixed the stare of the prisoner.

'Speak,' said Harahel. Scarlet witchlight crackled from his fingers and the man thrashed against the Librarian's grip but was unable to break free. 'Tell us everything.'

While the attention of the pirates was fixed upon the psyker, Sammael stepped behind the youth and crouched down to lay a hand upon his shoulder. The captive flinched as if struck.

'My companions speak truth,' the Grand Master said softly, keeping check the anger he felt at being defied. The young man had clearly been born and raised on Port Imperial, and Sammael tried to find some empathy with the youth. The young pirate knew no better than what he had been taught, fed lies since he was born. It did not absolve him of his guilt, but thinking of this made it easier for Sammael to sound conciliatory, keeping his ire from his voice. 'You have been damned by your parents, but we can cleanse your soul with confession. You do not have to suffer the same fate as your friend.'

'The gnawing! Make it stop!' the older man shrieked as Harahel exerted his power once more. 'The rats, they burrow deep. They chew on my lungs, feast on my guts!'

'What nightmares keep you awake, young man?' Sammael asked as the youth started shaking, eyes moving to the tormented pirate. 'What darkness will my Librarian find in the depths of your soul?'

The third prisoner leapt to his feet, seeking to drag his comrade free from Harahel's grasp. Malcifer was quicker, his elbow smashing into the man's already injured face, pitching him to the deck. Like a pouncing beast, the Chaplain fell to all fours over the man, one hand held against his chest. The pirate squirmed as Malcifer applied more pressure, the plastek breastplate protecting the man's chest bending inwards, cracking under the Chaplain's exertion.

'Who are the Divine?' whispered Sammael. 'Tell me about them and you will know peace.'

'I cannot, I swore,' the youth said. He started to babble, speaking names, talking about a promise made, though to whom he did not say. The young man scrabbled backwards across the deck, away from the Dark Angels, until he came upon a corpse, the chest of the woman ripped out from within by several bolt-rounds. He gave a quiet moan. 'Oh, come save me. Save me from these monsters!'

'Who do you call to, boy?' Sammael demanded, stalking towards the youth. The captive shook his head and kept repeating the call to an unnamed saviour. Sammael grabbed the youth's arm and with a simple twist dislocated the elbow, causing him to scream. The Grand Master's voice became harsh as he poured forth his scorn, every word filled with his contempt. 'They cannot save you, not from us. We are the Dark Angels, the First, Sons of the Lion. You belong to us now.'

'He will come, he will come for me,' gibbered the youth as Sammael released his hold.

'Tell them nothing!' bellowed the man pinned down by Malcifer. His next shout was cut short as the Chaplain leaned forwards, the breastplate buckling further, pushing the breath from the pirate's body.

'Tell me your name, young man.' Sammael reverted to his soft approach. The youth shook his head. 'Surely you can tell me your name?'

'I will say nothing,' the young pirate replied quietly, tears rolling down his cheeks.

'That is not true,' Sammael said, snatching hold of the youth's injured arm. He did not even have to exert a fraction of his strength to set the pirate to howling again. Sammael released his hold and glanced over at Harahel, realising that the old man had fallen silent. He appeared catatonic in the Librarian's grip, eyes glazed, mouth slack.

'There is little of use in his mind,' Harahel said, letting the inert figure fall to the floor. 'Names of family and companions. They call themselves the Divine.'

'We are not Divine,' yelped the boy, the Librarian's assertion filling him with dread equal to that he had shown to the Dark Angels. 'We are the Unworthy. The Divine will come for us, you will see.'

'They will not,' said Sammael. Terms like 'Divine' and 'Unworthy' did not sound like they were dealing with simple pirates. Suspicion crept into the Grand Master's thoughts, as yet formless. 'They have abandoned you.'

The words struck home, puncturing the last vestiges of defiance. The youth sagged to his knees, sobbing.

'Say nothing! They lie! They always lie!' The renegade under Malcifer gasped the words and weakly battered at the Chaplain's armour. 'Tell the bastards noth–'

With a loud crack, the turncoat's breastplate and sternum gave way, Malcifer's hand thrusting into the man's chest. Blood surged up the Chaplain's arm and spilled across the deck as his gauntleted fingers ripped out the pirate's heart.

'What is your name?' Malcifer rasped, standing up, the bloody organ in his fist. Harahel stepped up beside the Chaplain and raised a hand, tiny flickers of energy passing between his splayed fingers.

'Verekil,' the youth whispered, chin sagging to his chest. 'I am Verekil.'

'Good.' Sammael lowered to one knee beside him. 'That

was not so hard, was it? There need not be further pain. Tell us what we wish to know and your torment will end.'

Verekil nodded, eyes averted from the Dark Angels.

'How many ships do you have?' Sammael asked. He avoided the matter of the Divine and the Unworthy for the moment, allowing the youth to think about more mundane things. 'How many starships?'

'Four,' said Verekil. Sammael heard a growl of annoyance from Malcifer and knew what was passing through the Chaplain's thoughts: only three ships had been encountered so far.

'Good. Thank you.' Sammael reached out and, as gently as was possible, took hold of Verekil's injured arm. 'This will hurt, but not so much as it does now.'

He twisted the elbow back into place, a spat curse coming from Verekil as he pulled away from the Grand Master. The youth rubbed his arm vigorously, shaking his head.

'How many of you are there?'

'I don't know, five hundred maybe. Five hundred of the Unworthy.'

'And how many Divine?' Sammael asked with an encouraging nod. Verekil looked fearful again and the Grand Master thought for a moment that he would refuse to answer. 'Tell me, Verekil, how many Divine are on the station.'

'Most of them,' the youth answered. His expression was fearful that his ignorance would see him hurt again. 'Two hundred? I have never seen them.'

Fortunately Sammael's helm masked a moment of confusion. Perplexed, he mastered himself and continued.

'How can you fight alongside them and not know who they are?'

'They fight with the Overlord,' explained Verekil. 'On board the *Scar*.'

'And you are not on the crew of the *Scar*?' said Sammael, ignoring for the moment the mention of the Overlord.

'No! Only the Divine serve aboard the *Scar*. We are Unworthy.'

'And what else separates the Divine from the Unworthy?'

'They have ascended to the spire, where the Unworthy cannot go. The Overlord has chosen them from amongst the Unworthy and elevated them to Divinity.'

'Pseudo-religious nonsense,' Malcifer said over the vox, unheard by Verekil. 'This Overlord clearly maintains control through the deception that he can access a higher power.'

'Can we be sure it is nonsense?' asked Harahel, his voice heavy.

'There is no cause to jump to conclusions,' Sammael told them both, though the suspicion he had felt earlier returned. It was not unheard-of for demagogic leaders to affect godly influence, but the Grand Master was cautious to dismiss the claims of the Overlord without further investigation.

'Have you seen the Overlord?' he asked Verekil.

The youth's eyes lit up and he was suddenly animated.

'Oh yes, I have seen him four times! That's more than most of the Unworthy. He is a giant, like you, filled with the grace of the Divine. He speaks with the voice of the Divine and his words carry truth and wisdom. From him we learnt...'

'Learnt what?' demanded Sammael as the youth's voice died away. 'What did the Overlord teach you?'

'It is forbidden to speak of such things,' said Verekil. His expression hardened and Sammael realised that loyalty to the Overlord, or perhaps a greater fear, had suddenly bolstered the pirate's courage. The Grand

Master saw determination returning as Verekil set his jaw and turned away his gaze. It was time to move away from the subject of the Overlord.

'What defences protect the spire?' asked Sammael. 'What weapons do the Divine possess?'

'Jagrain was right, I have said too much,' replied Verekil.

'It is not too late to save yourself from damnation,' the Grand Master said quietly.

'There is no damnation, and there's no salvation neither,' Verekil whispered. 'Only oblivion.'

Sensing that he was losing control, Sammael glanced at Malcifer.

'You are the dedicated interrogator, brother,' he said to the Chaplain over the comm. 'You need to continue.'

Malcifer walked over to join the pair, the heart of Jagrain still in his fist. He let the organ flop from his fingers to the deck beside Verekil, flicking droplets of blood from the fingers of his gauntlet. Crimson spattered the young pirate, causing him to flinch.

'You will know pain, Verekil. Far greater pain than your companions endured. And you will speak to us. If only oblivion awaits then there is nothing to protect, no higher power to serve.' The Chaplain spoke coldly, his tone matter-of-fact. 'All that matters occurs in this world and you can save yourself needless agony.'

Verekil shook his head, hands forming fists in his defiance.

'Even if you do not speak, we will learn what we wish from the others,' said Malcifer, waving a hand towards the unconscious prisoners. 'You sacrifice your wellbeing for nothing.'

Still Verekil refused to speak, head bowed. Malcifer looked at Sammael and spoke over the comm.

'I can extract more information if you wish, brother, but it will take time.'

Sammael read the meaning behind Malcifer's words; a lengthy interrogation gave the enemy further time to prepare and could render worthless any intelligence gained. The Grand Master studied the youth for a moment, trying to gauge what the pirate knew.

'I do not believe he can furnish us with the information we desire,' said Sammael. 'He is just a low peon within the group.'

'The others?' Malcifer turned towards the unconscious men and women. 'I do not expect any swift success. The application of a higher authority has made their loyalty unthinking.'

'Then we must move on with what we know,' said Sammael. He drew his sword. Though Verekil could see nothing of the Grand Master's expression and had not heard his words, the pirate read correctly Sammael's intent and began to back away.

'Save ammunition,' said Sammael, pointing his blade towards the others. He returned his attention to Verekil. 'Be thankful that your ignorance shields you. Your death will be swift.'

Verekil opened his mouth to cry out but Sammael struck fast, lopping off the youth's head with one blow, the edges of the Raven Sword crackling with power as blood fizzed and spat along the blade. Harahel and Malcifer despatched the other survivors without hesitation and the three of them returned to their steeds.

Checking the scanner, Sammael saw that the sensor returns had strengthened. A sizeable number of foes – more of the Unworthy, most likely – were protecting the approaches to the main spire. It was time to bring in additional forces.

'Ravenwing. Brothers of the Fifth Company. Attend to orders,' announced the Grand Master. 'Prepare for the main attack.'

'The Overlord, do you think he is still here?' asked Harahel as they joined the two Black Knights by the doors.

'The boy's testimony gives us no clue,' replied Sammael. 'Yet his description of the Overlord makes me more confident that one of the Fallen is indeed in command here.'

'We must ascertain whether one of the ships we have crippled is the *Scar*,' said Malcifer. 'If one of them is the Overlord's flagship there is still hope.'

'I sense that the Unworthy will not be easily forthcoming with such knowledge,' said Harahel.

'I agree,' said Sammael. 'We must proceed carefully until we understand the full capabilities of the Divine. It is from them that we will learn the truth.'

'The truth?' Malcifer laughed. 'No, not the truth, brother. Yet we may unravel more of the lies that have been wrapped around these people.'

'There can be only lies when there is truth to hide,' argued Sammael. 'When we tear down the falsehoods erected by the Overlord, the truth will be revealed. And it is a weapon greater than any other.'

While he said these words, Sammael had a darker thought that he did not share. The truth was indeed a powerful weapon, and that was why the Dark Angels had such cause to fear it in the hands of others.

HOLDING THE LINE

There were three main routes of ingress towards the chamber where Cassiel guarded the elevator shaft. Araton swiftly divided the squadron to cover each approach, protecting the wounded sergeant until Brother Gideon and his escort arrived. For the moment, the pirates had pulled back from their attacks and appeared to be waiting for the Ravenwing to advance further.

Annael found himself with Sabrael on the platform of a rail transit station, positioned to cover both directions where the line disappeared into unlit tunnels. The platform was not high, only a metre above the line, and devoid of cover. There were small holes in the ferrocrete, left where furnishings or other fittings had been removed and the rail was littered with debris – broken ferrocrete, tattered rags and scatters of broken bolts and tools.

Ferrocrete ceiling blocks had fallen out and broken on the rails and platform, exposing the reinforcing girders within. There was rust on the metal, a lot of rust, and Annael was not certain of the chamber's structural integrity. Half-columns lined the walls on either side of the tunnel entrances but they appeared more decorative than functional, the plaster heavily cracked, exposing crumbling ferrocrete beneath.

On the wall opposite the pair of tracks were wooden frames, fragments of paper still fixed within, though what had been on the posters was now lost. The light fittings set at regular intervals on the curved ceiling were in poor repair, only a few of them giving out a fitful, flickering blue light. Now and then the power would fail, plunging the station into darkness for a few seconds before returning to cast jittering shadows from the immobile Space Marines.

'The Unworthy?' said Sabrael, referring to the term Grand Master Sammael had used for the enemy in his last broadcast. 'What twisted minds would cling to such a title?'

'It is fitting,' replied Annael. 'They have turned from the light of the Emperor. That makes them Unworthy of any mercy or consideration.'

'I do not think it is in reference to their rebellion, brother. Unworthy hints at aspiration unfulfilled, and one does not aspire to a position voluntarily forsaken. Our enemies consider themselves unworthy of something else.'

'Does it matter, brother?' Annael was content to wait in silence for the enemy or fresh orders, whichever came first, and found his squadron-brother's chatter a distraction. Even by voicing his ambivalence Annael realised he was playing into Sabrael's desire for attention.

'The motivations of the enemy are always worthy of consideration,' said Sabrael, his tone conversational though his words were an attempt to sound erudite. 'It speaks to their mindset and allows us to understand their tactics and capabilities. If we cannot comprehend why it is that our foes fight, what chance have we of knowing the means they will employ? Does their self-perceived unworthiness make them better or worse fighters? Do they hope to attain worthiness in battle?'

'Is that not our goal?' asked Annael, despite himself. There was some truth to Sabrael's opinion, though it was more a quest to discover understanding of himself than the foe that had occupied Annael's thoughts since Piscina. 'Glory and honour are the means by which we judge ourselves, brother. Without them, do we not consider ourselves also unworthy of our place amongst the Chapter?'

'You cannot compare the two,' Sabrael answered quickly, offended by the question. 'We have already been deemed worthy by those who brought us into the Chapter. Each of us is an anointed warrior of the Emperor, and that brings with it a certain amount of honour that cannot be removed. Our foes, scabrous and vile as they are, cannot measure themselves by the same standard. If they judge themselves against us, they will always be the Unworthy no matter their courage or efforts.'

Something about Sabrael's conclusion did not sit right with Annael. He considered the desperate rebels that had attacked the Dark Angels on Piscina. They were hopelessly outclassed and outgunned by the Space Marines, and the chances of achieving any meaningful victory were virtually nil. Had the Dark Angels force remained on the world the insurrection would have been put down swiftly, without any meaningful objective achieved on the part of the rebels. It seemed as senseless to Annael as the resistance of the pirates, yet there was something about the human soul that could not accept inevitability. To a Space Marine, to fight without clear purpose, even if devoid of the opportunity for ultimate victory, was as alien as surrender.

'If we are paragons of worth, as you say, then might our foes see worth in defeating us? We take no glory in killing lesser foes, so it must be the case that there is glory in killing a greater foe for our enemies. Our very presence gives purpose and meaning to our enemies. To kill a Space Marine, for those who have turned from the guidance of the Emperor, must be a goal in itself and one that brings worth.'

'Your philosophy is flawed, brother,' said Sabrael after a short while. 'We do not seek out the toughest enemies for the simple sake of proving our worth, nor do we shirk from slaying those who cannot match us simply because we can. We kill our enemies as part of a higher purpose, whether individually they are lesser or greater than ourselves. The Chapter and the Emperor are the higher purpose that drives us. Which brings more glory to the Chapter, to slay one greater foe or a hundred lesser foes?'

'I see your point, brother. We do not ascribe arbitrary value to individuals, but create it from the wider context of our purpose. A host of tough enemies may be slain and yet victory not achieved, whilst the death of a single less powerful individual may prove the victorious moment.'

'Then we are in agreement,' Sabrael said, his tone light-hearted. 'Our enemies do not gain worth simply by slaying a Space Marine, unless that death is informed by some greater purpose. In the case of these renegades, the purpose is survival. The selfish drive to live for the sake of living is all that sends this rabble into battle. They know that if they do not fight then they are dead.'

While he spoke, Annael monitored the sensor readings on *Black Shadow*'s display. They showed a strengthening return several hundred metres down the tunnel to Annael's left, towards the hub of the star fort. A smaller group was approaching from the right, moving slowly up the rail line on foot.

'Our philosophical discussion must wait,' he told Sabrael.

'Theory must give way to practice,' replied the other Space Marine. 'We are confronted by two groups, both of which pose a threat to the mission. One is larger but further away. Even as you analyse the tactical situation you are ascribing value to the individuals signified by the returns on your augur array.'

'This is not the time, brother,' said Annael, annoyed that Sabrael seemed intent on continuing the conversation despite the approach of enemies. 'We must focus on the mission.'

'Yes we must, brother.' Sabrael's voice moved from Annael's external pick-up to the vox-feed in his ear. 'Request permission to pre-empt attack. It is better to strike now than face assault from two directions.'

'Denied,' replied Araton, without hesitation. 'Remain in position.'

'Brother, further assessment reinforces my opinion that a pre-emptive attack is the best course of action in the current situation.' Sabrael's voice switched back to the external speakers as he addressed Annael. 'Araton's bloody-mindedness alters the context. There is no time to delay. If we strike now, we can eliminate the threat and return in time to counter the next attack.'

'I disagree with Brother Sabrael's assessment,' Annael said over the vox so that the others could hear. 'We have sufficient firepower to drive back a two-pronged attack.'

'Foolishness!' snapped Sabrael. His bike let loose a plume of exhaust as he powered up the engine and set off along the platform. 'The enemy can keep us stuck here without launching an attack, we must seize the initiative.'

'Sabrael, you are to remain in position!' barked Araton, but his words were ignored. Sabrael steered his bike off the side of the platform onto the rails, the thud of his machine's landing echoing along the station.

'Mobility and speed are our weapons, brother,' Sabrael argued as he rode into the tunnel. 'Do not surrender them lightly.'

Annael cursed Sabrael as the gleam from his armour receded down the tunnel and then disappeared. He did not like the idea of abandoning the position he had been given to guard, but was equally vexed by the thought of leaving Sabrael to attack alone. In the end, his hesitation made the decision for him – any benefit of Sabrael's counter-attack would be lost if Annael followed now. All he could do was protect the station and await his battle-brother's return.

Whether the enemy realised what had happened or not, the signal return from the tunnel ahead of Annael started to approach more swiftly. His audio pick-ups detected echoes from the incoming pirates; the scuff of footfalls and whispered voices. The noise grew swiftly louder, as the conversation fell silent and the sound of slapping feet quickened.

Annael opened fire into the darkness of the tunnel before he saw any visible target. From his position he could cover the first twenty-five metres or so and a scream announced that his speculative salvo had met a target. Something small and round flew out of the tunnel mouth and rattled across the rails for several seconds. It detonated with a loud bang and white flash, but the stun grenade was useless against Annael's autosenses, which had instantly dampened the audio and visual input from his armour to protect his ears and eyes. So it was that when a wave of warriors sprinted into view, rather than coming upon a disorientated foe they ran straight into a sustained volley of fire from *Black Shadow*'s twin bolters.

The hail of bolts cut a gouge into the press of men and women pouring from the tunnel. The Unworthy seemed heedless of the carnage as they scrambled and leapt over the fallen, blasting wildly with autoguns and laspistols, their shouts ringing from the curved walls and roof of the chamber. Ten of them had already fallen, but twice that number followed on, seeking the shelter of the platform lip.

One thumb pressing the firing stud again, raking fire moving left and right with his roaming gaze, Annael pulled a fragmentation grenade from his belt and armed it. With a measured throw, he tossed it toward the end of the platform. The grenade bounced once and then fell from sight onto the tracks. Like a flock of birds set to flight by the attack of a hunter, the pirates dashed in all directions to avoid the grenade. The thunderous blast reverberated down both tunnels, the clouds of fire and shrapnel catching the four slowest, turning them to ragged corpses.

Annael glanced at the sensor screen and could see from Sabrael's transponder location that the battle-brother had engaged the enemy to the right, though over the din of his own firing he could hear nothing from the far tunnel. More grenades bounced and rolled across the platform, surrounding Annael with flashes and bangs and smoke, but he continued to fire, pulling free his pistol to add to the hail of bolts screaming from his steed.

The unthinking desperation with which the Unworthy hurled themselves up the steps at the end of the platform and clambered from the rails gave Annael cause for concern. There were still two dozen and more piling out of the tunnel and he could not hope to bring them all down before they reached the passageway at his back. Had Sabrael remained at his post, the two of them could have withdrawn into the corridor and gunned down any foe reaching the entrance, but now Annael was caught between guarding the rear of Sabrael and the flank of the rest of the squadron. If he pulled back, he could not prevent the pirates continuing along the station to come at Sabrael from behind, but if he remained where he was there were so many foes some would inevitably pass by him if they wished, breaking the perimeter he was meant to protect.

'Sabrael, report progress,' he growled, firing a bolt into the face of a man who had snuck along the tracks and was pulling himself up to the platform. He fell back, half of his head missing.

'Three more to go, brother,' Sabrael replied. 'They ran away, the cowards. Returning to position in thirty seconds.'

'Return to position immediately. It is a diversionary attack to draw you away,' said Annael. Two more bursts of fire littered the platform ahead with blood, bodies and limbs. 'I need you here!'

The Unworthy appeared crazed, with wide eyes and wordless shouts as they charged along the platform. Realising that he would be overwhelmed, his options diminishing quickly, Annael decided that Sabrael had been correct about surrendering the initiative. Sitting where he was would not stop the renegades.

He revved hard and let loose *Black Shadow*, roaring into the foe like a black-armoured missile. Controlling the bike one-handed, firing his pistol in the other, he slammed through the enemy, breaking legs and shattering ribs. *Black Shadow* bucked and slid as a body passed under the front wheel and Annael accelerated, clearing the press of bodies. Braking, he skidded to a stop before the steps at the end of the platform. There were still more pirates coming out of the darkness but he had no time to worry about them – those already in the station were converging on him from behind. Evidently they were intent upon him, with no thought of breaking towards the rest of the squadron.

Tactically it made no sense, but that was to be expected. Sabrael's conclusion had been accurate. The Unworthy had no greater purpose or plan, they were simply seeking to kill as many of the Dark Angels as they could.

His bolt pistol emptied, he holstered the weapon and raced forwards again, taking the handlebars in both hands as he opened fire with the mounted bolters again. A woman bounced across the front faring, her screeching face passing within centimetres of Annael's as she thudded against him and span away. Las-bolts and projectiles whined around him and hands vainly tried to rip him from his steed, but he sped free of their grasp with ease, bringing the bike around again as he reached the passageway entrance where he had begun the engagement. A momentary glance at the scanner showed that Sabrael was on his way back but still three hundred metres away.

Looking up from the screen, Annael saw a spark of fire from the tunnel mouth. A missile screamed from the darkness, heading straight at him.

Acting out of instinct, he turned his left shoulder towards the projectile, to take the blast on his pauldron. The missile did not hit directly, but glanced from the curved plate and slammed into the wall behind Annael. Ferrocrete fragments and dust engulfed him as the missile exploded.

He opened the throttle, trying to find the missile firer with his targeter. There must have been two of the heavy weapons, for there had not been time to reload when a second missile powered from the tunnel.

Now moving, Annael was able to wrench *Black Shadow* to the right, avoiding the rocket, which hurtled into the passageway entrance. The crack and rumble that followed was far longer and louder than a missile detonation and as he ploughed through the enemy once more, Annael glanced back to see the archway collapsing.

Whether by intent or accident, the pirates were bringing down the chamber roof.

Ferrocrete and mangled steel fell across the station. A beam bracing the ceiling twisted and bent under the extra load, the screech of tearing metal sounding through the tumbling of ferrocrete blocks. The ceiling came down in a welter of jagged clumps of stone and plaster, sending debris smashing through the pirates and clattering from Annael's armour.

More and more of the station was crumbling, decades, perhaps centuries of poor maintenance taking its toll as pillars and supports crashed onto the tracks and platform. The only place for Annael to go was down onto the rails and he steered *Black Shadow* over the lip scant seconds before the whole of the platform was buried by an avalanche of masonry.

Swinging a lasgun as a club, a man smashed his weapon across Annael's face. The lasgun snapped and Annael did not even blink as he flung out a fist, turning the man's face to a bloody pulp, cheek and jaw shattered. Someone grabbed Annael's left arm and he let go of the handlebar to lift up the female pirate, hurling her into another enemy aiming a pistol at Annael's chest.

The detonation of another missile took Annael by surprise. The armoured chamfron of *Black Shadow* took the brunt of the explosion, metal and ceramite splinters cutting through the enemy who had been thrown back by the blast.

'Annael? Brother, are you alive?' Sabrael's voice seemed distant in Annael's ear. 'Annael, respond!'

'Still alive, brother,' snarled Annael, kicking out, the toe of his armoured boot crushing the ribcage of a man trying to climb onto the front of the Dark Angel's mount. Annael pushed *Black Shadow* forwards into the tunnel, firing the bolters in a steady stream to rip through the remaining renegades. 'Take no credit for that fact. I will demand restitution, brother.'

Sabrael's reply devolved into wordless static as more of the station roof fell down behind Annael, closing off the platform and track entirely. The Dark Angel dismounted as pirates swarmed around him, breaking bones with both hands as he waded into them with armoured fists.

'Sabrael?' There was no reply to Annael's inquiry and he switched channel with a sub-vocal command. 'Brother Araton?'

The comm was dead, the signal blocked by the tonnes of debris choking the station chamber. Annael grabbed the throat of the last foe – one who had been manning a missile launcher – and threw him against the tunnel wall, snapping his spine.

The only sounds were the rumble of the bike's idling engine and the patter and creak of settling debris.

Now that the immediate situation had calmed, Annael appraised the situation. He was cut off from the rest of the squadron, trapped in the tunnel. The only route out, if he wanted to maintain possession of *Black Shadow*, would be the next station. There might be maintenance access on foot somewhere in the tunnel, but Annael knew he would be shamed if he abandoned his mount. The loss of a mount was felt almost as keenly as the loss of a Space Marine, and Annael would give up a limb rather than be separated from his bike. The thought turned his mind back to Cassiel, who had done just that. The squadron was already one warrior down. It was imperative that Annael rejoined them.

Opening a panel in the left vambrace of his armour, Annael pulled free a cable and jack, plugging his vox-system into *Black Shadow*'s. The bike had a stronger transmitter and receiver, but with a snarled curse as static filled his ears Annael discovered that the last missile hit had damaged the communications array.

A normal soldier in his situation might have despaired, but Annael had no thought of fear. Though he was physically separated from his squadron and unable to contact any of the other Dark Angels, he dispassionately assessed his situation. Panic was counter-productive to mission success.

His greatest concern was that effort would be wasted trying to search for him in the wreckage of the transit station. Thus, he concluded, the first priority was to establish contact with his force. Once he could assure them he was still alive he could set about devising a plan to rejoin the attack.

A cursory search of the corpses revealed no hand-held communications devices. If the group had possessed some means of contacting other forces it was lost in the station. The most obvious solution to the communication problem was the star fort's internal system. If Annael could locate a console, he would be able to boost his bike or armour's transmitter. *If* the internal system still worked, which was far from likely given the general poor state of Port Imperial.

With no better plan coming to mind, Annael mounted *Black Shadow* and rode on through the darkness of the rail tunnel.

UNEXPECTED FOES

Mechanical thumping echoed along the corridor from a chamber ahead, as regular as a heartbeat. Steam leaked from cracked pipes overhead and rust was smeared along the walls as if daubed by some inhuman hand, mixing with patches of dark lichen. Droplets of water formed on the armour of Telemenus and his battle-brothers and mist condensed around the heat exchanges of their backpacks.

Moving through the quadrant designated grid-west, the squad had divided into two combat teams to cover the ground more swiftly. With Telemenus were Amanael, Cadael, Achamenon and Daellon.

'Water filtration plant?' suggested Cadael.

'Environmental system,' countered Sergeant Amanael. 'Humidity regulator.'

'Whatever it is, that pounding is annoying,' said Telemenus. The monotonous clanging masked the tread of the Space Marines as they advanced towards a sealed doorway at the end of the passage. 'Surely it is not meant to make such a din?'

'Anything to keep it working, I assume,' said Achamenon. 'One can let void shields and lighting fall to ruin, but breathable air is essential. I am surprised that they have managed to keep the station habitable for this long without the aid of tech-adepts.'

'Some of the tech-priests must have survived the secession,' said Amanael. 'Even if working under duress. To salve the machine-spirits of a star fort requires knowledge possessed by just a few.'

The passageway past the door was in an even poorer state, and even through his olfactory filters Telemenus could detect the rankness in the air. Mould and fungi grew in clumps where the walls met ceiling and floor, patches of drab greens and greys broken by brighter purples and blues. The bulkheads were heavily corroded and the decking underfoot had rusted away completely in places, leaving holes down into the crawlspaces beneath the Space Marines.

Picking their way around these, the five Dark Angels advanced.

'Strong life signals, through the next chamber,' reported Cadael. 'Not sure if it is hostile or background life.'

The doors lining either side of the passage were rusted shut. Achamenon tested the first and it only shifted after considerable effort, showering the Space Marine with dark flakes of oxidised metal. The room beyond led nowhere and held a few empty crates and nothing more.

'Press on,' said Sergeant Amanael, waving the squad forwards. 'These doors have not been opened in decades. No rebel could force them.'

The corridor took a forty-five degree turn to the left, angling directly towards the hub. Turning the bend, Telemenus could see the doorway at the far end was open. Roof panels had been torn away leaving piping and cabling hanging like bunting across the entrance.

Looking further ahead, the Dark Angel could see that the chamber was in a ruinous state, criss-crossed by a nest of jury-rigged wires and conduits. Bare cables sparked occasionally, lighting the darkness with blue glare.

'Touch nothing,' warned Amanael. 'Nobody can say what systems they have bypassed with this mess.'

Ducking beneath a pipe covered with a thin rime of frost, Telemenus stepped carefully, negotiating a path between the haphazard mass. The hum of exposed power lines buzzed through his autosenses and he registered a sharp rise in temperature and humidity. The conditions were perfect for the mould, which formed large slicks on the walls and a soft carpet underfoot. Spores drifted into the air at the tread of the advancing Space Marines, creating a cloud of fluttering particles.

'Atmosphere extractors and projectors are off,' Telemenus said, noting no breeze moved the floating spores. 'This environment is deliberate.'

'Who would want to live in this dank hole?' asked Cadael. He lifted up the auspex. 'Readings show this whole sector is the same, for about half a kilometre ahead and a kilometre to either side.'

'A micro-climate,' said Daellon.

'But for what?' Telemenus's question went unanswered.

A motor chugged hoarsely in the far corner, dribbling exhaust fumes, fuelled from a pipe jutting from a torn bulkhead. It was attached to a series of gears and chains that disappeared into the far doorway. Its purpose seemed to be to power the emergency door, which was closed.

'I have our answer,' said Amanael, stooping to inspect the crude machine. He pointed to a beaten metal panel poorly riveted on one side of the motor. Telemenus saw small blotches of red and green and as his autosenses improved the resolution he recognised the shape of pictograms. Their meaning was unknown but their type was immediately recognisable.

'Orks,' he muttered.

'It seems that not only humans can be Unworthy,' said Cadael.

'Brother Seraphiel, we have ork signs, quadrant four,' Amanael reported. 'Numbers unknown. Judging by the state of this place, they have been here for some time. Initiating cleanse protocols.'

'Acknowledged, sergeant,' replied the Fifth Company's commander. 'Continue with your advance and exercise standard doctrine.'

'Confirmed, sergeant, we will proceed.' Amanael gestured to Daellon, who was currently in possession of the squad flamer. 'Stand ready, brother.'

The sergeant pulled a lever on the motor, engaging the gears. The door mechanism snarled into life, the metal slab sliding sideways into the bulkhead, revealing a chamber much the same as the one in which the Dark Angels were standing. Daellon turned to face the way they had entered as Amanael led the squad through the doorway. As Telemenus stepped past, Daellon opened up with the flamer, bathing the mould and fungi with burning promethium.

The flames seared through the cabling, plunging the chamber into darkness, lit by the greenish-blue of the burning spores. Stepping backwards, Daellon played his flamer across the floor and ceiling, igniting everything. Fumes from the motor fuel line ignited, filling the room with a billowing ball of orange fire as Daellon rapidly backed away. The chain links melted through and the door crashed back into position just in front of Daellon, the last spurts of the Dark Angel's flamer splashing against rusted metal.

'Contacts!' barked Cadael. There were two doorways leading from the small room. He pointed to the right. 'Strong. Moving towards us. Directly towards us. Forty metres and closing.'

Telemenus readied his bolter as Cadael slung the auspex on his belt and brought up his weapon. He heard the noise of a door being slammed open and Amanael opened fire. Cadael turned to cover the other entrance with the flamer as Telemenus stepped up next to his sergeant, just in time to see an ork's head exploding from a bolt impact. Its body fell amongst the corpses of two more aliens, and there were twenty or more of the beasts rushing down the passageway behind.

Telemenus needed no order to open fire. He sighted past the closest ork and fired at another greenskinned creature just behind it, the bolt shell taking the alien in the shoulder. Amanael's next burst brought down the foremost alien and Telemenus had a clear shot at his target's body, his round hitting it squarely in the chest, ripping through flesh and organs. A following ork tripped over the falling carcass, Telemenus's next shot cracking open the top of its head as it fell, dead before it hit the ground.

With the orks only ten metres away now, Telemenus released his grip with his left hand and pulled out his combat knife, still firing. Amanael's chainsword growled into life beside him and the sergeant leapt forward to meet the orks as they burst into the chamber. His first swing took the arm off the closest alien as it raised a pistol to fire.

Telemenus sidestepped to his right, to get a line of fire past his sergeant and Achamenon. While the two Dark Angels went blade-to-blade with the greenskins, Telemenus continued to fire at the orks pressing in from the corridor, blowing off arms and legs, occasionally landing a clean shot in a torso or head.

A warning from Daellon and the sound of the flamer caused Telemenus to turn. His battle-brother fired another long burst down the other corridor, the flames dying out as the weapon's fuel canister emptied.

'I have you covered, brother,' Telemenus told Daellon, stepping up to fire through the doorway, his first salvo cutting down an ork that was covered from waist to shoulder in burning promethium.

He picked his shots carefully, ignoring the blasts from the orks' crude pistols and rifles. A lucky burst of orkish fire caught him full in the chest, cracking the emblazoned ceramite eagle on his plastron and sending his aim astray. With only one more burst left in his bolter's magazine he aimed high, stitching the three shots across the faces of the closest foes. A glance confirmed to Telemenus that Daellon was still fixing a new fuel canister.

The orks were moments away, firing wildly. There was no time to reload before they would enter the chamber and their numbers would count in their favour. Telemenus counter-charged, swinging his bolter like a club as he plunged through the doorway. The heavy casing cracked open the skull of the first, sending it sprawling to the floor with blood spattering on the walls. A spiked maul missed the Dark Angel's head by millimetres as he plunged his knife up to the hilt, burying it in the throat of the next ork. He could not avoid the next blow, the club smashing into his wrist. With a grimace, he held onto his bolter as pain briefly flared up his arm.

Surrounded by fanged, snarling faces, Telemenus rammed his helmet into one of them, forcing the creature back. Warning icons flared across his view as the orks fired their pistols at him and pounded on his armour with heavy cleavers and cudgels. His knife opened up the face of a third foe, sending long teeth spinning through the air, the slash ripping out the alien's eye. In return, a hooked axe head lodged into the flexible joint seal between his waist and left thigh, deep enough to bite into flesh.

'Die, xenos filth!' The wound angered Telemenus more than it hurt him. Forced to batter his foes to death in close combat, every ork that he felled would not count against his marksman tally. The thought of killing so many enemies and yet his laurel award remaining out of reach sent a fresh surge of anger through him.

An ork was trying to twist off his head, its arms wrapped around his helm. Launching himself backwards, Telemenus hurled himself and the ork into the wall of the corridor, crushing it against the unrelenting bulkhead. Dazed, it relaxed its grip for a moment, giving Telemenus the opportunity to stab backwards over his shoulder, his knife finding flesh and bringing forth a howl of pain.

'Clear the corridor, brother,' barked Daellon. Telemenus knew instantly what his battle-brother intended and flung himself back into the chamber, the ork still clinging to his back. Burning promethium scorched above him as he rolled across the floor, his weight squashing the last vestiges of life from the greenskin.

Freed from its grip, he pushed himself to his feet, hand moving for a fresh magazine at his belt. Ejecting the empty magazine from his bolter, he slotted home more ammunition, turning back towards the corridor.

The flamer blast had finished off the orks. In the passage there was nothing but charred corpses and burning bodies. Here and there a limb trembled or a hand twitched, but these were simple muscle spasms, not true signs of life. Any shots fired now would be a waste of ammunition.

Moving his attention back to the other entrance, Telemenus saw that the other three Dark Angels had pushed out, pressing the orks back to the adjoining room.

'Orders, sergeant?' he asked, taking a stride towards the others before stopping. It was risky leaving only Daellon and his flamer as rearguard.

'Secure your position and extend the perimeter, brothers,' came Amanael's reply.

'I shall lead,' Telemenus told Daellon, pushing past his battle-brother. 'Conserve your ammunition for when we encounter sufficient foes.'

'You mean I should leave the kills to you, brother?' said Daellon. He lifted up the muzzle of the flamer and waved Telemenus on. 'I would be no brother to deny you.'

The narrow passageway was short, not more than fifteen metres before it came to a T-junction. There was more evidence of the orks' salvaging and jury-rigging, panels torn from the walls to expose battered air pumps and vapour-spilling heating pipes.

'Brother, your leg?' said Daellon, reminding Telemenus of the axe still stuck in his hip joint. He pulled the weapon free and tossed it to one side, wincing briefly before the pain subsided. Inspecting the pierced ribbing, he saw the polymer expanding to close the breach, just as his blood cells were clotting to seal the wound in his flesh. Although it was not perfect, the joint would hold well enough for the moment, as would his leg.

''Tis but a scratch,' replied Telemenus, turning right while he motioned for Daellon to cover to the left.

After a just a few metres the corridor ended abruptly at a round doorway with a rusted lockwheel and a shattered datapanel in the bulkhead beside it. There was no window to check if he was correct but Telemenus assumed it was an airlock of some kind. Certainly it had not seen use for many years. Rejoining Daellon, he found that the left fork of the passage led to a stairwell. The two Space

Marines paused at the bottom and listened, but heard no signs of activity on the levels above and below.

'Nothing here, brother-sergeant,' Telemenus reported. 'Access to levels four and six. Shall we proceed?'

'No, brothers, return to our position. We will hold for you and proceed together. Sergeant Seraphiel is sending in Squads Actael and Mellusian to provide a cross-sweep to our position.'

'Understood, brother-sergeant.' Telemenus looked up the steps once more, hoping to see a foe skulking on the steps that he had not registered previously. There was nothing.

The sound of bolters echoed in the distance and the squad comm erupted into life. Telemenus and Daellon were running even before they heard the first words, pounding back down the corridor as they listened to their squad-brothers.

'Target the leader, Cadael. Achamenon, hold the left.' Amanael spoke quickly but calmly.

'They are cutting through the bulkhead, brother-sergeant.' This was from Achamenon.

'Throwing frag,' warned Cadael. The crack of its detonation rolled along the metal walls around Telemenus a second later. 'And another.'

The two Dark Angels sprinted across the corpse-choked chamber where they had first encountered the orks, striding over the mounds of the alien dead as a second fragmentation detonation echoed from the corridor ahead.

'It is still coming, brother-sergeant! Some kind of force-field?' Tension had replaced Cadael's calm as the ork leader apparently survived the Space Marine's attacks.

'Swap places, brother. Watch that archway on the left.' The buzz of Amanael's chainsword rang through the empty passageway as Telemenus and Daellon ducked beneath swaying fronds of moss and wire and squeezed through a narrow portal at the end of the corridor. They found themselves in what appeared to be an old water vaporisation chamber, the floor still covered with a few centimetres of algae-thick water. It was nearly fifty metres across and half as high. Nearly a third of the space was taken up with a festering mound of ork dung. Insects and small creatures buzzed and skittered over the disgusting hillock, which was obscured in places by forests of sprouting fungi with stems as tall as the Space Marines.

The flash of bolter fire reflected from the tarnished wall of a service duct off to Telemenus's left and the pair headed through the miasma of thick fumes and flies. Telemenus was grateful of the sealed environment of his armour; his suit had shut down all external air the moment they had entered the vat, but the stench would have been overwhelming.

The access hatch was barely large enough for Telemenus to squeeze through. He had to turn sideways and duck to manoeuvre through the opening, his bolter held out in front of him ready to fire. Straightening, he found himself in what appeared to have once been a pumping station, judging by the huge pipes that covered the ceiling, leading from the water vaporisation vat. The machines had long ago been dismantled, though large cogs, pistons and belts littered the rusty floor of the chamber.

The cavernous space was almost as large as the mustering hall on the strike cruiser; easily three hundred metres long and a hundred wide for most of its length, opening into a nave-like space at the far end where a massive drop-pipe entered from the ceiling. Once it had housed immense processors pumping human sustaining air to a large portion of the station. In the place of the pumps was now a jumble of roughly built hovels and workshops, walled and roofed with torn bulkheads and ceiling tiles, stained carpets draped over some, smoke-spewing generators and glittering electrical wires connected to several of the ramshackle buildings.

'A whole damned town of orks!' exclaimed Daellon as he came up beside Telemenus. 'Where are our brothers?'

'There, on the right,' Telemenus replied, pointing with his bolter towards a group of small huts about seventy metres away.

The other members of the squad had taken up a position near two shacks butting up against the wall of the chamber. Telemenus could see Achamenon on the roof, his weight causing the metal sheets to buckle as he moved from one edge of the building to the other, firing into the heart of the orkish settlement. Sergeant Amanael was on the ground with Cadael, keeping the area around the buildings clear of attackers.

There were scores of greenskins, clambering over rooftops and along swinging bridges held up by twists of cable. Many were the smaller aliens – the orks' slave species – swarming from building to building, pausing to take pot shots with their simple rifles. The larger orks were mainly on a more robust structure towards the far end of the pump hall, laying down scatters of fire from heavy weapons that fired hails of shells and blazes of green energy.

Telemenus spied a group of orks, fifteen or more, slinking through the gap between two workshops. Moving from one pile of debris to another, keeping to the cover of mangled engine parts and scrap, they were out of sight of the Dark Angels.

'Flanking force, brothers,' he warned, raising his bolter to fire at the skulking aliens. 'Engaging.'

He fired on the move, letting off single rounds as he closed with the aliens at a steady stride. Alerted to the new arrivals, the orks realised they had been found and made a dash for sanctuary behind a line of leaking drums. Telemenus's bolter fire followed them, cutting down one of the greenskins and wounding another before they reached the shelter of the barrels.

Daellon's flamer was of no use at this range and he moved ahead of Telemenus at a swift run, covering the ground quickly. The orks in the workshop realised his intent and a barrage of bullets screamed out of their hiding place, poorly aimed but effective from weight of fire. Daellon was forced to his right as rounds ricocheted from his armour, seeking cover at the corner of a small hovel made from piled crates. Metal splinters surrounded the Space Marine as the orks intensified their fire.

'Suppress these bastards, if you please, Telemenus,' said Daellon, his back to the wall of the shack.

'My pleasure, brother.'

He switched his bolter to burst fire and stopped, locking his armour into a stable firing position. The Dark Angel loosed off the rest of the magazine into the battered oil drums, the din of the bolts' detonations echoing back from the walls of the workshop. Reloading swiftly, he fired again, targeting the darker shapes of the orks beyond the wall of barrels.

The fire from the orks lessened under Telemenus's attack, though whether from casualties or distraction he did not know. Swapping out his empty magazine – noting he had only two reloads left as he did so – the Space Marine advanced again, snapping off short salvos every couple of seconds, keeping the orks occupied.

'Time to cleanse this damned filth,' snarled Daellon, rounding the corner of the shack with his flamer levelled. He broke into a run, bullets pattering from his armour, and unleashed a sheet of promethium into the workshop's interior. Burning flamer fuel and igniting oil filled the building with ruddy flames. Telemenus saw writhing, flailing figures dark against the wash of fire.

Some of the orks survived the flamer blast and burst out of the building, their guns chattering wildly as they charged towards Daellon. Telemenus switched quickly to single fire and aimed at the foremost alien warrior, the bolt knocking the creature from his feet as it hit its shoulder. Blood pouring from the wound, the ork snarled and pushed itself to its feet just in time for Telemenus's next shot. The round ripped out the creature's throat, felling it permanently.

With a glance to check his situation, Telemenus noticed more orks approaching from his left, at least a dozen of them. If he pushed on towards Daellon they would come at the pair of Dark Angels from behind and the two Space Marines would have only the burning workshop as cover.

'Fall back, brother, to me,' he told Daellon. 'We cannot break through here.'

'Damned if I retreat from orks,' the other Dark Angel replied. He fired another gout of flames into the charging orks, killing two and forcing the rest to turn and run. 'Not while I can still fight.'

'We will be surrounded, brother,' Telemenus said, breaking to his right, heading towards the blocky remnants of a pump engine. 'We cannot reach the rest of the squad.'

'Do as Telemenus says,' Amanael barked over the vox. 'Secure a position and we will pull back to you. The enemy are massing for a concerted attack. We cannot hold at our current location.'

'As you command, brother-sergeant,' replied a chastened Daellon.

Telemenus stopped beside the rusted carcass of the pump and checked the immediate area for foes. Several orks lay close at hand, missing limbs and heads, but he was certain they were dead. Able to inspect the enemy more closely, he saw that these aliens were scrawnier than most orks he had encountered. They had wiry limbs and thin fingers, their teeth not as prominent as most specimens he had examined. Their dress was strange, for orks, made from stitched human clothes, patched and armoured with thin pieces of metal and plastek.

Their weapons looked basically the same as the autoguns and lasguns of the Unworthy, though with typical orkoid embellishments of scrap fetishes, daubed paint and seemingly superfluous mechanical parts.

'These creatures are amongst the Unworthy also,' he concluded to the others. 'Not just allied with the pirates, but numbered amongst their cult.'

'So it seems, brother,' replied Cadael. 'The enemy commander is not averse to working with aliens. More proof of his sinful nature.'

Daellon reached Telemenus's position at a run, half a dozen orks a few metres behind. Telemenus fired into the group of greenskins as Daellon turned his flamer on them, and between the two Space Marines the alien warriors were cut down in short order.

'How much fuel do you have left, brother?' asked Telemenus as he eyed the indistinct figures of more orks gathering around the buildings ahead and to his left.

'Two more bursts and another canister,' replied Daellon, his voice grim as he took stock of what Telemenus had already noticed: there were several dozen orks massing for the next attack. 'Perhaps eight good bursts in total.'

'We cannot hold for long, brother-sergeant,' Telemenus announced. He could not see anything of the rest of the squad from where he was; Achamenon had left his rooftop post. 'What is your status?'

'Fighting withdrawal,' Amanael replied tersely, his words punctuated by the crack of bolter rounds. 'Brother-Sergeant Seraphiel, this is Amanael. Our situation is deteriorating swiftly. We must receive reinforcements or withdraw. What are your orders?'

Telemenus saw the three Space Marines past the burning workshop, the flames glinting from heavily scarred armour. Before they disappeared from view behind another shack he noted that Cadael was firing one-handed, his right arm hanging limply by his side.

The hall reverberated with a loud, guttural roar from the orks; a war shout that echoed across the settlement as the aliens gave voice as one. Telemenus knew well what the throaty bellowing of the greenskins signified.

The orks were readying for an all-out attack.

NO INNOCENTS

Glass splintered as Annael's fist crashed into the console screen. The Dark Angel growled in frustration as he glared at the inoperative terminal and mentally cursed the Unworthy for their lack of maintenance. It was the fourth communications console he had accessed without success and Annael was forced to conclude that the entire internal comms network was not functional; at least not in the outer towers of Port Imperial.

He was more than half a kilometre from the collapsed rail station and had abandoned the tracks after finding the second malfunctioning terminal, heading grid-north towards the central spire in the hope of establishing contact with another part of the Dark Angels force. He had not encountered any enemies, though on occasion he had heard distant, muffled explosions that he assumed were strike cruiser attacks in preparation for the assault on the inner sanctum of the enemy.

He desperately wanted to rejoin the other Dark Angels for the final attack. He could easily imagine the comments by Sabrael and others if he was absent from the battle at such a crucial time. Perhaps he would be the little lost boy, or the wanderer, or some other gently mocking title. With so little time spent with the company, despite his earlier achievements in the Fifth, his reputation would be badly hurt, the episode a blot on his honour that would be hard to overcome. It was a shameful situation, made worse by a quirk of construction that meant his only route back to the main force would mean passing through the inner fortress.

Mounting *Black Shadow*, Annael cursed Sabrael's disobedience. He would have strong words for his brother when they were reunited, if not immediately then when the battle was won. It had been Sabrael's irresponsibility that had plunged Annael into this debacle. It was an affront to the company that Chaplain Malcifer continued to tolerate Sabrael's wayward behaviour and if he did not receive satisfactory words from his brother, Annael resolved to bring the matter to Grand Master Sammael and, if necessary, to the Supreme Grand Master.

In a half-rage, Annael rode on, following a broad ferrocrete concourse that cut down towards the foundations of Port Imperial. Other than the communications relay, *Black Shadow*'s systems were working well, though the low ammunition warning icon reminded Annael that he was not well-placed to face determined resistance if he was able to access the central spire.

The dark tunnel lit by the lamps of his steed, he covered another half a kilometre, passing smaller passageways branching off to each side. Having consulted the broken schematic in his steed's cogitation engine, he knew that these junctions led only to self-contained hab-blocks with no connecting route back to the breach or the axis of advance the Dark Angels were taking. When he was roughly halfway along the connecting corridor his bike's scanner started showing a faint return, ahead and off to his left. It was indistinct, blurred by the intervening structure, but it was definitely an abnormal signal.

Bringing *Black Shadow* to a stop, Annael considered his options. It was impossible to tell from this distance whether the signal indicated hostiles, and their probable position meant that they were no threat to the Dark Angels attack, as cut off from the fighting as he was. Keenly aware of the difficulty he likely would face when negotiating his way through the central tower and his ammunition status, he was loathe to expend any more rounds in pointless battle but his instincts warned him against ignoring the signal return altogether. He reminded himself that he was Ravenwing now, and part of his role was to be the eyes of the Chapter. The hazy smudge on his scanner screen was likely to be irrelevant, but there was a chance that it might be a shuttle on stand-by, ready to bring a force of Unworthy to the attack. Remembering the conclusion of the fight at Hadria Praetoris, it occurred to him that it might also be an escape route for the enemy commander.

As eager as he was to join the main battle, his duty as a warrior of the Ravenwing overruled his personal circumstance. With good fortune the scanner response showed an active energy grid, which in turn might indicate functional infrastructure and a working communications terminal. Whatever it was, Annael realised he had to investigate.

His first attempt to locate the source of the signal brought him to a cluster of interconnecting living spaces that quickly became a dead-end. Backtracking to the main concourse he tried the next junction and after only a few seconds a dim light from ahead registered in his autosenses. On the scanner the reading became clearer, showing a scattering of returns that looked very much like life signals. Knowing that he could not afford a full confrontation with the enemy he engaged *Black Shadow*'s secondary engine. Running off a stacked crystal cell similar to the one in his armour's backpack the bike's growl quietened to a soft purr as the secondary core took over from the main motor. It was not quite silence but it would afford him the element of surprise should he need it, though at a cost of lower performance from his steed.

Edging forwards along the passage, which was barely a metre wider than his machine, the top of his helmet almost scraping along the metal roof, Annael risked a wide-spectrum scan pulse, judging that the Unworthy would not have the means to detect the millisecond burst of energy. His telemetric display updated a few seconds later as the readings were processed by *Black Shadow*'s cogitator, showing a maze of rooms ahead, each only a few metres square. They looked like pre-formed habitations that had been fitted at some later time onto the base of the superstructure, stacked three deep and five across on two levels. A labourer slum, he decided as he reviewed the schematic.

The scan also confirmed his suspicion of life signals, more than fifty crowded into the enclosed spaces. If they were enemy, they were doing their best to avoid the fighting, hiding out of the way in this disused part of the star fort. There seemed to be little movement, assuring Annael that his approach had gone unnoticed.

The tunnel came to an abrupt end after another twenty metres and Annael dismounted. He engaged *Black Shadow*'s self-protection system, ensuring that the machine would detonate its energy core if anyone tampered with the controls without entering the disarm sequence; standard procedure when leaving a mount unattended in hostile territory.

Annael took a last look at the scanner to confirm there had been no reaction to his presence and unholstered his pistol. There was only a single doorway at the end of the corridor, little more than a hatchway providing access to the rooms beyond. There was no other way to enter the chambers, and more importantly it was the only route of exit should he encounter enemies. Pausing beside the closed door, he listened for a moment and detected the soft murmur of voices.

The door was held by a simple latch bolt. He lifted the bar quickly and thrust open the door, stepping through with pistol held ready to fire.

Screams and wails greeted the Dark Angel as he was confronted by a group of people huddled together in the first chamber; wrinkled faces stared in horror and terrified infants bawled in their sudden fright. At a glance Annael took in the scene; five women and two men of advanced years and eight children ranging from babes to eight or nine Terran years old. They all looked haggard, skin pinched and waxy, hair lank and uncut, their clothes little more than rags. In the light of a bare glow-globe their pale skin seemed brittle and yellowing.

No threat was Annael's first thought, though he kept his bolt pistol raised.

'Stop that noise,' he commanded, instantly irritated by the mewling and weeping coming from the shocked children. In direct defiance of his demand, some of the older folk raised their voices in wordless lament, the racket intense inside the small metal-sided cube.

There were three more doorways, one in each of the other walls, through which Annael saw more of the ragged people. Soon there was a crowd clustering at each door, shouting and yelling in anger and fear.

'Silence!' he roared, his projected voice thunderous in

the close confines. His outburst had the desired effect on the adults, quietening them immediately though the infants showed no restraint in giving voice to their woe.

'Mercy, lord, show us mercy,' pleaded an elderly man crouched against the wall to Annael's right. The call was taken up by others for a few seconds, dying away as he swept the crowd with his lensed gaze.

He had little experience dealing with non-combatants, and had never encountered any as wretched as this group. There was little in his training to prepare him for such an event and he dredged through his memory trying to remember the Chapter doctrine on the subject.

Establishing control, he recalled, was the first priority. With the adults cowed by his presence already, that seemed to have been achieved.

Establishing rapport was the next stage in dealing with the situation. Discomfited by the thought of conversing with these miserable-looking folk, Annael turned his attention to the elder that had first spoken.

'You, what is your name?' he said, realising when the man flinched and trembled that he had barked the question like a threat. He modified his tone, addressing the man as if he were a novitiate or Chapter serf. 'Please tell me your name.'

'Quaron, lord,' the main replied in a quavering voice, the words as shaky as the man's outstretched hands. 'Forgive us, we were not expecting you, lord.'

'Stop calling me that,' said Annael, fearing that to allow them to continue using such a grandiose title made him guilty of self-aggrandisement. 'You may address me as Brother Annael.'

This pronouncement was met with confusion and blank looks. The assembled degenerates muttered amongst themselves and exchanged perplexed shaking of heads. Quaron, realising he had been selected as spokesperson, gingerly stood up on thin legs, one hand held to the wall to support himself.

'Brother Annael?' he said, brow knotted with worry. He grimaced as he spoke, fearing his words caused offence. 'Are you not the Overlord?'

'I am no overlord, Quaron,' Annael assured the man. 'I am Brother Annael of the Dark Angels Chapter.'

There was more murmuring and whispers and Annael heard 'Dark Angel' spoken over and over. The conversation subsided into silence and save for a few of the youngest children he was pleased to note that the infants had ceased their yammering. With deliberate care, he holstered his pistol and held out his empty hands in a gesture of peaceful intent. It did not seem to settle the nerves of the people but he thought it dishonourable to make any firm promise to do them no harm, not until he had fully appraised their loyalty and situation; he did not want to make himself a liar.

'Quaron, how do you come to be here?'

'We are the Unworthy, Brother Annael of the Dark Angels. We follow the teachings of the Overlord but still we do not become Divine. Are you kin to the Overlord, Brother Annael of the Dark Angels?'

Annael killed a snarled retort before he gave voice to it. These people were wholly ignorant of what was happening, seemingly unaware of the attack that was ongoing elsewhere on the station. That they identified themselves with the Unworthy was worrying, for Annael had at first taken them to be prisoners. Ignoring the people for a moment, he looked at his surroundings. There were threadbare blankets and thin pillows piled in one corner, and in the room directly ahead he saw a small ceramite-slate portable stove and several pots, dishes and cups. There were no weapons in evidence, though the piles of meagre belongs could conceal blades or pistols it was doubtful these poor souls possessed any arms capable of hurting him. Even so, he remained on guard.

Aside from the obvious degradation there was something else that jarred in his mind, though he could not pinpoint the source of his unease. In demeanour the people were subservient to the point of cringing obsequiousness. He detected human bodily waste and a faint trace of rotting flesh, indicating that the inhabitants were quite prepared to live close to, if not actually with, their own filth. The youngsters looked as miserable as the elders, who in turn displayed a lethargy beyond that expected of their poorly nourished state. Most of the adults moved with involuntary twitches in the face and limbs and he had already seen a few that would fall into a momentarily vacant state, glassy-eyed and open-mouthed. Aside from those easily attributed to age and injuries, he could determine no physical blemishes that might indicate some form of plague as cause for this strange behaviour and isolation.

This strangeness unsettled Annael, quite aside from the dilemma that had immediately occurred to him upon discovering the unarmed people: to leave them be or kill them? In his experience there had been three categories of interaction. There were enemies, allies and civilians. Enemies were to be slain, allies aided and civilians protected, where possible. By their own testimony, these people were the Unworthy, part of the renegade group. As such they were enemies of the Emperor and it was his duty to eliminate them. The fact that they were of no threat whatsoever weighed against this course of action. Regardless of their loyalties, it seemed dishonourable to slay them in cold blood, especially the infants who, given a proper upbringing by loyal servants of the Emperor could become useful members of the Imperium.

It was a conundrum Annael had never expected to face, and the fact that he could not reconcile the two courses of action vexed him further. Part of him wanted to leave, secure in the knowledge that there was no threat to the Dark Angels force present. Another part of him, the part that had slowly emerged over four centuries, had questions that needed answers. Answers he could only gain from the Unworthy.

He told himself that any information he gathered here could prove of use in the fight against the pirates; quirks of behaviour or belief to be expected or exploited. He also told himself that this was just idle justification to sate his curiosity and that he had no business remaining with these people any longer.

Rheumy eyes stared listlessly at Annael as this debate raged inside him. They could see nothing of the conflict in his features, and he stood as still as a statue, but his silence was starting to unsettle many of the older folk. Inquisitiveness conquered doubt and he addressed the old man.

'You live here, in this place, Quaron?' Annael could not believe that the Unworthy would voluntarily live in such poor circumstance with the whole of the station to occupy. 'Why do you not live with the rest of the Unworthy?'

'We cannot aspire, Brother Annael of the Dark Angels. I am old and will never be Divine. The young must cleanse themselves of their birthing sins before they can join the ranks of the aspiring.'

'You are exiles? Unable to fight for the Overlord?' Annael felt on firmer ground here. On New Macedon, where he had been born, some of the barbaric outhive tribes divided their communities along similar lines, the old left to care for the young while the able-bodied raided and traded with the other nomads. He saw badly-healed injuries and crippling deformities in some of the older people, though none in the youngsters, and guessed that they had all been warriors of the Unworthy before age or wounds had rendered them a burden rather than an asset in battle.

'Exile, Brother Annael? I do not understand.'

'Perhaps there is another that can speak with me,' Annael said, tiring of the old man's confused state. 'One that perhaps does not feel the weight of age so heavily.'

'I can speak with you, Brother Annael,' announced a scrawny-looking woman from the doorway to Annael's left. She had a blue shawl wrapped about her shoulders over a plain grey dress much stitched and patched. 'I am Halgeral Three-mother. Forgive Quaron, his mind withers alongside his body. Soon he will be reborn unto us.'

Ignoring this hint at heretical resurrectionist belief, Annael stepped towards Halgeral, the Unworthy shuffling and crawling out of his path with wheezing breaths and gasps to leave the route clear to the adjoining chamber. Halgeral motioned for those around her to make room and she backed away as Annael ducked through the low door. The room was much the same as the first, with carefully piled bedding. In the corner a tired-looking middle-aged woman suckled a child at her breast, her expression suspicious. Annael noticed the child's skin was thin and lined with veins, before the mother drew the swaddling over the babe's head to conceal it from his scrutiny.

Casting his gaze across the other inhabitants of the chamber he realised what had been nagging at his subconscious since his arrival. Amongst their rags the Unworthy wore strange necklaces and fetishes, that seemed to be made up of bones and animal scraps. Beside the nursing mother another woman was soothing a child with a rattle made of bones linked with copper wire. These morbid ornamentations were not surprising in themselves – many cultures throughout the Imperium revered ancestors by making artefacts from the deceased, and the Dark Angels were not alone amongst the Adeptus Astartes to house the remains of their heroes in reliquaries beneath their fortress-monastery – but it was at odds with what he had seen of the other Unworthy. He had seen no such beads and bangles on the foes he had slain.

Deciding the strange ways of these abandoned people were not his immediate concern, he turned his attention back to Halgeral. When she spoke there was a slight slur in her voice but she seemed the most lucid of all the adults.

'Come, I show you our good works so that you may know we do as the Overlord commands,' she said, turning away and gesturing for Annael to follow her.

Treading carefully between the women and children, Annael stepped after Halgeral into the next chamber. Timber trestles and boards lined the far wall, on which were arranged several long knives and serrated-edged saws, their blades stained dark. The surfaces of the boards were likewise covered with patches of deep red and black – old blood that had soaked into the grain of the wood. Instantly aware of the potential weapons, Annael moved his hand to his holster though he did not draw his pistol.

Halgeral ignored the blades and turned to the sealed door on the right. Above the crackle of the light fittings Annael could hear the hum of a motor close by, and when Halgeral opened the door a wave of chilled air washed past the Dark Angel, his suit monitors informing of a drop in the temperature by several degrees. Moisture clung to the inside of the door and rim as the cold air condensed on the metal. Halgeral stepped into the cool chamber with a smile and an enthusiastic wave.

'Come, see,' she said, beckoning again when Annael hesitated.

Stooping at the doorway, the Space Marine stopped, appalled by what he saw.

The room had been turned into a refrigeration unit by a machine set against the right-hand wall, spilling cold air from a coil of pipe that ran up to the ceiling. There were hooks hanging from the ceiling and on the hooks were carcasses, some intact, others dismembered.

Headless human corpses.

Shelves lined the other walls, stacked high with skulls, some flayed down to the bone, others with flesh and even scraps of hair still attached. Eyeless sockets stared at Annael as he absorbed the contents of the room further, seeing severed limbs, hands and feet piled neatly in one corner, flensed bones arranged in a metal crate opposite.

Disgusted, Annael backed away from the door, turning to find that the room had filled with the Unworthy outcasts behind him. They were looking at him with hopeful expectation, some of them smiling, others averting their gazes.

'The Unworthy are reborn through us, master,' Halgeral said behind him. The full import of her words sank in, deepening the Dark Angel's loathing. 'Is it not as you wish?'

'I am not your master!' Annael snarled as he swung back towards the woman, drawing his pistol. 'I am a brother of the Emperor's Space Marines. This... This is an abomination!'

Shocked, Halgeral fell to her knees, hands clasped to her chest. Tears welled up in her eyes.

'Forgive us, Brother Annael. We only hope to do the Overlord's bidding. If we are in error, please enlighten us. Is not the preparation correct? We will show the rites of rebirth! You will see, everything is as the Overlord commands.'

'I am not an ally of the Overlord,' Annael said grimly. 'This station, your home, has been ruled over by a renegade from the Imperium. He has lied to you.'

'No!' This outburst came from behind Annael and he twisted to see an old man with a long beard and bald pate pushing his way through the crowd of Unworthy. There was madness in his eyes and saliva flew from his lips. 'It is you that are the renegade! You defy the wishes of the Overlord!'

The man was irate, but he did not approach close enough to present a threat, but continued his tirade out of arm's reach. Annael stayed his hand for the moment, though every instinct in him was urging him to lash out, to destroy this coven of vile cannibals.

'The Overlord warned us that others would come, seeking to despoil our paradise. That time is now. We must seek the wisdom of the Overlord.'

There was a chorus of murmurs and calls echoing this sentiment.

'Seek his wisdom.'

'Let us hear his voice!'

'The Overlord commands.'

'Let his wishes be known to us.'

'How?' demanded Annael, stepping forward to seize the man by his tattered coat. 'How do you receive the wisdom of the Overlord?'

All eyes turned to the doorway opposite the refrigeration chamber, the Unworthy parting to form a path for Annael. He released his grip on the man and strode through the haggard crowd into the chamber he had seen earlier that he had assumed to be the food preparation area.

There was a ladder on one wall leading up to a hatchway, granting access to the chambers stacked above. Three stoves were arranged in the centre of the room, a bubbling pot on one of them. Glancing inside, Annael recoiled as he saw several hands bobbing about in the froth, skin peeling away, fat melting into the water. Beyond the stoves was an upturned box on which a ragged cloth had been laid, and upon this were arranged various trinkets and skulls. A shrine of some kind, but it was not the fetishes that drew his attention. Behind the bones and glinting jewellery, propped against the wall, was a bulky box-like device, its casing much tarnished and dented. Seeing a grille and a handset he recognised it immediately as a portable communications device.

'You are not to speak to the Overlord, intruder!' said the angry man, hobbling past Annael to stand between the Space Marine and the grim altar. 'His words are for our ears.'

'Step aside,' growled Annael, taking a stride. The man flinched but did not move from the Dark Angel's path. 'Step aside!'

'You will not defile our temple, outsider.'

'*Outsider…*' The word was whispered behind Annael, growing in volume.

'Enough,' snarled the Dark Angel. He grabbed the man's arm to push him aside, not seeking to injure him. The old man, who wore a necklace of finger bones Annael noticed, perhaps signifying someone of status amongst this disgusting cult, tried to resist. He lashed out at Annael's arm, his weak blows barely registering on his armour's systems.

Out of patience, Annael flung the man to one side. He was a lot lighter than the Space Marine had accounted for and flew across the small chamber, smashing face-first into the wall. He fell to the ground and lay in an unmoving, crumpled heap. Annael turned as the Unworthy surged towards him. He pulled his pistol, expecting attack, but the Unworthy broke around him, converging on their fallen companion.

'Is he dead?' one asked. There were nods from those around the man.

Annael detected no sorrow in the Unworthy as they lifted up the limp form, their aging limbs making hard work though the dead man had been so light to the Space Marine. The people started muttering, a hushed chant surrounding Annael as the Unworthy bore the body out of the room. A few remained, watching the Dark Angel, but they were as lethargic as when he had entered, no aggression in their posture or expressions.

He stepped up to the altar and lifted the vox-unit from the scraps and bangles around it.

'The Emperor provides,' he muttered with satisfaction, seeing that the device was of normal Imperial build, thankful for the gift of Standard Template Construct that meant the unit would work with the systems of his steed. There were several scratches and dents in the casing but a closer examination showed nothing other than cosmetic damage. As their conduit to the Overlord, the Unworthy had taken care of the device as best they could.

Ignoring the Unworthy drifting listlessly around him, Annael left the hab-units, closing the door with a resounding clang behind him. He was still not sure what to do with the degenerates. Though they were clearly corrupt and deranged, it still seemed to Annael to be dishonourable to slay them out of hand. There was also a practical issue. To conserve ammunition he would have to slay them all by hand or knife; a time-consuming activity that would keep him from the main battle. Fortunately, with the discovery of the vox-set he would be able to pass on the decision to one of his superiors.

Returning to *Black Shadow*, Annael placed the comm unit on the saddle of the bike, punched in the disarm code for the self-protection mechanism and opened up a protective plate beneath the display of his mount. Pulling free a cable, he plugged the set into the cogitator of the bike. The comm unit crackled into life.

'Praise to the artifices of the Machine-God,' he muttered, adjusting the channel dial in the middle of the set's front. With the unit to boost the bike's transmission power, he would be able to contact someone. Anyone. Lifting the mouthpiece to the speaker grille of his helm he carefully pressed the transmit button, wary of damaging the fragile device.

'This is Annael. Broadcasting from enemy device. Channel not secured. Send response.'

He waited for several seconds with no reply. Inspecting the unit, the device appeared to be functioning properly. He lifted the handset again but before he could speak there was a burst of static.

'Message received, Brother Annael.' A wave of satisfaction washed over Annael as he recognised the voice of the Grand Master. It was not until he heard Sammael that he realised how tense his isolation had made him. To be in contact with his commander was a relief, though he had been in no physical danger. 'State your position, brother.'

Annael read out the coordinates from the screen of *Black Shadow*. He felt he needed to apprise the Grand Master of what he had found, but was not sure where to begin.

'Grand Master, I have discovered a cadre of Unworthy non-combatants. Zero threat to the attack. They are... They eat their own dead, Grand Master.'

'Acknowledged, Annael. There are no depths to which these depraved souls will not plunge. Their behaviour condemns them, their extermination will be a cleansing.'

'How should I proceed, Grand Master?'

'I have despatched *Lion's Vengeance* to your position. Await the Thunderhawk.'

'And the Unworthy, Grand Master?'

'They are no threat, brother. Unless they hinder your extraction, leave them be. Save your ammunition and strength for harder foes.'

'Understood, Grand Master. How goes the battle?'

'Your timing is perfect, brother. All entries to the central spire have been isolated. Fifth Company squads have encountered unexpected resistance in the form of a tribe of orks. The extermination will commence shortly. You should be with us again in time for the final assault.'

'It is a blessing to hear that, Grand Master.'

'You will receive full debrief on the Unworthy from Brother Malcifer once the station is secured. Until then, do not speak of it with your brothers.'

'As you command, Grand Master.' Annael was not sure why the horrific rites of the Unworthy should be deemed a secret but he was not one to second-guess his superiors. 'I will await extraction.'

'Stand steady, Annael. You will soon be amongst your brothers again. Sammael out.'

The vox-unit clicked and fell to a quiet buzzing. He kept the unit plugged in, shifting it into his lap as he stepped across the saddle of his steed. He was alone again but now it did not seem so burdensome, knowing that he would be reunited with his squadron soon.

It took some time to turn around his bike in the close confines, a fact he had overlooked earlier he was ashamed to realise. Heading back to the main concourse, he waited patiently for the Thunderhawk sent by Sammael, glancing back now and then towards the hab-block of the Unworthy. They had not ventured from their chambers and he had a sickened feeling as he wondered what perverse rites they were performing over the body of the dead man. Despite his earlier misgivings and the order of Sammael, the more he thought about what they had become, the more Annael wanted to wipe out the depraved cannibals. He had used the word abomination and that was just what they were; abhorrent to any right-thinking servant of the Emperor.

The comm sparked into life, breaking through Annael's disturbed thoughts.

'This is Haeral, pilot of *Lion's Vengeance*. I have your position on scope, brother. Do not move from your location. Creation of extraction point commencing.'

The concourse shuddered from a shell impact, the roof caving in a hundred metres ahead of Sammael. Two more battle cannon blasts smashed a large hole through the ferrocrete through which the navigation lamps of the Thunderhawk blazed. The harsh blue of plasma jets lit the concourse as the Thunderhawk descended, stopping with its nose within the breach like a hound sniffing at the bolthole of its prey. With a whine of hydraulics the boarding ramp lowered, turning the rubble beneath to powder.

'Come aboard, brother.'

THE PURIFICATION

Hunkered next to the pock-marked shell of the pump, Telemenus fired again, placing a shot squarely into the chest of an ork pulling itself up a ladder to one of the roofs in front of the Space Marines. The alien fell back to the ground, landing on top of another ork. Pushing itself free of the body, the green-skinned warrior was an easy target for Telemenus's next shot, which turned the side of its skull into a blossom of blood and brains.

The floor of the pumping chamber was piled with the greenskin dead, many of them charred from the flamer; smoke from burning shacks choked the air. In the fire-light, the bestial warriors roared and raged, pressed back for the moment by the weight of fire unleashed by the five Dark Angels. The enemy waited in the shadows, red eyes glinting, perhaps sensing that their foes would soon be vulnerable to another charge.

'Last magazine,' Telemenus told the others as he reloaded.

'The laurels are yours brother,' said Cadael. The ragged

hole in the armour above his elbow leaked blood occasionally as he moved. He had little motion in the wounded arm and rested his bolter against the corner of the pump housing for extra stability as he fired with his other hand. 'You are a credit to the Fifth Company.'

'I have exceeded the mark by four kills already,' replied Telemenus. 'The tally will be higher shortly.'

'We may not see the award given,' said Achamenon. He pulled a grenade from his belt, armed it and tossed the explosive overhand, looping into a shed-like lean-to beside one of the workshops. Two seconds later the corrugated metal exploded outwards, showering body parts of the gretchin that had been cowering within. 'Still, the honour will be yours even in death.'

'One hundred thousand bolter kills is a remarkable achievement, brother,' said Amanael. 'It is a privilege to fight alongside you.'

Telemenus had never really considered the raw number of kills before; it had existed as only an abstract target to achieve. When he had gained the marksman's award at fifty thousand he had thought nothing of it, and now that he had earned the laurels for that award it seemed inconsequential. Despite their dire situation, there was only one thought in Telemenus's head.

'Each fallen foe moves me towards the golden skull for a quarter of a million kills,' he said to the others. 'Only seventeen brothers have ever reached that mark. A shame that I have not enough bolts for every foe we face here.'

'Have mine, brother. You can make better use of them.' said Cadael. He laid his bolter against the pumping machine and drew a magazine from his belt with his good hand, tossing it to his grateful battle-brother. Telemenus caught the magazine easily, slapping it to his thigh, the bonding plate on the side of the magazine sticking to his armour. Cadael left his bolter where it was and drew his knife, the monomolecular-edged blade shining in the light of the flames.

'Gratitude, brother,' said Telemenus. He sighted on a particularly bulky greenskin half-hidden behind a pile of debris from a toppled building. It was pointing at the Dark Angels and bellowing at its companions, no doubt giving the call to attack. Telemenus smiled as he pulled the trigger, sending three bolts into the ork leader's chest and head. It collapsed onto the rubble, howls of shock erupting from the warriors around it. 'Be assured they will not be wasted.'

'They are readying to come again, brothers,' warned Amanael. The sergeant gestured behind the squad, indicating the doorway to the vaporisation vat by which they had entered. 'Fall back on my command and we will make a choke point at the exit.'

The sergeant was not willing to meekly turn tail and raised his bolt pistol as a group of orks came running around a building only a dozen metres ahead, waving cleavers and serrated swords, guns spitting shells and las-bolts.

Telemenus was not sure for a moment what happened next. His sergeant fired into the press of aliens, targeting the closest. A massive detonation hurled orks in every direction, bodies ragged with cuts, limbs hewn away by the unexpected blast. Only after his autosenses returned did Telemenus see the telltale vapour trail of a missile. Following it back to its source, the Dark Angel saw Brother Nethor to the left, the squad's missile launcher on his shoulder. With him was the rest of Squad Amanael, advancing swiftly, their bolters spewing a storm of fire.

'Praise the Lion,' laughed Daellon. 'You took your damned time, brothers!'

'You have been entertaining most of these beasts, but not all,' came the reply from Saphael, the combat squad leader.

The growl of engines sounded across the pumping hall and black shapes darted through the flames: three Ravenwing attack bikes. In the armoured sidecar of each was mounted a heavy weapon, unleashing a furious salvo as the machines skidded into view between two buildings a few dozen metres in front of Telemenus. A beam from a lascannon sliced through an ork as it turned towards this new threat, cutting it in half, while bursts from the heavy bolters of the other two machines stitched bloody holes across more of the greenskins.

'And you have brought us more friends,' said Cadael. 'How thoughtful of you to share the glory.'

'The Grand Master insisted his company lent their aid,' Saphael told them as he and the other combat squad ran across the hall to rejoin their battle-brothers. The orks had been thrown into disarray by the unexpected attack and were caught between the Fifth Company squad and the attack bikes, ineffectually firing at both.

Halted again, Nethor fired another missile, the fragmentation warhead scything down three more orks as they broke into a loping run towards the squad. Telemenus sent a bolt into one of the greenskins as it tried to push itself up despite missing a leg. He turned to Nethor who was now standing to his left, his stance braced, firing on full automatic.

'A spare magazine, brother?' Telemenus said as he loaded the one given to him by Cadael. 'I am running a little short.'

'I am sure you are, brother,' replied Nemean. 'You have earned enough honour today, it is time you allowed the rest of us a fair attempt at the foe.'

'We will resupply when we link up with the rest of the

company,' Amanael assured them as Telemenus emptied the magazine into the remaining orks.

There were still thirty or forty orks still alive, and they were converging on the squad from ahead and to the right, snarling and bellowing. The attack bikes circled around to the left, preparing for another drive-past.

'I would prefer to defend myself than rely on the charity of others,' Telemenus complained, ejecting his spent magazine.

'That is why we have knives, brother,' said Cadael, holding up his blade. 'There is yet time for you to start earning the swordsman's award, yes?'

Hooking his bolter on his hip, Telemenus drew his knife and looked at it. In two hundred and twenty-three years since becoming a full battle-brother he had killed only four hundred and seven foes with it, compared to the immense tally of his bolter. Even in the press of melee he preferred his bolter, and many were the times that a point-blank shot had served him better than fifty centimetres of razor-sharp plasteel.

Telemenus looked at the orks, now barely twenty metres away, charging at full-speed despite the fire of his squad-brothers. Many of the aliens toppled and tumbled from the fusillade, and though sensing defeat the enemy struck with venomous spite, determined to exact some kind of payment for their fallen. The blade felt light compared to his bolter, flimsy and weak. It was no weapon for a true warrior, more useful for cutting into rations containers and prying open ammunition crates.

'Needs must when the Lion turns a blind eye,' he muttered to himself, launching himself at the orks as they closed with the squad. Around him the others met the attack with blade and bolter too.

With his right arm Telemenus batted aside a pistol shoved into his face, driving the point of the knife in his left hand through the eye of the ork. Amazingly, the creature did not fall, but wrenched its head back, pulling free of the blade with its eyeball still attached to the knife. A cacophony of impacts rang in the Space Marine's ears as the alien fired, a cloud of metal pellets scattering from Telemenus's helm, one of them ricocheting back into the open mouth of the beast, felling it as blood fountained from the top of its scalp.

There was no time to process the unlikely demise of the ork as another smashed headlong into Telemenus, trying to barrel him from his feet. His armour locked at the first moment of impact and the charging alien slammed into him with the same effect as running into a solid wall, its head bouncing from the Space Marine's midriff. Telemenus drove his dagger into its spine as it tried to stand, separating the vertebrae with a twist. Its legs paralysed, the ork collapsed while Telemenus pulled his knife free. With a sneer of distaste the Dark Angel stamped on the wounded alien's head, crushing it to a pulp beneath the tread of his boot.

While his squad-brothers spat battle-cries and sang litanies, Telemenus fought in silence, as collected and calm as if he were on a firing range. He saw the gleam of a powered axe just in time to dodge aside from the sweeping blade, cognisant of the danger posed by such a weapon, which would make a mockery of his armour if it struck. He lashed out with a fist, breaking the ork's jaw and cracking teeth. As thick blood trickled from its lips, the ork seemed to laugh; a laugh that was cut short by Telemenus's knife slashing across its throat.

'Hand-to-hand is so... barbaric,' Telemenus commented to the others as a maul smashed across his left pauldron, showering splinters of ceramite. He grabbed the handle of the weapon as the ork tried again, aiming for his face. With a twist of his arm the Dark Angel pulled the club from the alien's grip. The creature lunged forwards to regain its weapon, but was met by Telemenus's swing, the jagged head of the maul cracking open the side of the creature's skull. He let the bloodied weapon fall from his grasp onto the dead ork's body and stepped forward to confront the next foe. 'It is so brutal and wild.'

The roaring of Amanael's chainsword sounded to the Dark Angel's right, a second before the sergeant's weapon lopped the head from an ork ahead of Telemenus. Realising there were no more foes in front, the two of them turned, only to find that the orks were all dead. Amongst the heap of bodies lay Cadael, his armour awash with alien blood, his armour scored and cracked in dozens of places. Telemenus feared the worst and stepped forward, speaking his battle-brother's name. The toppled Space Marine pushed aside a corpse and sat up, shaking his head.

'You were supposed to watch my back, brother,' Cadael said as he offered up his good arm to be hauled to his feet. Telemenus assisted him and bowed his head in shame.

'Apologies, brother, I became distracted,' he said.

'You shall receive fresh instruction in squad combat doctrine when we return to the strike cruiser,' said Amanael. 'You have grown so fond of your bolter you have forgotten the lessons of the mêlée. It is fortunate that Brother Cadael has not suffered further injury.'

'Had Brother Nemeon furnished me with the ammunition I requested it would not have been an issue,' replied Telemenus. 'I would have been better placed to defend my brother if armed properly.'

'No harm suffered,' said Cadael, laying his hand on the arm of Telemenus. 'Your apology is accepted.'

'No.' Amanael's sharp word stung like a whip to Telemenus's pride. 'You are becoming insular and selfish,

Telemenus. Apology is not enough. You risk contempt of your brothers with this behaviour. You will make further amends as I deem required.'

'There is no contempt, brother-sergeant, I assure you,' Telemenus argued. 'I was distracted, that is all.'

'Your deeds speak differently to your words,' Amanael said, turning away. The Ravenwing attack bikes were advancing slowly towards the squad, moving between the piles of orkish casualties, the riders putting rounds from their bolt pistols into any alien that still moved. 'Offer no further argument, my judgement has been made. Do not embarrass us in front of the Second Company.'

'I submit to your will, brother-sergeant,' said Telemenus, lowering to one knee in deference to his superior.

'Good.' Amanael beckoned to Nemeon with a finger. 'Brother, give Telemenus a spare magazine, if you have one.'

Still shamed, Telemenus mumbled his thanks as Nemeon proffered the ammunition. He stood up, sheathed his knife and loaded his bolter, feeling better the moment the magazine slid into place.

'Sergeant Seraphiel is mustering the company grid-north,' said Saphael, pointing past the smouldering ruins of the ork settlement. 'About three hundred metres. We should move.'

'Good,' said Amanael. 'Take lead, brother. Apollon, accompany Brother Cadael until we can render him into the care of the Apothecary.'

'I can still fight, brother-sergeant!' protested Cadael as Saphael led the squad into the ruins.

'Only just,' replied the sergeant. 'If Gideon cannot improve the mobility in your arm you will return to the rearguard at the main breach.'

'Yes, brother-sergeant,' Cadael said with a heavy sigh. 'As you command.'

'I want to hear no more complaint or bickering,' Amanael said. 'We still have a stern test to face. These 'Divine' will not be as easy to defeat as the Unworthy, I am sure. We must keep our wits sharp and our weapons ready.'

The words were spoken to the whole squad but Telemenus felt them directed at him in particular.

'Yes, brother-sergeant,' he chorused with the others as the squad advanced into the fire and smoke.

STRANGE FORCES

Following behind Sammael, as the Grand Master and his command squad followed the circular transitway that ran around Port Imperial's central tower, Epistolary Harahel felt uneasy. The encounters with the cannibal cults had left him suspicious of some deeper motive behind the existence of the Unworthy. He had not spoken of the matter with Sammael or Malcifer but he was sure that they each harboured similar disconcerting thoughts.

He had mind-scanned a few of the Unworthy and found nothing more sinister than misguided teachings of cannibalistic resurrectionism. They had only ever eaten their own dead in the belief that the souls of the deceased would be reborn again in future generations. It was part of the Overlord's mechanism to control the renegades, making them believe they were a favoured people, cutting off contact with outsiders. It was an effective measure to instil fervent loyalty and fanatical devotion in the Unworthy, and having achieved higher status those who were selected to become Divine owed their success to the patronage of the Overlord.

The squad passed over an enclosed bridge, the tunnels of the rail system beneath. Through crystalflex panels in the ceiling Harahel could see the spire stretching up towards the stars, its surface pinpricked by windows, their white light harsh and sharp in the vacuum outside the station. Above the tower flickered three blue stars; the plasma engines of the *Implacable Justice* seen against the darkness as the strike cruiser orbited above Port Imperial.

In many of the spire's arching windows there were reflected flames from the starships' bombardment, the battery magazines and power housings ablaze while oxygen from the breaches fuelled fires that danced as shimmers in the distant windows. Amongst the ruin of the rest of the star fort, the central spire rose untouched; Sammael had not wished risking the death of the Overlord by attacking the tower directly. It was the starlight and tower lights and firelight that illuminated the transitway with rectangles of shifting brightness, the black-armoured command squad passing in and out of the darkness as they raced along the road. The metronomic changes between light and dark were almost hypnotic.

As the tunnelway dipped back towards the foundation plate of the station Harahel felt something at the edge of his perception. His instincts were telling him something was amiss and he pulled over his bike so that he could concentrate. Noticing this manoeuvre, Sammael brought the squad to a halt a short way ahead and over the comm made inquiries about the nature of the delay. Harahel said nothing but held up a hand to signal for the interruptions to cease.

He had come to a stop in one of the patches of light

from the overhead windows. Dismounting, the Epistolary looked up at the spear-thrust of the spire and then
closed his eyes, picturing the tower in his mind. He
allowed his othersense to strengthen, his mind flowing
from the confines of his head, his soul detaching from
its mortal vessel to seek the truth.

Blue sparks flared along the cables of the Librarian's
psychic hood and danced across the lenses of his helm.
He felt the warp opening up like a gulf beneath him,
the ground shifting to a maelstrom of energy under his
feet. Like quicksand sucking him down, Harahel felt the
warp drawing him in, trying to drown him. It was only a
momentary sensation and one that he had been trained
long ago to dismiss. The whirling gulf narrowed as Harahel exerted his will, drawing together the edges of the
ravine that sought to topple him into the immaterium.
Leaving only the tiniest cracks in his mind, through
which the power of the warp could pass into real space,
the Epistolary focused on the tower.

He could feel dozens, scores of minds. There were two
hundred and thirty-five, all of them adult humans, but
touched by something else. He did not want to delve
too deeply for the moment, but widened the crack into
the warp a little more to allow a greater flow of energy
into his mind. With this he was able to reach out further,
sensing the gestalt entity of the Divine.

All thought, all emotion, all life made ripples in the
warp. The lives and thoughts of a normal human were
brief flickers that barely registered. The minds of psykers
were like candle flames or bright bonfires depending
upon their power. Where there was similarity of purpose, the thoughts gathered, like attracting like. The
Dark Angels' purpose was like an iron curtain across
the warp, forged from faith and courage. It was a near-
impenetrable barrier. For the Unworthy, it had been

pools of despair, surrounded by a miasma of bleakness yet each of them had also lit the warp with a flickering spark of hope. The after-images of the orks' psyche was dimming, a roaring green wave that had pulsed and thrashed during the battle and was now subsiding.

From the tower, from the minds of the fighters within, Harahel sensed very little. There was a background buzz of blood and war, but that was only to be expected from a cadre of pirates and murderers. The Epistolary could not quite identify the binding sensation of the Divine, too few perhaps or maybe the Overlord had taught them techniques for shielding themselves from psychic attack; one of the Fallen could well know such tricks. Certainly the enemy were masked in some part by their false faith in the Overlord, shielding them from the warp as the pure faith of the Space Marines guarded their minds.

Seeking more power Harahel opened up the breach into the warp just a little further still, though nowhere near the boundary of his ability to tap into its energy. Even so, he felt nauseous, a sensation he had not felt for many years. His gene-seed-modified organs did not sicken easily and nor was his physiologically-improved body prone to dizziness or vomiting. Yet on touching the power of the warp and the minds of the Divine, Harahel felt something utterly corrupt. The feel of it was slick on his skin and cloying in his nostrils, stinging his eyes and making his ears ring.

He choked, coughing just once, before recovering. Even this momentary lapse had not gone unnoticed by Sammael.

'Brother, what is it?' the Grand Master asked. 'Is it psychic attack?'

'Worse,' Harahel replied over the command channel, his words for Sammael and Malcifer. He coughed again, trying to clear a lump in his throat that he knew was only in his mind. 'There is something more to the enemy than we know.'

'And of the Overlord?' asked Malcifer, turning his bike around and riding back to the Librarian. 'Do you detect the Overlord?'

'Alas, no, Brother-Chaplain,' Harahel replied with a shake of the head. Malcifer growled but the Librarian sought to dampen the Chaplain's frustration. 'It is not conclusive. The effect of the Divine forced me to break the scan before I was able to register on individual minds. It may be that we are dealing with one of the Fallen Librarians.'

This news was greeted with silence and Harahel knew well why it was such a cause for concern. All Fallen were corrupt, their treachery confirmed as such. Some had descended further than others, though, and there were some Fallen who gratefully accepted the judgement and mercy of the Chapter. Many of the Fallen were simply renegades, but also many of them had turned to the worship of the Dark Powers of Chaos. So far, every Fallen who had been a psyker was in the latter category.

According to the records of the Librarium, there had been twenty-eight psykers on Caliban when the Lion had returned from fighting Horus, and of those three were accounted for in the fighting, which left twenty-five psykers of varying skill, power and discipline. The Chapter had found seventeen in the last ten thousand years and Harahel considered it a good omen that they may have discovered another. Despite this, apprehending the Overlord would be dangerous. Combining the discipline of a Space Marine Librarian – and Harahel had no idea of the rank the Overlord had attained before turning on the primarch – and the raw power of the Chaos sorcerer, the Fallen Librarian would not allow himself to be taken meekly.

'Are you sure?' asked Sammael.

'Of course not, brother,' said the Librarian. 'Nothing we know at the moment is for sure. We have still to prove beyond doubt that the Fallen are still here, or were ever here. With that borne in mind, the conditioning of the Unworthy, the psychic barrier protecting the Divine, both point to the interference of a psyker. Whether present or not, I could only say if I press further with my scans.'

'Is that hazardous?' asked Malcifer. 'What threat does this psyker pose if you do so?'

'I am unwilling to risk a direct psychic confrontation at this time,' Harahel told them. 'For all that we can say, the Divine are also psykers, and it is a measure of talent that separates them from the Unworthy. It would be prideful to assume that my mind is strong enough to resist or defeat a foe that has access to the raw power of... of the Empyrean Dwellers to draw upon. Against such energy my psychic hood might prove insufficient defence.'

'What do you suggest we do?' asked Sammael. 'Should I alter the attack plan?'

'Not for the moment, Grand Master,' said Harahel. 'We shall be in the vanguard of the attack and so I will be on hand to deliver a fresher verdict once we have encountered the foe directly. You may wish to issue warning to the rest of the force, to be aware of possible psychic manipulation or attack.'

'Better to be prepared than sorrowful,' agreed Sammael. 'Is there any particular reason why we should remain at this place?'

Harahel looked around but neither saw nor felt anything remarkable about the stretch of bridge they were on.

'No, it is simply where we were when I felt the disturbance,' said the Librarian.

'What disturbance?' said Malcifer. 'A warp-related event?'

'No fear of a breach,' Harahel assured the Chaplain, realising that Malcifer was skirting around the subject of daemonic intrusion. 'There is nothing here to suggest the veil is any weaker. If the Overlord is a pawn of the Dark Powers he has not entreated them to send otherworldly minions at his behest. I think it is simply that the inner tower has wards placed upon it, to guard against psychic attack. It is dampening my powers and it was this effect that I sensed as we approached closer.'

'What could have such an effect at this range?' said Sammael. 'It is a powerful psyker that can suppress his abilities nearly half a kilometre distant. The tower itself would take immense reserves of psychic energy to shield.

'When we approached, you noted that Port Imperial's void shields were inoperative, correct?'

'Yes, there should be several banks of void shields protecting a star fort such as this. None were activated in defence of the station.'

'An intriguing possibility suggests itself,' said Harahel as he stepped across his bike. He and Malcifer rejoined the others and Sammael signalled for the squad to continue towards their rendezvous with other elements of the Ravenwing force. 'It is highly speculative, though. I should not waste time with idle chatter. We should concentrate on the execution of the battle plan.'

'Be brief, brother, and no distraction will be incurred,' said Sammael. 'Tell us what intrigues you.'

'Often when a star fort such as this is moved from system to system, it must be evacuated – it has no Geller fields to protect the populace while in the warp. Specialist teams from the Navigator houses and the scholastica psykana must be brought in to guide the fort through the warp whilst protected by battle psykers. Void shields utilise warp energy to create a defensive barrier, in effect an omni-directional warp portal that displaces incoming matter and energy.'

Harahel stopped, realising he was rambling slightly, telling his companions what they already knew. He focused on the point of his explanation.

'The sensation I felt was not dissimilar to the warp-suppression effect of a Geller field. The Overlord could possibly have used the warp cores of the void shields to create a Geller-type effect.'

'That seems to be a lot of effort expended to counter the rare eventuality that Port Imperial would be discovered and that it would come under psychic attack,' said Malcifer.

'You misinterpret my hypothesis, Brother-Chaplain,' said Harahel. There were sealed doors ahead and the squadron slowed. In less than a minute they would be back with other members of the company and the Librarian's speculation would have to end. 'The Overlord could be preparing to move Port Imperial through the warp.'

'A roving battlestation?' said Sammael, not quite masking his incredulity.

'A one-way journey, by my estimation. The field encloses only the province of the Divine, not the rest of the station. The areas inhabited by the Unworthy would be left open to the raw element of the warp. Perhaps that is even the Overlord's intent, to smooth passage with his infernal masters with a sacrifice of his people?'

'Disturbing,' said Sammael. 'Speak no more of this idea for the moment. We shall discuss it further when the spire has been won.'

'As you command, Grand Master,' said Harahel,

bringing his bike to a stop with the others while Daedis accessed the door controls.

The doors hissed open, revealing a plaza-like area at the conjunction of several corridors. The command squadron moved forwards to join the rest of the Ravenwing force at the area designated Assault Zone Alpha. Several Land Speeders floated close by, two attack bikes and two bike squadrons with them. To the left was a single passageway that gently rose up towards the central spire. It was one of half a dozen entrances that Sammael had identified as routes of attack. The Ravenwing and Fifth Company would assault together, the bikes and Land Speeders securing the main access and transit routes while the Fifth Company cleared the tower level-by-level.

Checking the chronometer display of his bike, Harahel saw there were forty-five seconds until the attack began. Letting just a chink open between his mind and the warp, he surveyed the tower beyond the gate at the end of the passage. He felt nothing; no life at all. Checking the digital display, he saw that the energy reading from his bike's sensors confirmed his psychic scan. There were no enemies directly guarding the doorway.

'The portal is undefended,' he said to Sammael, surprised.

'I know, and I like it not,' replied the Grand Master. 'Scans from the *Implacable Justice* place them at three main areas in the upper levels of the spire. We can expect the road ahead to have been prepared for us.' The vox-bead in Harahel's ear hissed as the Grand Master changed to the company-wide channel.

'The enemy have been expecting us for some time and have made suitable welcome, I am sure,' Sammael told his warriors. 'So far we have encountered dregs of this rebel force. The Divine who hold the central spire may be tougher opposition but they are no match for the Dark Angels. The Emperor is on our side and with the righteousness of our cause to propel us we shall overcome all foes. This cohort forms the last defence of Port Imperial and when they are vanquished victory will be ours. Strike hard, strike swift, strike sure. For the Emperor! Praise the Lion!'

'Praise the Lion,' whispered Harahel, pulling his force axe free. Its blade sprang into crackling life as he eased part of his psychic power through the crystalline matrix embedded in the weapon. 'Praise the Lion, indeed.'

THE DIVINE

The interior of the central tower was in the same state of disrepair as the rest of the star fort, a fact that surprised Telemenus. The squad, minus Cadael who had been deemed unfit for battle by Apothecary Gideon, had pushed into the spire with the other squads of the Fifth Company, advancing into a cordon set up by the swift-moving attack of the Ravenwing. Establishing a perimeter at the major transport hub at the heart of the tower, the Ravenwing had pushed up several levels via the system of conveyors and goods elevators that reached two-thirds of the way to the summit of the tower.

As expected, the foe offered no initial resistance and while several squads of the Fifth had been allocated to provide rearguard to the advancing forces, Squad Amanael was at the forefront of the Dark Angels' thrust. They currently occupied a split-level apartment complex in a subsidiary tower to grid-northwest of the main spire. Such furnishings as they discovered were mouldering, the wood of couches and tables rotted through, the painted plaster on the walls crumbling.

Having established their position, only a few hundred metres from a skybridge that linked the central tower to an offshoot complex believed to be the enemy command base, the squad were waiting for the Ravenwing to report back from their scouting missions.

Standing in a one of the living areas, through a window Telemenus could see the enemy-held complex, like a spar across a mast extending several hundred metres to either side of the tower, each end of the spar tipped by a hexagonal structure. He turned to the others as they cleared out the other rooms of the apartment.

'Why would the warrior elite live in the same squalor as the Unworthy?' he asked, of no one in particular. He prodded a dilapidated chair with the toe of his boot, causing it to collapse into a pile of splinters and dust. 'Surely the aspiration to the status of Divine is based upon a desire for superior accommodation, authority and privileges?'

'Do you seek such things, brother?' replied Amanael. 'Are the trappings of status your goal when you strive for the Chapter?'

'Of course not, brother-sergeant,' Telemenus replied quickly, still conscious of the chastisement Amanael had meted out after the confrontation with the orks. 'We are different. We are bonded together by brotherhood and service to the Emperor. Honour is the reward of dutiful service. You cannot compare this rabble with the Chapter, surely?'

'Many different people fight for many different reasons,' said Amanael. He nodded to Daellon to investigate a stairwell at the far side of the living space. The sweep was purely down to doctrine; no signal registered on the auspex within three hundred metres of their current position. 'Some fight for anger, for temporal gain or in a bid for power. Others are driven by survival, love and duty. Although our foes exhibit barbaric practices and have become piratical parasites it is an error to assume that they desire only physical reward. The names themselves, the Unworthy and the Divine, indicate that this particular nest of pirates has a spiritual core, however flawed it may be.'

'So the Unworthy aspire to become Divine out of a sense of higher purpose? If that is the case, why would they turn from the Emperor in the first place?'

'You are too simplistic sometimes, brother,' said Daellon, returning from his foray into the lower level. 'The Emperor alone knows how long this station has been renegade. The collapse of fundamental systems and the divergent society of the renegades suggest it is some considerable time, several generations. They did not become the Unworthy overnight.'

'Why does this occupy you?' asked Amanael. 'The corrupt nature of our foes is evident, why do you seek to understand their motives further?'

'Idle curiosity, brother-sergeant.'

'No curiosity is idle,' Amanael said, motioning for the other two Space Marines to follow as he headed back towards the apartment entranceway. He led them out onto the balconied landing overlooking the other apartments, the rest of the squad assembling in the concourse below. 'Do not allow the ways of the Ravenwing to colour your thoughts, Telemenus. One needs to know only enough about the foe to defeat them. Excessive interest in external cultures breeds doubt, and doubt brings dereliction of duty.'

'As you say, brother-sergeant.' Telemenus strode down the ramp leading to the others, walking beside his sergeant. 'Perhaps idle was the wrong word. I confess that since Piscina I have become vexed by the nature of treachery. If we are to guard against the forces of rebellion, and to see the seed of it in others, we must understand it. Do you not agree, brother-sergeant?'

'A would-be Grand Master,' said Amanael, 'who seeks greater understanding of the enemy. It is not our place nor our burden to think on such matters. Should you be honoured enough to be elevated to a position of command no doubt you will be occupied by these wider considerations. For the moment, be content that we act against the renegade and the heretic without mercy. It is not fit to wonder why they are misguided, nor is it your duty to seek empathy with them.'

Though he was not satisfied with this response, Telemenus knew better than to press the point further or ask more questions. He found it remarkable that Amanael, who had shown himself to be an insightful and gifted warrior and leader, could care so little about the motivations of their enemy.

A thought occurred to Telemenus as the squad departed the complex, heading back to the main through-channel that ran crosswise through the whole width of the tower. Perhaps it was Amanael's dedication and focus that made him such a good candidate for leadership. A warrior with his honours and history should have been promoted to the First Company half a century earlier, but Amanael steadfastly remained a sergeant in the Fifth and seemed not only content but proud of that fact. He revelled in his strict adherence to the Chapter codes, and although he always gave fair hearing to the opinions of the battle-brothers, Amanael also countenanced no lack of discipline or dispute.

'Hold position,' ordered the sergeant as they headed grid-north along the broad corridor. They waited for a short while before Amanael spoke again. 'We have fresh orders, brothers.'

The enemy headquarters could only be reached by securing the spar on which it was built. Scanner and Ravenwing reports had determined that the Divine were holding their positions at the entrances to the spar and fierce resistance was expected. The task of the Fifth Company was to drive a gap through the defenders, allowing the Ravenwing to pass through the enemy lines and attack from the rear. Amanael's squad were the closest to the grid-east entrance and they set off as other squads mustered for the attack.

Passing along connecting walkways and corridors, cutting through deserted rooms that seemed as abandoned as the rest of the station, the squad made swift progress. Two hundred metres from their objective Apollon called their attention to the readings on his auspex.

'Signals, in the chamber at the end of the corridor, on the right,' he warned. 'Unknown but significant number.'

'Full attack,' said Amanael.

'Should we not wait for the others?' suggested Nemeon. 'Attack in force?'

'We are nine warriors of the Adeptus Astartes, what manner of foe do you think we face?' asked the sergeant. 'Form up for attack. Achamenon and Telemenus take lead.'

Each side of the corridor was lined with wide archways, through which Telemenus could see large halls. He assumed that once they had perhaps been meeting chambers of the station's elite. He could see the ragged remains of banners and tapestries on the walls, their designs long-faded and obscured with decades of grime. Fifty metres ahead the corridor opened out into the broad concourse of a transportation terminal, covered with a large dome of crystalflex and plasteel. The tiled floor was heavily cracked, the panes of glass so smeared with a patina of filth that nothing could be seen of the stars beyond. Lampposts flickered and crackled, bathing the concourse in fitful patches of yellow light.

There were remnants of counters and desks spread across the open area and more faded banners hung from chains above, while others lay draped over what remained of the furnishings, slashed and burned. Above, a gallery stretched three-quarters of the way around the edge of the chamber and on the left Telemenus could see rows of lifeless cogitator consoles through a line of arched windows.

With a gesture, Apollon indicated a set of double-doors a dozen metres along the wall to the right. Telemenus and Achamenon took up position on either side of the entrance while the rest of the squad dispersed across the concourse, taking up positions to cover the other doorways and the balcony.

Telemenus inspected the doors. Like the rest of the wood on the station, they were eaten through by insects and rot, and slicked with moss. Despite their size, they seemed to be little obstacle to entry.

'After you, brother,' he said, motioning with his bolter to Achamenon.

The other Space Marine nodded and stepped squarely in front of the portal. With a single well-placed kicked he smashed through the wood, the doors tumbling from rusted hinges.

Half a second later an explosion engulfed Achamenon with a hail of red-hot shrapnel. The Dark Angel was thrown back by the blast, clattering to the tiled floor. Molten metal and jagged shards studded his armour from waist to helm, the ceramite outer casing of his plastron shorn away by the force of the explosion to expose inner fibre bundles and reinforced cabling.

Telemenus reacted immediately, stepping between his wounded battle-brother and the doorway, bolter ready, providing physical cover while one of the others attended to Achamenon.

The room beyond was large, bigger than even the pumping chamber where the orks had made their lair. It was a cathedral of some sort, its high-vaulted ceiling thirty metres above Telemenus's head. Rows of decaying pews stretched for a hundred metres, the floor covered with carpet that had once been red, the colour showing through in patches amongst a slick of dirt. The detonation of the trap had thrown up a huge cloud of dust and stirred hundreds of flies and beetles, which flitted back and forth in the dim red light of fixtures hanging like censers from the ceiling.

There was a shallow crater in the floor just behind the doorway and the nearest benches and fittings had been torn apart by the blast, a ring of black spread across the ground. Pieces of debris littered the doorway.

Beyond the main floor, the hall was raised up to a dais bordered by a rail of rusted ironwork. It was from here that the ministers of the Ecclesiarch would have held forth with their sermons and the remains of a stone altar – deliberately toppled and broken – dominated the centre of the raised area.

It was also from here, and on walkways lining the hall to the left and right, that the Divine opened fire.

In the moment before the hail of fire engulfed him, Telemenus glimpsed armoured warriors. They did not wear suits of power armour, but the figures he saw wore some form of exo-skeletal harnesses fitted with roughly cut metal plates. Their heads were encased with helms that hid their faces behind gold-mirrored visors. Fortunately for him, their weapons were no better than those of the Unworthy and his armour weathered the storm of fire for half a second before he retreated out of the enemy line of fire.

'Twenty-five, in superior firing positions,' he reported as he grabbed the arm of Achamenon and dragged him away from the door, Daellon and Nemeon sprinting past to secure either side of the breached door. 'Crude armour, basic weapons.'

The others in the squad opened fire as more of the enemy poured onto the gallery overlooking the concourse, their fire falling upon the Dark Angels from two directions. Telemenus raked the edge of the balcony opposite, forcing back the figures that appeared there.

'Brother, respond,' snapped Amanael, kneeling beside Achamenon.

Telemenus looked at the fallen Space Marine, knowing that what he saw was not encouraging. Blood pumped from several deep wounds at Achemenon's groin and stomach. The explosive must have had some form of shaped charge to punch through the armour, and the mangle of cables and flesh that had once been Achemenon's abdomen had been melted through as if hit by a plasma bolt.

As Daellon and Nemeon unleashed their bolters from the doorway into the shrine room, Telemenus looked between them into the temple-hall. With more time to study the environment, he noticed the coil of wires and suspicious-looking boxes threaded around the lines of pews; more charges. He turned back to Amanael, who was attempting to reach Apothecary Gideon on the comm, still knelt beside Achamenon.

'Brother-sergeant, our foes have made the whole area a deathtrap,' he said. 'You must warn the rest of the force.'

'I have already informed the Grand Master,' replied the sergeant, standing up. 'Daellon, see if the flamer can deal with some of the devices. Telemenus, ready frag grenades.'

Doing as he was ordered, Telemenus moved back from the door just as Daellon stepped out. The fire of the Divine greeted the Dark Angel but he was unde-terred, firing a three-second burst from the flamer before retreating. Detonations rocked the hall, sending a cloud of dust and wooden shards billowing through the open door.

'The damned fools placed the charges too close together,' said Daellon as more charges were set off by the detonations, cascading along the hall with a noise like a long roll of thunder.

'Attack!' snarled Amanael. His chainsword growled into motion as he stepped towards the door. 'Full attack!'

Apollon and Nemeon stood back-to-back near the centre of the concourse, firing up at the gallery. Under the cover of their fire, the rest of the squad assembled by the door. Daellon stepped aside to allow Nethor to take up his position. The Dark Angel angled his missile launcher through the doorway and fired. A moment later, Telemenus charged into the shrine on the heels of Amanael, sprinting to clear the door for the others. The missile exploded on the altar stage, hurling fragmented marble and shrapnel through the Divine lurking there.

The hall was lined with ferrocrete columns broad enough to provide shelter even for a Space Marine. Tele-menus headed for the closest as bullets whistled past, crashing into the pillar shoulder-first as he skidded to a halt.

Saphael and Menthius advanced more boldly, firing with the bolters as they strode to the left, picking out targets on the gallery above. The flare of their bolts lit the gloom, the spark of detonations flashing along the balustrade sheltering the enemy. Amanael stood just inside the door, snapping off shots with his bolt pistol, oblivious to the fire of the foe.

'Reward their defiance with death,' the sergeant told his squad, waving them on with his chainsword. 'Swiftly, brothers.'

Telemenus stepped out from behind the column and sighted on the Divine taking cover on the altar dais. Seeing them more clearly now, beneath their crude armour they wore much the same outfits as the other pirates. He realised that the harnesses were modified cargo-haulage suits, used by labourers for loading and unloading stores. The helms were also from the station's original personnel, intended for use outside the star fort to prevent blindness from star glare.

His bolt smashed through the golden visor of an enemy warrior, sending the Divine reeling back. From a raised pulpit at the right-hand end of the dais, two more manned a tripod-mounted heavy bolter. Explosive rounds shrieked into the pillar next to Telemenus as the Space Marine adjusted his aim towards this new threat. One of the heavy bolter's rounds hit him in the arm as he opened fire, causing his burst of fire to pass harmlessly over the heads of the Divine.

Reassessing his position, Telemenus moved back behind the column and emerged from the other side, sending a flurry of bolts into the heavy weapon position. The wooden rail of the pulpit turned to splinters and the Divine were cut down, the heavy bolter toppling over as one of them slumped across it, missing an arm.

A plasma bolt seared across the cathedral from the gallery above Telemenus. He watched it smash into the smouldering remains of the pew beside Menthius. The Dark Angel spun on his heel and returned fire, sending a flash of bolts over Telemenus's head.

'More enemies, coming from grid-west,' Apollon reported from back on the concourse.

'Brother Seraphiel, how long until you reach our position?' Amanael asked over the comm. The sergeant broke into a run, heading down the aisle between the burning pews towards the altar. 'Heavy resistance encountered.'

'Disengage and push through to the accessway,' came the reply. 'Squads arriving at your position in three minutes, they will provide rearguard.'

'Acknowledged, brother-sergeant,' said Amanael. Through a hail of enemy fire the sergeant leapt up the steps to the dais with one bound. His chainsword swept left and right, bolt pistol blazing in his other hand as he charged into the Divine.

'Plasma gunner still alive,' warned Menthius. 'Right above you, Telemenus.'

Glancing up, Telemenus readied a frag grenade.

'Watch this,' he said, stepping out from under the balcony. He tossed up the grenade, bouncing it from a column so that it arced easily over the rail of the gallery. Even before it detonated, he unleashed a fusillade of bolts through the wooden panelling lining the gallery, and a moment later the frag grenade exploded, sending bodies and debris tumbling around Telemenus.

One of the Divine crashed to the floor just in front of Telemenus. The enemy fighter wore a padded jerkin beneath his armoured exoskeleton, revealing heavily muscled arms pocked with scars, blisters and lesions on pale skin. The man stank of decay and filth, his clothes soiled, the struts of the exoskeleton showing spots of rust.

Disgusted, Telemenus turned away, focusing on Sergeant Amanael as he chopped his way along the altar platform. A warrior behind the sergeant, armour rent open by Amanael's chainsword, pushed himself back to his feet despite the horrendous gash across his chest. Telemenus fired a single bolt, hitting the man between the shoulder blades as he made a lunge for the sergeant, knocking the warrior down again.

The wheeze of actuators caused Telemenus to look back. The Divine behind him surged from the ground and slammed into the Dark Angel, the force of the impact forcing Telemenus back a step. Arms powered by the exoskeleton wrapped around the Space Marine in a crushing bear hug, lighting up Telemenus's visual display with a flurry of pressure warning icons. His bolter pinned beside him, Telemenus smashed his free arm onto the top of the Divine's helmeted head, cracking open the helm. Still the warrior did not release his grip, Telemenus's armour creaking under the strain; in seconds something would give way.

Reaching over the shoulder of his assailant, Telemenus drove his gauntleted fingers down into the power plant strapped across the warriors' back. The casing buckled and split and Telemenus closed his fingers and pulled, ripping out the mangled remains of the motor. Fuel ignited, swathing both fighters in a bloom of fire.

Though the inward pressure had stopped, the Divine's power frame was locked in position, fastened to Telemenus like a limpet. Two more enemies dropped over the balcony to Telemenus's left, the curved blades in their hands gleaming. Unable to move, Telemenus would be cut apart by the power swords.

Boosting as much power as possible to the muscle bundles of his armour, Telemenus seized hold of the Divine and lifted. His vision faded as energy was shunted from his autosenses, giving him just enough strength to rip the man's left arm away, flesh and exoskeleton together. The augmented man moaned as blood poured from his ravaged shoulder, a sound more of pleasure than pain.

Telemenus pivoted, twisting at the hips to hurl the Divine into his two companions, impeding their advance. In the moment this bought him, Telemenus raised his bolter and fired on full automatic, shredding the two warriors in a hail of small explosions.

'These bastards do not die easily,' said Daellon, coming up beside Telemenus. The other Dark Angel's flamer spat fire up into the gallery, promethium sticking to the balustrade and walls. 'Time to fall back.'

Telemenus reloaded and backed towards the doorway. The rest of the squad were pulling back, the fire of the Divine following Amanael as he jumped down from the altar dais and ran to rejoin the others.

'We must secure the entrance to the accessway,' said the sergeant, turning to snap off several shots from his pistol at the Divine still firing from the gallery to the left. 'Apollon, Nemeon, push forward.'

The squad emerged onto the concourse in quick succession, moving away from the door swiftly. Telemenus noticed that Achamenon had not moved from where he had been left. He glanced at Amanael, but the sergeant's attention was elsewhere, directing the squad to concentrate their fire on the enemy above an armoured door on the opposite side of the concourse. A missile from Nethor streaked past Telemenus's shoulder, exploding amongst the Divine protecting the portal.

Apollon and Nemeon reached the armoured door as the rest of the squad fanned out across the concourse. Daellon stood guard at the shrine door in case the enemy within decided to follow, his flamer shedding droplets of burning promethium to the floor.

Glass shattered behind Telemenus as more shots from the Divine erupted through the windows of the metriculator chamber. The enemy had entered from another doorway and taken up firing positions using the cogitators for cover. Telemenus shouted a warning as he spied the distinctive muzzle and barrel of a lascannon protruding between the casings of two of the cogitating engines. He brought up his bolter to fire as a beam of red energy stabbed from the lascannon, passing centimetres from the Dark Angel's head. More glass splintered and consoles exploded as he returned fire, bolts from his squad-brothers screaming past him as the others added their fire to the attack.

'Entranceway is sealed,' said Nemeon. 'Brother-sergeant, we need your melta bombs.'

Telemenus could spare no attention to the actions of the rest of the squad. Surrounded on three sides, his armour already much battered from previous engagements, he made a dash for the cover of a long, marble-topped counter facing the cogitator room. Splinters from the stone surface shattered into his armour as a foe opened up on Telemenus with a heavy stubber, the perforated barrel of the machine-gun spitting fire.

The Divine were no more than forty metres away, bobbing up and down from their cover. It was almost like the firing range on the strike cruiser. Telemenus pushed aside everything else, focusing on the targets in front of him, responding only with a grunt to acknowledge the assurance from Menthius that his back was covered. He became aware of the other Dark Angel beside him, firing up at the galleries.

Selecting single-fire mode, Telemenus targeted the lascannon first. The man wielding it was sheltering close to the doorway of the terminal room, not so well that he was completely hidden from view. Seeing a knee and lower leg poking around the edge of the cogitator, Telemenus fired. The Divine's shin shattered, toppling the warrior into view. Telemenus ignored him and fired his next shot into the lascannon that was still in the enemy's grasp. The bolt detonated the lascannon's energy cell with a bright flash.

Firing again, his next bolt punching into the shoulder of a warrior moving from one console to another, Telemenus heard a dull crump behind him: the sound of a melta-charge. He did not move, adjusting his aim through the console room to the doorway, where more Divine were arriving. Three shots in quick succession took down the next two enemies to appear, the bolts hitting their targets in the shoulders and throat where their armour provided no protection.

Something large and black sped into Telemenus's view. The Ravenwing Land Speeder strafed sideways across the concourse, its underslung assault cannon unleashing a blur of shells into the console chamber. Databanks and cogitators turned to spinning, lethal fragments. The Land Speeder gunner added the fire of his heavy bolter, the salvo chewing through the flimsy walls, tearing flesh and armour to pieces.

'Telemenus!' The Dark Angel realised it was the third time Amanael had called his name, so fixated had he been on his targets.

'Yes, brother-sergeant?' He tore his gaze away from the destruction being wreaked by the Land Speeder as it made another pass, bringing down the ceiling of the cogitator room with another two-second assault cannon burst. Telemenus saw that the rest of the squad were moving out through the molten remains of the entrance-way doors, heading into the passage beyond.

'Fall in, brother,' the sergeant said, standing at the threshold of the ruined portal. 'More Ravenwing forces will be here presently. Time to push on.'

Telemenus crossed the open space at a full run, still under fire from their attackers on the galleries above, though the weight of the enemy firepower was much diminished. As he plunged into the smoke-filled passageway after his squad-brothers, he detected the echo of roaring motors approaching behind.

The accessway ran straight to grid-east for three hundred metres, bare plasteel walls and mesh decking, a continuous light strip running its whole length. Thick stanchions every few metres supported the roof, and from behind these several dozen Divine were resisting the Dark Angels advance. Telemenus moved into position, reloading his bolter as he took cover behind one of the ferrocrete supports on the opposite side of the passage to Daellon.

Just ahead of him on his left, Nethor fired the missile launcher. The missile sped through the blaze of bullets filling the corridor to exploded against a stanchion halfway along the corridor. Though it filled the passage with smoke and shrapnel, the missile did not appear to have caused any casualties.

'Tracking is off,' complained Nethor, lowering the missile launcher from his shoulder so that he could inspect the boxy sighting array on its side. He gave the weapon a thump with the heel of his hand, shaking his head.

'Or perhaps just your aim, brother,' said Telemenus.

'Your wit is as sharp as your blade, brother,' replied Nethor, 'and used even less.'

Advancing two at a time, the squad moved along the passage, stanchion by stanchion, the rest of the squad unleashing suppressive fire before each pair moved. The Divine held their ground rather than fall back, and the corridor quickly filled with bodies and wounded.

When the squad had advanced nearly a hundred metres, the noise of engines grew louder and Telemenus felt the decking shake under his feet. He fired at a woman straight ahead of him, sending her ducking back into cover, and turned his head in time to see four black bikes of the Ravenwing speeding into the entranceway from the main terminus.

'Stand aside.'

Telemenus barely had time to obey the command from the Ravenwing biker before the squadron flashed past. The moment they were beyond the squad, the Ravenwing opened fire, their bike-mounted bolters leaving a trail of holes and bodies along both walls as they raced on without pause.

'You missed some!' Daellon shouted after the squadron as they continued towards the far end of the corridor, heedless of the Divine who had avoided the fusillade. The enemy fighters concentrated their fire on the retreating backs of the riders until they disappeared from view.

'Press on!' urged Amanael. 'Attack before the enemy recovers.'

'Squad Amanael, hold position.' The command from Sergeant Seraphiel came across the comm-net just as Telemenus stepped out of cover. 'Secure the entranceway but do not move forward. Ravenwing forces will secure the objective.'

'By the Lion's balls, they will!' snarled Daellon. The Dark Angel stormed from his position, flamer in both hands. Gunfire sparked from his armour as he pounded towards the enemy. 'Vengeance for Achamenon!'

Telemenus and Nemeon followed, ignoring the shout of Amanael as they ran past.

'You are blocking our fire,' shouted Nethor.

'Stand your ground!' Amanael's command was a roar across the comm, stopping Telemenus in his tracks.

Distracted, Telemenus saw too late a piston-boosted warrior rising up from the shadow of a stanchion behind Nemeon. The enemy warrior had a large axe in both hands. The edge of the blade shone with some form of energy field. As though time had slowed, while he brought up his bolter to fire Telemenus watched the axe swinging towards Nemeon. His shot left his bolter just as the axe head slashed into the back of Nemeon's helm. The bolt sped along the corridor as the power axe crackled, flares of light erupting from the blade as it carved into the skull of Nemeon.

Nemeon and the Divine went down at the same time; the former with half his head missing and the latter with heart and lungs blown out through splayed ribcage.

Daellon's flamer filled the passage ahead with a wave of fire, incinerating more than a dozen foes. Telemenus had no time to spare to check on Nemeon as he fired again, cutting down another enemy warrior.

'That is why you obey orders,' snarled Amanael, coming up beside Telemenus.

'I would spend a year in the penitentium rather than fight my way across this bloody station only for the Ravenwing to get the glory and honour,' said Daellon, firing again as he continued to advance down the corridor.

'Very well.' Amanael's quiet reply almost went unheard amidst the zip of las-beams and the crack of bolt-rounds.

'Really?' Telemenus glanced at the sergeant in surprise.

'As a squad,' Amanael continued, his voice an angry growl. 'We will settle this matter later. Show some discipline. Telemenus, suppression on the right. Menthius, on the left. Nethor, have you fixed that missile launcher yet?'

'Yes, brother-sergeant,' came the reply.

'Good. We are not Ravenwing, dashing about as we please. Let us show these glory-hounds the mettle of the Fifth Company.'

MISSION ACCOMPLISHED

It caused Annael some misgiving to ride past his former companions of the Fifth Company but the Grand Master's orders had been especially clear. While the Divine were occupied with the defence of the terminal hubs and accessway, Squadron Cassiel was to secure the chambers at the end of the jutting spar. They were to hold against counter-attack until Sammael arrived with other Ravenwing elements.

After rejoining the squadron, punching through the enemy perimeter had been straightforward enough. The Fifth Company had secured the ground well, leaving minimal resistance to oppose the Ravenwing as they had made their final push. In fact, so effective had Squad Amanael's suppression been, Annael and his brothers gained entry to the suspected enemy command area two minutes ahead of schedule.

The communications and control pod at the end of the accessway was a hexagon nearly two hundred metres across, on three levels. The squadron split as they left the accessway, Annael and Araton heading left while Zarall and Sabrael turned right. An outer corridor the height of the whole pod ran the circumference of the housing, the outer wall broken every few metres by slit-like windows, while sets of steps accessing the upper and lower levels ran from the inner side. At right angles to the accessway, blast doors sealed the central chamber.

From the open stairwells, Divine warriors fired at the incoming bikers. Araton was forced to make an emergency evasion as a missile sped from a set of steps leading down, passing between the two bikers before crashing into the outer wall.

Annael steered his bike to the right, directing his machine into the stairwell. He plunged down the steps, punching through the huddle of fighters like a bullet parting flesh. One of the Divine was nimble enough to avoid being crushed by Annael's mount, throwing himself aside as the Space Marine roared past. The Dark Angel turned in the saddle and fired his bolt pistol into the warrior's chest, holding tight to the handlebars as *Black Shadow* crashed down into the tunnel below.

Reaching the next stairway, Annael came face-to-face with half a dozen enemies piling down the steps to confront him. *Black Shadow*'s bolters cut down two and his pistol slew another before rider and mount reached the group of warriors. Strength bolstered by his lifting harness, one of the Divine leapt at Annael, landing awkwardly on the front faring of his machine, a pistol pointed into the face of the Dark Angel.

Annael braked and wrenched *Black Shadow* to the right, sending the Divine flying across from his perch to slam loudly and painfully into the inner wall. Something hit Annael from behind, pinging from the right heat exchange vent of his backpack. Ignoring the two warriors behind him, Annael gunned the engine and ran over the man in front as he pushed himself to his knees. *Black Shadow* bucked as the bike bounced over the reinforced harness of the enemy fighter, smearing tracks of blood from its tyres as Annael powered away. A few metres on, Annael slung the bike into a tight turn, bringing the mounted bolters to bear as the two surviving Divine took cover behind the open steps of the stairway. The sanctuary of their position proved false as a hail of bolts flew between the steps, scything down both men in a single salvo.

Completing a circuit of the pod, Annael cleared away one more group of foes before returning to the main level to reunite with the rest of the squadron. Araton and Zarall had taken up position to either side of the entranceway, ready to gun down any foes that broke away from Amanael's squad to follow the Ravenwing. This left Sabrael and Annael to guard their backs against any enemy concealed within the main chamber or upper rooms who might sally forth; the scanners detected no life signs but interference from the power lines and communications systems was affecting the sensor readings.

Annael waited patiently, keeping an eye on the stairwells a few metres in from of him, gaze flicking between the steps and the corner of the outer corridor ahead. Now and then bolter fire from the Fifth Company echoed along the accessway and occasionally the complex shuddered slightly as the boom of a missile explosion reverberated along the passage.

'Why do we not make the breach ourselves?' he asked. Growing swiftly bored of the inactivity, he switched the scan on *Black Shadow* to thermal. The energy grid stood out in stark yellow lines on the display, but it was impossible to tell if the darker red smudges in the closed rooms were people or activated terminals. 'There would be no risk of attack if we cleared every room.'

'The Grand Master has ordered that we secure only this area.' This seemed sufficient reply for Araton.

'I understand, brother, but why can we not fully secure the facility?' Annael persisted, turning in the saddle to address the rest of the squadron, occasionally glancing at the scanner screen. 'He has already confided in us the possible renegade nature of the enemy commander. What harm is there in conducting a full search?'

'We guard against undue discovery by other forces,' said Araton. Almost as if summoned by the squad leader's words, figures in dark green armour strode into view at the end of the accessway. 'Halt, brothers, proceed no closer.'

'We are here to secure the objective,' said one of the Fifth Company warriors. Annael recognised the voice from when he had been in the company.

'Telemenus, you should not be here,' he told the Space Marine.

'Brother-sergeant, this area is off-limits until Grand Master Sammael arrives.' Araton spoke formally, with no hint of anger. 'Return to your positions and defend the accessway.'

'If it is just the bloody same to you, we will wait at the objective,' the squad brother with the flamer announced, continuing forwards. Araton edged his bike into the Space Marine's path, blocking his progress.

'This area is not secure,' said Zarall. 'Your disobedience shames your company, and the whole Chapter.'

'We just wish to complete the mission,' said Telemenus. 'We have lost two brothers to get here, and we are so close it – makes no sense to guard an empty passageway.'

'Deepest respect to your fallen brothers,' said Zarall, 'but you cannot pass this point. Our honour would be stained if we did not enforce the command of the Grand Master.'

'Run along and do as you are told.' Annael felt himself tense as soon as Sabrael spoke. 'With speed and precision, this area has been seized and secured by the Ravenwing. We do not need you here.'

Annael knew that even Sabrael was not being deliberately dismissive of the squad's losses, but his tone verged on contempt. The flamer-armed Dark Angel turned, moving his gaze from Araton to Sabrael.

'Is that so? You have a damned loose tongue, brother.' Annael finally worked out that it was Daellon, who was known across the Fifth Company for his coarse language and forthright manner.

'Make apology, brother,' instructed Araton. 'Assure our brothers that no offense was intended.'

'If they have not the wit to decide that for themselves, what chance apology will be accepted?' replied Sabrael. Annael sighed and heard a groan from Zarall.

'We have also suffered loss,' Annael said quickly, trying to defuse the building confrontation. 'Our sergeant lies in the care of Apothecary Gideon, minus a leg. He may never ride again.'

'A sad loss,' said Sergeant Amanael. The Fifth Company sergeant looked at Araton. 'I see that you bear no sergeant's markings, brother. Do not seek to impede a superior.'

'Rank and superiority are not the same thing,' said Sabrael. 'Besides, we have specific orders from the Grand Master.'

Telemenus strode up to Sabrael. The Ravenwing biker did not move as the warrior of the Fifth Company leaned in close.

'Do not hide behind the words of the Grand Master,' said Telemenus, menace in his tone. 'Say what you really mean, brother.'

'Test me further, *brother*, and I shall demonstrate with actions, not words.' The humour had drained from Sabrael's voice. He leaned back in his saddle, one hand resting on the pommel of a short blade sheathed behind him. Sabrael's meaning was clear, for the blade he indicated was an honour sword handed to him by the Grand Master for skill at arms. If Telemenus wished to pursue the matter, Sabrael would call him out in an honour duel. Everyone in the Chapter knew that Telemenus was one of the best marksmen to have ever fought for the Dark Angels, but his blade-work was far inferior to Sabrael's.

The honour duel would be no contest.

The two squads stood for a moment in tense silence, neither willing to back down.

'What is the meaning of this gaggle?' Grand Master Sammael's irate voice cut across the comm as his jet-bike glided into view. His command squadron followed a few metres behind, coming to a stop as *Corvex* slid to a halt beside Sergeant Amanael. 'What are you doing here, sergeant? You, Araton, why are you not monitoring your scanners and keeping watch as ordered?'

'Apologies, Grand Master,' said Araton. 'The sergeant and his squad were attempting to pass the perimeter.'

'Why?' demanded Sammael, turning his attention to Amanael again. 'Did you not receive the command to secure position and hold?'

'Evidently not,' said Malcifer before Amanael could reply. The Chaplain stepped off his bike and approached Amanael. 'I do not recall hearing his acknowledgement over the comm. Is that not so, sergeant?'

Annael returned his gaze to the front, or rather to the rear of the squadron, and wondered what Amanael would do. He had a reputation of being quite a stickler for doctrine and duty, but Malcifer had, whether unwitting or deliberately, offered him a way to back down from the confrontation with honour intact on both sides. Annael was not sure the sergeant would accept it, given the warrior's past behaviour.

'That is correct, Brother-Chaplain,' Amanael said, speaking slowly as he chose his words. 'There was no acknowledgement signal.'

It sounded for a moment that Amanael was going to say something else, but the sergeant held his tongue.

'Very well,' said Sammael. 'Sergeant, return to the accessway and link up with the arriving Fifth Company forces. Araton, your squadron will remain on guard here. Stand by to respond if I call for you.'

'Grand Master, may we not secure the objective with you?' asked Sabrael, earning himself glances from the departing Fifth Company squad. 'It is an honour fitting for those who led the charge.'

'Sabrael, why am I not surprised that there is conflict between the Second and Fifth Companies where you are present? You will remain on post, as ordered, and be glad that I do not think your question insubordinate.' Sammael looked at each of the Ravenwing riders in turn, his gaze moving from one to the next without haste. 'Am I understood?'

Annael bowed his head as the stare of Sammael fell upon him. Sabrael had acted dishonourably, and the rest of the squadron realised they shared his shame.

'Understood, Grand Master,' they chorused, like unruly pupils chastised by their tutor.

'I am sure Brother Malcifer will elaborate at length once we return to the *Implacable Justice*.'

'Something for you all to anticipate with joy in your hearts,' said the Chaplain. 'An occasion that will make the longest sentry duty seem like the most exciting deployment you have ever undertaken.'

'If there are no other objections?' Sammael looked at the squadron, expecting no reply, and nodded. 'Good. Let us unmask the Overlord.'

THE INTERROGATOR

Even before the door to the inner chamber hissed open Sammael knew that the enigmatic Overlord of the Divine and Unworthy was not aboard Port Imperial. The Divine had made their stands at the transport hub and the accessway, not within the communications and command chambers themselves. Their strategy from the outset had been one of delaying the inevitable, not defending a revered leader to the last man.

The command chamber was not empty of foes, however. Half a dozen augmented soldiers rounded on the Grand Master and Harahel as they entered on foot. They had been working at the terminal cluster at the centre of the room and reached for lasrifles, bolters and a plasma gun that had been kept close to hand on top of the consoles.

'Hand-to-hand,' snarled Sammael, drawing the Raven Sword. 'Do not damage the data terminals.'

One of the Divine grabbed the plasma gun and fired at Sammael, aiming squarely for the Grand Master's chest.

The ball of energy exploded into streamers of blue light as it struck Sammael's personal field.

'Praise to the artifices of the Mechanicus,' he muttered, sweeping the Raven Sword two-handed through the leg of his foe, sending the warrior crashing to the ground. He raised his voice as he stepped over the body and glanced at the terminal where the man had been working. 'They are deleting the databanks – take them prisoner.'

The instruction was not soon enough to save the life of the foe Harahel had targeted; the Librarian's force axe swept off the man's head with a blaze of psychic sparks. One of the Divine scrambled for the doorway opposite the one through which the Ravenwing had entered, snapping off shots with his autogun. He stopped in the alcove, using a cogitator access terminal as cover.

A moment later, the doors wheezed open behind him, revealing the black-armoured form of Daedis. The Black Knight lashed out with the butt of his corvus hammer, cracking the Divine across the back of the neck. The man tipped forwards, helmeted head bouncing from the corner of the console before hitting the floor.

The others were subdued in short order, the last of them losing an arm to the Raven Sword just as Malcifer entered. The Divine fell to his knees, staring at the cauterized stump just below his elbow. Remarkably the man did not go into shock but turned hate-filled eyes on Sammael.

'Flesh is a prison, oblivion is release,' snarled the man. He opened his mouth to speak again but Sammael's boot crashed into his jaw, not hard enough to break bones but sufficient to force the man to the ground, his servo-harness whining in protest as he fell.

The Grand Master pulled off the man's helm, revealing a square-jawed face, handsome by most standards but for a blistering disfigurement around the left eye which gave the man a squinting appearance. Like the Divine Sammael had encountered earlier, the warrior had scars and lesions across his flesh, and a rash that made his greying skin leathery in patches.

'What were you deleting?' Sammael demanded, grasping the captive by the throat.

'Everything,' the man replied with a defiant grin. 'Communications logs, navigation records, everything. You'll never find him.'

'Find who?' Malcifer appeared at Sammael's shoulder, a skull-faced apparition whose voice was edged with anger. 'The Overlord?'

The man did not reply but the flicker of his gaze groundwards betrayed his thoughts.

'Allow me, Grand Master,' said the Chaplain, grabbing the exoskeletal strut that ran from the Divine's shoulder to elbow on his remaining arm. Malcifer lifted the man to his feet and then twisted, the metal of the harness biting into muscle and bone. 'Where is he?'

Grunting and grimacing, the prisoner said nothing. There was an insane gleam in his eye. Malcifer turned his attention to the stump of the other arm, cupping the wound in his hand, squeezing slowly. The Divine's eyelids fluttered and his lips parted as though caught between agony and ecstasy.

'Pain is an illusion,' the man moaned. 'Oblivion is reality.'

Malcifer's fingers dug into ravaged flesh, causing blood to bubble from the scabbed wound, dripping to the floor in a stream of droplets.

'His name,' said Malcifer. 'What is the Overlord's true name?'

'I do not know,' said the Divine.

'A lie!' Malcifer sounded triumphant, and with reason. Sammael's autosenses had detected the same momentary surge of pulse and flicker in the eyes that had been seen by the Chaplain. The captive certainly knew the name of the Overlord, otherwise he would not have felt the need to deny it.

'Anovel? Methelas?' There was another tiny movement at the mention of the second name, a miniscule furrowing of the brow and narrowing of the eyes. Malcifer released his grip and stood up, looking at Sammael. 'So it is Methelas who masquerades as the Overlord. At least we can confirm that one of the Fallen returned here after Astelan's departure.'

Sammael nodded and strode over to one of the other Divine. He picked up the warrior, the weight of the exo-harness no effort for the power armour of the Grand Master. Looking closely, Sammael saw that the servo-harness was not just worn like an exoskeleton; some of the bolts and rivets pierced the man's flesh. Old scar tissue grew around the threads of the bolts, skin fusing with metal like the bark of a tree growing round an obstruction, taking it into itself. Juts of bone, spurs grafted into the servos and joints of the harnesses, linked the man's nervous system to the machine in a crude imitation of powered armour. Surveying the other prisoners, Sammael saw this was the case with them all. The Divine had allowed the machine skeletons to become part of them.

Sickened, knowing that this had to be the work of the Fallen, Sammael was determined that his hunt would not end in this place. Sammael addressed Harahel and Malcifer across the command channel.

'Methelas has a plan greater than petty piracy,' said the Grand Master. 'Brother-Chaplain, what can you recall of Astelan's testimony regarding Port Imperial.'

'There is little detail,' replied Malcifer. 'Astelan, Methelas and Anovel took over the principal ship by force and subjugated the group already based at Port Imperial. I think it is not his testimony of Port Imperial that is of import, but what Astelan did at Tharsis.'

'Enlighten us, brother,' said Harahel. 'What happened at Tharsis?'

'Astelan staged a coup, after freeing the planet of rebels, riding atop the crest of popular opinion to replace the Imperial Commander by force. He then set about creating a *cultus personalis* about himself, including the creation of a warrior elite, his so-called sacred bands. The parallels are all too clear now that I think on them.'

'So Astelan and Methelas set about creating societies in some twisted image of the Imperium as it was during the Great Crusade?' Harahel grabbed the harness of an unconscious Divine and half-lifted her, the woman hanging like a child's doll in the Space Marine's grip. If not for the narrower shoulders and wider hips, and the slight protrusion of breasts, she would have been indistinguishable from the men, her arms heavily muscled, wrinkled skin and flesh covered with blisters and sores. 'Astelan was a heretic, to be certain, but Tharsis and its people were not corrupted. The stench of the Infernal Powers fills this place. The cannibalism, the unnatural hardiness and malady of the Divine, the fanaticism and craving for oblivion point to the basest of corruption.'

'Perhaps Astelan was not forthcoming in his reasons for the split from Methelas and Anovel,' said Sammael. 'We all know that the Fallen are not of one mind or one loyalty. Some are misguided like Astelan, believing their loyalty to the Emperor justified rebellion against the Lion. There are those Fallen wholly corrupted, sworn to the Ruinous Powers in body and soul. And there are those that run the whole spectrum between. Methelas is obviously of the unrepentant persuasion, embracing the dark masters who turned Horus on the Emperor.'

'It is well that we came here to learn such,' said Malcifer.

'If Methelas has some grander scheme, we must anticipate it and stop him.'

'Let us assemble the facts as we know them,' said Harahel. The woman in his grasp started to stir, groaning and shaking her head. Fumbling fingers released the strap of her helm, revealing a pinched face and short-cropped black hair. Boils puckered one side of her face, a mess of reddened skin and pus. Distracted for a moment, Harahel rapped the woman's head with the pommel of his axe, knocking her unconscious again. 'Methelas has assembled a fanatical army of warriors. He plans to move Port Imperial somewhere else, sacrificing the majority of his force in the process. The Divine are powerful in comparison to the Unworthy, but they are not so strong nor numerous to be effective on their own against a significant opponent. If Methelas has grand ambitions, he cannot achieve them with the Divine alone.'

Sammael nodded, accepting the Librarian's conclusions.

'They have been purging the databases of all information that might shed light on their master's plan,' said Malcifer, inspecting one of the consoles. 'It is a self-destructive last spasm of effort to protect their Overlord before succumbing to oblivion. They know that their master's plan has been thwarted by our arrival, and only his survival remains as a cause. It could take some time to break their will, but it can be done.'

Only the prisoners could answer the questions Sammael wanted to ask; the cogitator banks would be useless. It was all a matter of patience, finding the weakness and dread that every man harboured in the shadows of his soul. Even Space Marines knew fear; fear of failure, loss of honour and defeat. If a Fallen could be broken, the Divine were only a temporary challenge.

Sammael grabbed the wrist of the Divine at his feet,

the bars of the harness buckling in his grip. The Grand Master twisted slowly, pulling the man's arm up and back, rotating the shoulder painfully. Pneumatic pipes split apart, releasing a hiss of vapour as the servo-skeleton struggled to cope with the unnatural movement.

'Where is Methelas now?' asked the Grand Master, applying just enough pressure to keep the arm in its socket. 'Is he aboard the *Scar*?'

'Why should I tell you?' replied the captive. 'You will kill us anyway. Oblivion is peace.'

'Perhaps not,' said Sammael. The man had unwittingly revealed his fear, as all men did sooner or later. The Divine perhaps did not even realise it but Methelas's creed, his twisted version of the Adeptus Astartes doctrines, had left room for pressure to be applied. It was simply a matter of finding the correct purchase in the captive's psyche and applying appropriate leverage.

'Perhaps we will keep *you* alive,' said Sammael. 'We are very good at that. No oblivion, only torment and pain.'

There was hesitation in the captive's eyes, a brief chink of weakness in his veneer of contempt. Sammael saw his opening, his triumphant glare hidden by his helm.

'You believe me, do you not?' Sammael released the man, sending him falling to all fours on the decking. The Grand Master flicked the tip of the Raven Sword across three pipes linking the harness engine to the left side of the Divine, severing the connections. The man slumped sideways, effectively paralysed. 'We will feed you and water you like a plant, ensuring that you do not die of starvation of dehydration, though you will be forever on the brink of raving thirst and ravaging hunger. Slowly, part by part, your body will fail, but we can fix that as well. Anti-aging treatments and bionics will preserve your physical form, all the while trapping your soul in a prison of decaying flesh. The Overlord's gift to you, the toughness and stamina his blessing has brought, will become a curse. When lesser men would die, you will persist, on the brink of the oblivion you seek, able to feel its presence but never to reach out and grasp it.

'Madness will consume you, eating at your mind moment by moment, day by day, year by year, century by century.' Sammael could see the fear now, like a living thing trying to break out of the Divine. It writhed in his eyes and contorted his lips, burying its poisonous fangs into his heart and gut. Sammael poured his scorn into his words, feeding the dread, nurturing it to full strength. 'Yes, centuries will pass and still you will not attain oblivion. This weak, pained flesh will sustain you just enough, so that when insanity comes, there will be a part of you, the part listening to me now, that will survive. You will see the drooling, mewling beast that you have become, slavering in a cell for eternity.'

Sammael parted the other servo cables, hydraulic fluid spraying black across the man's skin as he slumped face-first into the deck. He was just able to turn his head, one eye gazing up as the Grand Master stepped over the prone warrior. Sammael planted the tip of the Raven Sword a few centimetres from the neck of the man, the blade sliding into the metal of the decking as its power-field disrupted the molecules of plasteel.

'Oblivion can be granted so swiftly,' Sammael said, crouching down, moving the edge of the Raven Sword fractionally closer to the throat of the Divine. 'The release you crave is moments away, if you but ask for it. A single word will grant your release. No more. Just one word, whispered so that only I can hear it. No one will know, and then oblivion shall claim you.'

'One word?' whispered the captive. Hope had pushed aside the fear and Sammael knew that he had broken the man. 'What word?'

'Where was Port Imperial to travel?' asked Sammael. 'Give me the name of the system and you will be free. Defy me and you will suffer.'

The man's lips moved, muttering something so quiet even Sammael did not hear it. The Grand Master crouched and leaned closer.

'Again,' he said.

'Thyestes,' murmured the man, the word nothing more than a breath.

'Well done,' said Sammael, standing up. With hardly any effort, he drew the Raven Sword across the throat of the Divine, blood hissing and boiling as it spat along the powered blade. The man slumped, still looking at Sammael. For a moment the Grand Master thought he saw peace in that grey eye, and then all life fled, rasping from the man's lips with his final breath.

'Thyestes,' said Malcifer. He looked at Harahel and then Sammael. 'I have never heard of this place before.'

'It means nothing to me,' confessed Harahel.

'Kill the others,' said Sammael, waving his sword at the remaining Divine. 'Scour the station database for mention of Thyestes. I shall return to the *Implacable Justice* and inspect our records.'

'What if he lied?' asked Harahel, gesturing towards the dead man at Sammael's feet. 'Allow me to inspect one of the others, to confirm that this place exists.'

'He did not lie,' said Sammael. He had seen the fear and the hope and knew that the truth had been told. 'However, do what you wish to satisfy yourself. I do not think you will be able to glean much more from these creatures. They are no less fodder for Methelas's plan than the Unworthy. Their ignorance protects them.'

'As it protects us all,' said Malcifer.

THE TRAIL IS FRESH

The view of Port Imperial dominated the screen on the main bridge of the *Implacable Justice*. With Harahel and Malcifer beside him, on the left, and Sergeant Seraphiel on his right, Sammael waited for the small flashes of blue to reach the grey structure. The gleam of the torpedoes' engines was lost against the fires raging across the star fort. From a few thousand kilometres starboard of the strike cruiser, the *Penitent Warrior* unleashed another shell from its bombardment cannon. For the previous thirty minutes it had sent a steady stream of rounds into the station, cracking open the armoured plates, smashing crystalflex domes and punching through the reactor housing.

'Twenty seconds to impact,' reported Judoc Pichon, standing a short distance from the force's commanders. 'Torpedo separation in ten seconds.'

'Very well,' said Sammael. 'Send word to the *Penitent Warrior*. Cease fire and make all speed for Rat One. Destroy target without delay. Sergeant Seraphiel will rejoin his company later.'

Seraphiel turned to look at the Grand Master, surprised by this announcement.

'You wish for me to remain aboard, Grand Master?'

'Yes, brother-sergeant,' replied Sammael. 'There is much we need to discuss. Your debriefing on Port Imperial is not yet complete and there are plans to set in motion for our next act.'

On the screen, the three blots of blue became brighter sparks for a moment, becoming dozens of tiny red stars as the torpedoes broke into their final approach warheads.

'The Fifth Company is to remain with the Ravenwing?'

'That is one of the matters we will discuss,' said Sammael, smiling reassuringly. 'I would learn your thoughts before I make a decision.'

'I am honoured, Grand Master.'

Sammael did not reply immediately. All eyes returned to the screen as the cyclotronic warheads hit their target. Blossoms of bright light grew across the towers and superstructure of Port Imperial, becoming raging spheres of energy. Lightning flashed from the expanding clouds of plasma and radiation, particles spewing in long streams like rivulets of burning ice as the ravening energies chewed through adamantium and ferrocrete, plasteel and armourglas. Like all-devouring whirlwinds, the cyclotronic tempests burrowed into the station's interior, the mass of the star fort fuelling the reaction, its own size speeding its demise.

A harbour spar broke away, repulsed by an exploding artificial gravity module, sent spinning towards the distant star. Arcs of electricity forked from the summit of the central spire, earthing through the tips of the other towers, so that Port Imperial looked like a massive inverted chandelier burning with flames of lightning. Supports melted and walkways buckled, foundations cracked and linking bridges collapsed. Its heart melted through by the warheads, Port Imperial fell in upon itself.

A second star shone at its heart as the plasma reactor overloaded, releasing the energy of a sun. The white heat devoured all that remained, turning everything into a slowly expanding cloud of gas and dust, the debris swallowed up by the detonation.

'The Unworthy know oblivion,' said Sammael.

'Falsehoods fed to them by the lies of the Overlord,' said Malcifer. 'If they are lucky they shall be taken by oblivion. If not...'

'What then?' asked Seraphiel.

'A conversation best left to another time and place,' Sammael said quickly, looking pointedly at the Chapter serfs attending their battle stations. Now was not the time for a discussion involving the vagaries of Chaos and the Sea of Souls. 'Pichon, set course and full-speed for the crippled frigate. Have the torpedoes reloaded, standard warheads, and prepare all batteries for close attack.'

'As you wish, Grand Master,' said Pichon, bowing low. 'I endeavour to please.'

'Come with me,' the Grand Master said to the others, striding to the entrance of the adjoining command chamber. 'Let us turn our thoughts to subsequent acts.'

Passing in, the other Space Marines followed Sammael. He waved them to chairs arranged around the hololith. Harahel was the last to enter, deep in thought, and Sammael sealed the door behind him as the Librarian stood at one end of the console desk.

The commander of the Ravenwing sat down at the head of the glass-topped table and gently rested his hands on the edge in front of him. He looked at each of the others in turn. Harahel seemed distracted, his eyes looking at something not inside the chamber. Malcifer was intent, brow creased by a slight frown as he sat hunched over the hololith. Seraphiel was attentive, keeping his gaze firmly fixed on the Grand Master.

'We are agreed that the lead to Thyestes is genuine?' he asked.

'For certain,' said Malcifer. 'Despite the efforts of the Divine, the datalogs showed several repeated journeys to the system by the *Scar*.'

'While it is in my mind, do we know anything more about this ship?' asked Seraphiel. 'Class, armament, crew?'

'A light cruiser of some kind, or possibly a heavy frigate depending upon how you wish to make the distinction,' said Malcifer. 'Torpedoes and lance batteries.'

'The ship was not expected to return,' murmured Harahel. He realised the others were looking at him and focused, eyes moving between Sammael and Malcifer. 'At least, the Divine I was able to scrutinise were not expecting the ship to come back to Port Imperial. The *Rapacious*, which is to say the starship designated Mongrel, was being re-equipped to fetch the Overlord and bring him back to the station.'

'If I understand your preliminary report correctly, the Overlord – which is to say the Fallen – Methelas, was planning to move the station through the warp to Thyestes. Am I right?' asked Seraphiel. 'Do we know when he planned to perform this feat?'

'Soon, but not immediately,' said Harahel. 'None of the heretics that survived knew the plan in detail. Indeed, it seems that Methelas wisely told them the bare minimum, keeping his plans to himself. The purpose of the transition, and why Thyestes is the target we can only guess at.'

'Anything on the system from our records?' asked

Sammael, looking at Malcifer who had been tasked with the investigation.

'Nothing remarkable,' said the Chaplain. 'The system is on our star charts, about fifty light years from our current position. Not so far to move Port Imperial without Navigators. One inhabited world, Thyestes Five. Last Administratum census was a little more than seven hundred years ago. Population between three and three-and-a-half billion. Self-sustaining agriculture and industry, widespread settlement across two main landmasses. Normal tithes rate, met more or less on target for previous seventeen hundred years. Imperium-standard technology level, Planetary defence force called the Thyestes Provosts. Three Imperial Guard regiments raised there about fifteen hundred years ago, no longer active. Last threat, ork attacks nearly two thousand years ago.'

'No priority supplies to strategic worlds?' asked Seraphiel.

'None. Utterly unremarkable, as I said.'

'Almost a backwater, one might say,' said Sammael. 'A world unlikely to register highly on anyone's scanners. If something were to happen there, nobody would notice for many years. Plenty of time for Methelas to establish himself as ruler. Who can say, it could be centuries before anybody in the Administratum realised all was not well, and another century or two before any response could be mounted.'

'In that case, it is a stroke of luck that has brought it to our attention,' said Seraphiel.

'It is unwise to attribute to luck that which has an alternative explanation,' said Harahel. The Librarian finally sat down, taking the chair to Sammael's right, and steepled his fingers to his chin. 'I am still collating the reports, but the account of Brother Annael and some of the images I gleaned from my psychic scans of the Divine suggests that the Overlord was not always alone.'

'We know from Astelan that a third Fallen frequented Port Imperial,' said Malcifer. 'The renegade known as Anovel.'

'Precisely,' said Harahel. 'Astelan parted company from the other two several hundred years ago, before his exploits on Tharsis. Why did he lie about the destruction of Port Imperial?'

'He is Fallen, it is in his nature to lie,' said Malcifer. 'He needs no reason or excuse.'

'Tharsis is only twenty-three light years from Thyestes,' said Harahel. Sammael sat back in his chair, surprised by this fact.

'I do not like the coincidence,' said the Grand Master.

'Conspiracy seems more likely than coincidence,' said Harahel.

'You think that when they parted ways, the three Fallen were not in fact separating, but instead instigating some wider plan?'

'Anovel certainly visited Port Imperial on several occasions during the lifetime of the Divine I interrogated,' said Harahel. He scratched his ear, and shrugged. 'That or another Fallen, but Anovel seems the most likely candidate.'

'Something does not sit right with me,' said Seraphiel. 'What does any of this have to do with Piscina?'

'I do not understand,' said Harahel.

'Seraphiel makes a fine point. We have forgotten where the hunt began,' said Sammael. He nodded with appreciation. 'Perhaps the hound not quite so close to the chase sees more clearly than the courser on the tail of the prey.'

'The testimony of Astelan, via Boreas, brought us to Port Imperial,' said Malcifer. 'It is Boreas that is the link.'

'What of the Fallen that travelled to Piscina?' said Sammael, his suspicions aroused by Seraphiel. 'We witnessed what happened in the wake of their arrival: anarchy. Boreas was led astray by a deliberate ploy of the Fallen, allowing them to enact their plan on Piscina without hindrance. It is from that point, and with that fact in mind, that we progressed to our current position. It must bear consideration that it may not have been by Boreas's hand that we were brought here.'

'For what other purpose?' asked Seraphiel. 'If it was Anovel, for the sake of argument, he must have known that we would destroy Port Imperial, and why risk our discovery of the presence of Fallen on Thyestes? It is a grand sacrifice to make, simply to distract the Ravenwing.'

'We must remember Boreas's words,' said Harahel. 'We thought him heretic, but perhaps he spoke a truth we did not see at the time. He said that the Fallen had been able to mislead him because the hunt consumed his thoughts, making him predictable. That is a warning we must heed now.'

'So we do not travel to Thyestes?' asked Seraphiel. 'Is it a distraction or perhaps even a trap?'

'I will not countenance this second-guessing,' snapped Malcifer. 'It is in confounding reasoned thought and through duplicitous behaviour that the Fallen are able to elude our attention. We can fall victim to over-analysis and circular doubt. The Divine believed Port Imperial was destined to travel to Thyestes. Whatever answers we seek, and perhaps Methelas himself, will be at Thyestes. To waste energy contemplating nebulous schemes is to fall prey to the very manipulation we seek to avoid.'

'Thank you, Brother-Chaplain, your words are timely,' said Sammael. He received a nod of thanks from Malcifer. Turning his attention to Seraphiel, Sammael continued. 'It is my intent to continue the hunt without reinforcement from the Chapter. To delay risks our quarry learning of our plans, or even the fruition of his. We cannot wait for the Rock to receive our message and meet us at Thyestes.'

'And it is your intent that the Fifth Company continue in the deployment alongside the Ravenwing,' said Seraphiel. 'I am honoured, but I must speak a note of caution. The closer we come to Methelas, the greater exposure of my warriors to the potential truth and the magnitude of the hunt. I am a sergeant of the Fifth Company but my first loyalty is to the Deathwing and Inner Circle. If the Ravenwing wish to continue unaided, I will pass suitable explanation to my warriors.'

'You have my gratitude for the offer, sergeant, but it is unnecessary,' said Sammael. 'The assistance of the Fifth may prove vital in apprehending Methelas.'

'I disagree,' said Malcifer. 'The confrontation between Squadron Cassiel and Squad Amanael is a demonstration of the tension that can arise when the Ravenwing operates for too long in the company of the uninitiated. It compromises the company's operational capabilities and weakens the morale and resolve of the Fifth.'

'Your objection has been noted, Brother-Chaplain, but until we know what manner of enemy we face, the Fifth Company provide a vital bolster to our strength. Sergeant, during transit to Thyestes, you must do all you can to ensure discipline is maintained. If you cannot keep your squads in check, Brother Malcifer will assume command in your place, with my full authority. Am I clear? Brother?'

'Yes, Grand Master,' said Seraphiel. He stood up and gave a nod of respect. 'Be assured that I will deal with any trouble promptly and effectively. In fact, with your permission I will return to the company as soon as practicable, to deal with those brothers who have shamed us'

'Ill-discipline and disobedience must be dealt with surely and strongly, brother-sergeant,' said Malcifer, also standing. 'I am willing to offer my assistance.'

'Not yet, Brother-Chaplain,' Seraphiel said with a smile. 'It serves my purpose better if you remain a higher, harsher authority to which I might turn if further pressed. Amongst my warriors, the name of Brother Malcifer carries more weight as a threat than a reality.'

'As you see fit,' Malcifer said with a short laugh. 'They have fought hard for little glory in these past encounters. My advice would be to allow them an opportunity to vent their disappointment a little. Their frustration is understandable.'

'Good advice, brother,' said Seraphiel. 'I have something in mind.'

'Remain at battle stations and prepare to receive warp transit orders shortly,' said Sammael. 'Let us hope that we run our prey to ground at Thyestes.'

'The Emperor wills it,' said Malcifer. He raised a fist to his chest, the gesture duplicated by the others. 'Death to the Fallen! Vengeance for the Lion!'

HONOUR

Three days from the translation to warp space, the Fifth Company and the Ravenwing came together aboard the *Penitent Warrior* at the behest of Sergeant Seraphiel. With the blessing of Grand Master Sammael, the veteran sergeant had announced a tourney, ostensibly to award Telemenus his marksman's laurels and celebrate the achievement; in truth the Dark Angels knew there had been some growing rivalry between the companies and the tourney offered opportunity for divisions to be healed and arguments to be settled between the Second and Fifth.

Annael was pleased that Sergeant Cassiel was recovered enough to accompany the squadron to the *Penitent Warrior*, his missing lower leg replaced by a crude but sturdy bionic. They were shuttled across by Thunderhawk along with the rest of the Ravenwing, minus the seven warriors who had not survived Port Imperial and the sixteen others in the apothecarion of the *Implacable Justice*.

The sergeant walked with a pronounced limp, swaying as if on a sailing ship in heavy seas, but seemed in good humour. Annael was keen for the sergeant to return to the squadron. Though he did not confess as much to Cassiel, he found Araton inflexible and lacking the natural qualities of a leader. Cassiel did not know how long his absence would last; possibly until he had returned to the Rock and received a more sophisticated augmetic limb.

Annael had been surprised that the tourney was being held so soon after the battle for Port Imperial, and said as much to his companions as the Thunderhawk prepared to set down in the launch bay of the *Penitent Warrior*.

'It is safe to say that we will not be seeing the Tower of Angels soon,' said Cassiel. 'In all likelihood our next warp jump will take us straight into fresh conflict. Seraphiel and Sammael wish all bad blood to be made good before the next battle.'

'Is it always like this, with the Ravenwing, jumping from one battle to the next without pause?' asked Annael. 'I know the company is fitted for extended patrol, but we have fought three serious engagements without proper resupply and refit.'

'Sometimes it is the way, though more often not,' said Zarall. 'Normally we would return to the Rock between missions like any other company.'

'The Grand Master is on the scent,' said Sabrael.

'The scent of what?' asked Annael.

'Prey,' replied his squadron-brother with a broad grin. 'The last time we fought like this we ended up capturing a renegade at Hellenis. Something happened at Hadria Praetoris, I would wager. It has been one warzone to the next ever since.'

'If traitor Space Marines were involved, that would explain our unseemly reception in Kadillus,' said Zarall.

'Such speculation is counter-productive,' said Araton. 'It is guesswork at best, and meaningless distraction at worst.'

'I think Sabrael is right, for once,' said Annael. His brothers were slow to reply, caught up in their own thoughts he assumed, and he continued. 'It makes sense really. The rebel leader that tried to escape by gyrocopter could have been a renegade himself, or an ally or follower of one.'

Annael realised that his squadron-brothers' lack of response was not accidental. They were pointedly ignoring what he said, glancing past him towards the rear of the Thunderhawk. Annael became aware of a figure standing at the end of the companionway leading to the rear of the gunship. He turned his head and was met by the scowl of Tybalain. The jewelled daggers piercing the scarred face of the Huntmaster sparkled like droplets of blood as the Black Knight approached.

'Loose talk,' growled the Huntmaster. Annael avoided the gaze of the veteran, realising that he had been chattering like an excited novitiate. 'Be sure to keep better control of your tongues in the presence of the Fifth Company.'

'Apologies, Huntmaster,' said Cassiel, placing a fist to his brow as a gesture of remorse. 'I have been too lenient with my brothers of late.'

'How you lead your squad is not my concern, brother-sergeant,' said Tybalain, the natural timbre of his voice a harsh rasp that made anything he said sound like an admonishment. He sat next to Sabrael on the bench opposite Annael. Sabrael, locked in his safety harness, looked uncomfortable though the Huntmaster did not spare the warrior a glance. 'If Brother Malcifer overhead your mutterings you can be sure he would have harsher words.'

'I will heed your wisdom, Huntmaster,' said Cassiel.

'Turn thought to the tourney instead of conspiracy,' Tybalain advised. 'Brother Telemenus earns the Fifth Company great honour with his award. It would be well to not allow the glory of the day to escape the Ravenwing.'

'You seek to set challenge?' asked Zarall, animated by the prospect. 'Against whom?'

'The Grand Master has named me seneschal for the tourney,' Tybalain said with a lopsided smile. 'I will contest with Sergeant Seraphiel, as champion for the Fifth. It will be close, but I think I have the bettering of him.'

'Would it be indelicate to offer advice against my former company?' asked Annael.

'You are Ravenwing now, brother,' said Cassiel. 'Speak without shame.'

Annael waited until he received a nod of confirmation from Tybalain.

'Seraphiel's right shoulder is not as articulate as it once was,' Annael said quietly. 'On Gomgrath an ork shell pierced the joint. Ever since, he has not been able to raise his arm more than level.'

'That is useful to know, brother,' said Tybalain, leaning forward to pat Annael on the shoulder. 'A skilled fighter can take advantage of such.'

The Huntmaster stood up, nodding to each of the squadron in turn before returning to his Black Knights sitting on the far side of the gunship's compartment. Sabrael breathed out heavily, evidently relieved by the departure of the Black Knight.

'He has the ear of the Brother-Chaplain and the Grand Master,' Sabrael said in answer to the inquiring looks from his brethren. This being insufficient explanation, the Dark Angel was forced to continue by the blank looks of the others. 'Surely each of you harbours the desire to become a Black Knight? Even a harmless incident such as this, a minor remonstration, could count in the tally against promotion.'

'You think you will become a Black Knight?' Araton's voice conveyed the same doubt that Annael silently harboured. 'You frequently flout doctrine and even disobey orders, Sabrael. You are no candidate for the upper echelons of the company.'

'And you are?' snapped Sabrael.

'Keep words soft,' cautioned Cassiel, raising a finger to Sabrael in warning. The sergeant pointed at the Black Knights where Tybalain had rejoined his squadron.

Sabrael nodded and remained silent, though his glare at Araton betrayed his thoughts.

Annael had not even considered moving on to the Black Knights. His transfer to the Ravenwing was unintended, and he harboured no particular ambition to ascend the hierarchy of the Chapter any further. If he was called upon to serve in the cadre of the Grand Master, he would be honoured, but he did not seek out favour or position.

It occurred to him that Sabrael's flamboyance was a means of attracting attention, though often of the wrong kind. Annael did not think Sabrael ambitious, not by the measures of ordinary men who might desire power. It was not authority or even respect that Sabrael desired. Instead, his squadron-brother seemed set on gaining glory, at the expense of all other consideration. Regardless of the work of the Tenth Company and the Chaplains, something still remained of the privileged son of nobility who had no doubt been the centre of attention since his birth. Fighting for decades as one amongst many had brought forth that hidden desire for recognition.

Looking at Tybalain, Annael knew that Araton spoke

the truth. The Black Knights were the bravest warriors, the most skilled riders, but they were also something else. There was hardness in their eyes that Sabrael lacked. Annael was well aware that there were greater truths than those he had already learnt from Malcifer and the Black Knights had been taught those truths. There was something unforgiving in their demeanour; unforgiving of themselves as if they harboured some deep guilt that they could not share. As with Malcifer and Sammael, the burden of knowing something great and terrible weighed on their minds and often showed through the facade of control.

These thoughts fled Annael's mind as the Thunder-hawk touched down. Today was not a day for grim contemplation, but a time of celebration. It was a tourney, and he was very much looking forward to the event.

Disembarking, they were led by orderlies of the Fifth to the grand hall, situated just below the command deck and officer's quarters of the strike cruiser. Clad in their black robes and boots, shoulders and heads covered with dark green cowls, the Ravenwing made solemn procession to the venue of the tourney, led by Sammael, Malcifer and Harahel, followed by the Black Knights. Each warrior bore a short blade at his hip and a bolter in his hands, ceremonially armed if not truly prepared for combat.

The Fifth Company lined the wall of the hall, standing beneath their squad banners with blades drawn and raised in salute as the Ravenwing entered.

'Make honour!' barked Sammael, drawing the Raven Sword. He raised the hilt to the level of his eyes.

Following his lead, like silver rippling along a snake's body, the Ravenwing presented their blades to the Fifth Company, squad-by-squad as they entered the hall.

Sammael led the Second Company to the left, where they lined up opposite the Fifth.

The formalities and schedule of the tourney were well-established by Chapter tradition. After a brief exchange of brotherhood vows between Sammael and Seraphiel, challenges would be issued and met first. Any Dark Angel present was allowed to call out any other warrior attending the tourney, whether of the same or different company, even a superior. It was often that a Space Marine with a grievance against his sergeant would seek redress at the next tourney, providing a valuable outlet for expressing dissatisfaction without being insubordinate. It was rare that superiors issued challenges to the lesser ranks; they had more straightforward authority to deal with warriors that spoke out of turn or otherwise tested the patience of a sergeant or officer.

The tourneys ensured that grudges were not borne and vendettas stifled, maintaining the discipline and fraternal relationships of a company. No reason needed to be given, and often challenges were fought as wager or simply for the honour of a squad or company. Once the matter of the challenges had been dealt with, and all scores settled, the attending Dark Angels could relax and enjoy the remaining festivities without harbouring any dissent with one another. Feasting, the award of commendations, recitals and the customary duel of champions would follow.

Sergeant Seraphiel, having instigated the tourney, was the presiding judge, and as the only Grand Master present Sammael would also stand witness to the challenges and their subsequent duels. Brother Malcifer finished the trio who would recognise the efforts of the challengers and challenged and ultimately arbitrated on who was victorious.

The Black Knights acted as marshals, providing the blunted training blades with which the duels would be fought and keeping watch to ensure the code of challenge was not breached by participants and spectators alike.

As host, Seraphiel invited the first challenger to make his presence known. Next to Annael, Sabrael stepped forwards, fist raised.

'I offer challenge!' shouted Sabrael. Though no explanation was needed, the challenger was allowed to make brief reference to the nature of his grievance if he desired. 'I seek satisfaction against Telemenus of the Fifth Company. He gave personal offense and through ill-discipline endangered the mission just completed.'

This caused a very non-traditional hubbub to course along the hall. Sammael and Seraphiel had a whispered conversation, the former shrugging and shaking his head throughout. It was most unusual for a warrior due to be honoured by the assembled warriors to be sought in a challenge, but evidently not against the code.

Telemenus stepped forward from the line of the Fifth, somewhat hesitantly.

'I intercede!' shouted Annael, stepping up beside Sabrael, earning himself a scowl from his squadron-brother. 'I have prior claim to satisfaction from Brother Sabrael.'

'How can such a claim be made?' demanded Seraphiel. 'The tourney has just this moment commenced.'

'Should proof be needed, I refer the brother-sergeant to communications logs recorded during the last mission,' said Annael. He briefly looked at Sabrael, lip curled with anger, before addressing the veteran sergeant. 'I made clear to Brother Sabrael a demand for recompense for abandoning his post against orders and my request.'

'What recompense do you seek?' asked Seraphiel.

'A full apology,' said Annael. There was little reaction from Sabrael, and Annael realised that his battle-brother was quite prepared to make a public apology if it meant that he could still humiliate Telemenus on the occasion that celebrated his marksman's laurels. Annael sought something else that Sabrael regarded more highly than his reputation, gaze flitting briefly to the sword in Sabrael's hand. 'And he must surrender the bladesman's honour, for his actions have brought shame to the title.'

There was a hushed murmuring, for this was a grave insult amongst the Dark Angels. Nobody could comply with such a demand and retain any dignity, least of all Sabrael. Annael had made it clear that he wanted to fight, and Sabrael realised as much.

'You do know what this blade is, brother?' asked Sabrael quietly, holding the ornate sword in front of Annael.

'It is the Blade of Corswain,' replied Annael, his voice equally soft-spoken. 'I do not need to be reminded of its pedigree nor its history. You are vain and ill-mannered, Sabrael. Qualities that disqualify you from bearing such an honour.'

'This sword marks me out as the best bladesman amongst the ranks of the company,' said Sabrael. 'You cannot hope to defeat me.'

'Still, that is my intent.' Annael raised his voice. 'The challenge is issued as before.'

'And accepted!' barked Sabrael.

'Then let us begin,' announced Seraphiel.

The two warriors stood in the space cleared between the two companies, ten metres apart, weapons at the ready. Sabrael had surrendered the Blade of Corswain to one of the Black Knights, so that both competitors were armed with short duelling blades, each a metre long with a broad crosspiece, basket guard and heavy pommel. The two would fight until one conceded defeat or two out of the three judges named a victor.

'Do not think to make a name for yourself at my expense, brother,' Sabrael said casually.

'It is time that you were taught some humility, brother,' replied Annael.

Seraphiel stood between the two of them. He checked that each duellist was ready, receiving nods from both.

'Commence!' said the veteran sergeant, stepping out of the way.

Sabrael attacked swiftly, as Annael knew he would. It was all Annael could do to bring up his blade to guard before his foe had advanced and was sweeping his sword towards Annael's chest. He parried and adjusted his stride, fending off Sabrael's next lightning-fast attack with the basket of his sword, mere centimetres from his face.

Sabrael backed away, stepping lightly from one foot to the other, always on the move, shifting balance from right to left and back again. It annoyed Annael that his brother was obviously toying with him, and there were some amongst the watching companies that started to shout condemnation. It was also equally clear to Annael that Sabrael had not been boastful. He was clearly one of the finest swordsmen in the Chapter, never mind the Ravenwing, and Annael would never beat him blade-to-blade.

There was little enough time to regret his challenge as Sabrael leapt forward, thrusting low towards Annael's groin. Annael managed to block the blow with the edge of his sword and span, slashing the point of the blade at Sabrael's head. His opponent ducked, the blade slicing air a few centimetres above Sabrael's scalp.

Annael jumped back as Sabrael's sword flicked towards his chest, and managed to fend off two rapid thrusts, though on the back foot he was not able to mount any offensive of his own. Sabrael's expression grew intent as he feinted low and then quickly raised his sword towards Annael's throat. In desperation, Annael ducked forwards, past the blade, driving the pommel of his own blade into Sabrael's chin. The blow knocked his opponent backwards to the floor.

'Win for Annael,' announced Seraphiel. Sammael and Malcifer were not so quick to declare victory though, as Sabrael rolled to his feet, stepping into the attack once more.

'A dishonourable strike,' said Sabrael as the two of them met blades and closed, faces less than a sword's width apart.

'Victory is honour,' Annael replied. He pushed hard, forcing Sabrael back and the two of them circled, wary of each other.

Annael parried the next attack and smashed the elbow of his sword arm back across Sabrael's face. Sabrael span with the blow, however, slapping the flat of his sword across the back of Annael's head, stunning him.

'Victory to Sabrael,' announced Malcifer.

All eyes turned to Sammael. The Grand Master stood with arms folded, dispassionate almost to the point of boredom. He slowly, casually shook his head, lips pursed.

'Your dirty tricks cannot help you,' laughed Sabrael. 'At least lose like a true warrior.'

Annael did not reply, but threw his blade, point first, at Sabrael. Surprised, his foe dodged aside, only to be hit in the midriff with Annael's shoulder as he charged full-speed. The two of them tumbled to the ground. Annael raining punches, blocked by Sabrael's upraised arms. Annael trapped Sabrael's sword arm between his left arm and his body, and rolled away, forcing the weapon from his opponent's grasp.

He snatched up the weapon as he rolled to his feet, spinning to present the blade point first at Sabrael. He was met by the other Dark Angel coming straight for him, a blade in his hand. Annael realised that Sabrael had snatched up the weapon he had thrown, too slow to stop the strike as it smashed into the side of his head.

'Victory to Sabrael!' declared Sammael.

Warriors converged on the two duellists, offering congratulations and commiserations in equal measure. Dropping his sword, Sabrael grabbed Annael in a tight embrace, pounding slaps against his back.

'You had me worried for a moment, brother,' said Sabrael, grinning broadly.

'For a moment?' Annael asked. His head started to throb from the victorious blow to his temple. 'Only a moment?'

'Do you think I have not faced brawlers before, brother? Class always beats aggression.' Sabrael pulled away as his arm was raised in victory by Seraphiel. The veteran sergeant dispersed the crowd, leaving the two fighters facing each other once more.

Sabrael winked as he bowed and Annael returned the gesture with more formality.

'For what it is worth,' Sabrael announced, growing serious, 'I offer apology to Brother Annael for my dereliction of duty. It was remiss of me to desert my post, and for that I offer sincere regret.'

Annael was expected to reply. He could refuse the apology, but after suffering defeat it would be very churlish. There was a hush from the surrounding Dark Angels as Annael weighed up his decision. He paused, thinking about what happened in the tunnel station. Had Sabrael stayed where he had been ordered, would the consequences have been so very different? It was impossible to say, and Sabrael had proven his quick wit and skill just moments earlier. The Ravenwing were not the Fifth Company. Independence of thought and improvisation were sometimes needed more than regulations and doctrine. Could he really blame Sabrael for what happened, or was it just one of those incidents of war that befell a warrior every now and then?

'Your apology is accepted,' said Annael, and he meant it. Through his skill at arms, Sabrael had proven his act justified, his argument backed up by the will of the Emperor. 'I retract my accusation. You are a worthy bearer of the Blade of Corswain, and you will bring honour to that sword many more times.'

The other Dark Angels pressed forwards again, shouting support as Sabrael was returned the Blade of Corswain. As Sabrael held the badge of honour aloft for all to see, Annael felt a tug at the arm of his robe. He turned to find Telemenus gesturing for him to follow. They moved out of the crowd, and Telemenus seemed humble, eyes cast to the deck.

'Thank you, brother,' said the warrior of the Fifth Company. 'In your place I would not have lasted a handful of seconds.'

'You are confused, brother,' said Annael, though he understood Telemenus's intent. Having fought already, Sabrael could not issue any further challenge. Each warrior could fight only once, to prevent bullying or glory-seeking. 'I did not act to preserve your honour. I know you Telemenus, and you are not so dissimilar to Sabrael. It was not to save your humiliation that I acted, but in an attempt to forestall Sabrael's victory. In that, I have failed.'

'Yet you have my thanks again, whether sought or not,' said Telemenus. Annael said nothing and the other Dark Angel eventually turned away, returning with his brothers to take his place against the far wall.

Standing next to Sabrael, back to the wall, Annael looked at his neighbour. Sabrael felt Annael's gaze and turned his head, a smile on his lips.

'I see Telemenus spoke with you,' he said. 'No doubt grateful for your intervention.'

Annael nodded but said nothing.

'I must offer thanks for the interruption also,' said Sabrael. 'It was childish of me to seek to spoil Telemenus's occasion. He has earned his laurels and I should not have sought to mar his moment.'

'I am happy to be of service,' said Annael.

'Also,' added Sabrael, nudging Annael with his elbow, 'fighting Telemenus was just a matter of honour. I actually enjoyed beating you, brother.'

'And I take no shame from the loss,' said Annael. He extended a hand and Sabrael took it. 'Brother.'

FOUR
THYESTES

GUILE AND SUBTERFUGE

The situation at Thyestes was painfully similar to events at Piscina. As Sammael started briefing Harahel, Seraphiel and Malcifer, it was clear to him that there was some greater plan at work than first appeared. Methelas's influence seemed to be everywhere, and the Grand Master had brought his two officers to council directly after he had ended his communication with Lasper Drazinoff, the Imperial Commander of the world. A hazy, static broken hololith of Seraphiel hovered between the Chaplain and Librarian as Sammael paced back and forth at the head of the console desk.

'Thyestes Five is a world embattled,' the Grand Master told his companions. 'The Imperial Commander is still loyal to the Emperor and is grateful for any assistance he might receive. There is no guarantee that Methelas has returned here, but someone has been fomenting rebellion for some time, over a decade in fact. Anti-Imperial factions have secretly been uniting for many years, leading to an outright rebellion that started two-hundred-and-forty-two days ago. Much of the populace has been corrupted by an anti-Imperial sect, and according to what Drazinoff has just told me there are remarkable correspondences to the Unworthy and Divine we destroyed at Port Imperial. If not currently leading the insurrection, I am convinced that Methelas must be sponsoring and supporting the uprising in some way.'

'We need to discover whether Methelas is here,' said Malcifer. 'As with Piscina, we cannot become embroiled in a prolonged engagement, unless it will serve to capture the Fallen.'

'Harahel, can you provide any assistance in this matter?' asked Sammael. 'Any inclination that Methelas may be on Thyestes Five?'

'There have been some reports of psychic activity logged by the local Adeptus Arbites, but nothing upon which to base a solid conclusion,' said the Epistolary. 'If you can get me closer to a probable location, I would be able to tell if someone as powerful as a Space Marine Librarian is tapping into the warp. From orbit, there is no way to be sure, not for someone of my limited rank and ability.'

'There still exists the option to send for the Tower of Angels,' said Seraphiel. 'Not to abrogate any decision on our part, but to better deal with the forces we are likely to face. Planet-wide rebellion is difficult to counter with less than two full companies.'

'Brother-sergeant, you are correct to be pessimistic,' said Sammael. 'Unlike Hadria Praetoris, we do not know the location of the enemy stronghold or command. There is no swift victory for the Dark Angels here. The insurgents are a powerful but dispersed forced, with no central authority or geographic location that has been detected. I believe that Methelas is responsible, and there will be a headquarters somewhere on Thyestes Five, but that is only suspicion. The Imperial Commander has access to sophisticated orbital stations, which have not furnished any usable information regarding the rebels' lines of supply, strategy or disposition.'

'Surely the planetary defence force have some idea where they might battle their foes,' said Malcifer.

'The Thyestes Provosts are waging a defensive battle, and losing badly,' said Sammael. 'Not knowing where they might be attacked next, the Imperial Commander and his men have been forced into an ever more defensive stance, retreating to keeps and bunker lines while the enemy bring terror to the wider populace.'

'This may prove a challenge too great for the force we have,' said Seraphiel. 'I return to my earlier point. The Tower of Angels can be contacted and greater strength, and wisdom, brought to bear upon the problem.'

'Time is against us, and not just in the possibility of wasting precious resources seeking Methelas where he will not be found,' said Sammael. 'As soon as the insurgency began, Imperial Commander Drazinoff sent word by astropath of the deteriorating situation. Sooner or later, the Departmento Munitorum will mobilise the Imperial Navy and the Imperial Guard and a military force will arrive.'

'Given that the nature of the threat is rebellion, the matter will come to the attention of at least one inquisitor,' said Malcifer. He clenched his fists. 'We stand between the beast and the abyss. On the one hand, if Methelas is here and we delay, we run the risk that one of the Fallen is captured by forces not of the Chapter.'

'That cannot be allowed,' said Sammael, shaking his head vehemently.

For ten thousand long years the Dark Angels had kept their secret from prying eyes. Inquisitors came and went, but the truth of the Fallen remained the sole property of the Chapter. Sammael's name would become as infamous as the likes of the thrice-cursed traitor if he was the first Grand Master of the Ravenwing to allow a Fallen to be taken into the clutches of the Inquisition. It would spell disaster for the Chapter and the Successors. The Unforgiven would be shamed across the galaxy for their failings; perhaps even destroyed for the measures they had taken subsequently to conceal their dark secret. In the eyes of their fellow Space Marines, and before the Emperor Himself, they would be dishonoured.

'An alternative peril is to engage in the fighting here, encountering only delays and casualties while Methelas makes good his escape,' said Malcifer. He shook his head. 'This is a decision that you alone can make, Grand Master.'

'Not without counsel,' Sammael replied. 'I refuse to choose between vague improbabilities. As with Piscina, we must cut through the fog and seek the heart of the matter. If Methelas is present, he must possess some form of base of operations.'

'Not if he intended Port Imperial to be his base, Grand Master,' interjected Seraphiel. 'We would be wiser looking for the ship that brought him here.'

'No,' said Sammael. 'Thyestes has considerable orbital augurs and defences. If the *Scar* committed any warlike act, it would have been easily destroyed. There are no warships currently in orbit, that much is certain.'

'But *Scar* was not due to return to Port Imperial,' said Seraphiel.

'Which means that there was something else for the ship and crew to do,' said Harahel. He cleared his throat, a sign of agitation. 'It matters not. If *Scar* was ever here, it arrived under cover and departed the same. The surest route, and the swiftest, will be to locate the enemy headquarters, whomever may be in command, and learn what we must from there.'

'And how do you suppose we succeed where the Imperial Commander and all of his forces have failed?' said Sammael. 'If you can find me a target I will lead the strike.'

'The rebels are fighting for an ideal, not territory,' said Harahel. 'Their attacks seem sporadic, random. They are perhaps politically motivated, but we cannot deduce from their locations any intent or scheme. Instead, we must lure the rebels into revealing themselves.'

'It must be carefully done,' said Malcifer. 'It is my worry that should Methelas learn of our presence here he will flee.'

'With the *Penitent Warrior* and *Implacable Justice* on hand, the orbital cordon is solid,' said Sammael. 'If Methelas is on the surface, he will be trapped. Brother-Epistolary, I still do not see how we can force the rebels to reveal the whereabouts of any base or headquarters.'

'We must give them something so valuable that they will take it to their most secure facility,' said Harahel. 'If we can offer up a prize worthy enough, they will take it back to their lair like ants delivering food to their queen.'

Sammael considered this for some time, trying to think of alternative courses of action. Eventually he nodded, liking what he heard.

'What do you propose we offer as bait to the trap?' he asked Harahel.

'We will use the Imperial Commander as the prize.' The suggestion was met with silence. Harahel looked from Malcifer to Sammael and back again. 'Why does my suggestion elicit such shock, brothers?'

'You cannot expect me to easily agree to sacrifice an Imperial Commander on the slim chance that his capture will reveal the identity of the rebel leader?' Sammael leaned on the hololith slab with both hands, shaking his head. 'The risks are too great.'

'He is only a single man,' said Malcifer, the words slow and quiet as he came round to the idea.

'The world is unstable enough already, and the loss of the governor could tip more people towards the rebellion,' said Sammael. The horror of Piscina IV's collapse was fresh in his mind and he would save Thyestes V that trouble. 'It might be the case that we leave the matter as it is for the moment. The Imperial Guard will arrive and their numbers will eventually grind down the opposition forces and bring the planet back under total Imperial control. At all times we stand ready to act should Methelas reveal his presence.'

'There is no conflict between the desire to hunt Methelas and the military needs of Thyestes Five,' said Malcifer. The Chaplain leaned back, clasping his hands in his lap. 'Regardless of whether the rebel commander is Methelas, if we can locate an enemy stronghold, we can decapitate the enemy command in a single stroke, as we did at Hadria Praetoria. If it turns out that one of the Fallen is leading the rebellion, then we will capture him and take him back to the Tower of Angels to confess his crimes.'

'There is considerable uncertainty in that proposal, Brother-Chaplain,' said Sammael, though Malcifer's argument was convincing. The Grand Master straightened and turned away, so that he did not see the eyes of the others upon him. He cleared his thoughts and tried to think objectively about the situation analysing his misgivings.

Using the Imperial Commander felt dishonourable. Whatever plan he concocted to deliver Drazinoff to the rebels, he could not do so with the compliance of the Imperial Commander. That would mean lying, and quite possibly collaborating with the rebels in some fashion.

Had he the luxury of this being just any other war, Sammael would have spoken up then, refusing Harahel's plan outright. As it was, he had a higher duty calling to him; the hunt for the Fallen. There were strong suspicions that Methelas was somewhere on Thyestes V, and if that was the case Sammael was beholden to his oaths as Master of the Ravenwing to use any and all means to bring his prey to account. His predecessors had sacrificed worlds to that cause, was he any less of a Dark Angel?

'How will we do it?' he asked, turning to Harahel, knowing that to ask the question was to give consent, if only for the moment.

'We will tell the Imperial Commander that we have solid information that his palace has been infiltrated by rebels and that they are planning another offensive soon,' said Harahel, his gaze distant as he thought through the scheme. 'You will suggest an alternative location where he will be safe with just a handful of guards. Meanwhile, the nature of this move will be leaked to the rebels. I am sure that the Provosts make unsecured communications all of the time, we simply need to replicate their carelessness.'

'So, Drazinoff will be intercepted by the rebels en route to this new location?' said Seraphiel. 'Rather than a few guards, it would be better that he is escorted by some of my squads. I shall take personal command and ensure that he is delivered up to the rebels without them becoming suspicious.'

'You agree with this ploy?' asked Sammael.

'If we are to do this, it is better it is done properly,' said the veteran sergeant. 'My approval is irrelevant, if you give the command, Grand Master.'

'Very well,' said Sammael. The others were making

it abundantly clear that they considered him the final and solitary authority, and by his word alone would the subterfuge be undertaken. In other company he might have suspected that his companions were protecting themselves against reproach, but he knew better. As he faced this almost impossible decision, all three were giving him that unequivocal support, whatever decision he made.

'Once Drazinoff is with the rebels, they will take him to their headquarters, we shall track them and the target is revealed,' said the Grand Master. 'Simple, yet effective.'

'There are no certainties,' warned Harahel. 'If Methelas leaves his lair to meet his captive we may not be aware of the fact.'

'We have to stay close to the bait,' said Sammael. '*You* will have to stay close to the bait. If Methelas makes a move, you must be on hand to detect him. I will have the Ravenwing on constant drop stand-by. We strike as soon as we are able. Seraphiel, your Fifth Company will remain on the ground after the failed escort, ready to respond and provide support.'

Sammael turned away again, conscious of the decision he had made. He told himself that removing Methelas, or whoever was leading the rebels, was the best way to bring peace to Thyestes V. Were he to be offered the choice, Drazinoff might well agree with the plan.

The Imperial Commander was not being offered the choice, and Sammael knew he risked greater tumult and prolonging the war if the ploy failed. There were too many variables for the plan to be justified in purely military terms: if Drazinoff was killed; if the Ravenwing were unable to track the rebels; if the enemy commander was not killed or captured. Yet Sammael was able to justify his decision all too easily when he considered the honour of the Chapter was at stake. Compared to the loss of a world, the loss of the Dark Angels' reputation was a tragedy that would endanger many more billions of lives in the longer term.

Faced with the machinations of the Fallen, Sammael had no other choice.

THE STAKES ARE RAISED

'Entering the forest,' Sergeant Atleus reported from the lead Rhino transport.

From his vantage point in the cupola of the fourth and final vehicle in the column, Telemenus could see the woods thickening to either side of the broad highway, the embankments to the left and right growing steeper and more overgrown with bushes.

Twenty metres behind the Rhino of Squad Atleus was *Castigator*, a Dark Angels Predator tank armed with lascannons and heavy bolters. The gunners in the turret and sponsons swivelled their weapons to and fro as they searched the woods for threats. Telemenus curled his fingers around the grip of the storm bolter in front of him and swung right in the cupola, sighting up the steep hill to the side of the convoy. He noticed the newly-painted laurels on the badge upon his arm and smiled inside his helm. To return to the Rock with such decoration would be a pleasure, though achieving the marksman's laurels had not provided the lift to his spirit he had expected.

The circumstances surrounding the recent campaign nagged at him.

'Sector clear,' he announced to Sergeant Amanael in the troop compartment below him.

Halfway between the rear Rhino and *Castigator* was Imperial Commander Drazinoff's personal carrier. Its basic chassis was the same as the Chimera transports used by the Imperial Guard and many planetary defence forces across the Imperium. This particular variant of the ubiquitous design boasted thicker armour plates fixed atop the roof where normally a firing hatch was located. A remote-operated missile launcher dominated the front of the vehicle, next to the rotating dish of an enhanced communications array. Whatever happened, the Imperial Commander wanted to stay in contact with his forces.

'Kaspor Gorge two kilometres ahead,' said Sergeant Seraphiel. The Fifth Company's commander was riding below with Squad Amanael. 'Scanners clear.'

During his briefing, Seraphiel had made it clear that the narrow gorge, nearly four kilometres long, would be the most likely site of an enemy attack. The vehicles would have little room to manoeuvre, and any ambushing foe would have the advantage of the heights rising up several hundred metres on both sides of the road. The downside of the area, from an attacker's perspective, was the rough terrain stretching for dozens of kilometres around the gorge; dense forest and a rocky mountain pass barred access to wheeled and tracked vehicles. If the enemy attacked, it would be on foot.

Telemenus had been confused by the emphasis placed on the gorge, and Seraphiel's description of it. While highlighting the unlikelihood of any rebel attack on the column, the company commander had seemed almost convinced that there would be trouble at Kaspor Gorge.

When Amanael had made inquiry into the under-strength nature of the column, Seraphiel had been keen to point out that secrecy and speed would be the best protection for the Imperial Commander, which accounted for the lack of close support air cover and the small escort.

The departure of the column had been timed to ensure that the vehicles reached the gorge just after noon, when the sun lit the steep valley in its entirety. Unfortunately, the weather was not inclined to cooperate. Dark grey clouds filled the sky, unleashing a steady drizzle of rain onto Telemenus, splashing from his armour and the top of the Rhino with a constant, irritating patter.

He moved the storm bolter to the right and left, scanning his sector, autosenses on thermal with full magnification. Small animals and birds fluttered between the trees, startled by the growl of the vehicles' engines, but he saw nothing else.

'One kilometre to Kaspor Gorge,' announced Seraphiel. 'Scanner clear.'

Given recent incidents, Telemenus had left unasked the questions he had regarding the transfer of the Imperial Commander. Though he could understand why a potential security breach amongst his staff had prompted the relocation and the involvement of the Dark Angels, it made little sense to him to move Drazinoff by land. A Thunderhawk would be far less vulnerable and a lot swifter.

At least he was away from the strike cruiser, he told himself. After the frustration of the last three missions – the rebels at Hadria Praetoris captured by Ravenwing, the withdrawal without action at Kadillus and the debacle that had concluded the attack on port Imperial – Telemenus was glad to have an objective that was clear and simple. With any luck, the rebels would find out about the convoy and try to mount some kind of kidnap attempt, giving him the opportunity to unburden himself of some of the dissatisfaction he had been feeling of late.

Despite his meandering thoughts, he remained alert, conscious of the wooded slopes giving way to steeper, rockier ground as they passed into the mouth of the gorge. He waited for Seraphiel to signal the all clear, scanning back and forth across the boulders and scree.

Telemenus heard the crack of a large gun firing a moment before Squad Atleus's Rhino was hit by a shell. The front of the transport erupted outwards, flinging the driver and armoured plates across the highway.

Acting despite the shock of the attack, Telemenus swung the storm bolter to look at the heights of the gorge walls. He saw something bulky and dark about two hundred metres ahead. There was a flash, just as he opened his mouth to give warning.

'Enemy veh–'

The shell hit the right flank of the Rhino, smashing into the tracks. The force of the blast lifted up the vehicle and Telemenus felt himself about to topple from the cupola as the Rhino flipped over. He pushed himself inside and slammed the hatch shut half a second before the transport crashed down onto its roof.

The transport compartment was not breached, but his squad-brothers and Seraphiel lay heaped on the roof-now-floor of the vehicle just to the rear of Telemenus.

'Report, brothers,' snapped Seraphiel, dragging himself clear as the Dark Angels pushed themselves away from each other. Telemenus answered his name as Amanael snapped out the roll-call, pleased to hear that everyone still in the squad replied.

'Some kind of vehicle with a battle cannon,' said

Telemenus. 'Two, actually, at least. One on each side of the gorge.'

'How could the rebels get a damned tank up there?' asked Daellon. The Space Marine made his way to the rear hatch, bolter in one hand. He jabbed his fist against the emergency release. Explosive charges hurled the rear doors away from the chassis and pale light flooded into the compartment.

'They were walkers,' said Telemenus, recalling the glimpse of the enemy in the moments before the shell had struck, of a monstrous, spider-like vehicle perched on the edge of the ravine. He joined the others as they clambered from their wrecked transport. The flipped Rhino had become a deathtrap, but Telemenus waited patiently while the others disembarked, half-expecting another mighty explosion to rock the transport.

'The only walkers on Thyestes Five are light recon units,' said Seraphiel. 'Where would the rebels get such vehicles?'

The question went unanswered as another booming retort echoed along the gorge. Telemenus's momentary relief that the shell had been targeted elsewhere was replaced by concern for his brothers in the lead Rhino. Right behind Amanael, he snatched a bolter from the rack beside the exit hatch and plunged out of the Rhino wreckage. As Amanael moved right with most of the squad, Telemenus veered to the left, moving around the inverted transport with Daellon, scanning the top of the gorge wall for more foes.

The walker he had first seen was lowering itself down the cliff with six mechanical limbs, serrated claws digging into the chalky rock. As it picked its way down the slope, the engine looked like an obscene metal spider with a turreted cannon atop its back. The machine was almost perpendicular to the floor of the valley and unable to fire, and Telemenus was grateful for this minor mercy.

Reaching the front of the Rhino, he saw where the third shell had been aimed. Smoke billowed from the rear grating of *Castigator*, thick and oily from the burning engine. The tank's turret was still operational though, the barrel elevating to target the crab-like walker on the far side of the gorge. The machine was silhouetted against the grey sky, its front appendages raised, tipped with spinning saw blades. A howl resonated along the defile, inhuman and drawn out, ringing with a metallic edge.

'Heretic engines,' muttered Seraphiel. 'Daemonically possessed war machines. Imperial Commander, remain in your transport for the moment.'

Whatever reply came from Drazinoff was made over the command channel, unheard by Telemenus and the rest of the squad.

'Troops moving to the front of the column,' Sergeant Atleus reported. His squad, only seven strong, Telemenus noted, fanned out through the rocks either side of the highway, following their leader. 'Armoured.'

'Renegade Space Marines,' warned Seraphiel. 'Betrayers of the Emperor.'

This pronouncement hit Telemenus like a fist in the gut, making him stop in his tracks. It was not the first time he had faced such foes, but the memories of his previous encounters were vague, half-remembered as though only a dream. The realisation that he faced former warriors of the Adeptus Astartes brought to mind a plethora of questions; questions he suppressed as he focused on the immediate situation.

'Damned traitors,' snarled Daellon. He disappeared back into the upturned wreckage of the Rhino and emerged a few seconds later, a plasma gun in his hands. 'This will prove most useful.'

'Incoming!'

The shout from Amanael sent the Dark Angels running from the Rhino. Moments later, the wreck exploded into flames as another shell from the machine atop the gorge wall hit the transport. Heat and smoke washed over Telemenus and secondary detonations rattled through the burning hull as storm bolter ammunition was cooked off by the flames.

'Not targeting the chimera,' he noted to the others. The observation came with a worrying conclusion. 'This is no opportunistic attack. They know we are escorting Drazinoff!'

'Traitor legionaires approaching from the north, three hundred metres. More walkers and battle tanks,' said Atleus. His squad were firing along the canyon at targets out of Telemenus's line of sight. The continuous hail of fire did not bode well. 'We must extract the Imperial Commander and retreat.'

'Negative!' shouted Seraphiel. He paused as *Castigator* opened fire, its twin lascannons sending bright beams of energy lancing through the torso of the armoured walker atop the ridge. A keening wail drifted down the gorge as the machine slumped to one side and scrabbled out of view, its churning claws sending chunks of rock and boulders rolling and bouncing down the slope. 'Sergeant Atleus, hold your ground. Squad Amanael, take out that other war engine.'

Nethor readied the missile launcher as the rest of the squad turned their bolters on the approaching mechanical beast. Through the magnification of his targeter, Telemenus could see the unholy conglomeration of metal, flesh and daemon more clearly. Sheathed in metal, there seemed to be muscle and bone beneath the hull of the machine. Dark runes emblazoned on the outer armour burned with black fire, trapping the ethereal spirits of the daemons inside the artifice of traitor tech-priests.

'Notice the rust and decay?' said Menthius. 'Recent acquaintances make it familiar.'

Castigator's turret turned towards the remaining war machine as Nethor opened fire with a krak missile. His aim was pure, but the warhead split against the armour of the daemonic engine, showering sparks and shrapnel against the cliff-face but doing no lasting damage. Telemenus raised his bolter, but knew he was helpless against the armoured monster.

The walker halted in its descent, digging in four of its claws deep into the stone. As it adjusted its stance, the machine's wide-muzzled cannon swung towards the Predator and the Space Marines standing not far behind the tank. Castigator's main gunner fired first as Telemenus and the others broke away from the battle tank, but the shot was too hasty, carving a gouge into the chalk below the abominable walker. The enemy walker returned fire, noxious smoke billowing from its gun as it sent a shell crashing into the side of the Predator. The battle tank skidded sideways, shedding track links across the highways as road wheels fell from their mountings and clanged onto the pitted ferrocrete. The heavy bolter sponson was a tangled mess of metal and flesh, the unfortunate gunner – Brother Amneos, Telemenus recalled – torn apart inside the weapon mounting.

His bolter no better than thrown stones, his armour no defence against the firepower of the mechanical beast, Telemenus snarled in frustration. Nethor was bracing himself, lifting the missile launcher to his shoulder.

'For Emperor's sake, take it out,' Telemenus snapped, stepping up beside his squad-brother. 'We cannot let it reach the convoy.'

The Predator's lascannons swivelled as they adjusted for their new position and let forth twin stabs of energy. The blasts sheared through one of the walker's legs, melting through the metal in a flash. A mixture of oil and blood spilled from the damage, splashing down the white slope in a slick of black and scarlet.

The firing from Atleus's squad attracted Telemenus's attention for a moment. The Dark Angels were still unleashing a steady hail from their bolters at targets further along the highway. Telemenus wanted to move forward to join them knowing that his superior marksmanship would prove valuable. Seraphiel's orders were clear, though, and Telemenus returned his gaze to the machine.

Recovering from losing its rear leg, the daemon engine ripped its claws free, letting itself slide down the white slope towards the column. Nethor lined up another shot with the missile launcher as the enemy walker ploughed onto the highway fifty metres in front of Squad Atleus. Twin beams of laser energy from the Predator obliterated a boulder that had tumbled along with the walker, turning it to dust and fragments but leaving no mark on the machine. The metal beast picked up speed, legs pumping as it headed towards the Space Marine force. Churning up the ferrocrete road with its claws, the half-daemonic machine leaked a trail of dark fluid from its severed limb. Telemenus lifted his bolter, ready to fire. He knew it was a futile gesture, and the thought of fighting against the other Space Marines following in its wake left him feeling cold inside, but he would not simply allow the enemy to attack without reply.

Nethor fired. The missile streaked over the wreckage of the lead Rhino to slam into the front armour of the walker's turret. The machine stumbled, swaying to its left, knees buckling with a hiss of hydraulics. The daemon-machine let forth a loud, plaintive moan. As the smoke of the missile's detonation cleared, a large gouge could be seen, running for two-thirds of the cannon barrel protruding from the turret. Bubbling, unnatural liquid dribbled from the wound, dripping like tar on to the hull.

'Again!' snapped Amanael.

'One more hit should finish it,' said Telemenus.

His satisfaction was short-lived though as the half-machine beast reared up on its three remaining legs, claw-tipped front limbs raised high. A piercing screech of defiance caused Telemenus's autosenses to momentarily shut out all audio input. When his hearing returned the noise of bolters firing and rounds pinging from metal filled the gorge. He added the fire of his weapon to his brothers' trying to hit the swaying pipes and cables that ran along its splayed limbs.

Atleus's squad switched their fire from the approaching renegades to the war machine lumbering into their midst. Armed with an autocannon, one of the brothers fired a salvo of shells into the approaching engine, buckling and cracking rusted armour plates but not penetrating into the machine's innards. Just as hope was beginning to stir in Telemenus's heart once more, it was quashed.

Without stopping in its stride, the daemon-tank lashed out with a claw the size of a Space Marine, smashing aside the Dark Angel with the autocannon. The unfortunate battle-brother was hurled several metres into the air and crashed down onto the road, where he lay unmoving. The squad's flamer set light to the remains of the turret but the war engine thundered on, heading straight for the *Castigator*. Bolter fire from Telemenus and the others sprayed harmlessly from its metal skin as it threw aside the smouldering remnants of the lead Rhino.

Clambering to the top of the battle tank, the enemy walker set upon the Predator, its front claws leaving ragged welts across the metal as it sought to drive its pincer-like appendages underneath the turret. Telemenus reloaded and fired again, desperate to pick out some weak point revealed by the enemy walker's elevated position. His rounds pattered harmlessly, sending up puffs of rust and slivers of metal but inflicting no real damage.

Daellon stepped forward, raising the plasma gun to the firing position. As the walker sank its claws through the top of the Predator's hull, the scream of tearing metal almost deafening, Daellon fired. The plasma bolt passed between the machine's legs, striking the armoured underbelly. Droplets of molten metal showered onto the roof of the Predator, but still the daemon-machine was not stopped.

Levering with its arms and remaining legs, the daemonic engine ripped free *Castigator*'s sloping turret. With a fluid movement, it tossed the turret aside, the wreckage sent through Squad Atleus. Roaring insanely, the mechanical creature slammed its claws down, smashing into the interior of the roofless Predator with blow after blow.

'We have to get Drazinoff,' said Amanael.

Telemenus moved slowly, recovering from the fugue of confusion that had gripped him since the first shell had hit the convoy. He broke into a run, following after his sergeant and Menthius as they dashed towards the Imperial Commander's armoured carrier.

'Fall back!' yelled Seraphiel, grabbing Daellon as he tried to run past. 'Protect yourselves.'

The war machine pounced, leaping from the back of the Predator to land on the roof of the Chimera.

Suspension cylinders exploded and rivets popped from their seals under the sudden weight. The walker swept out with a claw, driving a pointed tip into the shoulder of Amanael, hurling the sergeant sideways.

'Fall back!' Seraphiel's order was a bellow, cutting through the fog of madness that had descended on Telemenus. The Dark Angel looked up at the behemoth of flesh and metal towering over him and realised that his commander was right; there was nothing that he or his brothers could do to save Drazinoff.

'Help me with the sergeant.' Telemenus dragged his eyes away from the enemy at the shout from Menthius.

The other Space Marine had Amanael by one arm. Telemenus grabbed the other wrist and between the two of them they dragged the unconscious sergeant back along the road. Ahead of them, the dead and wounded of Squad Atleus were being pulled back by two of the battle-brothers, leaving two more to hold the front of the convoy. Splinters of rock surrounded them as the approaching renegades showered their position with bolter fire.

A flurry of explosions tore through the rocks and stunted trees where Squad Atleus were still holding ground. Depositing Amanael beside the wreckage of the squad's Rhino, Telemenus could just about make out the attacking traitors along the road. Figures in filth-daubed white and green power armour advanced in the wake of two Rhinos, the hulls of the vehicles encrusted with rust and filth like the walker. A Land Raider, almost twice as large as the troop transports, its heavy tracks grinding along the ferrocrete, loomed over the attacking column. From its back long pennants and tall banners fluttered, the white of the cloth heavily soiled and marked. A Space Marine in the top hatch directed the fire of a heavy bolter towards Squad Atleus, forcing them back into cover.

'Death Guard,' snarled Seraphiel. The name meant nothing to Telemenus, nor did the pale-green livery and dirt-smeared armour of the foe. It did not matter. The column was clearly outmatched. Just metres from Telemenus, the daemon engine was peeling back the top of the Chimera like an Imperial Guardsman opening a rations can. Las-fire erupted from the transport's interior as the Imperial Commander's bodyguard defended their charge.

'Better that the governor is not taken prisoner,' said Telemenus, thinking clearly for the first time in several minutes. He raised his bolter to his shoulder and sighted on the target. His finger rested lightly on the trigger of his bolter as the claw of the machine reached inside. It lifted out a slender, aging man dressed in dark robes of office.

For a moment Telemenus's cross hairs were centred in the forehead of the Imperial Commander; a sure kill.

'All brothers, withdraw,' ordered Seraphiel, stepping in front of Telemenus, the sergeant blocking the shot as he waved the front line of Space Marines to fall back.

The moment had passed. Telemenus moved his finger from the trigger and lowered his weapon when Seraphiel had cleared the line of fire, seeing that the walker had shifted. Its bulk now between him and the Chimera, the Imperial Commander obscured from view as the engine clambered back to the roadway with its prize.

'Thunderhawk extraction is on the way,' announced Seraphiel.

The words filled Telemenus with a mixture of relief and regret. It was not the first time he had been forced to retreat, but it felt like a more damning failure than before. The Imperial Commander was just twenty metres away and there was nothing he could do as heavy weapon fire from the Death Guard raked the convoy, forcing the Dark Angels to retreat further.

'What about Drazinoff?' demanded Amanael. The sergeant pushed himself to his feet, his armour ripped open from his left shoulder to his abdomen. Thick blood congealed in the wound, and the sergeant swayed for the moment, weak from the loss.

'We have failed,' Seraphiel replied. The flat statement sent a chill through Telemenus; words he feared more than death and injury. 'We had no idea the enemy had such strength. Fall back. There is nothing more that can be done here.'

Telemenus stood looking up the road for a few seconds while Seraphiel turned and started southwards, back towards the forest. It was almost too much to bear; to have glory snatched from him by the Ravenwing and now a damning failure to protect the Imperial Commander.

He saw a Space Marine from the vanguard of the traitor force reaching the wreckage of Squad Atleus's Rhino. Raising his bolter, he looked closely at the foe. The traitor's armour was a mish-mash of ancient marks, heavily reinforced and riveted in places. His helm was tipped by a long spike, the conventional front grille replaced with an armour-banded respirator tubing. Oil leaked from the joints and fungal growths were growing in the gaps between plates. The armour had once been white, but most of it was marked with filthy green mould and brown from coagulated oil.

Filled with hatred and disgust, Telemenus fired, putting a round through the cracked eye lens of the Space Marine. The Death Guard staggered back, half his helmet missing. Remarkably, the traitor did not fall, but turned towards Telemenus, bolt gun raised. Through the targeter magnification Telemenus could see that half the Space Marine's head was missing, one eye popped from the socket by the bolt detonation, the fleshy orb dangling on the warrior's exposed cheek. Even for a Space Marine the warrior's survival was unnatural.

'No time for that!' snapped Daellon, seizing Telemenus by the arm as he aimed again. 'We will be back for vengeance against these rotten bastards.'

Telemenus allowed himself to be led away, breaking into a quick jog with a final glance over his shoulder. The Death Guard were swarming over the remnants of the convoy. With a wordless, anguished shout, Telemenus tore away his gaze and sprinted after his retreating companions.

SILENT HUNTERS

'Understood, Paladin Two. Commencing close observation. Return to orbit.' Sammael sighed as the comm cut out. It was the third time since the Death Guard ambush that storms had forced his aircraft to abort their sensor tracking. Ten kilometres above the ground, far from the eyes and scanners of the enemy, the aircraft had proved invaluable in keeping the Death Guard force under scrutiny; for six days and twelve hundred kilometres north and east across the tundra of Thyestes V.

Now that the Death Guard were entering the Kurkarusk Mountains' cloud cover, storms and snow would mask the foe from the sub-orbital tracking of the Dark Angels. It was time for the Ravenwing to close the gap on their prey.

The ride had already been an arduous one, keeping within striking distance of the Death Guard without approaching too closely. Winter was fast setting in on this part of the world, and the further north the enemy travelled, the rougher the conditions for the Second

Company. The enemy had travelled so far it was impossible for Sammael to believe that they were not heading back to some headquarters or permanent outpost in the frozen north. He called Harahel and Malcifer to council as the order to move out was spread through the company.

The Ravenwing had been on the move constantly since the Death Guard ambush, subsisting off their armour systems, occasionally supplemented with high-protein rations. When the Death Guard force had split the evening before, just after sunset, Sammael had been forced to call a halt while the fighter jets scouted out the routes ahead. The Dark Angels had taken shelter amongst the pine trees that swathed this part of the taiga, sleeping fitfully for the first time in days. The recon flights returned with the information that one force was heading for the inhospitable permafrost beyond the mountains ahead, while the other was turning westward at some speed.

'I believe the enemy must have their base in the mountains,' the Grand Master told his companions. 'Any further north puts them on the polar icecap, which would provide ideal concealment but does not make sense from a logistical standpoint.'

As Sammael ordered the company to head north, the trio steered their mounts into the line, exhaust smoke drifting between the pines, tyres leaving deep tracks in the snow. The two Black Knights silently joined their masters, bringing the squadron up to strength. To the left and right, Land Speeders flitted through the trees, their anti-grav engines kicking up flurries of snow in their wake. A rumble of thunder rolled across the skies, the clouds darkening through the breaks in the tree canopy above.

'I concur,' said Harahel. 'The only alternative is that the

enemy know we are following them and are deliberately leading us astray.'

'Thank you for that thought, brother,' said Malcifer. 'Now that I think of that possibility, my optimism is quite diminished.'

'I said it was a possibility, not the likeliest scenario in the balance of probability,' replied the Librarian. 'The enemy have had ample opportunity to turn and attack if they knew of our presence.'

'That would make more sense than wasting fuel and time leading us a merry chase through the tundra and mountains,' said Sammael. 'That they have not done so stands testimony to the continued secrecy of our pursuit. We will close to within thirty-five kilometres, with a Land Speeder vanguard to keep visual contact with the enemy. There are dozens of mountain passes ahead, we must know into which one the enemy move. It is vital that we strike before the enemy can make any capital from their capture of the Imperial Commander.'

'Do we regard Methelas as the principal target now?' asked Malcifer. His bike hit something hard buried beneath a snowdrift, rocking the Chaplain in his saddle for a moment. Regaining his posture, he continued. 'The presence of the Death Guard reinforces my suspicions that Methelas is conspiring as part of some grander plan.'

'We cannot dismiss the similarities between the decayed state of Port Imperial and the particular affectations of the Death Guard,' Harahel said. 'It would not be the first time that Fallen have worked with members of the Traitor Legions.'

'The Cult of Decay is certainly a major influence in the rebellion on Thyestes, and I see its work now amongst the Unworthy and Divine on Port Imperial,' said Sammael. His knowledge of the Ruinous Powers was vague, but he was aware that some Chaos followers pledged their allegiance to a god of entropy and plague. In return for their sacrifices and obedience they became inured to pain and disease. The oblivion so valued by the Divine and their followers could be a euphemism for the Lord of Pestilence.

'If this is true, Methelas is to be numbered amongst those Fallen who embraced the Dark Powers,' said Malcifer. 'He will be exceptionally dangerous if cornered.'

'Not only by the bile and spite of his words. Methelas's psychic power will have been strengthened by daemonic pacts and other vile rituals,' said Harahel. 'Already we have witnessed the use of daemon engines. There could be other diabolic servants of Chaos summoned to the cause of the Fallen.'

'You wish to end the pursuit now?' said Sammael, concerned by the Epistolary's words.

'And risk the Grey Knights becoming involved?' Malcifer said harshly. 'I remind you, brothers, that the reason we are riding across this bleak, Emperor-forsaken wilderness is to ensure that no suspicion of the Fallen comes to the attention of the Inquisition.'

'I do not suspect full-scale daemonic incursion, brothers,' Harahel said hurriedly, realising his words had caused alarm. 'But it may be the intent of Methelas and his allies to bring about such a fate for Thyestes. We cannot be sure.'

'What we can be sure of is the fact that a swift and deadly strike will bring to an end whatever scheme Methelas pursues,' said Sammael. 'The presence of the Death Guard makes the enemy a more challenging obstacle, but it does not alter the fundamentals of the mission.'

'Attack fast, take Methelas and then withdraw?' said Malcifer.

'Exactly,' replied the Grand Master. 'I harbour no desire to seek extended confrontation with the Death Guard if it can be avoided.'

'What of the Fifth Company?' said Harahel. 'Do you think the Ravenwing alone will be sufficient for the task?'

'Seraphiel and the Fifth have returned to the *Penitent Warrior* and are on emergency drop-alert,' said Sammael. The forest ahead thinned to scattered trees, revealing the mountain range in all of its glory. Cloud-shrouded peaks jutted into the blue sky, the flanks of the mountains purple and red beneath the snowline, broken by the green of trees further down the slopes. A lake glittered in the foothills, reflecting the clouds above.

Deep within the catacombs of the Rock were tapestries and paintings from the ancient founding of the Chapter. They depicted the vast forests and majestic peaks of Caliban before the treachery that had destroyed the Dark Angel's home world. Looking at the mountains ahead reminded Sammael of those scenes, lost forever by the treason of the Fallen.

'It would be best if the Fifth Company were not exposed again to the traitor legionaries,' said Malcifer. 'The more they encounter the Death Guard, the more awkward questions stirred in their minds.'

'Let us hope that we are nearing the end of the campaign, for their sake,' said Sammael. 'If we swiftly conclude our business on Thyestes we shall return to the Rock in victory. Reunited with their brothers, and coming under the full scrutiny of the Chaplaincy, I am sure the brothers will soon be freed from doubts and curiosity. In the meantime, the presence of the Death Guard make for suitable distraction for the Ravenwing. As long as he is secured by the Black Knights or one of us, Methelas can be passed off as another Death Guard renegade.'

There were no objections to this conclusion and the command squadron rode on in silence. The forest gave way to snowfields, which gave way to foothills as the company trailed the Death Guard into the mountains.

A rotating shift of Land Speeders kept constant vigil on the enemy, ensuring that no matter how winding a path the enemy took, the Ravenwing remained just behind, unseen but ready to strike.

There was little to discuss for Sammael and his companions, until the nature of the enemy stronghold was known. They rode for days on end without speaking, each warrior alone with his thoughts, contemplating the meaning of the hunt and the peril of the Fallen. Sammael did not break these silences, though they made him uncomfortable. Being alone with his thoughts forced him to face the decisions he had made, the path he had chosen since becoming Grand Master.

There was one side of his tale, lit with glory and courage, recorded with praise and pride in the annals of the Chapter. These were the missions that the Chapter boasted of to their Successors, holding up Sammael and the other Grand Masters as beacons of hope in a galaxy benighted by enemies. The alien warlords slain, the heretic empires toppled, the mutant and psyker purged by the Raven Sword. These exploits were the face of Sammael turned outwards, that his company and brethren saw when they looked at him.

But the light masked a darkness; a darkness that resided in the hearts of all the Inner Circle. As glorious as Sammael's life had been, there were too many times when the shadow had called to him. The brothers sacrificed, the worlds left to ruin, the enemies unconquered so that the hunt could continue. It was these times that filled his thoughts, occupied his mind in the silent contemplation of his cell or the long road such as he now followed. It was the decisions made not for glory but necessity that filled his dreams, such as he had, and haunted his waking hours when sleep became impossible.

These last months had been particularly trying. The words of Boreas were etched in Sammael's thoughts, like a worm burrowing through rotten wood. He tried to expunge them, tried to leave behind the nagging of their intent, but Sammael could not be free of the truth they held.

What does it mean to be Dark Angels without the Fallen? We have come to define ourselves by them. Take them away and we are left without purpose. We have strayed far from the path, and it is my fervent prayer that you, Grand Masters of the Chapter, the wisest of us, can find the true course again.

The sun was setting and Sammael looked at the descending darkness and felt as though the shadow was a blot upon his soul. Boreas had been driven mad by what he had concluded, and now that madness had infected Sammael. While he had been hot on the trail, in the fiery heat of battle, the truth had been easy to put aside, his conscience simple to assuage. Now as twilight crept into the valley where the Ravenwing hunted their prey, Sammael wondered if he was right to risk a world for one enemy.

And in this, he was fortunate. Boreas had been alone, set adrift by the Chapter with no peer or superior to hear his doubts. His strength had been tested and without support had proven weak. Sammael was not alone. He was in the company of friends; the company of brothers.

'What is the righteous path?' he asked, looking at Malcifer who rode beside him, almost lost in the darkness.

'It is the most difficult path, brother,' the Chaplain replied carefully, understanding the weight of the Grand Master's question. 'To be righteous is a burden we all bear. I sense this is not idle philosophical questioning, Grand Master.'

'What is the righteousness that guides our hand this night, Malcifer?' Sammael asked, quiet and thoughtful. 'If we bring Methelas to account, what do we achieve?'

'You know the reasons, Grand Master,' said Malcifer, cautious if not a little worried.

'I know the sermons and the canticles and the catechisms, yes. I do not mean in general terms, but specifically, on this night, against this foe. I have put in grave danger the future of several billion servants of the Emperor. I feel it is justified, but I do not know if it is righteous.'

'Ah, well, that is a different matter, brother.' The Chaplain relaxed, his tone become conversational. 'If you wish to speak of specifics, I can assist. It was not you, nor I, nor any Dark Angel that placed Thyestes in danger. It was the enemy. Whatever contorted, vile plan he pursues, the one we hunt brought war to their world. Sometimes we must shatter the peace to being a lasting victory, but not tonight. Tonight we act to end war. In one strike, we can deliver this world from the evil of rebellion.'

'And Methelas, why do we seek his capture and not his death? In righteous terms?'

'Other than the salvation of his soul through confession and repentance?' Malcifer laughed, obviously thinking that this was righteous reason enough. The Chaplain continued nevertheless. 'Cast your mind back to how this particular hunt began. We seek a greater enemy than Methelas. The Fallen had struck a blow directly against the Chapter. This is not an esoteric threat, nor a philosophical supposition. With malicious intent, warriors of the Fallen attacked a keep of the Dark Angels, slaughtered recruits and stole precious gene-seed from us. The act was calculated to cause the most grievous damage possible, and it was guilt at allowing it to happen that drove poor Boreas to end his life and that of his brothers.'

'Vengeance cannot be righteous,' said Sammael.

'Not in itself, but in avenging the dead of Piscina, we have accomplished much. Port Imperial is no longer a scourge on the shipping of the Imperium, and whatever intent Methelas had for the station is now thwarted. Thyestes Five will be delivered from the shadow of treachery, whether Methelas is killed or not. These are indisputable facts. But in order to tread the truly righteous path, it is not enough to simply counter evil as one discovers it. It must be torn out at the root, and no root grows deeper than the vile master that leads the Fallen.'

Sammael had almost forgotten the involvement of the Chapter's nemesis. Malcifer, animated now by the topic, continued before the Grand Master could say anything.

'A number of paths lead away from Piscina. We know that our greatest foe was involved in the massacre somehow. We also know that the *Saint Carthen*, a ship connected to Port Imperial, was in the system. Methelas is connected to Port Imperial, which connects him to Piscina, which connects him to the chief of the Fallen. The web extends, becoming more complex the further one looks, but the Fallen are always interrelated on some level. That is the righteousness of the hunt, to continue the chase even when the trail grows dark.'

'Methelas leads us to him?' asked Sammael, heartened by the thought. The shadow lifted from him at the prospect of taking a step closer to apprehending the Dark Angel's most hated foe.

'Directly or indirectly, that is for certain,' said Malcifer. 'Three Fallen there were that knew of Port Imperial. Astelan is accounted for. Methelas, Emperor-willing, is upon the brink of capture. That leaves only Anovel. Even if Methelas does not take us to the corruptor himself, I believe that Anovel was commander of the *Saint Carthen*, working with Methelas.'

'That is a goal worth riding through the darkness for,' said Sammael. He steered *Corvex* close to the Chaplain's bike and lifted a fist, gently banging Malcifer's pauldron in thanks. 'To bring the great heretic to account for his crimes would shed light for eternity upon those who did so.'

'Yet that light must forever be hidden from those outside the Chapter,' cautioned Malcifer. 'It is not a glory that can be shared.'

'It is a glory one would take happily to the grave in the knowing.' Sammael grinned, imagining what it would be like to be the Grand Master who finally ran the most loathed enemy of the Chapter to ground. With this thought, he looked at the sun disappearing behind the mountains and found that the night was easier to face.

THE ASSAULT

Except for the distant whine of anti-grav motors from the patrolling Land Speeder, the forest was silent. Their black armour rendering them almost invisible in the darkness, the warriors of the Ravenwing gathered, leaving their bikes and attack bikes in the shadows beneath the tree canopy. The mountain slope was rocky, the forest floor covered in light undergrowth, only a faint carpet of snow and bushes. Above, twin moons shone down, half full, but their silvery light did not reach through the entwined pine branches above. With Araton, Zarall and Sabrael, Annael joined the rest of the company, ranks of dark statues facing the Grand Master amongst the trees. The Black Knights stood beside their lord, hammers couched in their arms. Only the glint of eye lenses in the darkness betrayed the presence of the unmoving sentinels.

When the company had assembled, Sammael stepped forward, head bowed. His words were quiet over the vox, thoughtful rather than theatrical.

'We have followed the trail of the hunt, from system to system and across the chill wilderness of this world. Our enemy have returned to their lair at last, unknowing of the vengeance that follows on their heels. They think they are safe, their fastness perched atop the summit of this mountain, but they are wrong. We are the Ravenwing and there is no hiding from our wrath.'

The Grand Master paused, resting one hand on the pommel of the Raven Sword at his waist.

'To outsiders, even those amongst our Chapter brethren, our steeds are the symbol of the Ravenwing. We are the all-seeing eye that roams wide. We are the blade that strikes swift. They are not wrong, but we are far more than that. The Ravenwing are the hunters that cannot be eluded. Our mounts have served us proudly, bearing us into battle, and we honour their spirits with our victories as we honour the company and the Chapter. Yet we are not beholden to machines. We must forego our steeds to negotiate the terrain ahead. The enemy reside upon the pinnacle, unreachable by our mounts unless we wish to drive into the teeth of their defences.

'We are a cannier hunter than that. On foot, we shall negotiate the slopes, coming upon our foes unseen. Though we relinquish our mounts, we do not depart from our honour and spirit. We are Ravenwing and the tenets of our company hold true tonight as they would any other time. Speed and surprise are our weapons. Daring and courage are our creed. I expect each of you to fight for glory and distinction, as hard as you would fight at any other time.'

Again the Grand Master stopped for a moment. Telemenus saw his hand tightening on his sword, the other forming a fist at his side. His voice grew more strident, edged with scorn.

'We have hunted long, pursuing a foe most hated. You

know that the rebels are bolstered by the presence of traitor Space Marines. These foes are beneath pity, worthy only of hatred. They have turned from the Emperor's light and seek to spread their vile darkness upon this world. War they have brought to the Emperor's domains, but in one night, one glorious battle, their darkness will be obliterated by the vengeful light of the Dark Angels. They have run as far as they can and can run no further. They seek to hide from retribution but it has found them. We are justice given form. The Emperor's wrath incarnate! For the Lion and the Emperor, show no mercy.'

'For the Emperor.' With the rest of the company Annael spoke the words with conviction, not a boisterous shout but a simple uttering of a fundamental truth. 'For the Lion.'

The squads broke at their leader's command, the order of the advance already known to the sergeants. With Araton as acting sergeant, Annael and the others fell into line, alongside the Black Knights of Tybalain. The Huntmaster lifted a fist in salute and set off into the night, quickly consumed by the darkness.

The ascent was long but not arduous. Annael's power armour made light work as he pulled himself over rocks and clambered along narrow ridges. Coming out of the trees, the Ravenwing found themselves on the shoulder of the mountain, the rock gleaming in the light of the twin moons. Looking up to the summit several thousand metres above, Annael could see nothing of the enemy stronghold. This was good, he decided, as it also meant that the foe could not see the warriors approaching from below.

The climb became monotonous, hour after hour, the temperature and air pressure dropping as the Dark Angels ascended the broken slopes and cliffs beneath the Death Guard's fortress. Ice slicked the rocks, but was no barrier to powered fingers delving into cracks and, on occasion, driving into the rock itself to create hand- and footholds.

There was no conversation, each Space Marine intent upon his path, measuring the distances and gauging the strength of the rocks above. Ice became a coating of snow; snow became deeper and deeper the higher they climbed. The moons dropped below the peak and the cliffs were shrouded in utter darkness. Suit lamps at minimal power glowed into life across the slope, dozens of tiny pinpricks of light. Annael fixed on Araton ahead of him, following the squad leader's every move precisely, as he in turn was following those in front.

After a particularly steep incline, the mountain shoulder flattened, a few hundred metres below the snow-covered peak. Moving quickly, the Ravenwing made their way across the snowy expanse, spreading out according to the orders of Sammael. With Tybalain's Black Knights, Annael and his squad headed to the left, cresting a ridge a hundred and fifty metres further on. Attaining the height of the ridge, the two squads crouched, surveying the ground below.

From this vantage point the enemy installation was easy to see. Two narrow ridges formed natural walls to the north-east and north-west, the compound finished with a ten metre-high revetment some five hundred metres away, down the slope. Twin towers guarded the armoured gateway, search lamps lighting a stretch of broken roadway before it turned behind a shoulder of rock and disappeared from view. In the snow-reflected gleam Annael could see the armoured shapes of Death Guard manning mounted lascannons and heavy bolters on the tower roofs. Any approach from that direction would have been met with a devastating crossfire.

'Not so much a fortress,' said Tybalain.

He was right. The enemy stronghold consisted of a network of fourteen prefabricated units, each no larger than ten metres square, linked together by covered walkways. Snow was banked up against the ferrocrete blockhouses and strings of lanterns hung along the walkways, spreading light over small patches of ice and snow packed down by the tread of heavy boots. Yellow gleamed from slit windows in the hab-units, now and then eclipsed by a passing figure, but Annael could see no movement in the open. In the shadows the bulky shapes of the Death Guard's transports sat, the snow around them melted by exhaust and engine heat.

'That is more problematic,' said Araton, pointing to the ridge on the opposite side of the site. Caught in the last light of the setting moons, a monstrous walker stood guard, as still as the buildings, clawed arms resting in front of it, multi-jointed legs furled beneath it like a spider lying in wait.

'Not for long,' Tybalain replied. 'Air strikes are incoming.'

'What do we do now?' asked Sabrael. He had the Blade of Corswain in his right hand, bolt pistol in his left. Annael unholstered his pistol and knife too, looking along the ridge line to where other Ravenwing squads were waiting for the attack order.

'After the air strikes, we head straight down,' said Araton, glancing towards Tybalain who nodded in confirmation.

'Clear and secure the nearest buildings,' said the Huntmaster. 'Remember that we need to take the enemy commander alive.'

'Why so?' asked Annael, eliciting surprised noises from his brethren.

'That is the purpose of the hunt,' said Araton, his voice

tainted by a condescending tone. 'We secure the renegades so that the Chaplains may learn of other traitors.'

'Apologies for the question, brothers,' Annael said quickly, feeling foolish. 'This is the first conclusion to a hunt I have witnessed.'

'And you are blessed because of it,' Tybalain assured him. 'So soon after your arrival, you will earn the greatest honour our company can know.'

'Though we can never speak of it to anyone, for shame,' said Sabrael.

'For pride,' countered Araton, 'not for shame.'

'You know well my meaning, brother,' said Sabrael.

'There is plenty of wide renown in other battles, Sabrael,' Zarall said softly. 'In this, our highest duty, we each know the measure of true reward, of service well rendered and honour upheld.'

'Of course,' said Sabrael.

They waited for a few more minutes, until the noise of jets to the south could be heard approaching quickly. They were not the only ones to hear the incoming craft, as armoured figures emerged from the blockhouses below.

'Stand ready,' said Araton.

Beside them, the Black Knights were already edging down the slope of the ridge towards the encampment. Araton held up his hand to stop Sabrael as he moved to follow.

'We move after the first strike,' said the squad leader. 'Not before.'

Shaking his head, Sabrael settled back on his haunches but did not offer vocal argument.

From the dark skies lascannon beams stabbed into the buildings, followed by the spark of launched missiles. Annael looked across the mountainside in time to see the war machine rising up, its battle cannon turning skywards moments before two missile trails converged on it position. The mechanical beast disappeared down the far slope amidst the detonations, an inhuman roar fading into the distance.

In the compound, the Death Guard were caught amidst missile blasts and lascannon fire as they ran for their transports. Bolter and plasma gun fire erupted from the Ravenwing squads close to the gate towers, hammering into the warriors manning the heavy weapons.

There was no time to take in anything more as Araton gave the order to attack, pushing forward down the ridge towards the Death Guard camp.

Thunderhawks strafed across the stronghold, raking heavy bolter fire and missiles into the prefabricated buildings, punching holes in the roofs and walls. A battle cannon shell caved in the end of the building fifty metres in front of the squad as they hit the floor of the depression, cracking apart the ferrocrete slab.

Annael saw shapes moving in the smoke and dust, and raised his pistol.

'Hold your fire,' Araton barked. 'All of you, mark your targets well. The commander is to be captured and the governor is in one of these buildings.'

Silencing a frustrated remark, Annael pounded across the stronghold with his brothers, wondering if he would know which enemy was their leader. The question became irrelevant as three power-armoured figures emerged from the darkness, opening fire on the Black Knights twenty metres ahead.

'This way,' Araton ordered, breaking to the right to move behind Tybalain's squad as they charged into the Death Guard, their corvus hammers gleaming blue in the night. Araton led the squad towards a ferrocrete blockhouse near the back of the encampment. 'Remember brothers, speed and surprise.'

Annael ran up to one of the slit windows and glanced inside. A single glow-globe lit the interior, which was bare save for metal crates and wooden boxes. The growl of engines rumbled across the depression and he looked across the camp to see lights blazing forth from the Land Raider.

'The governor!' declared Sabrael from the window behind Annael. 'In here.'

'Leave him!' snapped Araton. He pointed to a group of Death Guard breaking out of another building twenty metres ahead. There were five warriors, all in power armour though one stood out amongst the others. By the light of flames and flickering bolts Annael could see that his armour was dark, black even, a white cloak streaming from his backpack as he and his guards dashed towards Tybalain's Black Knights. The Huntmaster and his warriors were fighting their way into a breached blockhouse, unaware of the foes closing on them.

'We have to secure the Imperial Commander,' argued Sabrael, moving towards the door of the building.

'He is not the objective!' yelled Araton. The squad leader broke into a run towards Tybalain's position.

Zarall followed Araton without remark, leaving Annael conflicted between two courses of action. The desire to rescue the Imperial Commander and redress the loss of honour inflicted by his capture won through.

'Quickly now,' he told Sabrael, charging past his squad brother, smashing through the flimsy door with his shoulder.

Annael came face-to-face with a traitor, who was moving towards the door from inside. The stench of death swamped Annael's autosenses as he crashed into the warrior, flakes of rust and spatters of oil from the renegade coating the Dark Angel's black armour. The enemy

Space Marine lashed out with his bolter, smashing it across Annael's helm, knocking him sideways. Annael moved with the blow, his momentum slamming him into the wall, the ferrocrete cracking under the impact.

Another Death Guard, helm encrusted with barnacle-like growths, greenish vapour wheezing from the distended vent, seized hold of Annael's arm. A second later, Sabrael was there, the Blade of Corswain shining in the dim light of the cabin.

The power sword lanced through the chest of the Death Guard holding Annael, but the warrior was not moved by the blow. The other traitor kicked Sabrael in the midriff, sending him backwards into the wall, his grip on his sword lost. The spiked knuckles of the impaled Space Marine's fist crashed into Annael's mask, shattering the grille and breaking ceramite, and he tasted his own blood, mixed with foul pus from the decaying warrior's armour. He brought up his pistol, jamming the muzzle under the chin of the Space Marine as he pulled the trigger.

Pieces of helm, skull and brains showered over Annael, overwhelming his autosenses. Fighting the urge to gag, Annael prised himself free from the warrior's dead grip, but was too slow to defend himself as the remaining Death Guard fired his bolter.

The Dark Angel's chest plastron gave way under the welter of detonations and Annael felt his ribs and sternum cracking with it. Gasping for breath, he fell back, his hearts thundering in his ears.

Sabrael hit the Death Guard with a flying tackle, the two of them turning a pile of wooden boxes to splinters as they tumbled across the floor. Heaving in painful draughts of foetid air, Annael pushed himself to his feet. In the corner of the room he could see Imperial Commander Drazinoff bundled on the floor, rusted chains binding his arms and legs. He was a middle-aged man, sporting a ragged beard and unkempt grey hair, but it was not this that Annael saw.

The governor's skin was pockmarked with blisters, his eyes white with cataracts as they roved unseeing in their sockets. Blood trickled from lesions on his lips.

The bark of more bolter fire snapped Annael from the disturbing sight. Wincing with pain, he turned to see Sabrael standing over the remaining Death Guard, the enemy's bolter in his hand as he fired into the warrior's face.

'Pestilence has him,' gasped Annael as Sabrael tossed away the weapon and turned in his direction.

'It may not be too late,' said Sabrael. 'If we get him to Gideon swiftly.'

'Who's there?' Drazinoff demanded, trying to stand up despite his bonds. His voice was a thin whisper that became a wracking cough.

Sabrael snatched up the governor, easily heaving him over his shoulder, thick chains and all.

'Allies, Imperial Commander,' he said, setting off towards the door. He stopped just before the threshold and looked back. 'Can you move, brother?'

'Save the commander,' Annael said. The pain was subsiding as his genetically enhanced body and armour systems suppressed and tended the wound. 'I will follow.'

He reached the doorway with a few steps and stopped, finding Sabrael standing just beyond, as still as a statue.

'Lion's shade,' cursed Annael as he saw what had stopped Sabrael.

Beyond his squad brother, Annael could see the bodies of Araton and Zarall, lying alongside three Death Guard and several Black Knights. Their armour was rent open as if by some savage claw, steam rising from the grievous wounds. The snow was red with blood and flesh.

Now and then sparks of white energy flickered over the corpses, tiny lightning flashes leaping from the ragged edges of their armour.

'All brothers, converge on the gateway.' The Grand Master's command was terse, edged with anger. 'The target is escaping!'

Annael pulled his gaze from the splayed corpses of his brothers and saw the huge bulk of the Death Guard Land Raider moving past the buildings, its lascannons and heavy bolters cutting a swathe through the Ravenwing around it.

Sabrael let the Imperial Commander fall to the ground as he sank to one knee, head bowed. Annael staggered over to his squad-brother, the strength draining from his legs.

'Utter shame and dishonour,' Sabrael muttered, shaking his head.

'You can still save the governor,' Annael told his brother, sinking to the ground beside him, the last of his stamina spent. He felt light-headed from blood loss, his sight dimming, everything around him spinning and moving in and out of focus. 'The Grand Master will catch the prey, you will see.'

Sabrael grunted and stood up. He stooped to pick up Drazinoff, who was murmuring to himself, half-delirious, a fever-sweat soaking his face.

'Wait!' said Annael as Sabrael took a step.

With a last effort, gritting his teeth, Annael forced himself to his feet and stumbled back into the storehouse. He fumbled in the gloom for a moment until his fingers fell upon the hilt of the Blade of Corswain. Dragging it free from the Death Guard's chest, Annael returned to Sabrael, thrusting the sword hilt into his grip.

'This is yours, brother,' said Annael. 'As is the honour.'

'Yours is greater, brother,' said Sabrael as he turned away.

CONTINGENCY PLANNING

The drop pod was still shuddering from the impact as the door slammed down in front of Telemenus revealing a starry, cloudless sky and a wide expanse of snow. His descent harness snapped away from his armour with a hiss, releasing him from its embrace.

Needing no order from Saphael, acting-sergeant since the ambushed convoy, Telemenus leapt down to the ground, unslinging his bolter as he hit the snow. Half a kilometre to the west, the sky was lit by more drop pods and the streak of Thunderhawks plunging down from orbit.

'Sergeant Seraphiel was clear in his orders,' said Saphael as the squad mustered on their leader.

'Create a cordon but do not approach the target,' Zarall said, his disapproval evident. 'Are we really going to let the Ravenwing steal our glory again?'

'No,' said Saphael. 'Seraphiel lost us honour in his mishandling of the Imperial Commander's escort and we must restore the name of the company. If we see the enemy, we attack.'

'About time,' said Telemenus. 'Apollon, which direction?'

'North-west, brother.' Apollon pointed to the right. 'If we move fast we will be at the road leading from the enemy base within fifteen minutes.'

'It would have been easier if we had dropped directly to the site,' grumbled Nethor as the squad broke into a loping run, leaving billows of snow in their wake.

'Seraphiel would have noticed,' said Telemenus. 'Better this way. No interference.'

There were grunts of assent from the others. Following the debacle at the gorge, the squad, diminished in number and spirit, had returned to the *Penitent Warrior* to nurse their wounds and their pride. Losses were not easy to bear at any time, but the manner in which Amanael, Achamenon, Cadael and Nemeon had been killed or injured was a particularly sore wound from which to recover. It had been remarked that Sergeant Seraphiel had constantly shown poor judgement in his command of the company and his latest order to hold back from the battle was in a similar vein.

The squad ran on in silence, heading up the mountainside through the snowdrifts, leaving behind their brothers in the Fifth Company. They knew they were disobeying orders, a grave crime for which they were all prepared to be judged. It did not matter to Telemenus. Since Piscina, the company had lost pride and honour at every turn, playing second to the Ravenwing. The fresh laurels upon his armour were meaningless if the company was to return to the Rock in shame, and with the enemy on the loose an opportunity was presented to restore some measure of balance.

They reached the road, lined by low walls banked with snow, and turned north, towards the summit of the mountain. From this distance nothing could be seen of the battle that had raged there save for a pall of smoke that smeared across the stars. Like fireflies, the distant jets of Thunderhawks and fighters passed back and forth across the slope, sending reports of the enemy heard only by the Ravenwing.

Even in the night it was easy to follow the tracks left on the road by the Death Guard's vehicles. The road wound back and forth like a ribbon, but the Dark Angels were able to cut across the great loops, in places climbing rocky escarpments and ridges to speed their progress. After half an hour the pursuit from above was getting closer, the overflights of aircraft only a few kilometres away as they scoured the wilderness for their fleeing enemy.

'Let us ease haste, brothers,' said Saphael as they clambered over the stone wall onto the road once more. 'Better that we come upon our target prepared.'

Slowing to a swift walk, the squad strode along the road, Apollon with auspex slowly swinging back and forth in one hand, bolter in the other.

'Faint signal, directly ahead,' he reported. 'Heat source. Not strong enough to be a vehicle.'

'The quarry seeks sanctuary on foot,' said Telemenus. 'That makes the task simpler.'

'I can imagine the curses from the Ravenwing when we deliver their target to them, trussed like a hog ready for roast,' said Daellon. 'Nectar after the vinegar we have supped of late.'

Telemenus was less concerned by the reaction of the Ravenwing than he was Grand Master Zadakiel, commander of the Fifth Company. He was not entirely convinced their rogue action would be welcomed by their leader when they returned to the Tower of Angels, as good as the intention was to restore the company's honour. He kept his misgivings to himself though, his silence a sign of solidarity with his brothers. As a squad they would stand or fall.

The Ravenwing aircraft were close now, Thunderhawks moving slowly down the mountainside less than a kilometre away.

'We have to be close,' he said. 'Keep alert.'

His autosenses on full magnification, Telemenus scoured the darkness ahead, looking for any thermal signal. Apollon checked the auspex once more and gestured to a cleft in the rocks to the left. Silently, he stowed the scanner and took his bolter in both hands, all the signal the squad needed.

They moved into the defile two abreast, Menthius and Saphael in the lead, Telemenus and Nethor next, with Apollon and Daellon taking the last position. The crack in the mountain was about twenty metres wide, the sides swiftly becoming sheer, the floor of the rift littered with snow-covered rocks. Small, leafless bushes clung to crevices in the walls, but there was little cover.

Telemenus saw a faint blotch of orange ahead and whispered a warning to his brothers. The squad halted, spreading out across the defile as the smear of colour resolved into two distinct figures, heading straight towards them, their armour giving off clouds of heat from their backpacks.

'How should we proceed?' asked Menthius.

'A wounded target is easy to subdue,' replied Saphael. 'Open fire on my command.'

A few seconds later, the two figures stopped. They were close enough now to see in the starlight, one a Death Guard in filthy armour, the other slightly taller, his suit equally archaic but painted black. The latter wore no helm, his pale face lit by the stars, framed by long black hair. A white cloak draped behind him, tattered at the edges.

Telemenus felt Saphael shift beside him, about to give the order. He raised his bolter, expecting the command, but before the words were spoken the black-clad warrior raised a gauntleted hand towards the squad, crackles of energy playing across his fingertips.

'Psyker!' hissed Daellon, a moment before blue lightning streamed down the defile, crashing into Saphael. The squad leader was thrown black by the sorcerous blast, his armour ripping open from within as unearthly energy pulsed through his body.

Telemenus fired on the move as he darted to the right, away from the ripples of psychic energy crackling from the psykers fingers. His bolts flew true but seemed to slam into an invisible wall just in front of his target, detonating uselessly in mid-air.

The unholy energy coursed across the defile, seizing upon Menthius briefly, splitting open his armour, wisps of smoke drifting from the joints as he fell backwards. Telemenus suppressed a shout of grief, leaping to the right as the Death Guard aimed a meltagun in his direction.

Nethor fired as a boulder was turned to glass by the melta blast just behind Telemenus. The missile hit the Death Guard Space Marine in the chest, the shaped warhead breaking open his armoured plastron milliseconds before the charge exploded, cutting the renegade in half.

The psyker drew a long blade, its edges glimmering balefully with a sickening yellow light. Unperturbed by the bolts shrieking around him, he strode towards the squad. Telemenus could see that his skin was pale like a corpse, the bones of his cheeks showing through torn flesh, eyes red with thick veins.

'Brave but foolish, brothers,' the traitor declared in a

rasping voice. His words were accompanied by a gust of air that carried the stench of disease and rotting meat. 'Your masters have betrayed you.'

Giving up all thoughts of taking the warrior alive, Telemenus emptied his magazine at the ghastly apparition. As before, the bolts did not hit. Nethor steadied himself again for another missile shot, but was too slow. The psyker thrust his sword in the Space Marine's direction, a blast of churning warp energy flying from its tip to smash Nethor from his feet. His armour crumbled, turning to dust in moments, exposed flesh wrinkling and decaying beneath.

Apollon fell next, sent spinning to the ground by a fresh wave of psychic lightning that surrounded him with a cloud of energy. Telemenus skirted to his right, glancing at his battle-brother's twitching body.

'It is folly to oppose me, brothers,' the psyker spoke without malice, blood trickling from split lips as he uttered the words. 'Your sacrifice will go unremembered, your glory unrewarded.'

'I am no brother of yours,' snarled Daellon. A swirl of burning promethium engulfed the enemy warrior, setting fire to his cloak and hair. The psyker staggered to the left and raised his empty hand against the inferno. More sickly yellow light spilled from his open palm, pushing back against the gout of flames.

Fingers curling into a fist, the psyker seemed to grab hold of the streaming promethium, lashing it like a whip back at Daellon. The Dark Angel flung the flamer away and dived to the ground as its fuel canister exploded, showering the defile with burning liquid.

'You are all my brothers,' the psyker continued. 'If your blind masters had half the honour you possess, they would tell you the truth. I was once like you.'

'I know you, traitor,' said Telemenus. 'You have shunned

the Emperor and have no honour. You have the filthy heart of a heretic even if you were once a Space Marine.'

The psyker grinned, bearing a few rotted, pointed teeth, even as flecks of promethium continued to burn through the flesh of his face and flickered on his armour.

'Not just a Space Marine, *brother*. A Dark Angel.'

'Lies!' roared Telemenus. There was a fresh magazine in his bolter, his instinct performing the act even as his conscious mind had been occupied. He opened fire, the thunder of his bolter loud in the defile. The hail of rounds swamped the psyker with detonations, but he did not stop in his stride.

The bolter clicked empty in Telemenus's hands and he looked into that dead face and knew he was doomed. The psyker lifted his sword, the gleaming tip pointed at Telemenus's heart.

'May your soul take with it the torment of the newly-learnt truth,' said the warrior, his grin turning into a sneer.

Telemenus narrowed his eyes. He recoiled more at the realisation that the sinister creature in front of him had once been a son of the Lion than at the thought of impending death.

Nothing happened.

The psyker's brow creased in a heavy frown as he looked down at the weapon. His eyes widened a moment later and he turned, staring with shock up at the rocks over-looking the defile.

Telemenus followed his gaze. Three figures stood there, their armour as black as the night sky behind them, their outlines just a glimmer in the starlight. An axe head blazed into life, lighting the armour of Epistolary Hara-hel. The cables of his psychic hood buzzed with sparks of energy. Beside him a golden aquila gleamed; the crozius arcanum of Brother Malcifer. Between the two a long, silver-edged blade slid from a scabbard as Sammael unsheathed the Raven Sword.

'Back away, brother,' the Grand Master said, the words calming, cutting through the haze of confusion left by the psyker's shocking pronouncement.

Telemenus did as he was told, stepping back down the defile, eyes still fixed on the Grand Master. Below Sammael, the psyker looked like an animal trapped in a snare, head twisting left and right as he sought a means of escape.

Sammael jumped from the top of the defile, the Raven Sword held in both hands. As he thudded to the rock, the silvery blade plunged into the renegade's gut, erupting from his back. Pulling his sword free, Sammael swept the blade low, slicing through the psyker's left knee, toppling him to the ground.

Harahel and Malcifer followed the Grand Master into the defile. Sammael reversed his grip on his blade and drove it through the shoulder of his prey, pinning him to the rock. Harahel laid the edge of his axe against the chest of the psyker and energy flowed, coursing with white light through the traitor. A scream of agony and despair echoed from the rocks and Telemenus turned away, stumbling back towards the road, mind boiling with the unthinkable truth.

Behind him the shrieking abruptly ceased, but he knew that the psyker was not dead. A worse fate awaited the traitor.

No, he corrected himself.

The Fallen Dark Angel.

EPILOGUE

CONSEQUENCES

The five penitents sat with heads bowed in front of Sammael in the strike cruiser's reclusiam. They had not looked at him since he had entered. Two he knew well, brothers from his company. The other three were of the Fifth, but the extent of their deeds had been made known to him by Malcifer and Seraphiel.

'Sabrael, Annael,' he said, intoning the names slowly. They did not raise their gazes, but stared diligently at the tiled floor. 'In the midst of battle with the enemy, you shunned the duty of the Ravenwing. Our mission was to subjugate the traitor, yet you chose to act upon your own course to free Imperial Commander Drazinoff. Do you deny this?'

'No, Grand Master,' whispered Sabrael.

'I cannot deny the charge,' said Annael. His gaze flicked up to Sammael for a brief moment and then returned to the floor. 'Did we save the governor?'

Unseen, Sammael's lips twisted in a brief smile.

'He recovers after a fashion,' the Grand Master replied.

His smile faded. 'What have you to say in defence of your actions?'

Both Dark Angels said nothing.

'You offer no justification for your deeds?'

'We are subject to your will, Grand Master,' said Sabrael. 'Your judgement is the truth.'

'I see.' Their response pleased Sammael and made his final decision easier. He waited a moment, choosing the right words. 'Such behaviour cannot pass without consequences. You will each spend ten days in the penitentium.'

'Ten days?' Annael looked up in surprise. The movement caused him to wince and his hand moved to the bandaged wounds beneath his robe. 'Your leniency is unwarranted, Grand Master.'

'There is a greater punishment in store for the both of you,' Sammael continued solemnly. 'You have seen a deeper truth than most. It is not honour or glory to act without thought, simply obeying orders for their own sake. I place a great burden upon you, because you have shown the character and strength of will to bear it in silence, resolute and unyielding. I am short of Black Knights and you will serve me in that role.'

Sabrael's expression was one of confusion, while Annael showed relief.

'Some may think this reward for your ill-discipline, but do not take it as such,' the Grand Master warned. 'As Black Knights you will be subject to the highest demands of body and soul. It is an onerous duty, but one of which you are both capable. When you have passed the Seventh Rite of the Raven you will understand that truth is the harshest master to serve.'

The two Space Marines nodded and remained silent. Sammael moved his attention to the three others.

'Menthius.' The warrior of the Fifth was still swathed

in dressings, the flesh beneath burnt across much of his face and chest. He met Sammael's gaze with a look of deference. Next to him Daellon, his burns only superficial, nodded without looking up as the Grand Master spoke his name.

'Telemenus,' Sammael intoned as his gaze moved to the last of the Dark Angels. The Space Marine's hands were clasped fists in his lap, and his scalp was freshly shaven as a sign of penitence. At the mention of his name, Telemenus raised his face, a haunted look in his eyes.

'You have been brought before an even darker truth,' Sammael said, genuine sorrow filling him. The darkness of the Fallen had been cast upon them, despite his best efforts to shield them from the horrifying truth. All three had heard Methelas's claim. In a way, their squad-brothers who had been slain had suffered the kinder fate. All three had been brought directly aboard the *Implacable Justice* and segregated from the other battle-brothers lest a careless word spilled from their lips. They had borne their incarceration stoically, but there was no other course of action open to Sammael. 'You do not serve under the aegis of the Ravenwing and it is not in my power to pardon or punish you. I have spoken with Sergeant Seraphiel on the matter.' Sammael felt the warriors tense at the mention of their leader's name. 'I find myself in agreement with his judgement.'

Sammael stepped away and walked to the altar. He stood behind it and called for the three warriors to look at him.

'As with the Black Knights, you shall know the burden of knowledge,' he said slowly. 'I cannot guide you on that path, but there are others that will. Upon our return to the Tower of Angels you shall be rendered into the care of the Deathwing. May their teachings salve the wounds you feel in your souls. Serve in the First Company with honour, and expunge the guilt and shame that has laid its dark grip upon you.'

Their eyes widened as realisation dawned. There were no smiles, for as with Sabrael and Annael, they realised the expectation and duty being placed upon them. They accepted the news with grim nods.

When he had dismissed all five of the warriors, Sammael left the reclusiam, exiting through a small door behind the altar. He followed a short corridor and came to a metal portal. Opening, he stepped into the room beyond; a cell with bare plasteel walls and floor.

Malcifer stood to one side, his armour discarded for his robe though he still wore the skull mask of his rank. There was blood on his bare hands and on a slab-like table in the middle of the chamber Methelas lay chained. Harahel stood on the far side of the room, arms folded, eyes closed in contemplation. The Fallen turned his head and spat blood as Sammael joined Malcifer.

'There is no torture you can inflict upon me that will loosen my tongue, brothers,' he said. 'My patron guards my flesh and soul against suffering.'

'Many have claimed as much,' said Malcifer. 'They have been wrong.'

Sammael took two steps to stand at the head of the table looking down at Methelas's ruined face. He placed a hand on the brow of the Fallen, steeling himself against the touch of clammy flesh. Methelas struggled futilely against his bonds as the Grand Master leaned over, lips next to the Fallen's ravaged ear. When he spoke, Sammael's voice was a snarled whisper.

'*Where is he?*' the Master of the Ravenwing demanded. '*Where is Cypher?*'

The story of the Dark Angels continues in
Master of Sanctity.

ABOUT THE AUTHOR

Gav Thorpe is the *New York Times* bestselling author of 'The Lion', a novella in the collection *The Primarchs*. He has written many other Black Library books, including the Horus Heresy novel *Deliverance Lost* and audio drama *Raven's Flight* as well as fan-favourite Warhammer 40,000 novel *Angels of Darkness* and the epic Time of Legends trilogy, *The Sundering*. He is currently working on a new Dark Angels series, The Legacy of Caliban. Gav hails from Nottingham, where he shares his hideout with the evil genius that is Dennis, the mechanical hamster.